Claiming His Princess

MICHELLE CONDER
KATE WALKER
VICTORIA PARKER

First Published in Great Britain 2016
By Mills & Boon, an imprint of HarperCollins*Publishers*
1 London Bridge Street, London, SE1 9GF

CLAIMING HIS PRINCESS © 2016 Harlequin Books S. A.

Duty At What Cost?, *A Throne For The Taking* and *Princess In The Iron Mask* were first published in Great Britain by Harlequin (UK) Limited.

Duty At What Cost? © 2013 Michelle Conder
A Throne For The Taking © 2013 Kate Walker
Princess In The Iron Mask © 2013 Victoria Parker

ISBN: 978-0-263-92075-8

05-0816

Our policy is to use papers that are natural, renewable and recyclable products and made from wood grown in sustainable forests.The logging and manufacturing processes conform to the legal environmental regulations of the country of origin.

Printed and bound in Spain
by CPI, Barcelona

DUTY AT WHAT COST?

BY
MICHELLE CONDER

From as far back as she can remember **Michelle Conder** dreamed of being a writer. She penned the first chapter of a romance novel just out of high school, but it took much study, many (varied) jobs, one ultra-understanding husband and three very patient children before she finally sat down to turn that dream into a reality.

Michelle lives in Australia and, when she isn't busy plotting, loves to read, ride horses, travel and practise yoga.

To Paul, with love.

And "a big kiss" to Anne-Emmanuelle
for her wonderful friendship and even more
wonderful French translations. Thank you.

CHAPTER ONE

AVA GLANCED OUT of the car window at the sparkling summer sunshine bouncing off the exquisite French countryside and wished herself a thousand miles away. Maybe a million. That would land her on another planet where no one knew her name. Where no one knew the man her father had expected her to marry was about to marry another woman, and felt sorry for her in the process.

'It's time you stopped messing around in Paris, my girl, and came home to Anders.'

That particularly supportive comment had come only this morning, making her blood boil. His condescending words filled her head, drowning out the singer on the car radio who was warbling about wanting to go home. Home was the last place Ava wanted to go.

Not that her father's anger was entirely unexpected. Of course he was disappointed that the man she had been pledged to marry since she was a child had fallen in love with someone else. The way he'd spoken to her—*'A woman your age doesn't have time to waste!'*—as if turning thirty in a year meant that she was over the hill—made it seem as if it was her fault.

But Ava *wanted* to fall in love! She *wanted* to get married! She just hadn't wanted to marry Gilles—a childhood friend who was more like a brother to her than her own—and he hadn't wanted to marry her. The problem was they had played along with their fathers' archaic pledge for a little too long, sometimes using each other for a fill-in date when the need arose.

Oh, how her father would love to hear *that*… Somehow, after her mother's death fifteen years ago, her relationship with him had disintegrated to the point where they barely spoke, let alone saw each other. Of course if she had been born a boy things would have been different.

Very different.

She would have had different choices. She would have been Crown Prince, for one—and, while she had no wish at all to rule their small European nation, she would at least have had her father's respect. His affection. Something.

Ava gripped the steering wheel of her hatchback more tightly as she turned onto the narrow country lane that ran alongside Château Verne, Gilles's fifteenth-century estate.

For eight years she had lived a happy, relatively low-key existence in Paris; finishing university and building her business, stepping in at royal functions when her brother Frédéric had been absent. Now that Gilles, Marquis de Bassonne, was set to marry a friend of hers, she had a bad feeling that was all about to change.

Ava crinkled her nose at her uncharacteristically gloomy mood. Gilles and Anne had fallen in love at first sight two months ago and were happier than she'd ever seen either one of them before. They completed each other in a way that would inspire songwriters and she wasn't jealous.

Not at all.

Her life was rolling along just fine. Her art gallery, Gallery Nouveau, had just been reviewed in a prestigious art magazine and she was busier than ever. It was true that her love-life was a little on the nonexistent side, but her break-up three years ago with Colyn—the man she had believed she would eventually marry—had left her emotionally drained and a little wary.

At nearly twenty years her senior he had seemed to her to be the epitome of bourgeois intellectualism: a man who didn't care about her heritage and loved her for herself. It had taken a couple of years to figure out that his subtle criticisms of her status and his desire to *'teach'* her all that he knew made him as egotistical and controlling as her father.

And she really wished he hadn't popped into her mind, because now she felt truly terrible.

The only other times she'd felt this miserable had been during gorgeous evenings wandering by herself along the Seine, when she was unable to avoid watching couples so helplessly in love with each other they couldn't walk two paces without stopping to steal another kiss.

She had never felt that. Not once.

She frowned, wondering if she ever would.

After Colyn she had been determined only to date nice men with solid family values. Men who were in touch with their feelings. But they hadn't inspired much more than friendship in her. Thankfully her business kept her too busy to dwell on what she lacked, and if she was getting older...

Pah!

Stamping on even more mood-altering thoughts, she adjusted the volume dial on the radio and wasn't at all prepared when she put her foot on the brake to slow down for a bend in the road and nothing happened. Imagining that she had put her foot on the accelerator instead, she'd moved to correct the oversight when the car hit a patch of gravel and started to slide.

Panicking, she yanked on the steering wheel to keep the car straight, but the car had gathered momentum and in the blink of an eye it fishtailed and rammed into some sort of small tree.

Groaning, Ava clasped her head where it had bounced off the steering wheel.

For a moment she just sat there. Then she realised the

engine was roaring, took her foot from the accelerator and switched the car off. Her ears rang loudly in the sudden silence and then she caught the sound of one of her tyres spinning in midair. Glancing out through the windscreen, she realised her car was wedged on top of a clump of rocks and heather plants in full bloom.

Talk about a lapse in concentration!

She blew out a breath and gingerly moved her limbs one at a time. Thankfully the car had been going too slowly for her to have been seriously hurt. A good thing—except she could picture her father shaking his head at her. He was always telling her to use a driver on official engagements, but of course she didn't listen. Arguing with him had become something of a blood sport. A blood sport he was so much better at than her. It was one of the main reasons she'd snuck off to study Fine Arts at the Sorbonne. If she had stayed in Anders it would have been impossible to keep the promise she had made to her dying mother to try and get along with her father.

His earlier edict replayed again in her head. She couldn't return to Anders. What would she do there? Sit around and play parlour games all day while she waited for him to line up another convenient husband? The thought made her shiver.

Determined to stop thinking about her father, Ava carefully opened the car door and stepped out into the long grass. The spiky heels of her ankle boots immediately sank into the soft earth.

Great. As a gallery owner it was imperative that she always look impeccable and there was no way she could afford to ruin her prized Prada boots. Since she'd decided a long time ago not to take any of her father's money she didn't have any spare cash lying around to replace them. Another decision that had displeased him.

She stood precariously on the balls of her feet and leaned in to retrieve her handbag. Her phone had fallen out and when she picked it up she saw the screen was smashed. Unable to remember Gilles's mobile number, she tossed it back in the car in frustration. She could always call emergency services, but then her little accident would be all over the news in a heartbeat—and the thought of any more attention this week for 'the poor jilted Princess' made her teeth gnash together. Which didn't help her sore head.

No. She'd simply have to walk.

But standing on the grassy verge with her hands on her hips, she realised just how far it was to the main gates. Her beloved boots would be destroyed. Not to mention how hot and sweaty she would be by the time she got there. This was not the graceful and dignified entrance she had planned to make. And if one of those media vans she had seen loitering a few miles back saw her...

Wondering just what to do next, she had a sudden brainwave. A sudden and slightly crazy brainwave. Fortuitously— if she could describe running her little car into a ditch in such terms—she'd crashed right near a section of the outer wall that she had played on with her brother Frédéric and her cousin Baden and Gilles during family visits to the château in her childhood. Scaling the wall as revolutionary spies had been their secret game, and they'd even scraped out footholds to aid their escape from imaginary enemies.

Ava felt a grin creep across her face for the first time that day. She had to concede it was a tad desperate, but with Gilles's wedding only hours away that was exactly what she was. And, anyway, she had always loved to climb as a kid; surely it would be even easier as an adult?

'There's a woman stuck on the south wall, boss. What do you want us to do with her?'

Wolfe pulled up in the middle of an arched hallway in Château Verne and pressed his phone a little tighter to his ear. '*On* the wall?'

'The very top,' repeated Eric, one of the more junior members of Wolfe's security team.

Wolfe tensed. Perfect. Most likely another interfering journalist, trying to get the scoop on his friend's extravagant wedding to the daughter of a controversial American politician. They hadn't let up all day, circling the château like starving buzzards. But none had been brazen enough to go over the wall yet. Of course he'd been prepared for the possibility—the reason they now had this little intruder in hand.

'Name?'

'Says she's Ava de Veers, Princess of Anders.'

A princess climbing over a forty-foot brick wall? Wolfe didn't think so. 'ID?'

'No ID in her handbag. Says she had a car accident and it must have fallen out.'

Clever.

'Camera?'

'Check.'

Wolfe considered his options. Even from inside the thick walls of the château he could hear the irritating whine of distant media choppers as they hovered just outside the established no-fly zone. With the wedding still three hours away he'd better extend the security perimeters before there were any more breaches.

'Want me to take her back to base, boss?'

'No.' Wolfe shot his hand through his hair. He'd rather turf her back over the wall than give her even more access to the property by taking her to the outer cottage his men were temporarily using. And he would—after he had established her identity and satisfied himself that she wasn't a real threat. 'Leave her where she's perched.' He was about to ring off when he had another thought. 'And, Eric, keep your gun on her until I get there.' That would teach her for entering a private function without an invitation.

'Ah…you mean keep her *on* the wall?'

When Eric hesitated Wolfe knew right then that the woman was attractive.

'Yes, that's exactly what I mean.' For all he knew she could be a political nutcase instead of an overzealous journo. 'And don't engage in any conversation with her until I get there.'

Wolfe trusted his men implicitly, but the last thing he needed was some smoking Mata Hari doing a number on their head.

'Yes, sir.'

Wolfe pocketed his phone. This would mean he wouldn't be able to start the pre-wedding game of polo Gilles had organised. Annoying, but it couldn't be helped. He'd offered to run security for Gilles's wedding because it was what he did, and the job always came first.

Once outside, Wolfe found Gilles and his merry band already waiting for him at the stables, the horses groomed and saddled and raring to go. Wolfe ran his gaze over the roguish white Arabian that Gilles had promised him. He'd missed his daily gym workout this morning and had been looking forward to putting the stallion through his paces.

Hell, he still could. Taking the reins from the handler, he swung easily onto the giant of a horse. The stallion shifted restlessly beneath his weight and Wolfe automatically reached forward to pat his neck, breathing in the strong scent of horse and leather. 'What's his name?'

'Achilles.'

His mouth quirked and Gilles shrugged. 'Apollo was taken and he's a bloody contrary animal. You should enjoy each other.'

Wolfe laughed at his aristocratic friend. Years ago they had forged an unbreakable bond when they had trained together for selection on an elite military task force. They'd been there for each other during the tough times and celebrated during the good. Inevitably Gilles had started sprouting reams of poetry and Greek myths to stay awake when they'd spent long hours waiting for something to happen. By contrast Wolfe, a rugged Australian country boy, had used a more simple method. Sheer grit and stubborn determination. A trait that had served him well when he had swapped special ops for software development and created what was currently the most sophisticated computer spyware on the planet.

Wolfe Inc had been forged around that venture, and when his younger brother had joined him they'd expanded into every aspect of the security business. But where his brother thrived on the corporate life Wolfe preferred the freedom of being able to mix things up a little. He even kept his hand in on some of the more hairy covert ops some governments called consultants in to take care of. He had to get his adrenaline high from something other than his beloved Honda CBR.

'Always the dreamer, *Monsieur le Marquis*,' he drawled.

'Just a man who knows how to have balance in his life, Ice,' Gilles countered good-naturedly, calling Wolfe by his old military nickname. He swung onto the back of a regal-looking bay. 'You should try it some time, my friend.'

'I've got plenty of balance in my life,' Wolfe grunted, thinking about the Viennese blonde he'd been glad to see the back of a month ago. 'No need to worry your pretty head on that score.'

Achilles snorted and tossed his nose in challenge as Wolfe took up the reins.

'I won't be joining you just yet. I need to check on an issue that's come up.' He kept his tone deliberately bland so as not to alarm his friend, who should be concentrating on why he was signing his life away to a woman in matrimony rather than why a woman was currently sitting on one of his outer walls. 'Achilles and I will join you in a few.'

The horse pulled against the bit and Wolfe smiled. There was nothing quite like using all his skills to master a difficult animal, and he wondered if Gilles would consider selling him. He already liked the unmanageable beast.

* * *

Okay, so maybe it wasn't that much easier to scale a high brick wall as an adult, Ava conceded. In fact it had been downright scary and had shown her how unfit she was. Her arm muscles were aching in protest. It hadn't helped when she'd discovered the ancient chestnut tree she had been relying on to help her down the other side had been removed, and then two trained security guards wielding machine guns had happened upon her.

She hadn't considered that Gilles would have hired extra security for the wedding, but in hindsight she should have done. Naturally the men hadn't believed her about the car accident, and now all she needed was for one of those media helicopters she could hear to zero in on her and her joyous day would just about be complete.

It was all Gilles's fault, she grouched to herself, eyeing the uneven terrain at her feet where the magnificent tree had once stood. And surely they'd raised the height of the wall since the last time she'd climbed it as a tearaway twelve-year-old.

Shifting uncomfortably, she eyed the two killers camouflaged in street clothes below, glad she was conversant in English. She knew no self-respecting Frenchman would ever be seen mixing flannel with corduroy. 'If you would just check a couple of hundred metres up the road you'll find my car and realise that I am telling you the truth,' she repeated, struggling to hold back the temper her father had often complained was as easy to strike up as a match. Which actually wasn't true. It took special powers to induce her to lose the plot.

'Sorry, ma'am. Boss's orders.' That from the one who looked slightly more sympathetic than the other—although that was like saying snow was colder than ice.

'Fine. But I have a headache and I'd like to get down.'

'Sorry, ma'am—'

'Boss's orders,' Ava finished asininely, wondering what

the two men would do if she decided to jump. Not an entirely practical option since she would likely break her ankle.

It had clearly been an oversight on their part as children only to whittle footholds on *one* side of the wall. A mistake no self-respecting spy in their right mind would have made!

Ava briefly closed her eyes and gently tested the injury on her forehead. It felt so large she was sure the House of Fabergé would weep to get their hands on it.

A wave of irritation threatened to topple her off the wall and impale her on one of those raised guns, and as much as she told herself it was irrational to be irritated with these men, since this whole situation was her own fault, she couldn't dispel her growing agitation. In truth, she felt like a fool sitting atop Gilles's wall like a silly bird.

'And where is this boss of yours?' she queried, injecting her voice with a calm she was far from feeling.

'Coming soon, ma'am.'

So was Christmas. In four months' time.

A low rumble of thunder brought Ava's head around as she tried to locate the sound. Her view was hampered by soaring parkland trees and wild shrubbery, and the only thing visible in the distance were the rounded red brick towers of the château and a picture-perfect blue sky beyond.

Then a flash of white amongst the trees caught her attention, and she couldn't look away as a purebred stallion galloped into view. Ava's eyes drank in the beautiful creature—and then she felt slightly dizzy as her eyes took in its handsome rider.

Windswept sandy hair was brushed back from a proud face with a strong nose and square jaw, wide shoulders and a lean torso rippled beneath a fitted black polo shirt, and long, muscular legs were outlined to perfection in white jodhpurs and knee-high black riding boots.

She sensed he was absolutely furious, even though he hadn't moved a well-honed muscle. His narrowed eyes were boring into hers with the intense focus of a natural hunter. Even when the horse stamped impatiently beneath him, its nostrils flaring and its tail flicking with irritation, the man remained preternaturally still.

Ava's heart pounded and she found her fingers gripping the stone wall for support. Heat was turning her limbs soft. Of course it was the sun making her hot, not the ruthless-looking warrior staring at her with an arrogance that bordered on insolence.

'Are you the reason I'm still on this wall?' The confrontational words were out of her mouth before she'd known they were in her head and she could have kicked herself. She had meant to be pleasant, to make sure this ordeal was over as quickly as possible. She knew instantly from the firm jut of his jaw that she had well and truly put paid to that.

Wolfe didn't move a muscle as his eyes swept over the fey gypsy on the wall. He'd been wrong. She wasn't attractive. She was *astonishingly* attractive, and his soldier's eyes noted everything. High cheekbones, honey-gold skin, eyes as dark as night and thick sable hair pulled into a ponytail, wisps from which floated around a lush, sulky mouth that looked as if it was waiting to be kissed.

By him.

Impatiently discarding the unexpected thought, he let his eyes drift lower over a white cotton shirt the gentle breeze was using to outline her rounded breasts, and fitted jeans that hugged long slender legs. And bare, stocking-clad feet!

Achilles swatted the air with his tail, as if he too was disturbed by the vision, and then Wolfe registered her haughty, royally pissed-off question and recovered himself. She was an intruder, and she was ruining a rousing game of polo, and if she was upset she could stand in line.

'No.' He shot her a cursory look. '*You* are the reason you're still on that wall.'

Ignoring her hissed exhalation he swung out of the saddle and approached his men. He could feel her eyes following him and wondered at their exact colour, immediately irritated at the irrelevant thought.

He waited for Eric to fill him in on how they had come across her, and then indicated for him to pass over the leather handbag he held in his hand.

'Is the gun absolutely necessary?'

Her slightly bored question floated down from the wall.

'Only if I have to shoot you with it.' He didn't bother looking at her when he spoke. 'And keep your hands where I can see them.'

'I'm not a criminal!'

He ignored her little outburst and inspected her handbag. 'Find anything interesting in here?'

'No, boss. Usual women things. Lipstick, tissues, hair clips. No ID, as I said.'

He heard her exasperated sigh. 'I already told your watchdogs I had a car accident and my purse must have fallen out of my bag.'

'Convenient.'

'For whom? You?'

Wolfe gave her a stare he knew from experience made grown men think twice. 'You have an awfully smart mouth for someone in your predicament.' And he wished she would close it. The husky quality of her lightly accented voice was having an adverse effect on his body.

'I am Princess Ava de Veers of Anders and I demand you let me down from here immediately.'

Wolfe ran his eyes over her again, just for the sheer pleasure of it and because he knew it would put her on the back foot. 'What are you doing on a wall, Princess? Learning to fly?'

'I am a guest at this wedding and you are likely to lose

your job if you insist on leaving me up here. I'm probably sunburned by now.'

'By this watered-down version of the sun?' And on that golden skin? 'Unlikely. And honoured guests usually approach by the main gates. What outlet do you work for?'

Her brow crinkled. 'I don't—'

'Newspaper? Magazine? TV station? Nice camera, by the way. Mind if I take a look?'

'Yes, I do.'

He dumped her handbag on the grass and started checking through her photos.

'I said *yes*, I do mind.'

'Whether I look or not isn't contingent on whether you mind.'

'Why bother asking, then?'

He nearly smiled at the exasperation in her voice. 'Manners.'

She made a cute noise that said he wouldn't know what manners were if they conked him on the head.

Frowning at the photos on her camera, he glanced up at her. 'Nice celebrity shots on here. I repeat—what rag do you work for?'

She rolled her eyes. 'I am not a member of the paparazzi, if that's what you're suggesting.'

'No?'

'No. I own an art gallery. Those were taken at a recent opening night. Not that it is any of your business.'

Wolfe rubbed his jaw and pretended to consider that. 'Really? Given your current predicament, I'd say it's very much my business.'

She looked as if she was holding on to her temper by a thread. 'I do understand how this looks. And I even appreciate how efficient your men were at spotting me—'

'I'm so happy to hear that.'

'But—' she carried on as if he hadn't interrupted '—I am

who I say I am. My car is a couple of hundred metres that way, and your men would already know this if they had bothered to go and find it instead of holding their weapons on me as if I was a terrorist.'

Wolfe handed the camera to Eric. 'Oh, I'm sorry.' He didn't bother to hide the contempt he felt for her type. Haughty princesses—real or imagined—who thought their needs took preference over everybody else's. 'Did I forget to tell you? My men take orders from *me*, not you.'

Her pout turned even sexier. 'Convenient.'

He wasn't in the frame of mind to appreciate her wisecrack and nearly reconsidered his need to verify her identity before tossing her back over the wall.

'Eric. Dane. Take the Jeep and find her car. If it exists.'

She sniffed at his instructions and shifted her bottom on the wall. She must be completely uncomfortable by now. Serve her right.

'I told you to keep your hands where I could see them.'

She rolled her eyes. 'Do you think it might be at all possible that I could wait on the ground for your men to return? I promise not to overpower you while they are gone.'

The air seemed to buzz with the antagonistic heat she imbued him with, and her accent lent her sardonic words a sexy edge. She was a wicked combination of beauty and spirit, and not even the way she spoke down to him was enough to keep his libido at bay. A truly annoying realisation.

'I think I can handle you.'

Her eyes dropped to his mouth and Wolfe felt a kick of lust all the way to his toes. He waited, breathless, for the heat in his groin to dissipate, but if anything it got worse. Then her eyes blazed into his and the chemistry he'd been trying to ignore sparked like a live wire between them.

The way her eyes widened he thought perhaps she had read his thoughts, but that was impossible. Fourteen years in the business and Wolfe knew how to hide what he was feeling—hell, he'd learned how to do that by the time he could walk.

Perhaps she'd just felt the same burn he had. And had liked it just as little, if her wary gaze was anything to go by. Which gave him a moment's pause. If she was a journalist—or, worse, some sort of political stalker—she'd have already used that connection to manipulate him, not shy away from it as if she'd just been singed.

His eyes took in wrists that looked impossibly slender within the cuffs of her masculine-style shirt, then moved down along fine-boned hands and nails buffed to perfection. She didn't do hard labour. That much was obvious.

He knew instinctively she was who she said she was. It was in her regal bearing, the swanlike arch of her neck, in her sense of entitlement and the way she looked at him as if he was staff. His mother had often looked at his father like that and Wolfe had always felt sorry for the poor bastard.

She shifted again, her eyes on the ground. 'Do you have any suggestions on how I might get down from here?' And with a degree of dignity, her tone seemed to imply.

'Perhaps you'd like me to unfold my trusty ladder from my back pocket?' Wolfe mocked. 'Oh, dear. Left it at home.' He opened his hands, palms facing upwards. 'Guess you'll just have to jump into my arms, Princess. What a treat.'

His horse snickered and her eyes used the excuse to glance at the stallion before returning to his. 'Channelling your inner Zorro?' she asked sweetly.

His lips twitched. 'Only because I left my Batman tool belt at home.'

'With Robin?'

Despite his less than stellar mood he chuckled. 'Cute. Toss down the boots first.' The last thing he wanted was to be stabbed by one of those dangerous-looking heels, and by the gleam in her eyes that was exactly what she was considering.

'I have a better idea. Why don't I just go back down the way I came up?'

'No.'

Her lips tightened. 'It makes perfect sense. I can—'

'Try it and I *will* shoot you.'

'You don't have a gun.'

'I have a gun.'

She paused, her stillness telling him she was weighing up whether he was telling the truth or not. Her eyes slid down his torso and over his legs and he felt a rush of unexpected excitement, as if she'd actually touched him.

'You are being overly obnoxious about this,' she fumed.

'Not yet, I'm not.' Wolfe barely managed to suppress his rising aggravation at this physical response to a woman he already didn't like. 'But I'm getting close.'

'If you drop me I'll sue you.'

'If you don't hurry up and get down from that wall I'll sue *you*.'

Her dark brows arched imperiously. 'For what?'

'Trying my patience. Now, pass down the boots. Nice and easy,' he warned softly.

With an audible sigh she dropped her boots one after the other into his outstretched hands. The kid leather was warm from her touch.

'Now you.' His voice had grown rough—a clear indication that some part of him was looking forward to holding her in his arms. And what was wrong with that? He might not be interested in starting up another affair straight after his last one had ended so tastelessly, but he *was* male and this woman *was* beautiful.

'I'd rather wait for a ladder.'

So would he.

'Then you'd better settle in. I run security, not rescue.'

Again she glanced dubiously at the ground. 'It didn't seem

like such a big drop when I was younger. And what happened to the chestnut tree that used to grow here?'

'Now you're mistaking me for a gardener, Princess. What next?'

Her eyes narrowed. 'Certainly not for a nice man. Rest assured of that. And my correct title is Your Royal Highness.'

He knew the correct title. He might not be royal himself, but he'd met enough in his lifetime to know how to address one. 'Thanks for the tip. But I don't have all day. So let's go.' Time to stop thinking about the tempting swell of her breasts and her hot mouth.

'*You* don't have all day? Thanks to you, I'm impossibly late now,' she complained.

He beckoned her with his fingers. 'My heart bleeds.'

'You're really very rude.'

'Want me to leave you up there?' he prompted, fresh out of patience.

'Excuse me for being a little uneasy.'

Wolfe sighed and held his hands up again. 'I've never dropped a princess before.'

'You've probably never had the opportunity before now.'

He shook his head. 'You sure do know how to make yourself vulnerable, Princess.'

She muttered something in French, making him want to smile. She was all fire and…*attitude*!

Balancing on her hands, she carefully swung her leg over the wall, so that she was perched on it like a little chipmunk, her fingers turning white as she gripped the edge. Still she hesitated, lifting first one thigh and then the other to make sure the fabric of her jeans didn't catch.

'Want me to count to three?' he drawled.

She threw him a dark look, her eyes fixed firmly on his, and then they snapped closed and she launched herself off the wall.

Wolfe felt her svelte torso slide through his hands as he

caught her, his arms winding around her before she hit the ground. Her rib cage heaved as she dragged in an unsteady breath, the movement flattening her soft breasts against his hard chest.

Her arms clung tight around his neck, holding his face against the warm pulse at the base of her neck. His senses instantly filled with her heat and sweet perfume. He usually found perfume cloying. Hers wasn't, and was probably the reason he held her longer than he needed to. Held her moulded against him as if he'd been doing it his whole life. Held her long enough to wonder how it would feel to fit himself deep inside her.

Tight. Hot. Wet.

Wolfe's head reared back as his senses took over and he found himself staring into exquisite, wide-spaced navy blue eyes that made him feel as if he'd been hit by a land-to-air missile.

'You can put me down now,' she said a little breathlessly.

He could slide his hands down to her butt and wrap her legs around his waist, as well.

As if he'd spoken out loud the air between them thickened, and he felt every hot inch of her go impossibly still against him.

Almost embarrassed by a stupefyingly strong urge to crush her mouth beneath his, which had held him spellbound for— God—he hoped only seconds, he none-too-gently set her on her feet and stepped back from her.

It was only then that he noticed the slight swelling above her right temple.

'You should get that looked at,' he instructed roughly.

Her eyes licked over his face before meeting his, her breathing as uneven as his heart rate. 'I'm fine.'

'Put your shoes on. It's time to go.' He busied himself with collecting Achilles while his mind came back on line. By rights he should search her, to make sure she was clean, but, *hell*, he wasn't touching her again. Bad enough he'd have to put her on the back of the horse since Eric and Dane had yet to return.

He frowned, wondering what was taking them so long.

'I'd rather walk.' Her eyes flitted from the stamping stallion and back to him.

Realising he was functioning below par, and that had he been on a real military expedition he might well be dead now, Wolfe re-engaged his instincts and gave her a hard stare. 'You can try my patience, Princess, but I wouldn't recommend it.'

She blinked, as if she hadn't expected his curt tone. 'Unlike your men, I don't take orders from you.'

Wolfe widened his stance in a purely dominant move he knew she hadn't missed. 'We have yet to establish your real identity, so you either get on that horse or I'll use one of these reins to bind your hands and drag you behind.'

'I'd like to see you try,' she invited him coolly.

He couldn't believe this posh piece of work was calling his bluff. 'Would you, now?'

She balled her hands on her hips and drew his sight to her slender curves. Not a clever move in his currently cantankerous state of combined anger and arousal. Of course he wouldn't drag her, but he'd subdue her and throw her over his saddle.

He saw the moment she realised his threat wasn't entirely idle.

'Only men with very small appendages play the tough guy.'

'And only women who are incredibly stupid challenge a man they've never met to prove his masculinity. Fortunately for you, I don't feel the least threatened to prove myself by shrewish females.'

'What can I say?' She cocked her hip towards him insolently. 'You bring out the best in me.'

Wolfe breathed deep at her intentionally provocative manner. 'I'm sure that's very far from your best, Princess,' he drawled.

Her brows slowly rose and Wolfe realised he'd inadvertently revealed how attractive he found her. No doubt it was something she was used to and, like all women in his experience, would take absolute advantage of it given half the chance.

Something he didn't plan to do.

Aggravated by his one-track mind, he was about to end her rebellious stance by physically dumping her onto the horse when his phone rang.

'We found the car, boss. She's legit. Her purse must have been thrown from her bag because it was lodged under the front seat.'

Wolfe grunted a reply and told his men to meet him at the cottage.

He looked up in time to catch her superior expression and knew that she'd overheard his conversation. 'Seems you are who you say you are. Next time use the gate.' He brought Achilles alongside her and grabbed the stirrup. 'Give me your leg.'

'You're not even going to apologise?'

Her tone spoke of generations of superiority that made any apology Wolfe might have given die on his lips.

'Your leg?' he repeated, his eyes cool and guarded against the fire pouring out of hers.

Moving forward, she tossed her ponytail over her shoulder, caught her heel on a rock and pitched straight into his arms.

Already highly sensitised to her touch, and not sure if the move had been deliberate, to throw him off balance, Wolfe immediately set her away from him. 'And don't try using that sexy little body to garner any favours, Princess.'

'Trust me when I say that touching you is the last thing I would want to do.'

She presented him with her stiff back, gathered the reins

up in one hand and stamped her foot into his hand. Wolfe didn't know whether to be amused by her or angered, and perhaps if he hadn't been about to head off after Gilles's wedding to oversee an important software installation he might have hung around to test her lofty challenge. But he was, and he wasn't stupid enough to get involved with another highly strung female.

'Shift back,' he grated. No way was she riding in front, where she would be cradled between his hard thighs.

'You know, all that masculine muttering is entirely uncalled for. You are unquestionably the most irritating individual I have ever had the misfortune to come across.'

Wolfe was just about to tell her the feeling was entirely mutual when she twisted the reins out of his slack hold and dug her heels into Achilles's side. The horse responded like the thoroughbred it was and sprang into an instant gallop.

Wolfe couldn't believe it!

Not only had the little spitfire turned him on just by breathing, she had completely got the better of him. Neither of which had happened to him in… It had *never* happened before!

'Dammit!'

Cursing under his breath, Wolfe whistled sharply. If Gilles had trained his animals correctly the horse should come to a complete stop.

CHAPTER TWO

ONE MINUTE AVA was flying across the uneven ground with breathless speed and the next she wasn't moving at all. The horse did little more than twitch its majestic tail as she tried to urge him forward. By the time she worked out what had happened the overbearing *inbecile* was almost upon her.

'Come on, horse. Do *not* listen to him. He is nobody.'

'You look like butter wouldn't melt in your mouth, but you're a bossy little thing aren't you, Princess?'

'You are so arrogant.'

He settled his hands on his hips. 'That's rich, coming from you.'

'I am not arrogant,' she said in a voice that would have made her father proud. 'I am confident. There is a difference.'

He had the gall to laugh. 'And the difference would fit inside a flea's arse.'

Ava used her sweetest voice to call him a foul name in French, knowing he probably wouldn't understand her.

He shook his head and tsked. 'Temper, temper.' His gaze lifted to her hair. 'If I didn't know better I'd say there was a red streak running through that glossy mane of yours.'

A chauvinist. How original. 'I suppose you think I should be flattered you didn't say blond?'

'No, I would never confuse you with a blonde,' he said with mock seriousness. 'I like blondes.'

'Then I *do* consider myself flattered!'

She thought about flicking the reins to try and ride off again, but he read her mind and his jaw clenched. 'I don't make the same mistakes twice. Shift back.'

Ava noticed how big the hand was that gripped the reins and instantly recalled how they had felt on her body as he'd caught her. Once again her pelvis clenched, sending delicious ripples of sensation through her whole body. Surprised, and a little breathless, she berated herself for the physical reaction. He was Neanderthal man two million-odd years later, his blood supply no doubt taken up by all the muscles in his body instead of his head, where he needed it most.

He moved a small handgun out from under the back of his shirt and tucked it inside his boot, and she felt another traitorous thrill shoot straight to her core. Peevishly she hoped the gun went off and shot him in the foot.

'I'm sure many women get turned on by your barbaric tactics, but I can assure you I am not one of them.'

'Good to know.' He stroked the horse's neck in long, smooth sweeps. 'Since I'm not trying to turn you on.'

His eyes glittered up at her and made her heart pump just that little bit faster. Lord, she hoped he didn't know she was lying, because she *shouldn't* find this uncultured beast of a man so attractive.

Grabbing the pommel, he fitted his foot into the stirrup. 'Now, you can ride up in front between my legs if you want to, Princess. Who knows? It might be fun.'

Ava quickly scooted back and ground her teeth together when he gave a low, sexy laugh. His voice was rich and totally indolent, as if he was always thinking of ways to pleasure a woman.

He swung easily onto the great horse, his large frame filling the saddle. The horse shifted as it readjusted to take their weight. 'You might want to hang on.' He shot over his shoulder, drawing up the reins.

'I am.'

He glanced to where her hands gripped the saddle blanket before raising his eyes back to hers. Ava drew in a sharp breath at the impact.

'I meant to me.'

Ava had no intention of holding on to him. 'Dream on.'

He gave a half smile, as if he might do exactly that, clenched his powerful thighs, and the horse sprang forwards as if it had nothing more than a child on its back.

Instinctively Ava clutched at his shirt and found herself plastered up against the back of him. He was hard! And hot! Unable to help herself, she widened her fingers over his abdominal muscles as if she needed to do so to prevent herself from falling off. Colyn had always bemoaned the fact that she wasn't tactile enough for him, but right now she could barely resist the urge to explore this stranger's muscular physique. She thought she heard him blow out a hard breath and, slightly embarrassed at her temerity, quickly moved her fingers to his narrow hips. The roll of muscle there told her that he worked out. A lot.

Fortunately it took no time for the spirited stallion to make it to the main buildings. Unfortunately it was still long enough for the friction from the saddle and his body to make the space between her legs feel soft and moist.

Mon Dieu.

Yes, it had been a long time since she had been intimate with a man, but this one was *so* not her type…

Focusing on her surroundings, instead of the man she could feel with every cell of her body, she realised they weren't at the stables but at one of the side entrances to the main building.

About to ask what they were doing there, she stopped when he twisted around in the saddle, grabbed her under her arm and effortlessly lifted her off the horse. Ava felt the slide of his thigh all the way down her body and closed her eyes briefly to block out the rush of heat coursing through her. When her feet finally touched the ground she locked her knees to take her weight and had to force herself to push away from his heat.

'Any time you want to learn how to fly again, Princess, you just call me, okay?'

Ava curled her lip, but before she could come up with a pithy retort he had dug his heels into the stallion and was gone.

Thank God. It would take two top-of-the-line masseurs to work the tension out of her back after that!

'Ma'am? Are you lost?'

A footman materialised at her side, and it was only then that Ava registered that her 'captor' had set her down in a private part of the castle, far from the prying eyes of arriving guests. It was probably more because he was used to using the servants' entrance than out of any actual consideration for her, but even as she had the ungrateful thought she had a feeling she was wrong.

Wolfe stood on the lime-green lawn at the side of the white marquee set up as a servers' area under the shade of a weeping willow. He wasn't on duty, but his eyes scanned the throng of wedding guests holding sparkling glasses of wine and champagne and recapping the beautiful service they had just witnessed.

The men mostly wore classic morning suits, as he did, and the women were tastefully attired in afternoon dresses and sunhats. Later, at the evening reception, they would all change into their ballroom best.

It was only when his eyes finally found the Princess, in a small cluster of women waiting to talk to the bride, that he realised he'd been searching for her.

He cursed under his breath. His reaction to her was annoyingly primal. And annoyingly still present. The problem, he decided as he studied her, was that she had an element of the conquest about her. All that snooty standoffishness combined with her natural beauty was like a summons to any man who had red blood pumping through his veins. But while he enjoyed a challenge—possibly more than most men—some inner sense of self-preservation warned him to keep his distance.

He had very firm rules when it came to women and he never deviated from them. Keep it short, keep it sweet and, most importantly, keep it simple. This posh princess had *complicated* written all over her pretty face.

He'd seen enough relationships fall apart to last him a lifetime, and while logically he knew not all couples ended up on the scrap heap he wasn't prepared to take the chance. It was probably the only risk he wasn't willing to take, because when it all went pear-shaped the fall-out was usually devastating.

'I know that face. You're brooding about something.'

Wolfe glanced at Gilles, who had ambled up with two glasses of champagne in his hands. Wolfe took one and smiled. 'Just enjoying the frivolities.'

Gilles gave him a droll look. Previously they had both bemoaned any wedding they'd been forced to attend. 'I thought you were bringing someone with you today?'

Wolfe took a sip and tried not to wince as the warming liquid pooled in his mouth. 'Not while I'm working.'

Gilles lowered his own glass, amusement dancing in his eyes. 'She dumped you?'

Wolfe recalled the look on Astrid's angry face when he'd told her he wouldn't be seeing her again. 'Yep.'

'In…' Gilles glanced at his watch '…how many hours?'

Wolfe chuckled. He'd enjoyed Astrid's company for five busy nights while he was working in Vienna a month ago, and she had enjoyed his. When he'd tried to say goodbye she'd kicked up a stink. Accused him of using her. Wolfe's anger had surfaced then. He knew he had a name for being a heartless womaniser but he was simply honest. He didn't see the point in beating around the bush and pretending to feel things he didn't. And nor did he sleep with as many women as his reputation would suggest. He wouldn't have any time left over for work if he did.

'What can I say? She was one of the smart ones.'

Wolfe waited for his friend to start up another good-natured lecture about settling down. Anne, it seemed, had reformed the once bad-boy Marquis to the point where Wolfe now almost preferred her company to his.

'Well, that works out well for me.'

'It does?'

Gilles chuckled. 'Don't look so relieved. I wasn't about to try and reform the unreformable.'

'Thank God.'

'But I do need a favour.'

Favours Wolfe could do.

'Sure.'

'There's a girl I need you to keep your eye on tonight at the reception.'

Wolfe didn't exactly look at the sky, but he came close. 'Friend of Anne's, by chance?'

'Yes, actually. But, no, I'm not trying to set you up, you suspicious clod. She's the woman my father wanted me to marry.'

Gilles's words sparked a distant memory of a late-night chat from years back that Wolfe had completely forgotten about. He took another pull of his drink and wished it was beer in an icy bottle instead of champagne in a tepid glass. 'I'm listening.'

'Years ago my father and hers came to the decision that we would forge a strong union if we married when we came of age.'

'I think you "came of age" about ten years ago, my friend, and isn't that a little last century?'

Gilles's mouth twisted into an ironic smile. 'You've met

my father. Hers is worse. Anyway, the media have done a good job beating some life into the old story this past week, playing up the whole jilted fiancée thing, and Anne said it's been a bit rough on her.'

Wolfe knew what it felt like to be talked about behind his back. Even if the people in the small town he'd grown up in had been doing so out of sympathy rather than slander. At least for him and his brother, at any rate. 'What's wrong with her?' he asked suspiciously.

Gilles scoffed. 'Nothing. But I don't want you to sleep with her. Actually, I'd be downright angry if you did. She's gorgeous, and way too good for you. I just want you to keep an eye on her. Make sure she's having a good time.'

'Who is she?' he asked, premonition snaking down his spine.

'See the woman talking to Anne now?'

Wolfe didn't have to look to know it was the Princess from the wall and he nearly groaned. Anyone but her. But at least now it made sense why she had been so familiar with the estate. They were family friends.

Wolfe turned his back on the woman he was intent on avoiding for the rest of his life. 'I'm sure she can take care of herself.'

Gilles gave him a quizzical look and Wolfe cursed his curt tone. He had nothing against the Princess, really. Except for the fact that she'd occupied his mind all afternoon and made him want to push her sweet skirt up around her waist and take her up against the nearest hundred-year-old oak. He definitely didn't want to find out that Gilles had once been with her. Had they been lovers? The thought left a sour taste in his mouth.

'I'm sure she will, too, but as she's attending the wedding alone I thought you could keep your eye on her for me. You know—ask her to dance, make sure she has a drink.'

Today he'd been mistaken for a rescue service, a gardener

and now… 'You've got waiters for that, and I'm not a damned babysitter.'

Gilles's eyebrows shot up, but before he could say anything his new wife stepped around Wolfe and curled her arm through Gilles's. 'Babysitting who?'

Her green eyes met Wolfe's speculatively and Wolfe saw Gilles's eyes fall guiltily on someone behind him.

'I hope you do not mean me, Gilles?' Ava's tone was as lyrical and as superior as Wolfe remembered it.

Gilles stepped forward and kissed both her cheeks. 'Ava, you look as beautiful as ever.'

'I can see that you *do* mean me,' she berated lightly. 'And I can assure you I do not need babysitting.'

Her eyes briefly cut to Wolfe's with such aloof disdain it made him want to smile. He remembered her hands splayed over the ridges of his abdominal muscles as she'd clung to him on the horse. She might not like him very much, but he knew dislike wasn't the *only* emotion she felt.

'Of course you don't, *ma petite*.' Gilles humoured her. 'Now, let me introduce you to Wolfe, a good friend of mine.'

Unable to prevent himself from ruffling her regal feathers, Wolfe tilted his head. 'We've met. How's the head?' His eyes drifted to the wide-brimmed hat, tilted to one side to conceal the bruise on her forehead. The pale pink exactly matched a flirty two-piece suit that followed the line of her curves all the way to her perfectly shaped calves and slender ankles.

Exceptional legs, he thought, his gaze trekking slowly back up to her face.

She arched a brow that told him she hadn't taken kindly to his once-over, or to the implied intimacy in his tone.

'You know each other?' Gilles regarded Ava in surprise. 'No.'

'Oh?' Gilles cut his curious gaze back to Wolfe.

'Shall I tell him, or do you want to?' Wolfe drawled.

After briefly glaring all sorts of retribution his way, she

turned a serene smile on Gilles and Anne. 'It was nothing. I had a small problem with my car and your friend *kindly* provided me with a lift to the château.'

'A small problem with your car?' Gilles frowned.

Wolfe held her gaze as he felt the others turn to him and told himself to leave well enough alone. Ruffling her glorious feathers was not on his agenda, even if his body was demanding that he forge a new one—preferably starting with her naked on top of a set of silk sheets. 'What Her Highness means is that she had a car accident, climbed your outer wall and got captured by my men—'

'And stole your horse because you were being incredibly rude!' she provided, cutting Gilles's blustering in half.

Wolfe shifted his weight and stuck one hand into his pocket. 'And here I was thinking you stole him because you wanted to go for a ride.' He rubbed his hand across his abdomen, unable to stop himself from teasing her a little.

'I did think about it,' she murmured huskily, the quick dart of her pink tongue caressing her lower lip and sending a bolt of lust straight to his groin. 'But since he wasn't up to my usual standard I thought why bother?'

Wolfe laughed at her bald-faced put-down. Gilles was fortunately too worried about her accident to pick up on the subtext, but Anne's interested glances told him that she wasn't quite as obtuse.

'You weren't hurt?' Anne queried, concern lacing her words.

'A bump on the head,' Ava dismissed casually. 'Really, the whole thing was *incredibly* insignificant.'

Wolfe's lips quirked. 'You know, I wouldn't have described it that way myself.'

'No?' Ava held his gaze. 'Maybe you need to get out more.'

'Maybe I do,' he agreed, noting the line of pink that highlighted her lovely cheekbones. Maybe he needed to get out with *her*. No. He'd already decided not to go there. But, damn, he was enjoying sparring with her.

'But what were you doing on the wall?' Gilles interrupted with a frown.

'Well, trying to get down, obviously,' Ava returned pithily. 'Which would have been a lot easier if you hadn't removed that lovely old chestnut tree.'

Gilles gave a typically Gallic shrug. 'I had no choice. It was a security risk.'

Wolfe laughed right up until the moment she shared a warm smile with Gilles. Again he wondered at their history. Had she been in love with his friend? Was she still? Was that why Gilles had asked him to watch out for her? Was it possible she would cause trouble if he didn't? Questions, questions, questions. And there was really only one he wanted answered.

How responsive would she be in his bed?

His name suited him, Ava mused absently, nursing a flute of champagne as she willed the evening reception to finish.

Predatory.

Intense.

Arrogant.

And utterly transfixing when he turned those molten toffee-coloured eyes on her. Not to mention aloof and emotionally unavailable if the evening gossip was to be believed.

'They call him Ice, and apparently he has a heart as hard to find as a pink diamond,' one woman had said, giggling as she'd gazed longingly across the room at him.

Ava had rolled her eyes. She knew many women saw an unattainable man—especially a wealthy alpha male like Wolfe—as a personal challenge to go forth and rehabilitate, but she wasn't one of them. She was only interested in a man who was caring and considerate and who respected a woman as more than just a trophy to be admired and trotted out when it suited him. A gentle, sophisticated man, who was looking for love and companionship more than short affairs with a variety of women.

That thought reminded her of the luncheon she'd had with Anne last month. 'Hot' and 'divine' were words that had been bandied around when she'd talked about a friend of Gilles's called Wolfe. As had 'confirmed bachelor'. Ava remembered zoning out at that point, telling her friend she wasn't at all interested in commitment-phobes like her ex. Which put Gilles's 'hot' friend with the beautiful eyes and corrugated abdominal muscles firmly off her Christmas list.

Even if he *did* looked incredible in a custom-made tuxedo.

Oh, stop, she scolded herself. Lots of men looked incredible in tuxedos; they were the equivalent of a corset for women.

Of course lots of men hadn't made her burn just by looking at her, or made her want to touch them all over, but that was just bad luck. Or maybe it was more to do with how uncomfortable she felt tonight. Maybe she was just looking for a distraction from all the polite smiles and curious stares from many of the other guests.

Those who were friends knew that she'd never seriously been involved with Gilles, but they were intent on having a good time and she felt curiously lonely in the large crowd.

Her mind was intent on remembering the way Wolfe had held her in his arms that morning, with such breathless ease she hadn't been able to stop herself from imagining what it would be like to kiss him. Embarrassingly, she had even held herself perfectly still as if in anticipation of that kiss!

Pah!

She was just feeling a little strained after having to put on a brave face all day. And, okay, she was also a little intrigued by Wolfe. It had been a long time since a man had caught her attention. A long time since she had wondered about his kiss. A long time since she had felt the warmth of a man's loving embrace. Not that Wolfe's would be loving—but it would be warm…

Ava pulled a wry face at herself. Before today she wouldn't have said she had missed a man's embrace at all. But right now, watching this one they called Ice nonchalantly circle the room but not quite participate in the frivolities made her ache for it.

And don't try using that sexy little body to garner any favours, Princess.

Ava's lips tightened.

Arrogant.

Rude.

Unsophisticated.

Uncultured.

So why had she surreptitiously touched his body at the first opportunity?

Ava shivered and raised her champagne glass to her lips. Empty. *Drat.*

The doctor Wolfe had sent to see her—an unexpectedly nice gesture she still had to thank him for—had told her it would be best if she didn't drink tonight. Her position as 'jilted fiancée' in a room full of her peers told her it would be best if she did.

Taking another glass of Gilles's best from a passing waiter, she took a fortifying sip. It didn't surprise her that Wolfe had a reputation with women. A man who could lift a fully grown woman off a horse and lower her slowly to the ground with one hand held a certain *earthy* appeal.

For *some*, she reminded herself firmly. Not for her.

'My dance, I believe?'

For a minute Ava imagined the deep voice behind her was Wolfe, but it lacked a certain velvety-rough tenor and hadn't sent any delicious tingles down her spine so she knew it wasn't. Turning, she smiled at a nice English Lord who had been hounding her all night.

She didn't feel like dancing with him, but nor did she feel like triggering more gossip by refusing every man who approached her. Smiling with a polite reserve she hoped he read as, *Lovely, but be assured I'm not interested in furthering our acquaintance*, she stepped into his arms. Which was when she caught sight of Wolfe, watching her yet again from across the room. Her eyes immediately ran over the woman at his side, who looked young, happy and relaxed. By contrast Ava felt old, surly and uptight. Which was partly Wolfe's fault, she thought churlishly, because she couldn't seem to stop thinking about him.

And the fact that he had a beautiful woman at his side while he held his eyes on her only confirmed that the talk about him playing the field was true. Unless he had been watching her all night because of Gilles's silly request that he 'babysit' her. For some reason the latter thought aggravated Ava more than the former.

Five minutes later, feeling as graceful as a goose under Wolfe's constant regard, she sent her dance partner to fetch her a glass of water so she could find out. She didn't need an audience when she told Wolfe that his attention was not only supremely annoying but totally unnecessary.

Orientating herself in the vast room, she located him lazily propping up a wall in a dimly lit section of the ballroom, feeling ridiculously elated when she found the bubbly blonde was no longer running her fingernails up and down his powerful forearm.

He didn't say anything when she stopped in front of him, just looked down at her through a screen of thick dark lashes that made his mood impossible to gauge. Not that it mattered. She was here about *her* feelings, not his.

'You are eyeing me off because Gilles asked you, too, no?' She knew she'd mixed up her words—her English was always clumsy when she was agitated.

'I think the term you're looking for is *watching over you*.'

Amusement laced his tone and her spine stiffened in annoyance.

'I don't need watching.'

'I thought all women liked to be watched. Isn't that why you wrap yourselves up in those slinky dresses?' His drink swayed as he made an up-and-down motion with his hand.

Ava glanced down at her strapless jade-green gown, which was fitted to the waist and then fell to the floor in silky waves. 'My dress is elegant, not *slinky.*'

'Why don't we agree on elegantly slinky, for argument's sake?'

He was smooth, this handsome Australian, very smooth. 'I do not need babysitting,' Ava said, reminding herself that she had not approached him to flirt with him.

'I never said you did. In fact I told Gilles you could take care of yourself.'

'Presumably because I made off with your horse?'

'You didn't make off with my horse.' The pitch of his voice dropped subtly. 'But you did play a pretty dangerous game on him.'

Ava's heart kicked up a notch at his silky taunt. 'I'm quite sure I don't know what you mean.'

Wolfe smiled. 'I'm quite sure you do.'

He took a lazy sip of his beer and her eyes were drawn to the strong column of his throat when he swallowed. She looked up to find that his eyes had closed to half-mast as she watched him and her breasts grew heavy.

Determined to ignore the sensation, she continued. 'So, if you are not doing Gilles's bidding, why do you watch me?'

'Why do you think?'

His eyes toured over her body and she had a pretty good indication of why. Something hot and quivery vibrated up and down her spine. The memory of the feel of his hands on her torso returned. They were so large they had almost swallowed her whole.

Perturbed by the physical response he so effortlessly created in her, Ava shook her head. Compared to her he appeared so cool and relaxed, and yet she was sure if she touched him he'd feel as tightly coiled as a spring.

'I think you are a man who gets what he wants a little too often, Ice!' she challenged, deciding that he was messing with her head. The way he looked at her. The way his eyes lingered on her mouth. She knew he felt the chemistry between them and she wondered why she wanted to push him to show her. Even more she wondered what it would take to make this self-contained man lose control.

'Is that so?'

'Yes.' Ava tried to match his careless tone even though her heart was thumping inside her chest. 'The word in the powder room is that you steal hearts wherever you go.'

'Have you been talking about me, Princess?'

Ava felt her temper spike at his evasiveness. 'That's not an answer.'

His eyebrow rose at her sharp tone. 'You didn't ask a question.'

Wanting to stamp her foot in frustration, she decided the smart thing to do was to bid him goodnight. She'd already decided to ignore the way he made her feel, and yet here she was almost begging him to make her change her mind.

Dragging her eyes from his sensual half smile, she took a step back and curled a stray wisp of hair behind her ear. 'Fine. If you'll—'

His hand shot out and snagged her upper arm. His hold was gentle, yet uncompromising, and she couldn't prevent a gasp of surprise at the unexpectedness of it. 'Don't play games with me, Rapunzel. I guarantee you'll lose.'

Ava barely contained her temper. If anyone was playing games here it was him, not her. And if a small voice in her head was asking her if trying to get the better of him on the lawn earlier had not been a game—well, she didn't much care right now.

'You have that wrong.' She lifted her chin. 'I am not the

one playing games here.' Because deep down she knew it would be beyond stupid to invite this man into her life in any capacity.

He stared at her, finally letting the sensual heat she had felt in him all night shine through in his eyes. She couldn't look away, like a deer caught in headlights as he inexorably drew closer—only realising it was she who had swayed towards him when a glass of mineral water was thrust in front of her face.

'There you are,' Lord Parker puffed, pushing his chest out in Wolfe's direction.

Half expecting Wolfe to challenge him, Ava was absurdly disappointed when all he did was slide a thumb across the rampaging pulse-point in her wrist before releasing her. As if as an afterthought he bent towards her, his mouth close to her ear, his intoxicating scent making her breathless.

'Careful what you wish for, Princess. You just might get it.' He straightened and inclined his head in her direction. 'If you'll excuse me?' He mimicked the cool words she'd been about to serve him moments earlier before striding across the marble floor and into another room.

Ava let out a long pent-up breath. She should be glad he was gone. He was arrogant, obnoxious, and too cool for school—and yet he made her burn hotter than any man ever had before. It was a powerful aphrodisiac. All-consuming and tempting. And despite the fact that he had just warned her off some obtuse part of her still wanted to know what it would feel like to have those capable hands on her heated skin—her *naked*, heated skin.

'Ladies and gentlemen…'

The MC interrupted Ava's conflicting thoughts.

'The bride is about to throw her bouquet before the couple departs for the evening.'

A triumphant squeal rent the air as the bouquet was caught by one of Anne's American friends, followed by a stream of synchronised clapping as the bride and groom made their way upstairs. They would be spending the night at the château before leaving for their honeymoon after luncheon the following day.

Ava joined in the well-wishing but her chest felt tight. Anne and Gilles were so happy. So in love. An old fear that she would never get to experience that depth of emotion with someone special cut across the happiness she felt for them both.

Realising she must be more out of balance than she'd first thought, she decided to call it a night. Glancing around the room, she noted that Wolfe was nowhere to be seen and felt another stab of irritation at herself. She was torn between wanting him to want her and wanting him not to. It was as if she was somehow in thrall to him. As if her brain no longer functioned, or it functioned but was stuck in one groove, like the needle on an old-fashioned record player. The word *sex* was going round and round in her head like an endlessly exciting mantra.

Ava stared at her water glass and wondered if someone had drugged it. The last thing she wanted was sex with a man completely unsuitable for her hopes and dreams. Wasn't it?

Annoyed, she pivoted on her heel—and gasped when she nearly ran smack into the man who had occupied her mind pretty much the entire day and night.

'You're leaving before our dance,' he murmured silkily.

The balls of her feet hurt and she didn't want to dance. 'I did not think you played games.' She could barely hear her own voice above the sound of her thundering heartbeat. Had he been toying with her to heighten her awareness of him? If so, it had worked. She had never been more aware of a man in her life.

She saw his nostrils flare at her confrontational tone and something primal unfurled low in her pelvis, because she knew that he *did* play games. And even though it went against all her principles part of her wanted to play—with him—tonight.

'Maybe I want to feel you in my arms one more time.'

Heat rushed through her body as his husky words burned her up inside. *How did any woman stop herself from drowning under such blazingly sexual intensity?*

'Do you?'

As if sensing her near capitulation, he gave her a lupine smile. 'Yes.' He set her drink aside and swept her into his arms.

Ava's stomach flipped. She'd like to think that she'd *let* him walk her backwards onto the dance floor—although that would imply she still had some influence over her actions and she wasn't sure that she did.

'What about what *I* want?' The question was meant to establish some sense of control on her part, but she suspected that he knew what he did to her and had seen right through it.

He brought the hand holding hers towards her face and rotated it so that his knuckles gently drifted across her cheekbone. 'This *is* what you want, Princess.'

A cascade of sensations made her shiver and she told herself to tread carefully. Told herself that there was only one kind of man who parried around a woman all night and then approached her at the end. The kind her mother would have told her to steer well clear of. What it said about her wanting him regardless she didn't want to think about.

He was so sure. So confident. She should shoot him down in flames. Using his own pistol to do it.

Instead she braced herself against his magnetic sensuality and told herself she would walk away at the end of the song.

'One dance.'

CHAPTER THREE

DANCE? WOLFE DIDN'T want to dance with her. He wanted to possess her. And for a self-confessed non-game-player he had played a game of parry and retreat with her to rival all others.

Not intentionally.

His *intention* had been to avoid her. But once she'd entered the ballroom in a green dress that flowed around her body like a caressing hand he'd been lost.

Well, maybe not lost. More like mesmerised. And it had annoyed the hell out of him that he'd noticed that every other male in the room felt the same way. The married ones couldn't do anything about it, but the single ones had been lining up as if she was a participant in some secret speed-dating service.

He, on the other hand, had spent most of the night fighting the urge to muscle his way through the throng of wedding guests and throw her over his shoulder like the barbarian she had accused him of being. Hell, his body had been so attuned to hers he'd practically known every time she'd blinked.

Chemistry. He'd never experienced it quite so strongly. But he knew the quickest way to appease it would be to have her. So far he'd steadfastly stuck to his plan not to go near her but, hell, why not? He was only responding to her like any other healthy male who had held a beautiful woman in his arms and wanted her. Nothing complicated about that.

In fact it was so simple he didn't know why he was dwelling on it so much.

He would have had more to dwell on if he *hadn't* wanted her. And as for that instant tilting of the world he'd felt earlier when he'd caught her…well, it was only lust. Raw, pagan, blow-your-head-open lust. Perfectly rational. Perfectly normal.

Wolfe looked down into her face. Her cheeks were pink and her lips were softly parted as she breathed shallowly. His gaze drifted lower, to the firm thrust of her breasts, her aroused nipples, and then back up. Her gaze was slumberous but slightly guarded, as if she too were a little taken aback by the strength of this thing between them.

Without making a conscious decision to do so, he spread his hand possessively over her hip, pressing her closer. He knew the minute she felt his hardness because she made one of those softly feminine sounds that had his body jerking in response.

It made him want to spear his hand in her upswept hair and drag her mouth to his, but at the last minute the sounds of the party still in progress penetrated his desire-drugged mind. Instead he cupped her chin in his palm and brought her eyes to his. 'I want you, Ava. I want to kiss you until you can't see straight and make love to you until you can't move. I've thought of nothing else all day.'

A shiver raced through her and Wolfe felt as if he was poised on the blade of a knife as he waited for her response.

'I…' She blew out a breath. Swallowed heavily. 'Okay.'

Exalted, and no longer questioning his need for her, Wolfe grabbed her hand and fought to keep his steps measured as he led her off the dance floor.

She'd been allocated a room in the east wing of the château and he didn't pause for breath until, on the second-floor landing, he felt a soft tug on his hand.

Turning, he watched her run her hands down the sides of her dress, the nervous gesture only serving to mould it closer. 'Wolfe.' She cleared her throat. 'I'm not sure this is such a good idea.'

Wolfe wasn't sure about anything except that the sound of his name in her husky, accented voice twisted his insides into a mess. A very hot mess. 'Not sure what is such a good idea? This?'

He backed her against the stone wall and raised his hands to frame her face. Then he used every ounce of skill he possessed and leant down to claim her mouth with his.

Immediately his senses became overloaded with the rich, intoxicating taste of her. He'd known it would be like this. Overpowering. Overwhelming. Her ruby lips were so much fuller and sweeter than he had imagined, and when she parted them and pressed closer the instinct to ravage her consumed him.

His fingers dug into her scalp to hold her steady as he deepened the kiss, his tongue sweeping into her mouth to explore every corner.

'Wolfe, please…'

Her soft whimper of need inflamed him to the point of madness. He couldn't get enough of her. His hands shaped her slender curves, desperate to delve under the dress, and he was keenly satisfied when she ardently returned his hunger. Her uncertainty of moments ago was flung into the flames of a desire so bright it burned him alive.

She was sensational, and he ground himself against her in ardent anticipation. He couldn't remember ever feeling this frenzy of need before, and it was just dumb luck that a door banged somewhere along the corridor and brought him back to his senses.

Fighting for control, he grabbed her hand again and didn't stop until they were both breathless and inside her bedroom, the door firmly closed behind.

He hit the light switch and stared at her.

She stood in the centre of the historically preserved room like a pagan offering, her lips already moist and swollen from his kisses. She sucked in a deep breath and he thought he saw a shadow of vulnerability chase itself across her face.

It gave him a moment's pause.

He had avoided thinking about a woman in any serious capacity his whole life, after having to clean up the damage his mother had caused by her actions. But this wasn't serious. Making love—having sex, he amended—with Ava de Veers was not a threat to his wellbeing in any way, shape or form.

It was about pleasure. Mutual, unadulterated pleasure.

'I like the light on,' he rasped.

She moistened her lips. 'I don't…mind.'

Satisfied that he knew exactly what he was doing, Wolfe shoved away from the door and paced towards her. He stopped a breath from touching her and gazed into her wide-spaced smoky eyes, searching out any further signs of apprehension, promising himself he would stop if she showed even a hint of uncertainty. Fortunately he didn't have to test that theory, because her gaze could have melted iron when it met his.

His iron will.

Shaking off the insidious devil of doubt that told him once was never going to be enough with this woman, he curled one hand around the nape of her neck and pulled her up onto her toes. She steadied herself by placing her hands on his shoulders. The air between them turned to syrup as she tilted her head back into his hand, presenting him with the elegant arch of her neck.

Wolfe felt his lip curl upward as he thought of the recent vampire craze in the cinemas. Suddenly he understood the draw. Lust pounded through his blood and he brought his other hand up to trace the tender skin she had exposed to his hungry gaze. She opened her eyes, stared into his, and then did something he hadn't expected—she took charge and pressed her lips to his.

He let her sip and nibble at his mouth for maybe ten seconds before that primal feeling she dredged up in him took over. Then his hands and lips firmed and he forced her mouth wide, demanding that she cede everything to him.

And she did. Without hesitation. Her slender arms snaking behind his neck, her body arching into his.

Wolfe told himself to ease off before he scared both of them, but her mouth angled more comfortably under his and he didn't know how it was possible but she took the kiss deeper. Wrapped her sweet tongue around his and made his head spin.

Without really being aware of his surroundings he wrenched his jacket off and pushed her fumbling fingers aside to tear at the buttons on his shirt. Shucking out of it, he welcomed the bite of cooler air on his overheated flesh and the layer of sensation it added.

He released the dark mane of her hair from its tight coil and felt his heart wrench as it cascaded past her delicate shoulders.

Ignoring the swirling emotions ebbing and flowing through his mind, he cupped her breasts and moulded them in his hands. Soft and round, the nipples already poking through the silky fabric of her dress like tiny diamonds. He kneaded and shaped her, his eyes on her face as he roughly dragged his thumbs across both her nipples at once.

'Oh, Wolfe. *Mon Dieu.*'

Her husky groan urged him to draw the hidden side-zipper of her dress down until her pale, perfect breasts stood proud and taut in front of him.

'Ava, you're—' He swore as words failed him and bent to draw a dusky pink nipple into his starving mouth. The taste of her made him throb, and when she clutched his head to hold him closer he gave up any pretense of finesse, scooping her into his arms and yanking off the ugly floral bedspread before depositing her on crisp white sheets.

She leant up on her elbows and watched him through heavy-lidded eyes as he dragged the silky gown from her long legs and tossed it aside.

Wolfe took her in as he stripped off his remaining clothing: her wavy hair a dark ripple down her back, her sweet breasts rising and falling in time with her heavy breaths, her narrow waist, and the sheer purple panties that revealed more than they hid.

Her woman's scent rose up to tease him and he climbed onto the bed and came over her, his hands braced on either side of her face. 'Now, my lovely, I have you right where I want you.'

Her hands came up between them, curling into his chest hair. Her smile was full of womanly provocation. Her actions thankfully belying her earlier hesitation. 'You like to think you're in control, but I am stronger than I look.' She scratched her nails lightly against his skin like a cat.

She shuddered beautifully beneath him and turned her head to capture his mouth with hers. He groaned, sank into the kiss, let himself become absorbed by it. His free hand smoothed down over her torso, learning her wherever he went.

Her own hands were busy, stroking up over the muscles of his arms. When she pushed playfully against his shoulders he didn't budge. 'It feels like you're made of steel. You're completely immovable.'

'Where do you want me to go?' he growled with husky promise. 'Up?' He kissed his way along her neck and bit down gently on her earlobe. 'Or down?' His tongue laved her collarbone and dipped lower, circling ever closer to the centre of her breast.

Her eyes glazed over with desire.

'Ava?'

'Quoi?' She arched off the bed, her breasts begging for his mouth.

'Which way?'

She gave a low moan as he continued to tease her, and when she wrapped one leg around his lean hip he guessed her intention and let her flip him onto his back. She pushed up until she straddled his waist. 'Now who's got whom exactly where they want them?' she said, a look of triumph lighting up her face.

Wolfe grinned and repositioned her until her hot centre cradled his erection. 'That would be me.'

'Ohhh.' Ava spread her palms wide over his chest. 'I know you think—'

Wolfe leant up and suckled one of her peaked nipples into his mouth, cutting off whatever she was about to say. Her wet heat was shredding his control and the time for banter was well past. 'I think you're sensational.' He switched to her other breast and realised that he meant it.

Usually a woman was content to let him lead all the play in bed, but this was much more fun. And the taste of her cherry-red nipples blew his mind.

While she was distracted by his mouth he smoothed his hand down her belly and cupped her where she was open and already wet for him, her filmy panties no barrier to his questing fingers. Her eyes flew open as he found her and pushed a finger inside her slick centre. She cried out his name and balanced over him as she rocked against his hand.

Wolfe's erection jerked painfully but he forced himself to wait, enjoying having her at his mercy. Enjoying the astonished look of pleasure that came over her when he lightly circled her clitoris. And especially enjoying the way she flung her head back in ecstasy and screamed his name as she came for him.

He rode out her orgasm with her until her head flopped

forward, her long hair falling around his face like a silky veil. Needing to be inside her with an urgency that was shocking, Wolfe flipped her onto her back, chuckling softly when she just lay there in silent supplication.

'At least I know how to get your absolute cooperation now.'

Ava pushed her hair back from her face and stretched sinuously. 'What did you just do to me?'

'I made you come.' He rolled on the condom he'd pulled from his wallet and nudged her thighs wider, entering her on one slow, luxurious thrust. 'And now I'm going to do it all over again.'

It took every ounce of control he possessed to keep his movements even and gentle until her body had grown accustomed to his size, but when he felt her completely relax and take all of him fully he couldn't hold back, driving them both to the edge of reason a number of times, until with a sob she gripped his hips and forced him over the edge into a space that was so white-hot he felt as if their bodies would be fused for eternity.

His last coherent thought was, what did he do after an experience like that?

With sexual release came clarity, and Ava could barely believe what had just happened. Had she *really* just had sex with a man she'd met merely hours ago? A friend of Gilles's, no less?

Yes, she had. The evidence was still there in the tiny aftershocks of pleasure rippling through her core, not to mention the harsh breaths of the man lying beside her who looked as if he was choosing his best exit line.

She made a small sound in the back of her throat. 'I told myself I wasn't going to give in to this.'

Her voice had him rolling towards her and the bed dipped under his powerful frame. Ava's skin burned where his eyes raked over her, and as casually as she could she pulled the top sheet up to cover her nudity.

'Why did you?' His voice was gravelly. Sexy.

Was that a serious question? She'd done it because at the time she'd felt she didn't have a choice. As soon as he'd taken her into his arms she hadn't been able to help herself.

'Curiosity,' she said, the word sounding much better to her ears than, *I couldn't help myself.*

'That sounds a bit calculated.' His eyes narrowed as if he was assessing her. Judging her.

'Hardly.' Did he think she had set out to sleep with him?

Embarrassed by the thought, Ava wondered what happened now. Did they engage in polite conversation? Did he get up and leave? Well, he had to, because this was her room, but...

Unsure of herself, and hating the way that made her feel— as if she was standing in front of her father about to be told off for not living up to his expectations—she decided that she had no choice but to fall back on her usual tricks of feigned indifference or taking charge. Since indifference seemed too far out of her reach right now, she chose the latter.

'Please do not feel like you have to stay around because of me. You must be tired, and I'm not the sensitive type.'

Wolfe propped his hand on his elbow, a lazy smile curling his lips. 'This is your idea of pillow-talk?'

No. It was her idea of self-defence. She feigned a yawn. 'Or if you're not tired, I am.'

His golden-brown eyes grew flinty. 'Are you asking me to leave or telling me?'

'Isn't that what you were just thinking you should do?'

His eyes flickered from hers for the briefest of seconds, but it was enough for her to know she had been right in her assumption.

'Actually, I was thinking of inviting you out to dinner.'

His comment took her by surprise, and she was sure he was making it up. She swallowed heavily and pushed aside the tiny kernel of pleasure his words had imbued her with. 'I'd love to, but you're about five hours too late.'

He shook his head in amusement. 'Are you always this prickly after a bout of hot sex?'

Ava swallowed. She didn't know. She'd never had sex like that before. The whole thing both alarmed her and set her body on fire in equal measure. What had happened to her promise only to go out with men who wanted the same thing she did? Love. A family.

Hating the feeling of uncertainty that had her in its tight grip, and hoping she appeared as casual as Wolfe, she let her eyes drift over his stubbled jaw and broad shoulders. When she noticed a small patch of puckered skin right beneath his collarbone she frowned.

'That was a bullet from a semi-automatic.'

Ava's startled gaze met his. Was he serious?

He'd said it as if he was ordering a sandwich from a deli.

'Ouch!' Keeping her voice light to match his as she noticed another scar lower down, she said, 'And this?'

He wrapped a lock of her hair around his finger and started to play with it. 'Shrapnel.'

She pointed to another small mark on his arm. 'Spurned lover?' she queried flippantly, understanding on some level that these wounds weren't badges of honour for him, but represented the deep pain and suffering brought by the uglier side of the life he had once led.

'Accurate sniper.'

He brushed the ends of her hair across her upper chest, where the sheet stopped. Ava felt goose bumps shimmer across her skin and hoped he didn't notice.

'I take it you're not very good at your job?' she teased.

His eyes glittered with amusement. 'That's one way of looking at it.' He let go of her hair and replaced it with his fingers, his movements causing the fabric to drag across her sensitised breasts.

Anticipation made her body throb and, powerless to stop herself, she let her eyes drift lower, taking in the thin trail of hair that bisected his ripped abdomen and moving towards the magnificent erection rising straight out from his body—which was when she saw a jagged white scar that ran along his outer hip towards his thigh.

Her attention torn between the two, she was only vaguely aware of him chuckling. 'You sure you want to know about that one?'

'The scar?'

'That, too,' he teased.

She shook her head. 'What happened?'

'An unfortunate rendezvous with a piece of barbed wire, thanks to one ferociously competitive younger brother. Not very glamorous.'

'Glamorous!' Her brows drew together. 'None of them are *glamorous*!'

'You'd be surprised how many women find them a turn-on.'

She shuddered. 'I don't.'

'No?' He touched her face almost reverently, gently stroking around the bump on her head that—thankfully—pain-killers had taken care of.

Ava smiled and again surprised herself by touching her lips to his. Something flickered in his darkened eyes as she pulled back. It was some unnamed emotion, and the air between them seemed to pulse. She saw the instant Wolfe rejected whatever it was he was feeling and then, in a move that startled with its swiftness, she found herself flat on her back, with him once again braced over the top of her. He captured her hands in one of his and raised them above her head, the completely carnal smile on his lips making her heartbeat quicken.

'Wolfe, we probably shouldn't do this again,' Ava breathed, wishing there was a little more conviction behind her words.

Wolfe lowered his mouth to hers and nudged her thighs further apart with his knees, grabbed his last condom and slipped inside her wet, welcoming heat. 'We probably shouldn't have done it in the first place,' he said on a long groan.

CHAPTER FOUR

WOLFE SCOWLED AS he marched across the circular driveway of the château towards the outer cottage, the quartz driveway crunching loudly beneath his boots in the morning air. It was still early, the sky etched in palest blue with a ribbon of orange rimming the horizon.

Why the hell had he invited her to dinner? And would she take it to mean tonight?

He wasn't even meant to be in town tonight. He had a huge meeting first thing tomorrow morning in Hamburg. He didn't have time to wine and dine a woman. So he'd tell her. Apologise. Explain that he'd forgotten about the business meeting.

He winced inwardly. She'd no doubt think it was an excuse…but what else could he do?

An image of waking up beside her caused him to clench his jaw. After years of practice his body had clicked on just before dawn, and he'd come instantly awake to find a warm, sexy woman curled into his side, with her head cushioned on his numb shoulder and her hand curled over his heart, the soft skin of her upper back silky smooth beneath his rough hands.

No.

There was no way he could have dinner with her—tonight or any other night. The sex had been great—more than great—but he rarely visited Paris, and even if he did he'd have very little time to see her again. And the last thing he needed was another ear-bashing from a woman who wanted more than he could give.

Would Ava be like that? Start accusing him of using her even though they'd both agreed on short-term? He didn't know. And then he almost missed a step as he realised that he and Ava hadn't agreed on anything last night. They'd been too busy ripping each other's clothes off.

Wolfe grinned. Blew out a short breath. Last night had been something else. *She* had been something else. Hot beneath all that regal perfection. He knew if Gilles found out he'd slept with her he'd hop into him, but… His smile turned to a frown. Had Gilles ever held her so intimately? Come to think of it, had *he* ever held a woman so intimately after sex? Didn't he sleep on his stomach as a general rule?

No.

Entering into an affair with his friend's ex-fiancée wasn't going to work for either of them. Better to nip it in the bud now. Tell her it had been wonderful—more wonderful than he'd had in… What did that matter? It had been great. She had been great. But they were adults whose lives were vastly different.

Hell.

He stopped with his hand on the cottage doorknob.

He *had* to take her out to dinner. He might not have been one hundred percent truthful when he'd told her he had been thinking about asking her last night, but he wasn't a complete bastard. The least he could do after the night they'd shared was take her out for a meal.

So, okay, they'd go out. He'd choose a nice little out-of-the-way restaurant, make her feel special, take her home, maybe finish the night off with more sex—not that *that* was a deal-breaker—then he'd leave and his world would be right again.

Nice and simple. Job done.

He turned the knob and greeted his men as he entered the

cottage, not at all sure whether he should be bothered by the unusual level of excitement he felt at the thought of seeing her again.

Ava woke alone and realised immediately from the heat in the room that it was late. Then memory kicked in, facilitated by the lingering scent of Wolfe on the other pillow and the fact that she was naked.

She didn't know what had possessed her to sleep with him last night, but she knew she had definitely not been thinking with her head screwed on straight. No way would she have done all those things if it had been. No way would she have given herself so completely to a man she hardly knew if… A wicked thrill raced through her as images of Wolfe's magnificent body filtered through her mind and she frowned. She wasn't into cavemen, no matter how charismatic, and she had never been one to drool over a gorgeous face and body.

Before, a little voice chirped annoyingly.

Ever, Ava countered decisively.

She pushed her hair back from her face and smoothed out some of the knots caused by Wolfe's warm fingers. Her core pulsed with remembered pleasure and she groaned at her body's willingness to relive every erotic moment. Yes, there was definitely something to be said about all the dips and bulges of warm, sold muscle, and the man certainly knew his way around the female body. But so he should. According to Anne, he had enough experience for ten men. And she didn't have time in her life for someone like that. She was over shallow hook-ups where the male wanted sex and the female wanted a relationship.

Last night had been… Last night had been sensational, yes. But it was an aberration. One of those things out of the box that you couldn't quite explain but you knew you probably shouldn't have done. Too much champagne, too much anxiety about being at the wedding, too much overpowering testosterone in the form of one blond, godlike male.

Jumping out of bed to distract herself, Ava winced as long-unused muscles registered all that godlike male possession. He was just so big. So strong. When he'd manacled her hands and held her prisoner... Ava shivered and rejected her body's instant softening. But he'd just played with her and then he'd left. His actions spoke more loudly than his words ever could.

That old insecurity she'd thought long gone raised its knobbly head like a sleepy dragon and yawned. But she wouldn't go there. She'd dealt with that childish feeling when she'd moved to Paris, and it was no longer relevant to who she was now.

Maybe this whole business—her father's phone call combined with her emotional response to the wedding—had affected her more than she'd allowed herself to consider, made her act out of character.

Another one of Anne's comments snuck into her consciousness. 'Women drop like lemmings around him,' she'd said at lunch. 'But he lives a fast-paced life. According to Gilles, the man is never in the same city for longer than a few days at a time. It's like he's combing the globe for some holy grail.'

More like variety in his bed, Ava thought with a burst of asperity. And good luck to him. She hoped he enjoyed himself.

He did invite you to dinner, that devil's voice reminded her.

Yes, out of some sort of guilt, she told herself. He'd sensed her uneasiness after the sex and had made the invitation on the spur of the moment. It had been a nice gesture but his voice had lacked conviction. And his actions this morning only backed that up.

No.

She wouldn't be having dinner with Wolfe. He didn't really want to take her out and it would only be prolonging the inevitable. Also, she could think of nothing worse than forcing someone to do something they didn't want to do. That was her father's *modus operandi*, not hers.

Okay.

Shower. Get dressed. Hire a car. Drive back to Paris. She had a meeting with a new artist she was sure was going to be a pain in the backside but who had the potential of van Gogh and she couldn't be late.

She didn't have time to dwell on a man who had taken as much pleasure as she had without any promises for the future.

When the right one came along she would know it, and until then—well, she was nearly thirty. She didn't have time to waste time on casual encounters with ripped Australian security experts. And if fate was kinder than it had been yesterday she wouldn't run into him this morning and would be spared the whole awkward morning-after thing.

Feeling more like her normal self after a shower, she smiled as she crossed the marble foyer and propped her small suitcase beside the front door. Bending down, she'd retrieved the thank-you note she'd written to Anne and Gilles, which she planned to leave with Gilles's butler, when she heard a dark voice behind her.

'Leaving so soon?'

Ava wheeled around, her hair flying over her shoulders in a slow arc. Wolfe stood in the arched doorway, ruggedly handsome in worn boots, black low-riding denims and a basic white T-shirt that drew her eye to every solid inch of him.

Placing her hand against her chest, Ava tried to smile into his hard face. 'You scared me.'

He crossed his arms over his chest. 'Obviously.'

'I…ah…' God, she sounded like a silly debutante! And why did he look so angry all of a sudden? It wasn't as if she had been the one to walk out on *him* before the birds had started chirping. 'I have a busy day lined up.'

* * *

Wolfe could tell instantly that Ava had put last night behind her. It was in the regal tilt of her head, the squared shoulders and the way her gaze didn't quite meet his. Not to mention the small, reserved smile she bestowed on him, as if all that had passed between them last night had been polite conversation instead of intimate body fluids. It was the same smile he'd seen her give plenty of other men the night before, and to say he felt infuriated by it would be a grand understatement.

He recalled the way she'd told him he could leave her room after sex. At the time he'd thought she had been politely trying to *give* him an out, but what if she'd been trying to *get* him out instead?

'On a Sunday?'

Her chin came up, most likely because of his sceptical tone. 'Yes.'

'And what about dinner?' he asked casually.

It appeared she had a guilty conscience, because her gaze cut to the left before returning to his. 'Tonight?'

Damn.

Wolfe read her meaning in that single word and knew she had no intention of having dinner with him, that night or any other. He didn't like it. 'Yeah. You, me, a bottle of red. Or do you prefer champagne?'

'Actually, I have a meeting with someone this afternoon, so I won't be able to make tonight.'

Someone she was sleeping with, perhaps?

Wolfe raked her slender figure in a floaty summer dress and lightweight sandals and tried to rein in his uncharacteristically possessive response as his mind immediately stripped her naked.

On some level he knew he was behaving completely irrationally. Really, he should be rejoicing that she didn't want to complicate things between them by prolonging the inevitable, because—well…he knew his interest in her would wane at some point.

'And it's probably better this way, don't you think?' she said a little too quickly.

'Better what way?' He refolded his arms and rocked back on his heels. No way would he make this easy for her.

Her gaze snapped irritably to his and then cast over him, lighting little bushfires in its wake. 'Better if we forget dinner. Forget last night.'

'Forget last night?' Wolfe wasn't sure if this had ever happened to him before. A woman waking up after a night of phenomenal sex who not only didn't want to have dinner with him but looked as if she never wanted to see him again either.

'Oh, come on, Wolfe.' Her slender hands fitted around her hips just as his had done last night. 'I'm sure this isn't a novel concept for you. In fact it's probably a relief.'

His eyes rose to hers as he forced himself to focus. A relief? Yes, it *should* have felt like a damned relief. The fact that it felt more like an insult only increased his aggravation.

'You think I pick women up and sleep with them every time I go out?'

'I don't know.'

And she didn't care, if he read her tone correctly.

'But why are we arguing? Did you want more from last night than just sex?'

He stiffened, suddenly uncomfortable as she turned the tables on him. Saying no just felt wrong, but… 'No.'

She nodded quickly, as if she'd expected his answer. Wanted it, in fact. Did *she* do this all the time? Pick up men for a night of no-strings sex? The idea made his stomach knot.

'Great, so we're on the same page. Last night was lovely. I had a good time. Hopefully you did, too.'

She shrugged almost apologetically and he had an unpleasant moment of wondering if this was how women felt when he walked away from them. But then with all the previous women in his life he'd established the parameters from the start. Perhaps he was just reacting badly because this time he hadn't done that.

'What more is there to say?'

Ava's challenging question brought his mind back to her.

'Clearly nothing,' Wolfe ground out. 'You seem to have it all worked out.'

She mashed her lips together, as if confused by his tone, and Wolfe warned himself to stop being stupid. This was the perfect scenario, wasn't it?

The sound of footsteps coming down the grand staircase drew his eye, and then he heard Ava swear in French.

'Gilles is coming. I don't want… Can we just pretend this never happened?' She tinkled a laugh. 'Yes, the wedding was gor— Oh, Gilles. *Bonjour*. Where's Anne?'

Wolfe thought about telling her never to try her hand at acting. She looked as innocent as someone trying to make off with the family jewels.

He narrowed his eyes as Gilles put his hands on her waist and gave her a kiss on each cheek, disturbed by the unexpected urge to pull him off her.

'As quaint as Anne finds the ancient staff bell in our room, it didn't work this morning—so I've been sent in search of coffee.'

'What a fantastic idea.' Ava nodded enthusiastically. 'I think I might join you.'

'You want one, Wolfe?' Gilles rubbed his eyes, as if he hadn't had much sleep.

Wolfe knew how he felt.

'No. I've had enough coffee to last me a lifetime.' Ava's pout firmed, and Gilles threw him a quizzical look.

Deciding it was past time he left, he shoved his hand into his pocket for his keys and felt the phone he'd put there to give to Ava.

'This is for you.' He held out a silver smartphone. 'I took

the liberty of placing your SIM card into a spare after my
men found yours broken in your car.'

'Oh.' She looked confused by the gesture. 'You didn't have
to do that.'

He knew he didn't. He'd wanted to.

He turned it on and passed it to her, before informing
Gilles of his plans to hit the road earlier than he'd intended.

While Gilles tried to convince him to reconsider, Ava's
phone beeped a string of incoming messages. They both
turned to see her frowning at it.

Wolfe immediately felt his guard go up. 'What's wrong?'

'My father has left ten messages. Excuse me while I retrieve them.'

She dialled a number and pressed the phone to her ear at
the same time as Gilles's butler hurried into the foyer.

Momentarily distracted when he handed Gilles a piece of
paper, Wolfe returned his gaze to Ava in time to see the colour leach out of her face.

She turned almost blindly to Gilles, her breathing erratic.
'Frédéric has been involved in an accident. Gilles...' Her voice
trailed off when Gilles looked at her, and if possible she lost
even more colour. *'Quoi?'*

Wolfe didn't think she'd realised that she had reached out
and was gripping his forearm in a talonlike hold.

Gilles shook his head as if in a daze.

Hell.

'I need to speak with my father. Find out what hospital
he is in.' Ava's shaky hands fumbled with the phone, and it
would have dropped if Wolfe hadn't swiftly bent to catch it.

'Ava, he's not in hospital.'

'Ne sois pas absurde, Gilles. The accident sounds serious.'
She shook her head, unable to say more.

Wolfe cursed under his breath.

'Ava—'

'No.' She held up her hand and cut him off, backing away

from both of them, so disorientated she would have bumped into the wall if Wolfe hadn't reached out and grabbed her by the elbows.

'Breathe, Ava,' he instructed levelly. 'In. Out. That's it.'

Her gaze cleared a little and her body went rigid as she pushed his hand away. 'I'm fine.'

Wolfe's mouth tightened. 'Give me the phone,' he ordered. 'I'll call your father.'

She swallowed heavily, her navy eyes bruised. He would have wrapped his arms around her then, pulled her in close, but she was so rigid she might as well have been wearing armour. He'd thought he'd sensed fragility in her—the same as he'd sensed last night—but if he had it was long gone.

Ignoring the voice in his head that told him he should butt out of her affairs and mind his own business, he scrolled through her phone. When he couldn't find an entry under 'Dad' or 'Father' he glanced at her. 'What's his name?'

'It's listed under "The Tyrant".'

Her chin came up, as if defying him to make a comment; the action told him that the moniker hadn't been given in jest. But was her father really a tyrant? Or was she just another spoilt little girl who threw tantrums when things didn't go her way? And why did he even care?

Dumping a lid on the list of questions forming in his mind, he quickly dialled the number and introduced himself when the King answered on the first ring. 'Your Majesty, this is James Wolfe, head of Wolfe Inc. I have your daughter here. Yes, Gilles is with her. Ava?'

She took the phone with a shaky hand. 'Sir—'

Her voice trembled and despite trying to keep himself detached the sound of it cut Wolfe to the quick.

'Of course. *Oui.* I can get a flight. Yes. Okay.' She rang off and frowned at the phone as if she didn't know what it was doing there.

'Ava?'

She glanced at Gilles as if she didn't know what he was doing there either.

Shock. She was going into shock. Wolfe recognised the signs.

'I have to…' She gave a tiny shake of her head, collected herself. 'I… Frédéric has died. He… I have to organise a flight home.'

Gilles barely blinked, but Wolfe could see his friend's utter devastation below the façade of calm. 'Wolfe, can we borrow your plane?'

'Of course. But there's no we, Gilles. I'll take her.'

'Frédéric was a good friend. I'll—'

'You should be with Anne—'

'I can organise myself,' Ava cut in.

Wolfe's hands clenched into fists when Gilles put his arm around her shoulders. 'Don't be silly, Ava. You can't be alone at a time like this.'

'Shouldn't your priority be to your new wife and your house guests?' Wolfe hated himself for reminding Gilles so flatly. Hated himself for the stab of jealousy over a woman he'd never planned to see again.

'Would you two stop?' Ava demanded. 'I am more than capable of—'

'Getting on my plane and letting me escort you home,' Wolfe commanded.

She scowled up at him. 'I don't want to put you out.'

Wolfe didn't know if she was being stoic or just obstinate, but he knew he wasn't letting Gilles take her to Anders. 'Too late,' he growled.

When the butler approached Gilles again Wolfe stepped closer to Ava, invading her personal space. 'Is that your only suitcase?'

She stepped back. 'I told you before. I don't get off on barbaric men.'

Her view of him grated but he pushed his feelings aside. 'Do you really have time to argue?'

'No.' His words seemed to trigger something inside her and her eyes grew distant. She paced. Looked at Gilles and then turned back to him. 'Fine. You may take me.'

Wolfe mentally shook his head, almost awed at the way she'd managed to turn her acceptance into an order.

Ava was functioning on autopilot and barely registered Wolfe buckling her seat belt while the plane taxied down the runway. Somehow he had got her to Lille and on board a plane without her conscious awareness of it.

Her brother was dead.

The news was shocking. Indescribable.

A helicopter accident. Ava couldn't think about it, her mind incoherent with grief. Her brother was the rock of the family. The future heir. He was five years younger than her and, while they had struggled to be close after her mother died, she had always looked out for him. Anticipated that he would always be there. He couldn't be gone. He was only twenty-four.

She shivered and felt a soft blanket settle over her shoulders. She clutched it.

Wolfe placed a glass of water on the table in front of her. 'Do you need anything else?'

She shook her head. 'I'm fine.'

'So you keep saying.'

But he didn't push it, and Ava was grateful. She watched him return to his seat. When he'd come across her in the foyer her heart had turned giddy at the sight of him. It had taken a lot of effort to remind herself that there was no point in seeing him again and even less in sleeping with him! His increasing anger at her response had thrown her a little but then he'd confirmed that, no, he didn't want more than sex from her, and she'd known she had made the right decision.

After they arrived in Anders she would likely never see him again, and that fact made her feel instantly bereft.

Her mind linked the feeling with a time when she was fourteen and her father had continued with a state trip even though she'd been hospitalised with chicken pox. He'd monitored her condition from afar, as usual, but coming so soon after her mother's death his behaviour had done little to alleviate her loneliness and her sense of powerlessness at being alone.

That same sense of helplessness and loneliness engulfed her now, and she pushed it back. Her father would expect her to demonstrate more fortitude than that.

More childhood memories tumbled into her mind, like dice on a two-up table. Memories of Frédéric as a boy. Of her mother.

Rather than becoming *more* available after her mother's death from cervical cancer, Ava's father had withdrawn and focused on his work, seeming not to know how to connect with her. He had been fine with Frédéric. Ava had grown more and more resentful of the disparity in the way in which he treated his children, and more and more determined to show him that his views of women were archaic and demeaning.

But nothing she did ever seemed to be good enough for him. Perhaps if she'd been more like her mother, had been able to put his needs first, they might have seen eye to eye. But Ava couldn't. She had witnessed her mother's sadness whenever her father chose duty over family, and it had made her want something entirely different for herself.

Now, with Frédéric gone—a thought that just wouldn't stick in her head—she was next in line to the throne. She could only imagine how her father must be cringing over that, and she felt slightly nauseous at the prospect of having to step into the role.

Wolfe's voice telling her to refasten her seat belt cut across her tumultuous thoughts, and she glanced outside her window and saw the Anders mountain range as they came in to land.

Imposing a rigid shut-down on her fears about being home, she blanked her mind and switched to cool indifference. From the plane doorway she could see her father's royal guard standing alongside a line of official black cars, and she nearly turned and asked Wolfe to restart the engine and fly her some place else. Really, she felt about as strong as a daisy in a hail-storm—and she hadn't even seen her father yet.

Sensing Wolfe directly behind her, Ava had a debilitating urge to turn and rush into his arms, have him tell her that everything would be all right. But that was weak, and Wolfe was the wrong man to lean on in this situation. She wasn't special to him, and he wasn't the type to sit back and go unnoticed. He was used to taking charge, and there was no way she was going to let him sideline her in front of her father. She had been handling things on her own for a long time now, and she could handle this, as well.

Images of last night, of falling asleep in his arms after their wonderful lovemaking, filtered through her mind and made her pause. Then the empty space he'd left in the bed that morning intruded and stiffened her resolve. It would be a mistake to think she could rely on James Wolfe even for a short time.

'Thank you for the use of your plane but I can take it from here.'

'I told you I would take you home and I will.'

His hot toffee eyes glittered down at her dangerously, and his controlled voice told her he was as determined to have his way as she was.

'I am home.'

'Ava—'

'Wolfe. I'm fine. Really.'

'You don't look fine. You look like you're about to break apart.'

Did she? She'd have to work on that between here and the palace. Practising now, she squared her shoulders and stared him down. 'I'm not. I thought I told you already. I am not the sensitive type.'

Wolfe arrogantly slashed his hand in the air to cut her off in a move that was reminiscent of something her father would do. 'It's not open for discussion.'

That was *exactly* what her father would say, and *exactly* the reason she couldn't have Wolfe with her. That and the sudden sense that if she let him Wolfe would hurt her as Colyn never had.

'No. It isn't,' she agreed tightly, hardening herself against the sheer force of his will, the sheer force of her desire for him, which appeared to be even worse now that she had experienced what passion really was.

For a moment neither one of them moved, facing off against each other like two adversaries in a gunfight.

Wolfe's mouth tightened as he made to turn away from her. Then his fist clenched and his eyes, when he brought them back to hers, were seething with frustration. 'You are without a doubt the most infuriatingly stubborn female I have ever met.'

His voice, for all its aggression, was as soft as silk and sent a flash of fire beneath the surface of her skin.

He was without a doubt the most beautiful, the most powerfully dangerous male she had ever met, and she was afraid she would dream about him for ever.

CHAPTER FIVE

'Did Matthieu say what my father wanted to see me about, Lucy?'

'No, ma'am.' Lucy, her new lady's maid, returned from the wardrobe with two jackets for her to choose from.

Ava shook her head and immediately felt terrible as Lucy's face fell. Two weeks home and she still wasn't used to being waited on hand and foot again. She felt sorry for the young girl whose services she'd barely used.

She glanced at her reflection and smoothed her messy ponytail. She hadn't done her hair properly in days, but her father had requested her presence and she would not let him see her as anything less than perfect.

'You don't like my choices, ma'am?'

'I love your choices.' She gave Lucy what she hoped was an appreciative smile. 'But it's hot. In fact, why don't you take the afternoon off? Go and see your boyfriend.'

The girl bobbed her head deferentially and Ava sighed heavily and headed out.

She hated being home.

Hated the cold stone walls of the palace that felt more like a prison. She had barely seen her father since she'd returned, which wasn't necessarily a bad thing—except she had barely seen anyone other than staff, and it had given her far too much time to dwell on her grief.

Glimpsing bright summer sunshine through the long row of Gothic windows as she moved from one hallway to the next made Ava feel bleak. It just felt wrong. The sky should be grey, not blue.

Her brother was dead. The royal duties she had always shied away from were upon her, and there was no escape.

As her father had said, the people needed hope in these black times and she was it. They looked upon *her* to lift them out of the bleak mood caused by the loss of her brother—and, more than that, Ava now knew that her father was ill. One day, sooner than she had expected, she would be Queen— and the thought was completely overwhelming.

What did she know about running a country? Having all those people depend on her? It was criminal how little she knew, and even though that was mainly due to her father's chauvinistic views that women were trophies, not leaders, it gave her no pleasure that he now had to rely on her to preserve Anders' future as an economically viable entity.

And what of her gallery? It was closed for the whole of August, but she had dithered about what to do with it. Although of course she knew in her heart that she would most likely have to close it. It was devastating to think that the life she had built for herself could be so easily dissolved. As if nothing she had done in Paris mattered.

Steadying her breath, she hid her pangs of dismay and a gnawing sense of foreboding behind a smile as she stepped inside her father's plush outer office and greeted his personal assistant.

'He's waiting, Your Royal Highness.'

'Thank you, Matthieu.'

She tried to relax her face as Matthieu opened an inner door and Ava saw her father, as always, behind his enormous rosewood desk. He looked pale and more drawn than usual, and Ava tried to keep her immediate concern from showing in her voice. 'You wished to see me?'

'Yes, Ava. Take a seat.'

'You're starting to worry me, sir,' she said, sitting in one of the leather-bound chairs opposite, wondering why he had greeted her in English. 'Have you received bad news from your physician?'

'No.' Her father's response was clipped. 'I've received disturbing news from the security expert who brought you home from France.'

Wolfe?

Ava's heart leapt behind her rib cage as an image of him that seemed all too close to the surface of her mind clouded her vision. For two weeks he had filled her thoughts right before sleep took her, and he was the first thing she thought of when she woke up. Even on the morning of Frédéric's funeral, when she had felt at her lowest.

Ava sighed. She really needed to stop thinking about those hours they'd spent in bed together. Her dreams of him left her feeling weak and needy, and the man probably couldn't even remember her name, let alone conjure up her image in his head.

Unlike her good self, who could not only conjure up his image oh, so easily, but his scent as well—woodsy and masculine. It was so vivid that he might as well have been in the room with her right now.

'What does Wolfe have to do with anything?'

She had tried to keep the query light, but a sudden fear that her father knew that she had slept with him came at her from left field. Surely Wolfe hadn't told anyone? The tabloids? Could her father's health withstand a salacious story about her at this time?

'I have to do with a lot of things, Your Royal Highness.'

The deep, familiar drawl from the man filling her head space had her twisting around in her seat to where he stood across the room, his body half turned away, as if he'd been doing nothing more than studying the scenery outside the high arched windows.

'But in this case it's about your safety.'

Her eyes drank in his beautifully cut black trousers and white dress shirt that pulled tight across his wide shoulders. He'd had a haircut, the shorter style drawing even more attention to the roguish quality of his perfect bone structure.

Those remembered toffee eyes were fixed on her face, touching her mouth ever so briefly, and Ava felt singed all the way through.

'What about my safety?' She hated that she sounded as breathless as she felt.

'Monsieur Wolfe has some news concerning your car crash at Gilles's château.'

She heard the underlying censure in her father's tone and guessed that he was angry she hadn't told him about the accident herself, but she had no time to ponder that as Wolfe prowled towards her, his loose-limbed gait impossibly graceful for a man his size.

He effortlessly dominated the large room and as he drew closer she realised that her heart was racing. He, of course, could have been a mummy for all the emotion he displayed.

Using years of practice to keep her expression from revealing any of her inner turmoil at having this man—her one-night lover—in the same room as her father, Ava forced herself to maintain eye contact with him. 'Such as?'

'Yesterday I spoke to the mechanic who repaired your car,' he informed her, a touch of fierceness lining his words.

'Why would you do that?'

'A hunch.'

'A hunch?'

'Yes. One that paid off. You didn't crash because of a loss of concentration. You crashed because a vial of potassium permanganate mixed with glycerine had been dropped into your brake master cylinder.'

Ava's brow furrowed. 'Is there a layperson's version of that?'

'Your brakes were tampered with.'

Did he mean deliberately? 'Maybe they were worn.'

'Yes. With a special chemical compound that, when it got hot enough, rendered your brakes useless.'

Ava struggled to digest what he was saying. 'You think my car was deliberately sabotaged?' The very idea was ludicrous. It was true that Anders had once experienced conflict with the neighbouring country of Triole, but that had died down years ago. Her brother had even been set to marry the young Princess of Triole when she came of age.

'Not only that,' her father interjected. 'We now know that Frédéric's helicopter crash was not an accident either.'

'What?' Ava's startled gaze flew to her father. 'I... How is that possible?'

Wolfe's voice was hard when he answered. 'A section of the rotor was altered in such a way that the pilot had no chance of detecting it.'

'You're suggesting Freddie was *murdered*?'

'Not suggesting. Stating. And whoever did it went after you, too.'

Ava reflexively pressed her hand into her stomach. This was too much to take in. 'But that is absurd. Who would do such a thing?'

'Enemies. Freaks. Stalkers. Shall I go on?' His tone was deadly serious.

'Monsieur Wolfe has kindly agreed to investigate that side of things.'

'Wolfe.'

He'd corrected her father. Something no man ever did. Half expecting him to put Wolfe in his place, she was surprised when her father nodded.

Men!

'Really? You volunteered?' Ava didn't bother hiding her incredulity. 'Why would you do that?'

'Ava!' Her father's reprimand at her outspokenness was loud and clear in the still room. 'Wolfe hasn't volunteered. I have hired him.'

Of course. She thought asininely. *Why would a man who keeps his affairs short and shallow volunteer to help out a woman he is clearly finished with?*

It galled her to recall just how many times she had checked her mobile phone for a missed message from him over the past weeks. She could have called him, she supposed, but pride had stopped her from even considering it. Calling him would only prove that she hadn't been able to move on from their night together while he had.

'Why would you do that, sir?' Ava turned her back on Wolfe to try to block out the overwhelming physical attraction she still felt for him. 'Why not use the local police?'

'It's a question of trust, Your Highness,' Wolfe answered.

His frigid formality made her feel despondent, and that in turn made her feel annoyed. 'We don't trust our own police force now? We're a peaceful nation, *Monsieur* Wolfe,' she said, stamping her own formality on the situation. 'No political uprisings anywhere.'

'True. But in this situation you don't know who is intending to hurt you. I won't.'

His tone was bold and confident and she wished she shared his assurance. After the way she had dreamt about him for two weeks she wasn't so sure. Although she did believe he wouldn't hurt her in the way he was referring to.

His thick lashes acted like a shield against his thoughts and Ava couldn't wait for the meeting to end. 'I'm not sure I believe this.' She appealed to her father. 'It could just be coincidence.'

'Chemical compounds kind of mitigate that possibility, Your Highness.' Again Wolfe answered for her father.

'I trust Wolfe's judgement on this, Ava.'

Over her own? What a surprise.

'Fine.' She waved her hand dismissively. 'Is that all, sir?' She needed to get out. Back to the sanctuary of her suite. Wolfe's steely indifference was like a red rag to her overly sensitised senses.

On the one hand she was glad he was treating her like a stranger, but it made her feel inadequate when all *she* could do was remember the feel of his body when it had been joined to hers, his hands on her skin, his mouth... Oh, his mouth!

And Frédéric had been *killed*. Someone might be trying to kill her as well...

'No, that is not all.' Her father brought her attention back to him. 'Wolfe has also been hired as your personal bodyguard for the duration of the investigation.'

The breath stalled in her lungs and the room spun. 'I don't think I heard you correctly, sir.'

Neither did Wolfe.

Her *personal* bodyguard?

He glanced at Ava's shocked expression and hoped his own didn't mirror it. The King had requested that he organise personal security for her, not that he be responsible for her himself. He didn't have time for that kind of grunt work on top of his corporate responsibilities. And guarding a woman who already occupied too much of his head space was not something he'd let any of his staff do.

'I know you don't like security being assigned to you Ava,' the King said. 'But things have changed. You are now the Crown Princess and you need to be protected at all times. This situation highlights how important that is.'

'Yes, but we have our own security detail.'

Her father sighed, as if he was settling in for a familiar battle. 'I believe hiring an outsider is the best course of action until this situation is resolved. Wolfe comes highly recommended and is a personal friend of Gilles.'

'I disagree.'

Determination vibrated through her voice and got Wolfe's back up.

The skin on the back of his neck prickled and he resisted the urge to rub it; he was a master at not giving in to those physical signs that demonstrated when a man was under extreme stress. He had tried to convince himself that his sleepless nights with Ava on his mind were just because he had a niggle about her accident. He'd assumed that once that niggle had been investigated and the King was apprised of the danger surrounding his daughter he'd be able to re-establish his normal routine.

The driving need that had hit him in the gut as soon as Ava had stepped into the room made a mockery of that. It wasn't ruminations over her accident that had kept him awake—and hard—for the past two weeks. It was her.

Absently Wolfe wondered if she had relived their night together as much as he had, and whether she'd be interested in taking up where they had left off.

What?

He silently mocked his wishful thinking. By the look of her she'd prefer to run him through with one of those swords lining the King's private study.

Maybe he just needed to get laid.

And, no, not with her. If he took her on as a client—

'Wolfe is clearly too busy, sir. But I'm sure there's another person out there just as capable.'

She was right about him being too busy, Wolfe thought, but there really was no one else he would trust with her life.

Feeling that he no longer had a choice, he gave the King a curt nod of acceptance.

'No!'

The King cut an irritated look at his daughter. 'Ava, this

is not open for discussion. My word is law, and it's time you realised that you have a responsibility, a *duty*, to your country. You *will* do it.'

Did that mean she didn't want to? Wolfe wouldn't have been surprised. He understood the fickle nature of women better than most.

She stood beside the window with her arms crossed and the afternoon sun turning her hair a deep glossy brown. Wolfe could feel her frustration, her fury, in every tautly held muscle of her slender body.

His own body flushed with heat as he took her in, and he couldn't help resenting the effect she had on him. He didn't want to be this caught up by the sight of a woman. *Ever.*

'I'll need absolute control,' he said, overlaying unwanted thoughts with the professionalism he prided himself on. 'Access to everything.' Wolfe addressed his words to the King. 'Every nook and cranny and secret entrance and exit to the castle. Ava's diary. Her itinerary. I'll employ my own chef to do her meals, and I want the final word on everything she does and every person she sees.'

'You're asking a lot.'

Wolfe knew what the King was saying. *This is my daughter and you'd better not stuff up.* 'Yes, I am.'

'Perhaps Monsieur Wolfe would like my firstborn, as well?' Ava said, injecting her voice with bored insolence, tapping her foot agitatedly on the marble floor.

The King nodded his agreement before addressing his mutinous daughter. 'I have organised a ball in your brother's honour this coming weekend and you will need security for that.'

'It's too soon,' Ava whispered softly.

Her arms enfolded her waist in a protective gesture her father didn't seem to notice, but it tugged at some unwanted place inside Wolfe's chest.

'It's not too soon. And the ball is not only to honour your brother's life—it is to find you a husband.'

A *husband*?

Wolfe's eyes locked on Ava's face, which had suddenly turned ashen. His own gut felt as if it was twisted up with his intestines, and a flash of adrenaline rushed through his system as if he'd just been physically assaulted.

'I can find my own husband, sir.'

'Not now that you're Crown Princess, you can't,' the King rasped. 'The stakes have been raised, Ava, and you've had more than enough time to find a suitable partner and Anders badly needs a celebration *and* an heir.'

The tension in the room as Ava stared at her father could have cracked the Arctic shelf. Wolfe thought of the island paradise he had planned to visit next week, after his round of meetings. The warm sparkling blue waters of the North Atlantic. A new set of sun loungers that edged one end of his lap pool.

'Do I even need to be in attendance, sir?' Ava stared down her nose at her father with bored enquiry. 'I'd hate to mess around with your plans.'

The King's eyes hardened. 'Don't be smart, Ava. You have a duty to do. You know that.'

'And is it *my* fault that I am entirely underprepared to carry out that duty?' she retorted.

Her words were underscored by a subtle vulnerability that called to every one of Wolfe's protective instincts and threatened his determination to remain detached from everything at all times. It was an aspect of his nature that had never been challenged before—regardless of what he had seen and experienced. It was the reason he had acquired his nickname.

Instead of following that troublesome thought down what could only be a dead-end street set with an ambush, he focused on what he could see and hear. The facts.

'You chose to run around Paris for eight years.' The King's face had the motley hue of a man on the edge.

'Because I didn't have any choices *here*,' Ava returned icily.

'I won't argue with you, Ava. You need a husband. Someone who understands the business and can support you when you need it.'

Wolfe noticed the King's hand shook slightly as he picked up his water glass. 'Wolfe, if you would accompany my daughter back to her quarters? I'm sure you'll want to get started on the best way to carry out your duties as soon as possible.'

Wolfe wasn't sure about anything right now except two things. His need for this woman was stronger than it had ever been, and taking on the role of her personal bodyguard was absolute insanity.

Ava rounded on him as soon as he'd followed her into her private sitting room. *"I'll need absolute control. Access to everything."* She mimicked his voice, her tone scathing. 'Are you kidding me?'

Wolfe couldn't stop himself from running his eyes over her slender curves as she stopped in the middle of the room, her body vibrating with tension.

Had she lost weight?

He studied her face. Her cheeks were flushed, her mouth was tight and she had dark smudges under her eyes that told him she had been sleeping as poorly as he had. All the same, she looked magnificent, and he wanted to take her in his arms and kiss her so soundly it was all he could do to remain where he stood. 'It's for your own good.'

'According to some so is whale oil, but you won't find me firing a harpoon any time soon.'

Wolfe sighed, realising this meeting was going to be even more difficult than he had anticipated. 'Ava, this doesn't have to be awkward.'

She paced away from him and then turned back sharply.

'Don't mistake my fury for awkwardness, Wolfe. I can't be-lieve you've agreed to take this job.' She paused and locked her eyes on his. 'You know, if you wanted to see me again you could have just picked up the phone.' Her navy eyes glit-tered challengingly.

'My taking this job has nothing to do with whether I want to see you again. And I believe it was you who cancelled din-ner,' he reminded her stiffly.

She gave a dismissive shrug. 'I didn't see the point in going out with you when it was a spur-of-the-moment request made out of guilt.'

Wolfe contemplated her answer. Was that why she'd can-celled? 'It wasn't guilt.'

She arched a brow. 'No? So why run off so early? I don't even think the birds were up when you left.'

Wolfe's mouth tightened at the insouciant boredom he heard in her voice. It was the same tone she'd used with her father before. 'I left because I had to provide last-minute de-tails to two of my men before they left on another job.' And he'd wanted to surprise her by replacing her damaged phone with one of his.

Her eyes flicked to his briefly, as if she hadn't consid-ered that. But why would she? In hindsight, it had probably looked bad to her, waking up alone after the passionate night they had spent together. Which, he acknowledged to himself now, was another reason he'd left. He'd woken up with such a strong sense of wellbeing his instinct had been to pull back. It was so ingrained in him he hadn't even thought to ques-tion it at the time. Hadn't *wanted* to question it. Now, look-ing at it from her point of view, her reactions that morning made more sense.

'I'm sorry if I hurt you,' he murmured sincerely.

Ava's chin came up and her eyes shot sparks at him. 'Hurt me? You didn't *hurt* me, Wolfe.'

Wolfe's mouth tightened at her vehemence.

'Quite the contrary. In fact you did me a favour, because I didn't have time to have dinner with you and…' She shrugged again. 'It's too late now anyway.'

Was it?

Yes, of course it was.

'You're right.' For one thing he was now her bodyguard and she was his client, and for another he wanted her just a little too much for comfort. 'That ship has definitely sailed.' Wolfe paced the length of an antique rug, agitated by the situation he had inadvertently created for himself. 'And your father wants you to marry!' Which would effectively remove her from his orbit altogether.

'Something you'll never do!' The heated statement was almost a question.

'Something I'll never do,' he agreed. He'd spent his adult life avoiding that particular institution, and he'd never felt any need to reconsider his views.

Ava nodded sharply, as if somehow his response had been predictable, and Wolfe ground his teeth together. This situation—his total physical awareness of this woman, his total *agitation* at this woman—was going to make his job almost impossible. Never before had he felt as if he was at the mercy of his emotions as he did with Ava, and he hated the feeling that he was not as in control as he would like to think he was. So much for his old nickname. Thank God his army mates couldn't see him now!

Ava started pacing in front of the high bevelled windows again, as if she had too much energy that was searching for an outlet. Her fitted trousers pulled tight across the rounded curves of her backside.

'You do realise if my father knew of our history together there is no way he would let you guard me?'

Wolfe brought his attention back to her face. 'So will you tell him or will I?' he asked silkily, irritated with himself and

with her hot-headed stubbornness. She threw him a look and
he swiped a hand through his hair. 'Will you just sit down?'

'Another order? Let me just set you straight on something,
Monsieur Wolfe.' She set her hands on her sexy hips. 'If you
think I am going to do everything you tell me to do you have
another thing coming.'

Her accent had thickened with her agitation and it drove
his mind right back to the bedroom.

Wolfe released a slow breath. 'Believe it or not, I'm trying to help you.'

'Oh, that's right—my own personal protector.'

He crossed his arms and waited for her to run her anger
out, determined not to get into any more arguments with her.

Seeming to sense his newfound resolve, she prodded at it
like a child poking its fingers inside a lion's enclosure. 'So,
do I get to order you around, as well?'

'I work for your father.'

Her gorgeous mouth thinned. 'Two peas in a pod. How
cosy.'

'All that energy you're burning up is just going to tire you
out unnecessarily,' he offered amiably.

'You should be glad I'm using it up on pacing,' she snapped.

Wolfe's body caught fire at her words. *Down, boy.* She
didn't mean *that* was an alternative. It would probably never
be an alternative again after today. No, it definitely *couldn't*
be.

He watched her ponytail trail over the soft skin of her neck
before he sat on the edge of the low, plump sofa that was surprisingly modern in a room that dated back centuries. 'Take
your time. I have all night.'

She crossed her arms over her chest, pushing her breasts
up so they swelled just above the opening of her shirt. 'Well,
I don't. So I'd like you to leave.'

'I need to ask you a few questions first.'

'You're really pushing your luck.'

'Maybe we should clear the air about that night at Gilles's wedding.'

'Us having sex, you mean?'

Her cool indifference again made him wonder just how many other men she had spent the night with, and the fact that he was at all interested only added another layer of heat to his spiralling annoyance. Was she just like his mother, willing to slake her lust whenever the urge arose and with any man handy? The thought made him sick.

'Yes.'

Her eyebrows rose at his churlish tone and she leant back against the windowsill. 'What's to clear up? Have you forgotten how it's done?'

'Ava—'

'Oh, don't worry, Wolfe. I'm not about to strip off my clothes and ask for a repeat. Unless that's what *you* want? Is that why you took the job?' Her voice dropped, lowering to a sultry purr. 'Are you going to order me to take my clothes off, Monsieur Wolfe?'

'I don't sleep with my clients,' he informed her sternly, ignoring the lie his body's response begged him to make of that statement.

She raised a mocking brow. 'My father will be chuffed to hear that. He's not into men, as far as I know. Although every family has their secrets.'

Her unexpected humour broke the rising tension between them and Wolfe laughed. 'Tell me, Princess, what is it about me being your bodyguard that you hate the most if it isn't our history?'

She threw him a droll look. 'Do you have a spare year?'

Wolfe took a deep breath and offered up an olive branch. 'Why don't we start over?'

'Pretend we've never met?' she asked, somewhat dubiously.

'If that works for you.'

She shrugged. 'As long as you don't order me around I can do that.'

Could she? He wasn't sure he could. 'Good. Take a seat.' He spoke briskly, indicating the sofa opposite him. 'I need to ask you some things to help my investigation.'

When she didn't move Wolfe frowned. Was their cease-fire over so soon?

'Ava?'

'You can call me ma'am. And I believe you just issued another order?'

Yes, perhaps he had.

'So did you,' he ground out.

'You didn't say I couldn't order *you* around.'

'Av— Dammit, you need to cooperate or I can't do my job.' His mind conjured up the last time he'd teased her by telling her that he knew how to make her cooperate and he swallowed. Hard.

'So quit.'

'No.'

'Why not?'

'I've given my word to your father and there's no one else I'd trust with your safety.'

'What do you care about my safety? We're strangers.'

Wolfe sucked in a silent breath. Seriously, the woman would try the patience of a saint. Reminding himself to keep control, he settled back more comfortably on the sofa. The cat sleeping in the corner rose and stretched, sniffed him and then crawled onto his lap.

'Hey, mate.' He stroked it absently. 'You look like you've seen better days.'

'He belonged to my mother.' Her mouth turned down slightly at the corners, indicating that she was still affected by the loss. In some way he envied the fact that she cared.

The cat nudged his hand. 'I take back what I said,' he told the cat. 'You're in top condition for a man your age.'

He looked up to find Ava watching him. When their gazes collided she flushed, and he wondered what she had been thinking.

'I think I hate you.'

Well, that was definitive, and unfortunately the feeling wasn't mutual. 'I'm not your enemy, Ava,' he said softly.

The words *but someone is* lay unspoken between them.

Her shoulders slumped as if she had the weight of the world bearing down on her. 'Can't my father answer your questions?'

'That depends on whether he knows anything about your love-life. From what I saw of the interaction between you two before I would have said you're not that close.'

Her eyes narrowed suspiciously. 'Why do you want to know about my love-life?'

'Everyone in your sphere will be investigated.'

'Even you?'

'I have an alibi for the night Frédéric was killed.'

'Really?' She finally sat down and crossed her legs. Slowly. 'What is it?'

Wolfe regarded her wryly. 'And I don't have any motive for wanting to kill you.'

Yet.

She smiled, clearly sensing his frustration. 'Am I getting to you?'

'You don't want to get to me, Princess.'

'No, I want you to quit.'

'Get over it.'

Suddenly her gaze turned serious. 'Are you planning to investigate my artists?'

'Of course.'

'Be nice. Some of them are sensitive.'

'Unlike you?' It was both a statement and a question.

'Unlike me.'

He didn't believe her. Just the fact that she cared about her

artists told him more than anything else. And then there was
the look of concern that had briefly crossed her face when
she'd first walked into the King's office. She had a heart. She
just guarded it well. He could relate to that. He'd put his in
a box years ago, and that was exactly where he intended it
to stay. It was a timely reminder to keep his head on straight
around this woman. She got to him as no one else ever had,
and that made her dangerous and him volatile.

'Who was your last lover?'

She threw him a look.

'Before that,' Wolfe said gruffly.

Her eyes widened. 'You want a list?'

No, he did *not* want a damned list. 'Yes.'

She looked as if she was about to tell him to take a hike.
'A lovely American took my virginity when I was eighteen
because he thought it would be fun to bed a European princess. Then I met a novelist who wanted to write the great
Parisian novel. We were quite serious—unbeknown to my
father—but three years ago I realised that we weren't after
the same thing and we broke up.'

Wolfe could tell that both men had hurt her and he wanted
to run them through with a blunt instrument.

'Did you love him?' The question was irrelevant and he
hoped she wouldn't pick up on that.

'How is that relevant?'

Damn. 'If you're going to question me at every turn this
won't work.'

'I already know it won't.'

'Ava…'

She huffed out a breath. 'I thought I did at the time. Now…
I'm not so sure.'

He wanted to ask what had happened since to make her
question that but he wasn't sure he really wanted to know.
'And since then?'

The look she gave him made his stomach knot.

'Apart from the Anders football team…' She recrossed those long legs in the other direction and stared straight at him. 'You're the lucky last, Monsieur Wolfe.'

Wolfe sucked in a litre of air at her admission, ignoring her snipe about the football team. How had he so completely misread her? But he'd known, hadn't he? He'd needed to believe she was as sophisticated and jaded in the art of seduction as he was. It had made it easier to let her go after the night they'd spent together. Made it easier to believe that what was between them was nothing more than mutual biological gratification. Not that it had worked exactly…

He stood up and startled the cat, who promptly jumped down and crossed to Ava. She reached down, her movements as graceful as the animal she scooped into her arms to cuddle.

'I'll need to see your itinerary for the next few days,' he said gruffly.

She didn't look up. 'I'll have Lucy forward it to you tomorrow morning.'

Wolfe moved to the picture window and stared out at the acres of grass that ringed the palace to the sprawling mountains beyond. Incredibly, he was thinking how happy he was that she'd never slept with Gilles.

Hell.

If he was going to protect her he had to stay on task. He had to stop thinking of her as a person. As a desirable woman. And he especially had to stop thinking of her marrying some stupid fool her father was planning to choose for her.

CHAPTER SIX

AVA WASN'T SURE how she was supposed to find a husband when she compared every man she came across to Wolfe. Not that she had taken her father's oppressive statement seriously. She had no intention of letting herself be bullied into a convenient marriage just to suit his wishes. Not on something this important.

Fortunately she was getting a reprieve from having to pretend to go along with it in the arms of her debonair cousin Baden.

'Quite the *soirée* your papa has put on for you, cuz.'

'Yes,' Ava agreed flatly, glancing around the gilt-edged ballroom filled to the gills with beautifully attired guests. Alcohol consumption had lifted the mood considerably since the beginning of the night, and even though she hated being here she had to admire her father's opportunistic streak.

He was a man who didn't stop until he got what he wanted. And he wanted her married, it seemed. In a hurry. Of course the supreme and lately suppressed romantic in her knew that there was every possibility she would meet someone tonight and fall in love at first sight. After all it had happened to Anne and Gilles. But... Her eyes drifted to Wolfe, standing nonchalantly towards the back of the room.

There was her problem, right there.

He was supposed to look like one of the guests. Undercover. What he looked like was a man who could kill with his bare hands and not put a crease in his bespoke tuxedo. But perhaps that was only because she knew it was true. Perhaps to the other women watching him so closely he just looked like a sexy, rakish male who was good in bed. Something else she knew to be true...

As if sensing her appraisal, he meshed his eyes with hers. Ava felt the impact of his stare from across the room. She couldn't fathom the effect he still had on her. It was instantaneous and totally consuming. She sensed that he felt it, too, but he had much more control over it than she did. Or the attraction just wasn't as strong for him as it was for her. Given that he was only here because her father was paying him, she put more weight on the latter.

And at night dreamt of shedding him of the former...

'Who is he?'

'Who?' Ava gripped Baden's hand and swung him so that Baden had his back to Wolfe.

'The cowboy leaning against the wall who hasn't taken his eyes off you all night.'

Ava glanced over Baden's shoulder as if she was searching for whoever he was talking about. 'I don't see anyone special, but then Father has every single man on the planet in attendance tonight. How are you enjoying the evening?'

Baden scoffed. 'It's a little soon after Freddie's death, but... You're trying to change the subject, dear cousin. There's a story here you don't want me to know about. Come on.' He tickled her ribs as he'd used to do when they were children. 'Tell Cousin Baden.'

'*Arrête*, Baden. This is hardly the place.' Ava hadn't meant to snap, but Baden wasn't the most socially savvy individual at the best of times. 'You're letting that wild imagination of yours run away with you again.'

'I don't like him.'

'I don't either,' she grumbled, knowing that it wasn't dislike she felt for James Wolfe, but something else entirely.

If only he wasn't so arrogant. So self-assured. So lethally male. Ava sighed. Who was she trying to kid? She loved those aspects of Wolfe's nature. Colyn had never been so overcome with passion that he had dragged her from a dance floor and kissed her senseless the way Wolfe had.

'You slept with him, didn't you?' Baden mused. 'I can see it in your eyes.'

Pressing her fingers to her forehead, Ava wondered if it was possible for a headache to materialise out of thin air. 'Please, Baden…' There was no way she was going to confirm anything to her blabber-mouth cousin. 'Keep your voice down.'

'You don't want your papa to find out?'

'He's…' Ava struggled to come up with some plausible reason as to why Baden might see Wolfe around the palace over the next little while without informing him as to why he was really here. 'He's trying out for a staffing position, I believe.'

'You slept with the hired help. You naughty girl.' Baden laughed. 'Not that I can't see the attraction. All that hard muscle!'

Ava cringed as she realised that Wolfe had moved to within hearing distance. 'Would you *please* keep your voice down?' she pleaded.

'What position is he going for?'

'I don't know and I don't care. Ask Father.' Ava knew that he wouldn't, because he had never had an easy relationship with her father.

Baden sipped his wine. 'How is the old tyrant bearing up?'

Relieved to be talking about anything other than Wolfe, Ava latched on to the change in topic. 'You never know with

Father. But honestly I think he's in denial. Hence the party tonight.' She swept the lavish ballroom with a rueful glance.

'And you? How do you feel about being Anders' first Queen?'

Baden knew her life at the palace had never been easy. It had always been something that had bonded them together since he had lost his own father, her father's twin brother, when he was five. Then his mother had deserted him, taking his baby sister with her, and he hadn't seen either of them since.

'Oh, I'm definitely in denial.' She gave a dismissive shrug, not wanting to dwell on the future when she still had no answers about how to handle it. 'Can you excuse me? I need the powder room. Why don't you ask the lovely Countess over there to dance?'

Baden followed her gaze and raised an eyebrow. 'Because she's ugly.'

'Baden!' Ava rebuked him again. 'That's a terrible thing to say.'

'If you don't like the truth, don't get in the way of it.'

Ava gave him a look that told him exactly what she thought of his tasteless comment, and then kept her gaze down as she wound her way purposefully through the throng of guests. She didn't have a specific destination in mind but somewhere quiet and—

'I told you not to go outside.'

The sound of Wolfe's deep voice directly behind her shimmered down her spine.

Ava looked up and realised she had been so preoccupied with Baden's horrible comment that she had walked outside the glass doors leading to her mother's rose garden. A golden moon hung like an enormous balloon on the horizon, and fairy lights twinkled strategically from various trees and bushes, giving the summer evening an ambient glow.

'I needed some air.'

'Is it any wonder?'

She stopped walking and looked back at him. 'What does that mean?'

'It means I'm surprised you're still standing after all the dancing you've done. Husband-hunting looks like difficult work.'

Ava glared at him. Really, she wasn't in the mood for the uncivilised version of Wolfe tonight. 'Why are you even here still?' she asked, her English skewed by her testiness. 'I thought you were the best, but so far you haven't come up with anything, and it has been a week already.'

A long week, in which she had once again locked herself in her room in a petulant sulk. Partly she still wasn't ready to embrace the duties her father wanted her to take on, and partly she had been hoping that Wolfe would get so bored he would quit.

'Unfortunately the invitation I put out over the internet for the bastards responsible to come forward hasn't seemed to work. Maybe I'm losing my touch.'

'Maybe you never had it.' As soon as the words were out she regretted her provocative tone because his golden eyes sparkled with amusement. 'Now, that's just plain nasty, Princess. Fortunately my ego is strong enough to withstand that kind of a slur.'

She snorted. 'Your ego is like a cockroach. It could withstand a nuclear holocaust.'

Completely unprepared for Wolfe to throw his head back and laugh, Ava struggled to prevent a smile from forming on her lips. 'Stop that.' She absolutely loved his deep chuckle. 'People are looking.'

Not waiting for him to follow her instructions, she continued down the stone steps past small clusters of guests enjoying the fragrant garden.

'So, any contenders you need me to vet for you?'

Wolfe's lazy drawl sounded too close, and Ava stopped and swung around to face him.

It took a minute for her to ascertain his meaning and when she did she gasped. '*You're* vetting my future husband?'

'It's part of the package.'

Ava bit back the first retort that came to mind, knowing it wouldn't lead anywhere good. 'Well, it's a useless part,' she informed him shortly. 'Just because my father says something should happen it doesn't mean that it will.'

'You're against marriage?' His brow rose in surprise.

'No, I'm against marriage without love.'

'Ah, a romantic. I somehow didn't take you for that.'

'You don't know me very well, that's why,' she said stiffly.

The look he gave her told her that he knew part of her very well, and was remembering it just as vividly as she was.

Ava felt a blush creep up her neck and quickly added, 'And you don't have to be romantic to want to fall in love.'

'No, just deluded.'

The wealth of emotion behind his brief response made her hesitate. Everyone had a story that coloured their actions and decisions, and she had a sudden urge to know what his was. 'Is it that you're afraid of intimacy, or that you like variety too much to settle down?'

'Since I'm not afraid of anything, and I move around continuously, I think it's safe to go with the latter.'

Ava studied his brooding expression and knew he was afraid of one thing at least—revealing anything personal about himself.

'Choosing that kind of lifestyle would indicate that you're running away from something.' She watched his response to her comment and just saw bland enquiry. Then another idea popped into her head. 'Or is it more that you're searching for something to add meaning to your life?'

The slight narrowing of his eyes was the only sign that she might have punctured his cool reserve in some form.

'Why complicate things unnecessarily, Princess? It's always better to lead with the head, not the heart.'

His use of the word *Princess* in his sardonic drawl told her it would be pointless to push him. He was a man who did what he wanted regardless of anyone else. 'You should take coffee with my father,' she said with measured indifference. 'You'd get on well.'

His piercing gaze scanned her face and she knew he'd picked up on the bitterness that was never far from the surface at the mention of her father.

'What's up between you and your old man?'

About to tell him that she didn't answer personal questions either, Ava found herself responding anyway. 'The truth is we've never seen eye to eye. He is a man who is very set in his ways. Very practical and logical. I was never his idea of the perfect daughter.'

'Why not?'

She could see his curiosity was well stirred and paused. She never talked about her relationship with her father—or lack thereof. Ever. But some small part of her wanted Wolfe to understand her. She'd seen the look on his face when she'd revealed how few lovers she'd had in her twenty-nine years— as if he'd expected there to have been a cast of thousands— and she hated that she cared what he thought of her. But it was senseless to deny that she didn't—at least to herself.

'I was too much of a tomboy growing up. Too impetuous. I liked bareback horse-riding and climbing trees and he wanted me to dress in pretty clothes and speak only when spoken to. I did like the pretty clothes, but…' Her voice trailed off.

Wolfe gave her a small smile. 'The speaking when spoken to…?'

She returned his smile, but it felt hollow. The pain of the past still had too tight a grip for her to find any lightness in those memories. 'Not so much. When my mother died he got worse. My brother was sent to a military academy to start his leadership training and I was home-schooled because my job was to look pretty, not to go out and work. Nothing I ever did was good enough in his eyes. Do you know he's never once visited my gallery in Paris—?' She cut herself off with a self-conscious laugh when she realised just how much she had revealed to him. Why not blurt out that she was afraid she'd never find love either, and tell him *all* her deepest fears?

'Does that make you feel like you're still a disappointment to him now?'

Ava felt her stomach churn. 'No. I don't need his praise. I'm not a child.' She cleared the strident note out of her voice. 'But I resent that he wants everything his way.' She bent and sniffed at one of her mother's prized flowers, the scent faint now in the late evening. 'Why do you think he wants me to marry?'

'To make sure the monarchy is secure.'

'To make sure there is someone beside me who can do the job, you mean.'

'You think he doesn't believe you're capable?' Wolfe's brows rose in surprise.

'I'm a woman. That speaks for itself as far as my father is concerned.'

Wolfe seemed to consider this and Ava moved farther along the path, wishing she'd never let this conversation progress as far as it had.

'Do you?'

His question stopped her and she glanced back at him. 'Do I what?'

'Think you're capable?'

'Yes,' she said, internally cringing at the defensiveness in her tone. She had a Fine Arts degree and a Master's in Business and while she might not know everything involved in running a country, she… 'I run a successful gallery.' Which surely counted for something.

'A small business,' he dismissed, shoving his hands in his pockets and strolling closer. 'It hardly translates, wouldn't you say?'

A wave of heat coursed through Ava at the slight. She might struggle to feel worthy in her personal relationships, but hadn't she always backed herself professionally. 'No, I would not say that.' She didn't even try to keep the indignation out of her voice. 'Do you know how hard I had to work to prove myself in Paris? To make my *"small"* business successful?' She straightened her spine. 'How difficult it was to get anyone to take me seriously? To get artists to trust me to work for them when everyone just expected me to be a vacuous party girl?'

She was breathing so hard when she'd finished she nearly missed Wolfe's soft grin.

'Oh, you are *horrible*!' she spluttered. 'You were playing devil's advocate with me!'

'You have a fire in your belly I guess you would never show your father.'

It pained her to acknowledge he was right. She had built a wall up where her father was concerned and she used it to keep him out. To show him that she didn't need him. More than that, she was afraid he would shoot her down in flames if she tried and failed in replacing Frédéric.

She was a grown woman who had never got over wanting her father's approval. She'd moved to Paris so she could avoid facing that.

Feeling dismayed by her unexpected realisations she shook her head. 'He doesn't respect me.' And, boy, did that hurt.

'So make him.'

Ava's startled gaze connected with Wolfe's.

'And if you stop pretending you're not sensitive about things when you are, that might help.'

She felt her mouth fall open at his gentle ribbing and quickly snapped it closed. She wanted to argue that she'd mastered that unwelcome aspect of her nature years ago, but just looking at Wolfe made her awash with a certain type of sensitivity she couldn't deny.

She turned away, only to have him grasp her shoulders and turn her back before she'd taken a single step. He reached out and secured her chin lightly between his fingers, his eyes glittering down at her in the glow of the mood lighting. 'Maybe you need to think of your duty as being to your people now, Ava, not your father.'

Her breath caught. He hadn't called her Ava since that morning at Gilles's. Trying to hold on to her equilibrium, and reminding herself that there was nothing intimate behind his unexpected tenderness, she gave a rueful quirk of her lips. 'I never looked at it like that.'

'Because you're focusing on the past. That's gone. It's only the future that counts.' His tone was firm, the words delivered with such a resounding sense of resolution she knew he had said them before.

'You're right.' She let the silence build between them as her head spun with ideas. His words *'make him'* settled inside her. Perhaps if she stopped reverting to the recalcitrant teenager she had once been that would be a start. 'I cannot keep fighting my father. It is not only futile, but he's sick. And I do have obligations now that require my full attention.' She released a noisy breath and smiled wearily. 'Do you think perhaps I have felt sorry for myself for long enough?'

Wolfe's head came up, surprise lighting his gaze, as if he hadn't expected her to admit to such a flaw. Then he laughed. 'You're one out of the box, Princess.'

She smiled back at him, warmed by the admiration in his voice. Warmed by the fact that he somehow made her feel valued.

She was instantly transported to the single night they had

shared together. As much as the passion between them had shocked her, it had also thrilled her. She wondered— *No, Ava.* Not only was Wolfe not interested in fostering a long-term relationship with a woman, he had said himself that their *'ship'* had *'definitely sailed'*.

CHAPTER SEVEN

'WE ARE NOT stopping, Ava, and that's that.'

Ava knew her father's face had taken on the stony hue that had used to scare her as a child, but she steadfastly kept smiling at the sea of people waving flags along the tree-lined boulevard as the royal coach trotted slowly down the centre of Anders.

Every year citizens and tourists came out in droves to celebrate Anders Independence Day, with a plethora of sumptuously themed floats and gaily designed costumes. This year there was a more sombre mood to the proceedings, with many of the floats carrying her brother's picture. It made Ava want to reach out to her people to make up for Frédéric's loss. After her conversation with Wolfe three nights ago she knew that she could either let her insecurities control her or…try.

So she had.

And it felt like a blessed release finally to make some of the hard decisions she hadn't realised she'd been actively resisting. One had been to inform her artists that she would be helping them find new representation when her gallery closed down the following month, and the other had been to start sitting in on business meetings with her father's advisors. The workload was intense, and there were aspects of ruling her country that made her head spin, but she felt as if she was making inroads. Slowly.

Slow inroads into everything except her relationship with her father. Just this morning he had been lecturing her about making a decision on the five 'expressions of interest,' as he referred to the marriage proposals he had already received on her behalf, without even considering her view. As far as he was concerned she should bow down to her destiny, and he saw nothing wrong with the fact that one of those proposals had arrived from a man she hadn't even met!

But Ava wasn't ready to compromise on that point. And with Wolfe sitting opposite her, sublime in a designer suit, his gaze scanning back and forth over the joyous crowd, she didn't even want to think about it.

Instead she marshalled her determination to make her father respect her and kept a calm smile on her face as she addressed him. 'I need to walk some of the way.'

Her father nodded benevolently to his people. 'I won't repeat myself, Ava.'

'I know it's not the way we've traditionally done the avenue ride,' she said. 'But if I am going to rule Anders it's important to me that our people don't see me as a distant figure. Especially since I have lived in Paris for so long.'

Her father glanced at Wolfe. 'Tell her it's too dangerous.'

'The King has a point,' Wolfe conceded. 'It is never a good idea to make last-minute changes to your itinerary.'

Ava felt her stomach plunge as he sided with her father, instantly recognising the emotion that gripped her as a feeling of betrayal. After the gala ball she felt as if they had formed a friendship of sorts. She had enjoyed his company as he had escorted her to and from meetings, had enjoyed him sitting in with her to ensure her safety, and been surprised and thankful when on a couple of occasions he'd offered some keen business insights that had been beyond her understanding at the time.

Most of all, though, she loved how when everyone else had left for the day he brought her a cup of her favourite tea without her having to ask. Nobody, she had realised that first time, ever did anything for her without her having to ask first.

She looked across at him, willing him to understand. 'But it *can* be done.'

Her father's face tightened. 'Why are you always so determined to defy me?'

'This is not about defiance, sir,' Ava insisted, holding back her tendency to disconnect from her father in order to keep her goal in sight. 'If you can give me one good reason why I shouldn't walk amongst our people then I'll listen.'

'It's a break in tradition.'

'Why can't I start a new one?'

'A safety risk, then.'

Of course Ava knew he was right, but she also recognised that fear was debilitating. 'Is it important to rule safely, Father?' she asked softly. 'Or with integrity?'

Her father turned from the window and stared at her, his expression pained. 'You always were a smart child, Ava, but you're still not leaving this carriage. Wolfe—' he spoke while still smiling and waving '—stop her before she does something stupid.'

Ava hated the fact that yet another man held something so important to her in his power. She lifted her chin, wondering how she would react when Wolfe sounded the death knell to her idea. It was important to her on so many levels…

Fortunately her determination wasn't to be tested on this as Wolfe, his expression stern, broke her steady gaze to address her father. 'My job is to keep her safe, Your Majesty, not to stop her.'

'Thank you.'

Wolfe turned from the narrow window that had once formed part of a parapet when he heard Ava step into the small room he was using as an office. He'd thought she would want to make an early night of it, worn out after walking for miles that day and thrilling her people with handshakes and good wishes. On the contrary, she looked fresh and still buzzed, dressed in some sort of yoga outfit that left little to his hyperactive imagination.

He knew why she was thanking him, but she'd put him in an impossible position with her earnest request and he was still fuming about it. 'It was a foolish thing to do.'

'Maybe.' She threw him a brief smile. 'But I needed to do it and you understood that.'

'I understood you had a crazy idea and it came off okay this time. Next time it might not.'

'Life's a risk, no?' She cocked her head. 'I would have thought your job was full of them.'

'Calculated risks are different from spontaneous reactions.'

'It wasn't a spontaneous reaction,' she said indignantly. 'I'd thought about it all morning.'

'Next time you might want to share that,' he said dryly.

'Okay.' She shrugged. 'I take your point, but it doesn't stop me from being happy that I did it.'

Wolfe grunted in response and made the mistake of moving to stand behind his desk. He'd had to train himself to ignore her delicious scent all week, but this close, in the confines of this suddenly overheated room, it was nearly impossible to do.

When she didn't make a move to leave he glanced at her. 'Was there something else?'

'Yes. Do you have any news on who might have killed my brother?'

'No.' He had some leads to go on but he had no intention of telling her that. Keeping a client apprised of his intel was not the way he operated.

'Okay, then.'

Her slender fingers trailed over the top of his desk, but just when he thought she was going to give him a break and leave she swung back towards him.

'I'm going for a walk outside. Just in case you need to know.'

Of course he needed to know.

'If you go I'll have to go with you.'

Her eyes met his. 'Okay.'

Her voice had a husky quality, and all he wanted to do was haul her across his desk and push that stretchy top up her chest. 'I suggest you get a jacket. It's cold outside.'

'I don't know where you get your weather information from,' Ava said ten minutes later, her sneaker-shod feet crunching the gravel footpath underfoot. 'It's not cold at all.'

She shrugged out of her lightweight jacket and draped it loosely over her shoulders. 'I love these cloudless summer nights in Anders. The cicadas singing and the mountains in the background. When I was small I used to lie on the grass with my mother and count the stars. It's not possible to do that in Paris.'

'No stars?'

'It's not the stars; it's the grass. If you so much as look the wrong way at the lush lawns in a Parisian park a *gendarme* will come over and slap you with a misdemeanour charge.' She wagged her finger playfully. 'One can look but never touch.'

Wolfe knew exactly how that felt.

'Even princesses?'

She threw him an impish grin. 'Afraid so. The only people who get special treatment in Paris are the Parisians.'

Wolfe laughed, finding himself relaxing under the vast velvet sky, intrigued as Ava relived her time in Paris and made comparisons between France and Anders. He'd found himself making similar comparisons between Australia and Anders during the week. It was most likely because it had been years since he'd spent so long in one place, but as much as he would have said he was a beach lover he found the small mountainous nation of Anders surprisingly serene and peaceful.

'How do you feel about being back?' he asked.

Ava stopped walking and turned to face the mountains, their high peaks barely discernible in the night sky. 'Two weeks ago I would have said I hated it, but now…now it's growing on me again.'

She hesitated, and he could see her wrestling with herself about whether to continue. Surprisingly he wanted her to. He liked listening to her talk.

'Because?'

'Because I've missed the fresh scent of pine in the air and the tranquillity of being surrounded by every shade of green. It feels like home, and being here has made me realise that I miss that more than I allowed myself to think about.' Her hand trailed a clump of lavender and she raised her fingers to her nose and inhaled the sweet scent. 'The only fly in the ointment is my father,' she continued, almost to herself. 'He's so determined that he's always right it becomes exhausting trying to deal with him at times. What about you?' she asked lightly.

'No. I find him easy to get along with,' Wolfe deadpanned.

She stopped in the middle of the path and arched her brow. 'You know what I mean.'

He did. He just had no intention of talking about his parents.

Stepping off the path onto the well-tended lawn, he walked a short distance and laid his palms against the trunk of an ancient pine tree. He wasn't sure if she would follow, but then he heard her soft tread on the pine needles and felt glad that she had. 'They say if you hold your hands against the trunk like this you can feel its secrets.'

'Really?'

She spread her fingers wide against the trunk beside his and stirred up all sorts of unwelcome responses inside his body.

'What do you feel?'

Wolfe paused, quite sure she didn't want to hear what he was really feeling. 'Bark.'

She laughed and shook her head. 'And for a minute there I thought you were going to go all deep and meaningful on me.'

'Mmm, not me.' Wolfe caught her lingering gaze and moved back to the worn path.

'You grew up on a farm, didn't you?'

'Yep.' He hoped his short answer gave away just how little he wanted to talk about his past.

'What was it like?'

No such luck...

'Dusty.'

'Pah!'

He glanced at her and couldn't help chuckling at her disgusted expression.

'Do you know you close up like a crab whenever I ask you anything personal?'

'Clam.'

'That's what I said.' She studied him as if she was trying to work him out. 'Why do you make it so hard to know you?'

Wondering what to say to that thorny question, Wolfe was relieved when his cell phone vibrated in his pocket. He pulled it out and saw that it was his brother. 'Excuse me, but I have to take this.' He pressed the answer button. 'Ad-man, what's up?'

His brother hesitated on the other end of the line. 'Oh, sorry, bro. Have I caught you in the middle of a run?'

It took Wolfe a second to understand his brother's comment, and then he became conscious that his breathing was tense and uneven. *Great.* 'Just work. Don't tell me you're still in the office, too?'

'With you living it large in a European castle, guarding a beautiful maiden, where else would I be?'

Wolfe told his brother he'd trade places with him in the blink of an eye but even as he said it he knew he was lying. Quickly changing the subject, he tormented his brother a little more and then ran through a few work-related issues before ringing off.

'Well, that was convenient.'

Wolfe lifted his gaze to the woman who was slowly driving him mad and realised that other than his brother she was the only person who had ever teased him about his behaviour.

Feeling overly hot, even though the air temperature had dropped a couple of degrees, he focused on the small cluster of flowers she held in her hands, not unlike a bride waiting to walk down the aisle. Shaking off that disconcerting image, he made his voice curt when he spoke. 'We should head back inside.'

'Okay.' She sniffed the small posy and fell into step beside him. 'Was that your brother?'

He thought about changing the subject, but knew if he did her interest would only grow, not wane. 'Yes.'

'You sound close to him.'

'I am.'

'So, no sibling rivalry?'

He shook his head. 'We're less than two years apart so we did everything together.'

'Does he travel around like you?'

'No. He's based in New York.'

'Does he have a wife? Kids?'

Wolf stopped so abruptly she'd taken two more steps before she noticed.

'This is starting to feel like an inquisition.'

She shrugged one slender shoulder. 'I'm just trying to know you a little better.'

'By asking questions about my brother?'

'You won't answer questions about anything else.'

That was because he had never seen the point in talking about himself. And, if he was completely honest, because he was starting to like her in a way that transcended the physical and that scared him. It was dangerous to bond with a client. It caused sloppy work and unrealistic attachments to develop.

'Look, don't worry about it.' She gave him a half smile that seemed paper-thin. 'When you're like this…' She gave another one of those Gallic shrugs that drove him bonkers. 'I forget you work for my father.'

If she had tried to wheedle information from him, or tried to make him feel guilty, he would have held his line. Faced with the stoic indifference he now knew she used to mask her true feelings, he caved. Or perhaps it was just that she looked so beautiful in the light of the crescent moon.

'What do you want to know?' he asked, not a little gruffly.

'What do you want to tell me?'

Wolfe blew out a breath. It was so typical of her to make him work for something he didn't even want.

'My father died ten years ago.'

Ava stopped and looked at him. 'I'm sorry. Were you close?'

Had they been close? Probably not, if he had to think about his answer. 'At times.'

'And your mother?'

Wolfe turned to continue walking. 'I don't know where she lives. She left when I was younger.'

'Oh. That must have been hard.'

'It is what it is.'

He felt her glance and knew she was seeing more than he wanted her to. 'Is she the reason you avoid long-term relationships?'

There was a lengthy silence in which he realised even the cicadas had stopped singing. As if they too were waiting with bated breath for his answer. Wolfe made a sound in his throat at the uncharacteristically fanciful thought and nearly missed her next word.

'Love?'

He did not want to talk about this with her. It was time

to end the conversation. 'Love is the most unstable emotion I've ever come across,' he said fiercely. 'My mother didn't just leave once. She left over and over. And every time she returned she told us how much she loved us. It was the only time she ever said it.'

As soon as the bleak words were out he regretted them. The look of pity on Ava's face only made the feeling ten times worse.

'Where did she go?'

Wolfe thrust his hand through his hair and promised himself next time he'd stick to monosyllabic answers or none at all, as he usually did. 'We never knew. Sometimes she would meet a man in town and take off, other times she just went on a "holiday".'

'But that's awful. What did your father say? Was he even there?'

'He was there,' Wolfe said grimly. *Usually out on his tractor, ignoring reality.* 'But he didn't say anything. When she came back, sometimes months later, we all just pretended she'd never left.'

'That hurts the most, no?' Her delicate brows drew together in consternation. 'I used to hate it when my father would go off on extended business trips, or lock himself away in meetings and then totally ignore how it made us feel.'

'I wasn't hurt by her actions,' Wolfe denied. 'But Adam was. Whenever she'd go he used to run away and try and find her.' He hated remembering those hours of searching for his brother, worried about whether he'd find him alive or dead in the hot, arid bushland that surrounded their farm.

'But not you?'

Wolfe realised with a start that she had somehow sucked him back into the past against his better judgment, and he felt excessively relieved to find they had arrived back at the palace. 'No. Not me. I was older. I understood.'

She looked up at him with such a penetrating gaze he felt every one of his muscles grow taut.

'Understood what, Wolfe?' Her gaze bored into his. 'That you were a child who couldn't rely on his mother's love?'

CHAPTER EIGHT

AVA VACILLATED BETWEEN the two evening gowns laid out on her hotel bed. She could smell the fragrant Parisian air through her open window, and outside she knew the night sky was streaked with pink and orange, the Seine sparkling under the glow of the street lamps that had just gone on.

She tapped her foot in time with her favourite jazz album, blaring from the hotel's sound system, trying to feel okay about her coming dinner with Prince Lorenzo of Triole and not to torture herself about where Wolfe had got to last night.

For a whole week he'd barely uttered a word to her—ever since he'd opened up about his childhood and she'd made that rash statement about his mother. The words had been out of her mouth before she'd thought it through, but she had felt so outraged on his behalf. And clearly he'd felt outraged by what *she'd* said, because he had stopped sitting beside her in meetings and had even stopped making her evening cup of tea. It was a silly, inconsequential thing to care about, but it had come to mean a lot to her. His support had come to mean a lot. Somewhere along the way she had forgotten that she was just his client. Forgotten that, although they had been lovers, they had nothing else between them.

The devil on her shoulder told her he'd been out with a woman. That he was a man with a large sexual appetite he had not slaked for weeks. Her hands knotted into fists and she forced herself not to think about the heaviness in her heart. Forced herself to concentrate on the *crucial* task of choosing a gown for the evening. She smiled wryly at Lucy, who clutched the ornate mahogany bedpost with a dreamy expression on her face.

Ever since Ava had submitted to the changes in her life and accepted Lucy's help their relationship had blossomed into the beginnings of a genuine friendship.

'Which do you think, Lucy?'

'Depends on the look you're going for. The silver is stylish and understated, while the red is very "look at me". Very racy.'

Which would Wolfe prefer? The thought winged into Ava's mind before she could stop it. The silver. He'd want her to blend into the background.

'The red,' she said decisively, angry with herself for wanting to dress to please Wolfe. And *racy* might help pick up her mood. Ava rolled her shoulders to ease the tension her warm bath had failed to alleviate.

'Great choice.' Lucy beamed. 'Prince Lorenzo will find you irresistible!'

The sound of the music being clicked off made Lucy's last words ring loudly in the sudden silence. Lucy gasped, her hand pressed against her chest. 'Monsieur Wolfe!'

'Leave us, Lucy,' Wolfe commanded icily.

Lucy hesitated, her eyes darting to Ava's.

Ava handed Lucy the red gown. 'If you could have this pressed and return it when it's done, Lucy, that would be lovely.'

She could tell instantly that Wolfe was in a dangerous mood; the expression on his face was as black as his clothing.

After waiting for Lucy to close the sitting room door, she turned to face him. 'I didn't hear you knock.'

'That's because I didn't.'

Their eyes connected and Ava couldn't have looked away

to save her life. Then he prowled to the other side of the room and slammed her window closed before turning to face her. 'Big night tonight?' His eyes fell on the silver dress draped over her bed.

'A state dinner is always important.' Her heart thumped in her chest and she moved to sit on the stool facing the dressing table, started unwinding her hair from the topknot she'd put it in while she bathed. If nothing else it gave her hands something to do. Although she knew he was angry, she had no idea why. 'Did you want something?'

Now, *there* was a loaded question. But it wasn't one Wolfe was in a state of mind to answer. Not with her wearing that flimsy midnight-blue kimono that perfectly matched her eyes and most likely nothing underneath.

He was in a foul mood and he knew why. He was frustrated with the lack of progress he'd made on her case—and frustrated with himself. He'd lost focus somewhere in the middle of last week and stopped thinking of her as a job. Somewhere along the way he'd started to admire her work ethic, her commitment to master a duty she'd never thought would be hers…and then he'd gone and exacerbated the situation by spilling his guts to her.

'Understood what, Wolfe? That you were a child who couldn't rely on his mother's love?'

Wolfe silently cursed as her nosy question replayed once again inside his head. That's what you got for opening up to a woman. Psychobabble and a week-long headache.

He'd made a mistake—too many where she was concerned—but as long as he made the other night his last he could live with it.

Now all he had to do was to reinstate the cool professionalism he was renowned for and get back on task.

In some ways he had hoped taking last night off would help with that. He'd met a mate in Rome at a nightclub he'd hated before he'd even made it past the officious bouncer. When he'd hit the dance floor with a super-sexy Italian girl his head had started aching from the loud music and his body had all but yawned with boredom. Boredom? At breasts bursting out of a short dress that would send any normal man into a frenzy of desire? Ridiculous. Or so Tom had informed him.

'Wolfe?'

His name falling from Ava's delectable lips was like a husky invitation to his senses. In his mind's eye he imagined her rising gracefully from the cushioned stool on which she sat. Saw her loosen the sash on her robe, knew that it would fall halfway open, catch on the crest of her nipples and hold, revealing the temptation of her flat belly and the brunette curls he longed to bury his face in. She would hold his gaze, tilt her cute nose and saunter towards him. Then she'd arch her imperious brow, wrap her arms around his neck and pull his mouth to hers.

Of course she didn't do any such thing.

Instead she picked up her hairbrush and ran it through her hair in long, languid strokes. Wolfe glanced sideways and saw the discarded jodhpurs and billowy white shirt she had worn riding earlier that day with suitor number two hundred and one, and all he wanted to do was ride *her*. Hard.

For nearly three weeks he'd held it together. Held his desire for her at bay. Held his self-control in check. Why was it pulling at him now? Making him sweat?

But he knew, didn't he?

Lorenzo, the urbane Prince of Triole, wanted her—and her father had decided he was the one. He'd asked Wolfe to do a special security check on him to clear the way. Tonight Lorenzo would no doubt try to stake his claim on her. Knowing how much she sought her father's approval, how much she wanted to do the right thing by her country, he was very much afraid she'd go along with it. Not that he should care. It wasn't as if he had made a claim on her himself.

'Wolfe?' Her voice had risen with concern at his delayed response to her question. 'Do you have news about who caused Frédéric's accident?'

'No.' Wolfe grated harshly, holding up the crumpled piece of paper he'd printed out five minutes ago. 'I'm here about this.'

She glanced at the document before cutting her eyes back to him. 'Am I supposed to know what *"this"* is?'

'Your itinerary.'

'Oh, that.' She turned back to the mirror dismissively. 'You told me to tell you in advance when I planned to make changes to it.'

'I remember telling you it was dangerous to change it.'

Her nonchalant shrug ratcheted up his tension levels. 'It's going to be a lovely day tomorrow and—'

'You've been to Paris before,' he interrupted impatiently. 'Hell, you lived here for eight years. Why do you need to go on some convoluted walking tour?'

'I have not been here for nearly a month. I want to see the city again.'

Wolfe bit back a string of curses at her determined expression. 'Look out of the window.' He gestured to the one behind him without really seeing anything. 'To the right the Eiffel Tower, to the left Notre Dame.'

'Actually, that's Hôtel de Ville to the left. You cannot see Notre Dame from that window.' She regarded him steadily. 'Have you ever actually walked around Paris before, Wolfe?'

'Sure. I've strolled from the airport to the car and from the car to whatever building I needed to enter.'

'Well, that at least explains why you don't understand my need to reconnect with the city,' she said. 'I might not be back here for some time and I want to wander up through Montmartre to Sacré Coeur, have lunch, and check out the new installation in my gallery before it is disassembled.'

'You agreed to let *me* decide when you could visit your gallery.'

'I've changed my mind.'

'You're angry because I'm calling the shots.'

'That has nothing to do with it. Did you have fun last night?'

The unexpected question threw him, and he watched through narrowed eyes as she rose and slowly approached the bed, gripping the bedpost in a provocative pose he wasn't even sure she was aware of.

'I can fit in Sacré Coeur, but you're not walking around Montmarte and your gallery is off-limits until I say so.'

He had leaked a fake itinerary to a couple of key suspects and the one she had devised for herself came too perilously close to it for comfort. Letting her have her way would put her in danger, and he couldn't live with himself if something happened to her. If she should—

'Look at you,' she said testily, her knuckles white where she gripped the bedpost. 'You are frustrated and angry with me and yet you won't show it. So controlled. So cool under pressure. Maybe the rumours are true and you *are* made out of ice.'

She turned, flicking her hair back over one shoulder in a quintessentially feminine gesture that dared a man to follow through with his baser instincts. Wolfe was not in the mood to let such a direct challenge go uncontested.

Within seconds he was on her, the flat of his hand slamming loudly against the wardrobe door as she was about to open it. 'You think I'm made out of ice, Princess? How quickly you forget.'

She spun around, her eyes wide, her breaths punching the air. Was that fear or anticipation he read in her dilated pupils?

He looked at her. At the silvery striations in her dark eyes and the tiny row of freckles that lined one side of her upper lip. Unable to help himself, he slid a hand into her hair and tilted her face up to his. Their eyes clashed in a battle of wills. He told himself to back off, settle down, but his gaze dropped to her soft mouth and he couldn't think of anything else but kissing her. Taking her.

Her nostrils flared as if sensing his need, and instead of crushing her lips beneath his he lightly brushed against them.

Once.

Twice.

She moaned and tried to draw his tongue into her mouth, but he'd thought about kissing her like this for weeks and now he didn't want to be rushed. He slipped his other arm around her waist and drew her against him, all the while teasing her lips with his. She twisted in his hold, her mouth moving beneath his as if she was as desperate for the contact as he was. As if she'd thought about this as often as he had. His hands swept over her back, cupping her firm butt and bringing her in closer against his pulsing hardness.

Her own hands were just as busy, roaming his chest, curving around his shoulders, burning him wherever she touched.

The sensation of her velvet tongue flicking against his threatened to drive him to his knees, and he pressed her against the wardrobe and wedged his leg between her thighs to keep them both upright. Her head thudded lightly against the wardrobe door and he cupped the nape of her neck and urged her mouth to open wider. She was like molten silk in his arms, sliding against him, urging him on with her husky whimpers for more.

Wolfe had felt his control slipping the moment he walked into the room. Now he had none. Even the thin barrier of their clothes was too much between them, and his hands stroked over her, shifting the slippery fabric aside as he sought the sweet perfection of her breasts.

For God only knew how long he was lost. A slave to sensation. A slave to her soft scent and even softer body. A slave to her heat, to the tug of her feminine fingers in his hair. If there was some reason he shouldn't be doing this he couldn't think of it.

Behind him he heard the snick of the latch as the door was quietly opened.

Thrusting Ava behind him he spun, his gun drawn, but even as he did so he knew he was at least two seconds too late.

The maid gasped softly and nearly fainted, but other than the sound of his own ragged breathing you could have heard a feather float to the floor.

So much for not making any more mistakes, Ice.

Hell.

If he needed a clearer example of just how poorly he was doing at the job of protecting her he didn't want to know what it was.

Wolfe stood motionless at the back of yet another extravagant ballroom and knew that despite donning yet another squillion-dollar tux he was doing nothing to blend into the glitterati of Paris. He was too angry with himself to care.

He should never have kissed her.

Now it was not only uncomfortable to watch her in the arms of another man, it was downright impossible. How his father had taken his mother back time after time Wolfe didn't know. He only knew he couldn't do it. If Ava chose someone else—Lorenzo—then she could have him.

Hell.

Of *course* she was going to choose someone else. That was the whole point of these elaborate tea parties and gala events. She was husband hunting and he thanked God he wasn't on her list.

Didn't he?

Of course he did. Even posing that question was a sign that he needed to step back. A very long way back.

And he would. In fact he already had. In—he checked his watch—fifteen minutes everything would have changed for the better. He blew out a long breath and dragged in some perspective with his next inhalation.

He knew how it felt to feel that someone you loved didn't love you, and… Oh, hell. He couldn't keep thinking like this. It felt as if his precious rules were in tatters, and he'd already thought and spoken more about his past in the last week than he had in twenty years. Next he'd be imagining that lust was love, and then where would he be? Hung out to dry like his old man, that was where. Talk about perspective.

It was a cliché that the client often fell for the bodyguard. It was just a hot mess if the opposite occurred, and he *fixed* hot messes—he didn't create them.

Telling himself she was just like any another woman wasn't working either. He wanted *her*. Not just any woman. *Her*.

When he had taken this gig his arrogant fat head had led him to believe he could control himself around her. *Yeah, right.* He'd proved in her hotel room two hours ago that he showed about as much control around her as a shark in a blood bath.

As a special ops soldier he had been trained to dig deep when every bone, muscle and tendon in his body was screaming for rest. He was trained to hold his line under extreme forms of torture no man should ever have to face. Apparently they hadn't thought to train him to resist desire of this magnitude. Of course in reality he *could* resist her—there was simply some part of him that didn't want to. And that was the part that scared him the most.

Ten minutes.

He shifted his weight to the balls of his feet and searched the baroque-style ballroom for her. She wasn't hard to find in that showstopper of swirling scarlet that hugged every inch of her lush curves—those it managed to contain anyway. If she'd wanted to make a statement of availability she'd succeeded. And Lorenzo was in the market and had the correct weight to buy.

But not Wolfe. His life was mapped out just as surely as hers. Work, women and play—in that order. It was a great life. A life any man with his head screwed on right would envy. A life he had never questioned before and, dammit, still didn't. That soft, sexy sound she made every time he slipped his tongue into her mouth was nothing he wouldn't forget with time.

Raucous laughter from somewhere behind him brought him out of his daze. Where the hell was she? The ever-moving crowd kept blocking his view, but even so his sixth sense told him she wasn't there.

An icy chill slid down his spine.

Glancing to the left, he caught the eye of one of his team acting as a waiter. Jonesy subtly signalled towards the patio doors leading to the gardens. His mouth tightened. He'd told her not to leave the room. No doubt the perfect Prince of Triole had taken her outside, and that wasn't going to happen on *his* watch.

Furious with himself for yet another lapse in concentration, Wolfe wove a determined line through the throng of guests until he was outside. Giving his eyes a moment to adjust to the dim light, he strained his hearing for the sound of her voice. Then he saw the flash of her strapless gown through the trees and the matching red stripe down the side of the Prince's trousers. His and hers. Perfection in the making, he thought acidly.

Lorenzo had caught her hands in his, the expression on his face one of earnest concentration. Was he about to propose? Wolfe didn't wait to find out.

'Nice night for a stroll, *ma'am*.'

Ava stiffened at the sound of Wolfe's voice behind her and tugged her hands out of Lorenzo's. She knew Wolfe was reprimanding her for going against his orders, but she didn't care. Since he'd walked out of her hotel room she'd been more determined than ever to find Lorenzo attractive. She didn't want Wolfe to be the only man who could make her melt with mindless passion, because she knew he was determined to stay unattached for ever and she needed the opposite. She *wanted* the opposite! And wanting something more with him was just asking for heartache. Especially when the look on his face as he'd stormed out of her hotel room had left her in no doubt as to how appalled he was by the attraction that still simmered between them.

He moved now, blocking her way, his legs set wide apart, his hands clasped behind his back. He was so intensely male he took her breath away and, try as she had all night, she couldn't forget the way it felt to be pressed up against all that hard muscle.

Previously she would have said she wasn't a woman who could get turned on by a powerful man. But of course previously she hadn't met Wolfe. Hadn't felt this explosion of chemistry that made her tingle and burn. Hadn't felt such a strong need to be with someone not just sexually but…always.

She let out a silent, shaky breath she hoped he wouldn't notice and stared him down.

'Prince Lorenzo and I would like some privacy, Wolfe.'

'I need to talk to you.'

Ava shook her head. Talking was a bad idea. Forgetting about what had happened in her hotel room was what was required. 'Not now.'

Wolfe cut his eyes to Lorenzo and she knew he was on the verge of ordering him to leave. Only Wolfe would consider doing that with a man who was second in line to the throne.

'Wolfe, please.' She hated the way she sounded as if she was begging but she was. She couldn't do this any more. First thing tomorrow morning she was going to contact her father and tell him to organise another bodyguard. Wolfe could still head up the case if he liked, but she knew there was absolutely no way she could feel anything more than friendship for any man she met while Wolfe was by her side. Even when he wasn't with her she thought of him, ached for him. She was starting to fear that no one would measure up to him. *Ever*.

His jaw clenched, as it always did when he was annoyed with her, and if possible his expression grew even more remote.

God, he was impossible! That kiss back in her hotel room… Her lips parted…

Don't think about it, she ordered herself.

Not easy when he blocked her path, giving her no choice but to either wait for him to step aside or turn around with her tail tucked between her legs and retreat back inside as he wanted her to do.

Ava knew which option she *wasn't* going to take.

Stepping closer to him was a mistake, though, as her senses became immediately overloaded with the faint trace of musk and man—a combination that instantly flooded her body with heat and need.

She shivered and Lorenzo placed his hand on her shoulder. Straight away her undisciplined mind compared its size and texture to Wolfe's. It felt cool, where Wolfe's always felt so warm it bordered on hot, and it didn't make her want to wind herself around him until she didn't know where she ended and he began.

'Are you cold, *piccolina*?'

For a minute Ava thought Wolfe might do Lorenzo damage, and she quickly smiled her reassurance at Lorenzo before throwing Wolfe a baleful stare. 'We can talk later. Right now I need you to move out of my way.'

In more ways than one, her mind quipped unhelpfully.

Ava waited, remembering the time he had threatened to toss her onto his horse. Back then she hadn't believed he'd really do it. Now she knew better. Wolfe always got the job done, no matter what.

He glanced at his watch and then stepped aside, but it didn't feel as if she had won a major victory.

In a fit of frustration she tightened her hold on Lorenzo's arm in an attempt to disconnect her senses from Wolfe.

Oh, who was she kidding? She'd done it to send a message to Wolfe that his rejection of her hadn't affected her in the slightest. That she didn't *need* him. But silently she accepted that if Lucy hadn't interrupted them they'd have made love again. And she couldn't dislodge the sensation that it just felt so right to be in Wolfe's arms.

'Ava?'

'I'm sorry, Lorenzo. I was...you were telling me about how we could integrate the telecommunications networks between Anders and Triole?'

Ava let him fill her head with possibilities and murmured appropriately, but her heart wasn't in it and, feeling Wolfe's steely silence behind her, she experienced an overwhelming need to escape both men and take stock. And she would have done exactly that if Wolfe hadn't cleared his throat and stepped forwards again.

'Ma'am.' His voice was dark and official. 'We need to have that talk now.'

Ava glanced from Wolfe to the burly man in an expensive suit and with a grim expression standing beside him. Did he have news about her situation?

Excusing herself from Lorenzo, Ava waited for Wolfe to speak.

'Ma'am, this is Dan Rogers. He's a security specialist who has worked for me for a number of years. He'll be taking over your security detail from now on.'

It took a minute for Wolfe's words to sink in, and when they did Ava's stomach bottomed out. 'You're quitting?' She couldn't believe it. He'd told her he would *never* quit, and she realised with a start that she'd come to rely on that.

'Not quitting. I'm rearranging the team to better utilise our skill-set.'

Ava heard what he said but she didn't believe it. This wasn't about skill-sets. This was about that kiss in her hotel room.

With her thoughts and feelings swirling around inside her like leaves in a whirly wind, she said the first thing that came to mind. 'My father won't like it.'

Wolfe's jaw clenched and released. 'I'll deal with your father.'

Before she could think of anything else except the sick feeling growing in the pit of her stomach he turned to the other man.

'Take care of her. Once she's secure for the night call me and I'll come and give you a complete brief.'

The man nodded.

Wolfe nodded and then turned his eyes briefly to hers. 'Goodbye…ma'am.'

Ava closed her eyes and leant her head back against the butter-soft leather seats inside her limousine. She was alone in the car, having forbidden her new bodyguard from riding with her. He hadn't liked it, but she'd given him the super-special superior look that had never worked on Wolfe and he'd acquiesced.

Now she felt horribly alone and hankered for something familiar. Something to anchor her in a world that kept moving and changing at a pace she was struggling to keep up with. She'd had so many decisions to make lately she was completely exhausted. No wonder she felt so out of sorts. Life-changes usually happened one at a time and with some sense of order. Didn't they? At least that had been her experience to date. But these past few weeks nothing had been as it should. Least of all her.

In a split-second decision she knew Wolfe would call a

'*spontaneous reaction*' Ava instructed the driver to take her to her gallery, and immediately felt better.

The restless energy flowing through her was somewhat appeased at the thought of seeing Monique's new works. They'd been installed two weeks ago, and viewing them on her smartphone wasn't the same as standing back and inspecting them in person.

She smiled as her change in plans was relayed to the other two cars. No doubt Wolfe would have a kitten…but he had chosen to abandon his post and there was nothing he could do about it. She imagined the conversation they might have if he were here. Was it wrong to enjoy their mental tussles with each other so much?

When the car stopped Ava didn't wait for her chauffeur to open her door but did it herself, breathing in the sweet damp air of Place des Vosges.

Her new bodyguard stopped beside her. 'Ma'am, I'd like you to wait a few minutes before heading inside.'

Ava considered that briefly and then realised why. 'Is Wolfe on his way?'

'Yes, ma'am.'

Ava cursed. 'I thought you were in charge now?'

'I am. However—'

'Never mind. And, no, I won't wait for your boss to join us.'

Pivoting on her heel, she set off across the square to the row of shops she knew like the back of her hand. Her footsteps echoed in the quiet night that was only broken by the low hum of fast-moving cars on the main road and the squeak and clunk of a garbage truck as it rattled along the cobbled streets.

Dan reached the solid metal door to her building before her and held his hand out for the key. 'I'll do that, ma'am.'

A car door slammed somewhere close behind her but she ignored it.

'I can do it.' It might be the last time she ever did, and she wanted to take in every moment.

'Ava!'

Wolfe's hard, angry voice made her fingers fumble the key, and that made her mad. He wasn't going to ruin this for her by muscling his way in. She wouldn't let him.

Of course her stupid key chose that moment to become stuck and, frustrated, she twisted it in the opposite direction. Wolfe's harsh, 'Get back!' confused her, and then a strong arm wrapped around her middle and yanked her sideways seconds before a deafening bang exploded in her ear.

CHAPTER NINE

SHE SCREAMED AND then lost her breath as she felt as if a giant boulder had fallen on top of her.

'Secure…the…area.'

Wolfe's deep voice, laden with pain, instructed the men running towards them. Ava coughed as she tried to breathe the filthy air around them, but her lungs were constricted. Feeling winded, she tried to twist onto her back and realised that it was Wolfe who was smothering her with his body.

When he shifted she dragged in a bucketload of acrid-smelling air. 'What…?'

'Ava. Don't move.' Deft hands ran over her body with mechanical efficiency, and when he was satisfied she wasn't seriously injured he hovered over her, his movements somehow lacking their usual fluid grace.

Hearing a ringing sound in her ears, she peered around to see that the front of her building was completely blown apart. The fire door she had installed as a precaution lay crumpled as if a giant fist had tried to punch holes in it.

Bewildered by the chaos and devastation around her, and only peripherally aware that Wolfe's men surrounded them, Ava glanced at Wolfe. '*Mon Dieu*, you are hurt.'

Ignoring the pain in her hands and hip where she had hit the pavement, she reached out to the jagged tear down the sleeve of his jacket. The white shirt beneath was already turning crimson under the glow of the street lamp that remained intact like a silent sentinel above them.

'Get her…into the car,' Wolfe rasped, shrugging out of his torn jacket.

'No.' Ava tried to reach for him, her only thought to help him, but he slashed his hand in the air.

'Now.'

His voice brooked no argument and before she could do anything his men had gripped her arms and steered her back towards the limousine. She could hear Wolfe ruthlessly issuing orders and the distant wail of a police siren. Concerned voices filtered through the dust and smoke and then faded away as Wolfe's men held back any curious onlookers drawn by the explosion.

Within minutes of the police arriving Wolfe was beside her in the car, wearing a black leather jacket; nothing about his appearance suggested that he'd just thrown himself on top of her as a bomb had blasted glass, bricks and plaster all over him.

He seemed calm and eerily controlled.

By contrast Ava couldn't stop trembling. She was to blame for what had happened. Wolfe had told her not to change her itinerary and she hadn't listened. She had wanted—what? The comfort of the familiar? To get back at Wolfe for leaving her? To make him come after her?

She let out a shaky breath. Right now all she knew was that she had put those assigned to take care of her in danger and she felt awful.

On top of all that the threat to her life was obviously real! Somehow she had held on to the notion that Wolfe was wrong. But it wasn't he who had been wrong, it was her.

'I'm sorry,' she whispered helplessly. 'I feel terrible.'

'It's not your fault.' His voice was clipped, withdrawn. It made her feel worse because she could tell he was blaming himself.

Tears welled behind her eyes but she told herself not to get emotional. That now was not the time. But emotion was stronger than logic even on a good day. 'That is nonsense. I should have—'

'No! *I* should have.' His eyes met hers and he stopped. 'Where are you hurt?'

'I'm okay.'

'Ava.' The way he said her name was a warning that he was going to go completely macho if she didn't cooperate, but all she could think about was how much she loved the way it sounded on his lips.

'My wrist.' And her hip. And she could really use a glass of water.

As if she'd spoken out loud he retrieved a bottle from the mini-bar and untwisted the top.

'*Merci.*'

After she'd finished he took the bottle. 'Give me a look at your hands.'

Shaking, Ava held them out and he gently felt along her wristbones. She winced as he pressed on her tender palm, but he continued his inspection undeterred.

'I don't think bones are broken, but your palms are badly scraped.'

'They'll heal,' she dismissed, catching his brooding frown.

'Thankfully.'

His phone rang before she could ask what would happen next and he released her hand to answer it.

She closed her eyes as the night-dark city whisked by. Wolfe didn't try to touch her or talk to her again but she wanted him to. She felt chilled, as if she'd never be warm again. And for once she didn't argue when he took complete control of the situation. Right now it was easier to sit back and let him do what he did best.

She stole a glance at his austere profile. His jaw was packed with tension, his expression tough. He would do anything to keep her safe because he *had* to, and all she wanted was for him to do it because he *wanted* to.

With a start she realised just how much she trusted him to take care of her. How much she trusted him to have her best interests at heart.

'Please don't be angry at Dan,' she said, suddenly realising that she might have put the other man's job at risk. 'He tried to stop me.'

'I'm not angry at Dan,' he said flatly.

No. He was angry with her. With himself, perhaps.

'You won't fire him?'

'Your concern for his future is a little misplaced. Your behaviour tonight could have got him killed. It could have got you— Hell! What were you thinking?'

Although his words were angry his tone sounded more... devastated. And that sent her own sense of guilt higher.

'I wanted...something familiar. Closure.'

'Closure?'

'I felt restless after you left and I knew I wouldn't sleep. It seemed like a good idea.'

He shook his head. 'I should have told Dan to physically waylay you.'

'Why didn't you?'

His gaze was intense when it connected with hers. 'I didn't want him touching you.'

Ava swallowed at the raw admission.

'Just another mistake on my part.' He blew out a breath and turned away from her, his hands knotted into fists on his thighs.

'Do you think any of Monique's paintings survived?'

He looked at her as if she'd grown another head, but then his expression softened. 'Unlikely. Your fire door sent most of the explosion inward instead of outward. It tells me that whoever set it was more rank amateur than stalwart professional.'

'Do you have any idea who it might be?'

'If I did I'd have my hands around their throat right now.'

'Me, too.'

He shook his head at her, a reluctant smile forming on his lips. 'You are one tough lady, Princess.'

Ava's nose crinkled. She wasn't great at accepting praise even when she felt like she deserved it, but she couldn't deny the warm glow Wolfe's words lit up inside her.

When the car stopped it was a good excuse to refocus her thoughts. Glancing outside, she could see they were on some form of airstrip, but it was too dark to make out exactly where they were. The only source of light was coming from the open rectangular door of Wolfe's private plane.

Wolfe waited for his men to flank the car before opening the door. He glanced around, his eyes scanning the darkness. He was so fierce. So sure. He braced himself against the car as he leant down and beckoned to her. 'This way.'

Careful of her injured palms, Ava scooted across the soft leather, still warm from his body. The softly falling rain chilled her bare shoulders and arms as she stepped out of the car.

Immediately Wolfe moved into her space and lifted her into his arms.

'I can walk.'

'My way is quicker.'

His tone told her he was readying himself for an argument, but frankly Ava didn't have the energy and wasn't sure of how capable she was of making it up the steps under her own steam anyway.

She sighed and rested her head against his chest, her eyelids too heavy to stay propped open. No doubt he was taking her back to Anders, but she'd much prefer a tropical island far away from the outside world if she was given the choice.

Once on his plane she kept her eyes closed, and only opened them when she felt Wolfe gently lower her onto a soft mattress.

The doctor Wolfe had sent to her at Gilles's was waiting and Ava struggled to a sitting position, with the reams of fabric from her torn and dirty gown twisting around her legs.

He followed Wolfe's instructions and checked her wristbones before efficiently sticking a number of plasters over her scraped palms. 'These will feel stiff and sore for a couple of days, due to the bruising beneath the scratches, but they should heal fine.'

'Check her left hip. It's bothering her.'

Her eyes flew to his. How did he know it hurt? 'It's fine.'

'Check it.'

Ava only flinched once during his gentle ministrations, grateful when he deemed it only a light bruise.

'What about you?' She glanced at Wolfe but he was busy checking an incoming message on his phone.

'I'm fine. Thanks, Jock. Tell Stevens to get us airborne as quickly as possible.'

It was only after he said it that Ava became conscious of the whine of the aircraft. Seconds later they were racing towards the sky.

Her eyes traced the smudges of dust covering Wolfe's sandy-blond hair and moved down over his snowy-white shirt beneath the leather jacket.

'You're shivering. Here.' Wolfe pulled a brand-new white shirt out of a small closet, his movements as clipped as his tone. 'I don't have anything for you to wear and both your clothes and your lady's maid are back at the hotel. Can you get changed yourself?'

'Into a shirt?'

'It's all I have here.'

Ava stared at it, the events of the night crashing in around her. Tears pricked behind her eyes and she bit her bottom lip. Hard. She felt scarily vulnerable and needy. The feeling brought both Frédéric's and her mother's death into sharp focus inside her mind.

'Come here,' he said gently.

Wolfe gripped her shoulders, but Ava was afraid if she gave in to the comfort he was offering she would break down completely and never let him go. She shook her head. 'I need to use the bathroom. I'm filthy.'

He looked as if he wanted to argue but then released her. 'Bathroom's through there.'

As the enormity of what had happened hit her full-on Ava had to concentrate to make her legs carry her the short distance across the plane.

Once inside the pristine bathroom, she used the amenities and eyed the shower stall despondently. It would take too long to shower with her hands bandaged, but she would love to just wash the night away if she could.

Don't think about it, she ordered herself. *Then maybe it will all go away.*

She felt like crying.

Reaching around to the side of her gown, she let out an impatient growl as her clumsy fingers fought to drag the zipper down. Then she heard the unmistakable sound of fabric tearing and a sob rose in her throat. The once beautiful gown sagged and fell to the floor and it took all her effort to remain standing. Crying over a dress when someone was trying to kill her…when someone had killed her brother… Pathetic.

Telling herself to get a grip, she kicked off her heels and stuffed her arms into Wolfe's shirt. She knew immediately by the linen smell that he'd never worn it, and that made her want to cry even more.

Dashing at her useless tears to hold them back, she nearly screamed aloud when she couldn't even do the simple task of sliding buttons into buttonholes. Her fingers were hampered by the thick bandages and the length of the shirtsleeves that dangled past her wrists and refused to stay pushed up her arms.

'Oh, damn, damn, *damn*.'

'Ava? Are you okay in there?'

Ava stopped cursing and stilled. '*Oui.* Fine.'

The door opened regardless and Wolfe stood framed in the doorway, with his hands on his hips. He'd changed into a clean shirt that hung out over soft denim jeans. *Magnificent* didn't even begin to describe him.

Wolfe felt as if someone had just tried to squeeze every drop of blood out of his heart as he took in the sight of her standing in the middle of the bathroom, pale and regal, clutching the sides of his shirt together, her torn gown like a puddle of blood circling her bare legs and feet. Tear-marks tracked down her dirty face and her lower lip was trembling as she tried to hold herself together.

He'd never met another woman like her. One who faced life's challenges with grit and determination. One who wasn't afraid to face the truth about herself and, when she set her mind to something, just gathered her courage, rolled up her sleeves and got on with it.

Something tugged in the region of his heart. She was beautiful and strong and…*special.* The word anchored inside his mind and wouldn't budge. It didn't help that she looked as sexy as hell in his shirt.

'I can't do up these damned buttons,' she complained, her voice rough as she worked to hold back tears, her brow furrowed.

'Oh, baby…' Wolfe didn't have a lot of experience dealing with female tears but he acted purely on instinct as he stepped into the room and closed his arms around her. Something satisfying was released inside him when she buried her head against his chest and sniffed. It felt as if she belonged there, but he immediately dismissed the rogue thought. That kind of thinking was totally against his rules.

Her arms slid around his back and he ignored the bolt of discomfort that shot up his spine as she inadvertently touched muscles that had been crushed when part of the wall of her gallery building had landed on top of him.

'Do you know why I chose Paris?'

Her soft voice was muffled against his shirt front and she reminded him of the bunch of newborn kittens he and his brother had once found abandoned in one of the back sheds on their farm. He and Adam had secretly fed them until they had grown too big to be contained. His father had wanted to drown the lot of them, but both of them had begged him to reconsider. Then they had made signs and taken the kittens to the local mall, and stayed all day until the last one had been given away.

The stupid memory made him feel suddenly vulnerable, and he cleared his throat and smoothed his hand up and down Ava's back to distract himself. 'No. Why?'

'It's my mother's city. She grew up here. After she died my life became like something out of a Dickens novel. My father didn't know how to deal with a teenage daughter so he didn't. Since Frédéric had been sent to military school, I...I...'

'You had no one.'

'No.'

A raw sob ripped from her throat and, remembering her stoic reaction to the news of Frédéric's death, Wolfe guessed that she had probably never let herself grieve the loss. The futile destruction of her gallery would be just one more injury for her to try to cope with.

The need to comfort her overrode any sense of self-preservation he had left. Gathering her close, he cradled the back of her head and soaked up her tears, absorbing as much of her pain as he could. When the storm had passed she shifted even closer and every muscle in his body tensed in response.

'You must think I'm a weak foo— Oh, my God. Why did you not tell me I looked like this?'

Wolfe glanced over his shoulder and saw her horrified

reflection in the small bathroom mirror. He eased her away from him and pushed her mass of hair back from her face. 'Really? I thought you were just going for the Panda of the Year award.'

'Yes. With dreadlocks,' she scoffed, dashing at the dusty tear-smudges on her cheeks with the back of one hand. The other was holding her shirt blessedly closed.

'Here, let me.' Still taking most of her weight, and trying not to think about how good she felt leaning into him, Wolfe reached around her and wet a facecloth with warm water. He tilted her chin up and gently wiped as much of the grit and smudges from her face as he could. His muscles knotted as he thought of how close she had come to dying, but he forced himself to relax. Right now her needs took precedence over his rage.

She must have sensed the change in him because she gave him a half-hearted smile and started fumbling with the tiny buttons on his shirt.

Damn, he was going to have to do that for her, as well.

Gently knocking her hands aside, he reached for the top button of the shirt. 'Let me do that. It will be quicker.'

Her beautiful red-rimmed eyes met his and sweat broke out on his forehead. He needed to think of something else.

First, remove the dust cover, then release the tension on the recoil spring.

Okay, he started disassembling an AK47 in his head. That was definitely something else.

His fingers felt feeble as he forced the buttons into their holes and he paused when he accidentally brushed the sweet-smelling skin between her breasts.

Slide the hammer back.

What the hell were these buttons made of anyway? Plasticine?

Gas tube off—

No, idiot. Adjust the front sight post first.

Oh, what the hell.

There was no way cold hard metal could compete with the memory of the weight of those round breasts in the palm of his hands and he gave up, giving his mind permission to conjure up the bumpy texture of her nipples when they were aroused into tight peaks, their colour, their flavour…

Finally reaching the last button, and completely disgusted with himself, Wolfe was glad he didn't have that useless AK47 handy or he might shoot himself with it. He'd been as good as useless to her tonight anyway.

With professional detachment he ignored the question in his head about whether she was wearing panties and lifted her into his arms, hoping to God she couldn't feel his thundering heartbeat. He strode into the plane's bedroom and placed her quickly on the turned-back bed.

About to tell her he'd leave her to rest, he realised she hadn't moved, but sat huddled right where he'd put her.

'Ava…' He said her name on an exhalation. She looked so washed-out and unhappy he couldn't stop himself from placing his knee on the bed beside her and rubbing his hands over her shoulders. 'Baby, lie down.'

She shook her head and her lower lip wobbled again.

'Come on, Princess. Time for sleep.'

He eased her down on the pillows and smoothed her hair back from her face, determined to let that be the end of it.

'Wolfe?' Her voice, barely a whisper, was laced with fatigue and shock. 'Could you stay with me? I mean…just for a minute.'

Could he stay with her? Sure. *Should* he stay with her? No.

Wolfe closed his eyes and held himself still. It would be a monumental mistake to say yes. He wanted to stay. All too much. Which was why he shouldn't.

'Okay.' His hand slipped to the side of her face, caressing the cool skin of her cheek, her jaw. Before he had time to think about it he eased in beside her and leaned his back against the headboard. Without a word he gathered her close and felt her whole body sigh as she arranged her limbs to slot perfectly against his own—as if he'd been made specifically for this purpose. Specifically for her.

A sensation of warmth spread inside his chest and a lump formed in his throat. Without being truly conscious of it he stroked her back. 'Sleep, Princess. I'll be here.'

Had he really just promised that?

After promising himself he'd keep as much physical distance from her as possible?

Well, yes, but there was time to re-implement that plan once he had her on his island. His house wasn't huge, but it was big enough to get lost in, and once he had her safe he'd be able to lock himself away and get to work.

So, yes, he would stay for now, give her the comfort she had sought and failed to receive as a lonely teenager, and then he'd get up. Pore over the intel his team would have sent him about the bomb. He had a suspicion he knew who was behind the attack on her life, given the people he had deliberately leaked Ava's bogus itinerary to, and it was time to find out if his instincts were correct.

Releasing a slow breath, he willed his pain-racked body to fake relaxation. Earlier, when he had spotted Ava in front of her building it had been like running over moon grass instead of smooth pavement trying to reach her. His instincts had been screaming that he should have sent somebody over to check the gallery earlier that night. He hadn't—another slip-up—and he'd nearly lost her. Hell, a newly minted grunt could do a better job of protecting her than he had.

She made a light snuffling sound in her sleep and he realised he'd been stroking her hair. He untangled his fingers and pulled his hand back, wincing when a strand caught in one of his chipped fingernails.

Seriously, it was time to stop mooning over those blue,

blue eyes and the honeyed taste of her mouth and remember she wasn't a goddamned date.

He cursed low under his breath as he realised he'd given himself this same pep talk once before. Then it had been as effective as trying to milk a cow while wearing gardening gloves. Something else he and his brother had tried once. And what was with all these childhood memories streaming into his consciousness as silent and insidious as floodwater?

His gaze slid to Ava's face. A soft wave of her hair had fallen across her cheek and he gently moved it back. The lump in his throat returned with interest.

Dammit, he had to pull back. If he didn't do white picket fences he certainly didn't do bluestone rock with a moat and a drawbridge! But there was nothing he could do to stem the flood of feeling her near-death had opened up in him. He'd do anything to protect her. He knew it. And it was only sensible that he hated that feeling.

About to move off the bed, he felt her arm stretch and settle across his waist. Helpless to do anything else, Wolfe watched her sleep.

CHAPTER TEN

AVA HADN'T HAD any time to feel embarrassed over her crying stint. Once they'd landed Wolfe had hustled her from the plane and led her to a waiting Jeep. She knew instantly that they weren't in Anders, where she had assumed he had been taking her. It was the humid night heat and the smell of eucalyptus in the air.

'Where are we?'

Wolfe stopped beside the black Jeep. 'An island.'

Ava gave a short laugh. 'You're kidding?'

'No. Why?'

She shook her head, wondering if she was still dreaming. 'No reason.' She knew she must have been dreaming that Wolfe had sat with her during the whole flight and stroked her hair. Ava hesitated before preceding him into the car. 'Which island?'

'Cape Paraiso. It's a small private island off the west coast of Africa.'

She studied the carved planes of his profile in the starry sky, noting the sense of ownership in his voice. 'Yours?'

'It was on sale. Get in.'

Ava already knew that Wolfe hadn't grown up wealthy, which meant he was a self-made man, and she couldn't help but like how unassuming he was about his success.

She stifled a yawn as the car zoomed along a rough track.

She gingerly held on to the door to stop herself from sliding against Wolfe's solid frame, but he didn't even notice as he scrolled through some sort of document on his phone.

'Do you have any ideas as to who is responsible yet?'

He glanced at her briefly, his expression guarded. 'I'm working around the clock on it.'

Ava let him read. The wind was up and it rustled through towering hardwood trees. The glint of the moon shone silvery streaks on the inky ocean. She could just make out a solid stone house that looked to be set into the side of a cliff, and as they drove closer she saw that it was finished with a tiled roof and acres of glass.

When the car had pulled into a short circular driveway Wolfe jumped stiffly from the Jeep. Her eyes followed him as he walked around the front of the car. If she wasn't mistaken he was very much a man in pain. She remembered the blood on his torn jacket before he'd changed out of it and reluctantly acknowledged that she had become so absorbed in the horror of what had happened she hadn't thought about his injuries at all.

Wolfe hovered by her side.

'I'm okay. I can walk.'

After a brief pause he nodded. 'Follow me.'

The tiles were cool and slightly gritty with sand beneath her bare feet, but Ava had only a moment to admire the massive front door before she was inside a foyer-cum-living area that could comfortably house his plane and the Jeep and still have room to spare for an ocean liner.

'Wow!'

'You like it?'

Ava glanced at him. 'It's enormous.'

'The size is deceptive. This is the largest area because of the aspect. Are you hungry?'

Her hand went to her belly and she shook her head. 'I couldn't eat anything.'

He nodded. 'I'll take you to your room.'

She followed him along the narrow hallway.

'This corridor leads to the bedroom. The other one leads into the kitchen, gym and pool area. The house is all on one level so I doubt you'll get lost.'

He led her down a long hallway that had various other hallways leading off it and she wondered absently if they shared the same idea of size. 'Is it just us?'

He stopped outside a closed door and threw it open. 'Yes. The island is completely private. The couple who caretake for me live on a larger island about an hour away. Wait here.'

He stepped into the room, flicked on the light and checked the double glass doors leading to an outdoor area. When his gaze returned to her she became intensely aware that she was standing in the middle of a bedroom wearing nothing more than one of his shirts and a teensy pair of knickers. Every cell in her body seemed to vibrate on high alert and she wondered if he was at all affected by her. On some level she knew he had to be, but he was so good at controlling himself. It made her want to rip her shirt open and push all that stony self-control to the limit.

'I don't have any women's clothing and I can't send out for any. That shirt should do you tonight. In the morning I'll lend you some T-shirts and shorts of mine.'

'Merci.'

'I'd also prefer you didn't go outside. The whole house is alarmed and I don't want you tripping it.'

Without waiting for her acquiescence he strode to the door. 'You should have everything you need in the *en suite* bathroom, but I will be next door if you should need anything else.'

Like him?

The impulsive thought jumped into her mind and she smiled brightly. 'I'm sure I'll be fine.'

Or at least she wouldn't tell him if she wasn't.

Wolfe nodded. 'Goodnight then.'

Feeling wired after her rest on the plane, Ava turned her interested gaze to the room. It was large and airy and continued the strong Spanish feel of the other rooms, with terracotta floors inlaid with handcrafted mosaics, brightly coloured rugs and light timber furniture.

She'd dearly love to take a shower, but that seemed impossible with her bandaged hands. Nor could she go outside. Glancing around the stylishly furnished room she found nothing to distract herself, not even a TV.

With nothing to do she freshened up in the bathroom as best she could with her cumbersome bandages and lay down on the comfortable bed, willing herself to sleep again. Her mother had always said she could do anything if she put her mind to it, but it seemed that sleep on command wasn't one of those achievements.

Thinking of her mother made her feel sad again. Sad and alone. She had been the only person who understood her need to shine in her own right. Her need to stand on her own two feet.

Wolfe understands you.

The sneaky little thought crept sideways into her brain and transported her back to the bed on his plane. Rolling sideways, she shifted restlessly and felt bereft in the empty bed. Snuggling into his big body had been… It had been… Ava felt her pelvis clench in response. Yes, it had been heavenly. He was so warm. So solid. And this bed in comparison was cold. Empty. Exactly how she felt right now.

What would he do if she went to him…naked? Would it matter that he would never love her the way she desperately wanted to be loved?

Irritated with herself, she rolled onto her back and stared at the dark ceiling. Why, oh, why couldn't she get that man out of her head?

And why couldn't Lorenzo affect her half as much? Marrying him would solve every one of her problems. He was the spare to the heir in his own country, so he understood the pressures she would face as Queen. And he was kind. Considerate. The perfect gentleman.

But she didn't love him and he didn't love her. Although it was possible that love would grow; it often did in arranged marriages.

And it often didn't either.

'Oh, shut up!' Ava told the insistent voice in her head.

She would have to sleep with him. Take him into her body. And that just felt...

Wrong.

'Yes, yes. I get it.'

And talking to an empty room wasn't going to change anything. Feeling horribly alone, and miserably vulnerable after the night's events, Ava felt a desperate urge to leave a message for her father. To reconnect with him in some small way. Something her mother would no doubt be immensely happy with.

About to reach for her phone, she realised she had no idea where it was. She knew she'd had it in the limousine on the way to her gallery because she'd ignored an incoming message. Or had that been during the dinner earlier? She couldn't remember, but no doubt if she had left it in either place one of Wolfe's efficient men would have picked it up for her.

If they had where would they have left it? The living room? The kitchen? No way would they come to her room and disturb her.

Mulling over her options, Ava decided to take a look; she knew she wouldn't sleep anyway, and maybe she would fix herself a glass of warm milk in the process.

Feeling marginally better now that she was taking action, she stepped out of her room, feeling a bit like a thief as her bare feet padded silently on the tiled floor.

Hoping she was headed in the right direction, she stopped

when she noticed a triangle of light spilling into the hallway ahead of her.

Wolfe obviously wasn't in bed yet. Or maybe it was the driver of the Jeep. Maybe he could help her.

Cautiously moving forward, she felt a sense of trepidation tightening her throat as every horror movie she had ever seen vied for supremacy in her head. She leaned around the open doorway and her hand flew to her mouth to stifle her shocked gasp.

Wolfe was standing in a small utility room, naked to the waist, his back covered in a crisscross pattern of fresh welts and bruises. A large medical kit stood open on the marble benchtop, bandages, scissors and blood-covered swabs strewn around it. A white gauze bandage he had clearly applied himself ran the length of his left triceps.

As if in a daze she connected her eyes with his in the wide mirror. 'Oh, my God. That looks terrible.'

When it had felt as if a wall had fallen on her it *had*, she realised, but Wolfe had taken the brunt of the impact. Broken pieces of brick, wood and plaster had turned his bronzed flesh into a checkerboard of pain. The shock of the night returned full force and, feeling sick to her stomach, Ava moved into the room.

Wolfe spun around, presenting her for the first time in weeks with the sight of his magnificent hair-roughened chest.

Ava barely noticed.

Her eyes slid past his impressive pectoral muscles to where his bruised back could be seen as clear as day under the fluorescent light.

'It looks worse than it is.'

Her eyes met his. 'I very much doubt that.' Her hand covered her mouth again. 'Wolfe, I am *so* sorry.'

Swearing softly under his breath, he reached for the shirt he'd dropped onto the floor.

'I told you it wasn't your fault.' The words were more like

a grunt, but he didn't move to cover himself with the T-shirt as she stepped into his personal space.

'Much.' She gave him a stilted smile. 'What is this cream for?' She picked up the opened jar on the vanity behind him and smelt it.

'It's arnica. It's a natural remedy that takes a lot of the pain out of bruises.'

'So you *do* feel pain?' She tried to make light of it to curb how truly awful she felt about his injuries.

'Not if I can help it,' he said flatly.

She cocked her eyebrow at him and noticed him stiffen when she dabbed her finger into the jar. 'Turn around,' she instructed on impulse.

He shook his head, swallowed heavily. 'I can take care of myself.'

Ava understood his need for self-sufficiency. On a much smaller scale she too had decided it was safer to rely only on herself, but for some reason she wanted Wolfe to know that she was there for him just as much as he had been there for her.

Finding it hard to maintain eye contact with him as he towered over her, Ava nevertheless held her ground. 'Everyone needs someone, Wolfe.'

'I don't.' His words sounded gritty. Empty.

'Yes, you do. You're just too afraid to admit it.' Ava twirled her finger. 'Now, turn around. Please,' she added when it looked as if he wouldn't comply.

He shook his head in mock resignation. 'Anyone ever tell you you're a bossy little thing?'

'Hmm, there was a man once who might have uttered something similar.'

'What happened to him?'

'I threw him in my dungeon.'

'Then I better not cross you,' he said gravely.

'A smart man.' She laughed. 'Who knew?'

He scowled at her but there was a twinkling of humour in his toffee eyes. Her breath caught as she took in his male beauty, but then he turned and she could barely stop herself from wincing when she saw his back again. 'Tell me if I hurt you.'

'You won't.'

Their eyes met briefly in the mirror and she knew he was right. If anyone was going to get hurt here it would be her.

Ignoring the maudlin thought, she concentrated on being gentle as she touched him.

She felt him tense up at her first touch. His hands braced against the vanity unit, but other than that he didn't move as she worked the cool cream into his discoloured skin. 'Weren't you wearing one of those special vests?' she asked to distract herself while she worked.

'Kevlar is better against bullets than bombs. Although it hurts like a son of a bitch to get shot.'

And she knew he knew what *that* felt like.

He was so strong, this warrior of a man who had shielded her so well all she'd ended up with was a bruised hip and sore hands.

Fortunately her plasters didn't hinder her fingers from spreading cream onto him, and by the time she'd worked her way down to the base of his spine she felt his muscles start to relax.

And then other sensations started to creep into her consciousness. Sensations like the fact that his warm, toned flesh was beneath her fingertips. Like his size. The fact that she was standing so closely behind him she would only have to move a centimetre to be plastered against all that heat.

Just like that lust unfurled like a flower low in her pelvis and turned her insides to liquid. She glanced at his face in the mirror and found his eyes were shut tight, his knuckles as white as the basin he gripped. It was as if he was holding on to his control by a thread. As if her touching him was affecting him the same way it was affecting her.

Without allowing herself any time to think about it, she leant forward and placed her lips along the indent of his spine, feeling rather than hearing his sharp inhalation. He smelt of soap and the cream now absorbed into his skin. And all man. Ava breathed deep, careful not to press against his bruises but unable to stop kissing him on every undamaged section of his back.

He was tall, so much taller than her, and she had to stretch to reach the base of his neck. As soon as her lips found their mark a deep sound rumbled through his body and he spun towards her, his hands gripping her waist to hold her back.

A tap dripped in the quiet room but neither of them paid it any attention.

Ava knew her eyes showed how aroused she was but she didn't try to hide it from him. She knew he would never want a future with her, but at this point she didn't care.

Last week she had pledged that she would dedicate her life to her country. But that seemed irrelevant tonight. Tonight they had both nearly lost their lives. Tonight she just wanted to be a normal woman with a man who made her feel so much.

'What are you doing, Ava?'

His deep growl sent a frisson of awareness straight to her core.

She spread her hands wide over his magnificent chest. 'What does it look like?'

'It looks like trouble.'

She smiled. 'I want to make love with you, Wolfe.'

His nostrils flared and his fingers bit into her waist. Like a sinuous cat Ava arched towards him, powered by the knowledge that he seemed to be as aroused as she already was.

When he continued to stare at her, unmoving, she wondered if perhaps she'd misjudged him. Misjudged the depth of the chemistry between them. Misjudged his infinite self-control. The old feeling of not being good enough swamped her, but just as she might have withdrawn he hauled her up onto her toes and claimed her mouth with his.

Ava sighed blissfully against his lips. Her body knew his, trusted his. When he groaned and slanted his mouth to widen hers she didn't even think of holding back. She had wanted him to touch her—had wanted to touch him—for weeks, and it felt as if her whole body just melted into his like a boneless mass.

Possibly she was just being driven by the need to be physically close to someone right now. The ghosts of those she had loved and lost lay heavy in her heart after her horrifying ordeal. But she didn't care. She had never wanted a man the way she wanted James Wolfe.

'I want you, Ava.' His voice was as rough as a cat's tongue against her ear. 'God knows I've tried to resist you. Tried and failed. If you don't stop me now I won't be able to.'

Ava gazed into eyes as black as the night sky outside. He was giving her a message, she knew it. He wasn't the one for her no matter how good it felt to be with him.

Maybe it would have been smarter to heed that warning. Maybe it would have been smarter to push him away. But her body refused to cooperate. Something inside her sensed that he needed her equally as much as she needed him, and that feeling was stronger than any maybe.

'I don't want you to stop.'

CHAPTER ELEVEN

IT WAS AS if those passion-drugged words had unleashed a beast inside him. Wolfe forgot all about the gut-wrenching pain in his back and instead could only feel the gut-wrenching ache in his body. For her. Only for her.

Before, when she'd looked at him so guilelessly and told him that everyone needed someone, he had vehemently denied that he did. But right now his body made a mockery of those words. Her concern over his injuries had completely undone him. No woman had ever treated him so tenderly before and it was appalling how badly he wanted to soak that up.

As if in a dream state Wolfe smoothed his hands down over her thighs, encouraging them up around his hips. 'Put your legs around my waist.' His voice was so rough it was barely recognisable as he hoisted her higher.

'I hate it when you get macho,' she teased, locking her ankles together and squeezing his hips.

Wolfe's eyelids grew heavy as he felt her heat against his abdomen. Her breathlessness inflamed him even further. 'You want me to put mine around yours?'

Her husky laugh turned into a low, keening cry as he adjusted her so that she rocked against his erection exactly where he knew she needed it the most. A deep sense of satisfaction hit him hard at the thought that he could please this spirited woman so easily.

He kissed her all the way back to his room, only breaking contact to switch on the side lamp and lie her back on his bed.

This was what he wanted—what he had dreamt of since Gilles's wedding. Ava, hot for him. Spread out on his bed, aroused and waiting for him to take her. To possess her.

The warning in his head that he wanted her just a little too much was driven out by the sheer, unequivocal desire to take and brand her as his own.

Forgetting all about technique and—heaven help him—finesse, he pulled the front her shirt open, uncaring as some of the buttons tore free.

Her breath caught, pushing her breasts higher. Her nipples were already standing up and begging for his mouth. 'I need a shower.'

'No.' He shook his head slowly, his eyes drinking in her naked perfection. 'You need me.'

And he needed her. So badly it was a physical pain. He needed to be inside her and he gave up trying to work out why.

When she was naked, spread out before him like this, it would take a whole army to pull him off her, and he had the insane urge to beat his chest and chain her to the bed so that she could never leave.

More than a little disturbed by that gut-wrenching notion, Wolfe shoved it aside along with his jeans. Nothing, not even the whispered warnings of self-preservation in his head, was going to stop him from taking her now. He climbed over the top of her, his mouth nipping her skin wherever it landed.

Her hands stroked up his arms, trying to pull him down over her, but he resisted. He had no intention of rushing this. Instead he straddled her hips, imprisoning her legs with his and brought his hands up to cup and pleasure her breasts.

She tried to arch into his caress, but she was effectively trapped and he smiled. 'I know you hate this type of macho stuff.' He lightly brushed over her nipples as if by accident, enjoying that little catch in her breath. 'So feel free to tell me to stop at any time.'

Her eyes flew open. 'I should…I should…'

She stopped breathing again as he circled ever closer to her rigid peaks. She squirmed, making his erection throb, but he deliberately held off giving her what she wanted—what he wanted—building the anticipation between them, making them both burn.

Her hands stroked down over his chest towards his throbbing erection, a look of power and delight tilting her smile.

'Uh-uh.' He secured both her wandering hands in one of his above her head and dropped a kiss on her open mouth, lingering long enough to tease her with his tongue.

'You said "I",' he reminded her.

'I will never speak to you again if you don't put yourself inside me right now,' she vowed.

'What about this?' he asked, watching her face as he rolled a nipple between his thumb and forefinger.

She sighed in rapture, her body tightening as if she was a weapon he was fine-tuning.

He let go of her wrists and brought both his hands into play to pleasure her gorgeous breasts. The sight of her like that was highly erotic. He let his eyes roam over her flushed face and chest, enjoying her pleasure as he slowly increased the pressure to a torturous level.

'Oh, that. Oh, yes. Don't stop. Wolfe!'

Her arms fluttered and moved down, her hands sculpting his chest and abdomen until finally one was cupping him while the other palmed his aroused length. The bandages on her palms were cool where her fingers were hot. He bit back a pleasurable oath, his eyes closing as he continued to tug on her sweet nipples and absorbed her sensual touch at the same time.

'Wait,' he advised softly. 'Ava, baby, if you keep doing that I'm going to lose control.'

He shifted out of her hold, smiling as the sound of protest she made in the back of her throat turned to relief when he took the tip of her breast into his mouth.

She writhed beneath him and he released her imprisoned legs to stroke his hand between her thighs. She was hot and wet, so close to her climax he could feel the tiny tremors of her release beneath his fingers.

'Not yet, baby. I want to be inside you when you come.'

'I can't help it,' she moaned. 'You've pushed me too far.'

'Not yet, I haven't.' He urged her legs wider and positioned himself at the apex of her body. 'But I intend to.'

On a single powerful thrust he surged deep, pausing just long enough to let her expand around him before moving again. She whimpered desperately and dragged his face down to hers.

A primal sense of satisfaction rushed through him as he established a steady rhythm, rolling his hips against hers and causing a string of sensual spasms throughout her body that sucked him in even deeper.

Driving into her, Wolfe didn't stop until he felt her go still, poised on the edge of her release. He held her there as long as he could, but she moved against him, sobbing as her climax consumed her, her inner contractions forcing his own body to speed towards a release that burned hotter than the West Australian sun.

Wolfe woke and knew instantly that he'd overslept—something he hadn't done since before his army days. And in his arms was a woman who twisted his insides into knots Houdini would struggle to break out of. He thought about his inflexible rules: short, sweet and simple. Only one of them had been upheld last night, and it wasn't short or simple.

He lifted a strand of her hair and closed his eyes as he breathed in the soft floral fragrance, ignoring the screaming pain in his back from muscles still stiff from lack of use.

He'd ignored them the night before, too, when they'd been screaming from overuse. He'd lost track of the amount of times they'd made love, each time eclipsing the last in a way he would have said was impossible. And it wasn't just the sex he'd wanted, he realised uneasily. He liked her. He liked spending time with her. Watching her. Listening to her. Being challenged by her. Somehow, in a short space of time, she had come to mean more to him than any other woman ever had. More than he wanted her to. More than he was willing to think about.

She gave a small moan and snuggled deeper into his shoulder. Irresistible.

'What time is it?'

He glanced down and smiled as her eyes remained scrunched closed. 'I take it you're not a morning person?'

She rolled onto her back and shifted her head onto the pillow. 'Not really. You?'

'Always.' He propped up on his side. 'In fact I'm never up late, even after spending most of the night awake. I think you're making me soft.'

She glanced briefly down his body. 'I hope not.'

Wolfe gave a chuckle. 'Witch,' he said against her mouth, and her lips opened under his in a way that made him think about taking her again.

Remember the rules, a timely voice reminded him forcefully.

Yeah, the rules. The ones he was breaking faster than a politician broke election promises.

He jumped out of bed and reached for the jeans he'd discarded on the floor the night before. 'How about you take a minute to wake up while I fix something to eat?'

'Oh, Wolfe, your back looks terrible.'

He glanced over his shoulder. 'It'll heal.' He yanked a T-shirt over his head and his belly clenched as he saw Ava staring in that region. 'How are your hands?'

'*Quoi?*'

He couldn't prevent a crooked smile from curling one side of his mouth when she looked at him with dazed eyes. 'Your hands? How are they?'

She made a great show of looking at them, but he suspected she was trying to hide her blush from him. She never blushed, as far as he knew, and the sight was pleasing on a purely male level.

'Sore.'

'I'll take a look at them after breakfast,' he promised, grasping her wrists lightly and dropping a kiss against each bandage before he thought better of it.

Ava paused in the doorway of the kitchen and watched Wolfe flip something in the frying pan. His lithe, narrow-hipped frame drew her eye like a flame drew a moth.

He turned as if sensing her and gave her a lazy grin. 'The clothes fit, then?'

Ava glanced down at the oversized T-shirt and board shorts she'd had to roll twice at the waist to keep them up. 'I think that might be a grave exaggeration, but they're not falling off.'

His gaze lingered on her legs. 'Eggs, bacon.' He cleared his throat. 'Tomatoes in two minutes. It's not *nouvelle cuisine.*'

'I don't need anything fancy,' she assured him.

He gave her such an open, clear-eyed smile before turning back to the stove that Ava felt something inside her shift and fall into place. Shell-shocked, she couldn't move.

She loved him.

She had been trying to ignore the feelings burbling away inside her for so long but…*mon Dieu*, she had loved him from that first night. Had she? A lump rose in her throat as she recalled how gentle he had been with her mother's cat. At the time she'd told him that she hated him but she hadn't. Not even then.

'You okay?'

Ava glanced up from the terracotta tiles to find Wolfe holding a spatula and wearing a frown. 'Fine.'

'Well, that's a surefire answer saying that you're not.'

'No. I am.' She strolled into the room as if she hadn't just made a discovery that would irrevocably change her for ever. She couldn't tell him. Not only were her emotions too new, she didn't know how to tell him. And she was pretty sure he wasn't feeling the same thing she was, so she smiled instead. 'Really. I was just thinking of last night.'

'Good to know I make you scowl.'

'The other part.'

'Come here.' He pulled her in close. Kissed her mouth.

His warmth made her heart swell but she didn't let herself think it was more than it was. 'The eggs are burning,' she said faintly, wanting space.

His gaze was piercing, as if he was trying to read her, and she painted on another smile. 'I'll get the orange juice.'

'I've made fresh coffee, as well.'

Coffee. Yes. That would help her jumbled thoughts.

She opened the fridge. Funny, but when she had imagined realising she was in love with someone it hadn't been anything like this. She'd imagined she might be at a restaurant, or in bed, somewhere cosy, wrapped up in her lover's embrace. One of them would say it and then the other…they'd smile, share the moment…

'It's right there.'

Ava started as Wolfe reached around her and pulled a carton from the door, his other hand resting on the small of her back.

'Are you sure you're okay?'

'Positive.' Positive she might never be okay again. That was what she was positive about. Because Wolfe wouldn't want her love. He wasn't a man who wanted any woman's love. In fact if she told him how she felt it would probably send him running in the other direction.

* * *

Ava pulled her foot up onto a wooden chair and hooked her arm around her knee, nursing what remained of her coffee in both hands. They'd decided to eat their food outside by the infinity pool, but although the view was magnificent she had barely paid it any attention.

'So, tell me why you joined the army,' she asked, intrigued by some of the stories he'd told her about the time he'd spent with Gilles when they were younger.

Wolfe set down his fork and pushed his empty plate away, reaching for his own coffee. He took his time stretching out his long legs, his jeans riding so low she could just see the ridge of that fascinating muscle that wrapped around his hip-bones where his T-shirt didn't quite cover him.

'Couldn't think of anything else to do with my time.'

'Really?' She dragged her eyes back to his face as if she hadn't just been ogling him. She didn't believe a man with his keen intelligence would make such a decision so casually. If she had to guess she'd say it had something to do with his need to protect everyone around him. Like his brother. His father. 'That was it?'

His eyes narrowed, as if he could discern her thoughts. 'Don't make me out to be some sort of hero, Ava, because I'm not.'

Even without the cool words she could see the sudden tension in him and wondered if it was because this was the first personal question she had asked him since that night he had talked about his family.

Trying not to let his response completely ruin the mood between them, Ava cast her eyes over the golden cliff-faces and tiered flowerbeds that tripped down towards a horseshoe-shaped blue lagoon. 'Wow, this view is really something. Is the whole island this beautiful?'

'The other side gets the wind straight off the Atlantic, so it's a bit scrubbier, but basically yes.'

'Do you come here often?'

'Not as often as I'd like.'

Ava sighed. 'It's so relaxing here. It's as if the real world is another planet. If I had my way I'd stay for ever.'

The scrape of wood against terracotta brought her eyes back to him.

'It's deceptively dangerous. That cove down there is relatively sheltered, but the island can get twenty-five-foot waves at times, and then the beaches are littered with seaweed.'

His tone was much darker than it needed to be and Ava suspected he was talking about more than just the island. She suspected it was a warning for her not to fall for him, but if it was it was not only too late but completely unnecessary. What did he think she was going to do? Stalk him?

'And speaking of for ever...we didn't use protection last night.'

Ah, so *that* was what had triggered his tension. Ava felt her stomach bottom out. She hadn't even thought of it. She'd been so absorbed by her feelings for him, by her anxiety about what to do...

'I can see you're shocked.' He gathered up their plates, the harsh sound of cutlery sliding against porcelain jarring her. 'If you're pregnant it will change things.'

She *was* shocked—but more because the prospect didn't make her nearly as unhappy as he thought. In fact it made her feel elated to think of herself carrying his child. Something she definitely wasn't prepared to admit when his face had taken on all the levity of a thundercloud.

'What do you mean?' And still her silly, hopeful heart beat just a little faster as she waited for him to declare his love for her. Ask her to marry him.

'You'll have to cancel any plans you have to marry the Prince of Triole, for one thing.'

Quoi?

Ava stared at him. He thought she was going to marry Lorenzo? And he'd still slept with her! Controlling her temper by a thread, Ava arched her brow. 'No?'

One of the knives on the plate he was holding clattered onto the tiles but neither one of them broke eye contact to locate it. 'No. You'll be marrying me.'

'*You?*' She hadn't expected him to say that and it threw her off balance. 'I already told you I wouldn't marry without love.'

He paused, his brows pulled together. 'Not even for a child?'

Dull colour flooded her cheeks and a breeze rustled the nearby shrubs. Trap a man who so clearly wanted his freedom? 'I'd rather be a single parent.'

He glared at her. 'Since I don't hold the same view you'd better hope you're not pregnant. Because if you are you *will* marry me, Ava.'

'You'd better hope you're not pregnant. Because if you are you will *marry me.'*

Wolfe leaned his elbows on his desk and cupped his face in his hands. What an idiot.

Before, when she'd been sitting on his deck, he'd been looking at her and thinking how lovely she was. How much he enjoyed having her in his home. In his life. Then she'd mentioned for ever and he'd broken out in a cold sweat. It was as if she'd read his mind.

Panicked, he realised that in making breakfast and playing house with her he was not only still breaking all his rules with her but grinding them into the dust for good measure. This must have been how his father had felt about his mother. How else to explain why he'd taken her back over and over? Wolfe had vowed never to let a woman mean so much to him that she weakened him in the same way. But that had nothing to do with Ava, did it?

Hell, he'd acted like an ass and he owed her an apology. A big apology.

After checking once more for updates on the bomb blast that had ripped her gallery in half, he scoured the house and found her walking on the beach.

She was a vision of loveliness, with his large blue T-shirt swamping her lanky frame and her mane of dark hair rippling down her back. Watching her, Wolfe felt a now familiar tug in his chest and knew he was in trouble. Deep trouble.

Not that it would do him any good to think that way. She'd made it pretty clear before that she saw him as nothing more than a temporary entity in her life.

'I'd rather be a single parent.'

Just the thought of her vehemence made him see red. Made his anger— He stopped. Blinked. What the hell was wrong with him? Had a brick from her building landed on his head last night and messed with his brain? Surely nothing else could explain his seesawing emotions.

Ava's soft laugh reached him from across the sand and forced his attention back to the present moment.

She turned slightly to twist her hair out of her face and Wolfe forgot all about his apology when he saw that she was on her phone.

When had she got that? And, more importantly, hadn't he told her not to use it while she was here?

Totally off balance, he let his frustration and volatile emotions morph into savage anger. 'Dammit, are you stupid? You don't make calls on a mobile phone.'

Ava spun round at the sound of Wolfe's harsh voice and nearly dropped her phone in the water. She could still hear Baden's voice but could no longer make out the words, her attention totally focused on the furious expression on Wolfe's face. Her breath caught and she felt as if she was thirteen years old and being confronted by her disapproving father.

'I have to go.' She disconnected the phone just as Wolfe reached her.

'What do you think you're doing?' he said, breathing fire and brimstone at her.

'Ice-skating?'

'Dammit, Ava. I told you not to make mobile phone calls from the island.'

She frowned, pretty sure that he hadn't. 'No, you didn't.'

'Yes. I. Did.'

'No. You. Did. Not. But anyway I didn't make a call. I received one.' She'd found her phone on Wolfe's chest of drawers after breakfast and checking her messages had helped take her mind off just how futile her feelings for him were.

'Answering it works the same way,' he said through gritted teeth. 'It gives away our location to anyone with the equipment to utilise it.'

'You use yours,' she felt stung into retorting.

'Mine's encrypted.'

Ava shoved her hands on her hips. 'Well, nobody told me that.'

Wolfe shook his head and ground his jaw as if she were a complete imbecile. 'I *knew* this wouldn't work.'

'I have no idea what you're referring to, but I've had enough of your overbearing attitude for one day,' she fumed. 'And, so you don't have to worry, it was just Baden checking up on me after the bomb. I hope that is not against your rules?'

She stalked off in the direction of the house. This was exactly like her father, judging her and finding her lacking. It hurt. Despite everything she had promised herself she had given Wolfe the power to hurt her. She had no one else to blame but herself.

As she passed the pool she glanced down at the phone in her hand and in a fit of pique her father would say was incredibly impulsive tossed it into the water.

'Dammit, that was a fool thing to do.'

She spun around, not realising that Wolfe had followed so

closely behind her. 'Like climbing that dumb wall at Gilles's. I wish I'd never done that either. Maybe then we would never have met.'

'We would have met.'

Caught off guard by his brooding tone, she felt all her anger leave her body and for a minute stood in front of him feeling strangely lost.

She needed a cup of tea. Yes, that would help her regroup. She glanced once more at the rippling pool as she stalked off. It *had* been stupid to toss her phone in it, particularly since she still had messages to check.

'What are you doing now?'

Ava opened a cupboard near the kitchen sink in search of mugs. 'Making tea. Do you want some?'

'No. The cups are above your head.'

'Do you have lemon verbena, by any chance?'

Wolfe expelled a long breath and some of the tension seemed to leach out of him. 'I have no idea.' He strode to a cupboard and started rifling through containers. 'No. Will peppermint do?'

'Yes.' Their eyes connected. Held. 'Thank you.'

Wolfe watched her pour boiling water into a mug and berated himself for letting his frustration at the situation cloud his objectivity. No wonder he hadn't located her brother's killer yet.

And she'd been right before. He *hadn't* told her not to use her phone. He'd *meant* to. But that wasn't the same thing. And mistakes like that got people killed.

Could get her killed.

Now he'd have to change their location. Find another safe place. Because he wouldn't risk her life, no matter how small the chance that the killer had the skills to track her to the island. He didn't know who he was dealing with and it was time to act as if he had some sort of a clue as to how to do his job.

He blew out a breath.

He needed to apologise to her. Again.

Without giving himself time to decide if it was a bad idea, he wrapped his arms around her from behind.

She stiffened but he didn't let go.

'I'm sorry for yelling at you. I behaved like a jackass.'

'Yes, you did.' She sniffed. 'Why?'

Now, there was the million-dollar question. 'I was jealous.'

Her eyebrows shot up. 'Of Baden?'

'I thought you were talking to Lorenzo.'

Her eyes softened and Wolfe felt more vulnerable than he ever had, even as a kid walking up to the front door of his house after school and wondering if his mother would be home.

Her throat worked and he was sure she was about to say something soft and mushy. He wanted to hear it so badly he ducked his head and kissed her breathless. He wasn't sure if she had been about to tell him that she loved him but he couldn't have coped if she had.

Because it wouldn't be real. They had grown closer through forced proximity and sex, but that wasn't love. And he couldn't bear to hear her say it when she didn't mean it.

A memory of his mother tucking him into bed and kissing his forehead when he was about five punched him in the head. Her warmth...her soft touch...

He felt a yearning open up inside him and doused it by slipping his hands beneath Ava's baggy T-shirt and appeasing a much more basic need. He stroked her breasts until she arched into him.

This.

This was something he knew he could trust in.

He lifted her onto the bench and yanked the shorts down her long legs, shifting her forward so that his erection was cradled in the notch between her thighs.

'That feels so good,' she groaned, wrapping her arms around his neck.

Wolfe kissed her like a starving man and carried her back to his bedroom.

'After the bomb?'

'Mmm?' Ava felt Wolfe shift to his side and let her body collapse against him.

'Ava, baby, wake up. I need to ask you something.'

'Mmm? Do I have to?'

'Yes, come on, baby. Back to the land of the living.' She sighed, enjoying the way his hand stroked her hair from her face.

'Okay, I'm back, General. What it is you want to know?'

'You said before that Baden was checking on you after the bomb?'

Ava frowned. The urgency in his voice was more than clear. 'Yes.'

'Did you tell him about it?'

'No.'

'You're sure? Now, think, baby. I need you to be certain.'

'I'm not a child, Wolfe.'

'Don't go getting surly on me again.'

She arched a brow. 'Me? Get surly?'

'Okay, okay.' He cupped her face in his hands. 'This is important. I need you to be one hundred percent certain.'

'Why would I tell Baden when he already knew about it?'

Wolfe closed his eyes briefly, as if he was in pain. Which he might be considering his bruises and their recent lovemaking. 'He shouldn't know.'

Ava pushed his hands aside, the nape of her neck tingling. 'I don't see how he couldn't. It must be all over the media, and my father would have told him.'

Before she'd even finished speaking Wolfe was off the

bed, shucking into his boxers and jeans. 'Dammit, where's my phone?'

'I saw it in the kitchen. Wolfe…?'

'Stay here.'

Ava stared after his departing figure and only paused to sweep up the T-shirt he hadn't bothered to put on before racing after him.

He was on the phone but speaking too quietly for her to take in more than, "Yeah…" and, "Get back to me."

'Want to tell me what's going on?'

Wolfe had his soldier's face on when he turned to her. 'You might want to sit down.'

Ava did, but only because his intensity was starting to make her legs feel rubbery. 'You think it's Baden.'

Wolfe pulled a chair in front of hers and sat down, his hands gentle as he held hers. 'I know you don't want to believe this, but your father just confirmed that Baden hadn't been told about the explosion.'

'But it must be all over the internet by now at the very least.'

He shook his head. 'No. I had it suppressed. As far as anyone knows a car ran into the front of your gallery.'

Ava stared at Wolfe's hands, absently noting how beautiful they were. Then her eyes rose to his. 'Baden would never have hurt Frédéric.'

Wolfe sighed. 'I'm sorry, Ava. I know you won't want to hear this but my team have been closing in on him for a few days now. He's mentally unstable. Did you know that?'

Mentally unstable? Ava shook her head.

'He's been diagnosed with schizophrenia. And his psychological transcripts reveal that he blames your father for the death of his.'

Stunned by what he was telling her, Ava shook her head. 'No. His father died in a boating accident.'

'Your father was driving it.'

'I know, but… You think Baden believes *he* should be the heir to the throne in Anders?'

'That's what it looks like.'

'But why do something now? Why not get rid of me and Frédéric years ago?'

'He might not have considered it. He might be off his meds. Or perhaps your father's illness has made him panic.'

Ava refused to countenance Wolfe's ideas.

'How could he expect to get away with such a thing?'

'That's the part only he knows.'

His expression grew remote and she felt him mentally withdraw from her when he stood up.

'All you need to know is that it's over. You can go home.'

CHAPTER TWELVE

'IT's OVER. *You can go home.*'

Ava shivered. She knew Wolfe meant more than the threat to her life was over, and it made the four-hour flight to Anders interminable. She spent the whole time thinking about every way imaginable to tell him that she loved him and didn't want him to leave, but came up empty.

She'd nearly blurted it out in his kitchen, when he'd told her he was jealous, but he'd tensed up like a lone lion with a pack of hungry hyenas approaching and distracted her. She suspected that move had been because he had guessed what she'd been about to say and didn't want to hear it. And why would he? It wasn't as if she would be giving him some prized gift he'd waited his whole life to receive.

And on top of that her period had arrived midflight. She didn't know how she felt about that, having thought all afternoon about what it would be like to carry Wolfe's baby. But she knew she hadn't been relieved to find his bathroom well stocked with female hygiene products. Though that had been a timely reminder that he was a man who enjoyed women. And plenty of them. And knowing why, knowing that his mother had left him over and over and no doubt given him a healthy dose of abandonment issues in the process, didn't make the reality of his choices any easier to bear.

Still feeling torn about what to do when the plane finally

landed, she moved to the open doorway and paused. A fierce wind whipped her hair around her head. She saw her father and, surprisingly, Lorenzo waiting beside one of the palace cars, and she wished she was wearing more than one of Wolfe's shirts tied in a knot at the waist and a pair of his jeans rolled at both ends.

She felt Wolfe come up behind her and turned, expecting that he would accompany her down onto the tarmac. As soon as she saw the remote expression on his face she knew instantly that he wasn't going to. And, unlike the last time he had flown her home, she would have welcomed his support now.

'You're not coming,' she said unnecessarily, straightening her spine as if his actions meant nothing to her.

Wolfe hesitated and then shook his head. 'No. I have another job to go to.'

Oh. She hadn't thought of that. 'Where is it?'

'That's confidential.'

And dangerous. He didn't have to add that.

Ava gripped the inside of the open doorway, remembering all those scars on his body.

'I won't be back.'

She nodded slowly, feeling as if her stomach was about to upend its entire contents all over his shiny shoes. He looked at her warily, as if he was expecting her to kick up a fuss and stamp her feet—beg him to stay, perhaps. And she wanted to. She wanted to do all those things. But she wouldn't.

For one thing her father was waiting with what looked like the entire police force in attendance, and for another…Wolfe was too closed. Too distant.

Saying *I love you* seemed like too big a leap to make in the face of his implacable regard, and it wasn't as if it would change the outcome in any way. He was leaving. He couldn't make that any plainer.

'I can see that.'

His eyes snapped to hers, as if he was surprised by her lack of argument. 'I can't give you what you want, Ava. I'm sorry.'

He was sorry?

Ava shook her head at his pitiful comment. No way was she accepting that cop-out. 'How do you know? You haven't even asked what I want.' She knew there was an edge of frustration in her voice but she couldn't contain it. 'The truth is, Wolfe, you don't want to give me what I want because you have trained yourself not to need anyone. To be like that island you own. But you're not, and if you're honest with yourself you'll realise that your mother's actions hurt you just as much as they did your brother. Maybe more.'

She glanced up quickly, wondering if her words had affected him at all. If he got just how ruthlessly he'd disconnected himself emotionally.

'I'm fine as I am.'

That would be a no, then…

Ava sighed. He really was like an immovable rock, and she realised there was nothing left to say. The fact was Wolfe didn't love her and, as she had so often had to do lately, she had to face the reality of her situation.

Closing her eyes briefly against the quivering sensation in her bottom lip, she straightened her spine, marshalling her indifference to protect herself as she had so often done in the past. But it wasn't easy. Wolfe had crashed through her protective walls with the force of a military tank and all she wanted was for him to take her in his arms and tell her he loved her.

'Okay, then.' She turned to go, her feet leaden.

She hadn't made it two steps when he grabbed hold of her arm and stopped her. Ava felt her heart soar and searched his face for some sign that he was about to—

'You'll let me know if there's a child, won't you?' His voice was gravelly, strained.

Right then her hopes and dreams were well and truly shattered. She knew he would have 'done the right thing' if she *had* been pregnant, and it was with some irony that she realised that while she had fought marrying someone else for convenience she had never considered that the opposite could happen. That someone would have to marry *her* for convenience.

'There won't be,' she replied woodenly.

He frowned and dropped her arm. 'You can't know that for sure.'

'Yes, I can,' she said wearily. 'I got my period on the plane. Nice stash of female hygiene products, by the way.'

'My staff stock my plane, not me.'

Okay, that was something…sort of.

When he didn't immediately walk away she glanced up again and found his expression fierce.

'Ava, I still want you.'

She stared back at him while those words sank in and then she just felt angry. 'I don't know what you want me to say to that, Wolfe.' Because apart from begging him to stay what could she say? That he should do what she wanted him to do? Be what she wanted him to be? Wasn't that what she had railed against her father for her whole life? 'It doesn't mean anything. It's only lust and lust fades over time. Isn't that what you believe?'

'Yes.'

God, she hoped he was right. Because she felt as if her heart was being cleaved in half with a toothpick.

'Ava?' Her father materialised at her side. 'Is there a problem?'

'No.' Swallowing hard, she braced herself to look at Wolfe one more time, her eyes tracking over his features like a laser beam, trying to trace every fine detail of his handsome face. 'Goodbye, Monsieur Wolfe. I hope you find what it is you are searching for.'

Turning away before he saw how painful it was for her

to walk away from him, Ava let her father escort her from the plane, resolved to face whatever the future had in store for her with the same dignity and grace her mother would have shown.

CHAPTER THIRTEEN

WOLFE HAULED HIMSELF out of the sparkling blue sea and flopped onto the hot sand. The sun beat down on his head with relentless precision and a hermit crab scurried towards the ocean in search of safety.

The only sounds he could hear were the languid ebb and flow of the incoming tide and the intermittent squawk of overhead birds as they dived for fresh fish.

By rights he should have felt happy and relaxed, but he didn't. He hadn't felt that way for three days. Not since flying out of Anders and ordering his pilot to return to Cape Paraiso instead of flying him to the round of meetings he'd had to put off to guard Ava.

Ava.

When he'd left her back in Anders he had somehow convinced himself that he would be fine. That he would get over her. Right now he felt very far from fine. And his sense of loss when she'd told him she had got her monthly period on the plane made a mockery of his assertion that he would get over her.

'I hope you find what it is you're searching for,' she had said at the end.

The trouble was he hadn't been searching for anything. She'd been right in her first assumption that night at the gala ball. He was running. Filling up his life with work and activities so he would never have to face how empty his existence really was. So he'd never have to think about what he really wanted.

But that was unavoidable now, it seemed, because he couldn't think about anything else. He couldn't think about anything other than Ava.

He shook water from his hair and let his hands dangle over his knees.

The fact was he missed her.

She was everywhere on the island. In his kitchen in the morning when he made coffee, on his deck when he stood beside the pool and searched for the silver phone he'd removed a week ago, in his bed at night when he rolled over and found it empty, on the beach... He wasn't sure how she had infiltrated every part of his mind so profoundly in such a short space of time but there was no doubting that she had.

And if he kept up obsessing about her like this the next thing he'd think was that he was in love with her.

Hell.

He *was* in love with her.

Why keep denying it? He'd known it for a long time—he'd just refused to face it. Fear had kept him immobile. Fear of needing her more than she needed him. Fear of ending up a lonely shell of a man like his father. Fear of facing the fact that, yes, he *had* been just as devastated as his brother every time his mother had done her disappearing act.

'Understood what, Wolfe? That you were a child who couldn't rely on his mother's love?'

Oh, hell.

His heart had known the truth. His heart had kept pushing him towards her. His heart had wanted to protect her and care for her. His heart had insisted that he trash his dodgy rules every time he'd looked at her. It was his head that had come late to the party.

But was it too late?

Wolfe stared blankly out to sea. The way he saw it he had two options. He could take the risk, tell her how he felt and hope she didn't have guards cart him away, or he could keep his pride intact, travelling the world by himself until he slowly did become that empty shell of a man he had spent his life trying not to be.

He ran his hand through his hair. Hell, that wasn't even a real choice.

'I think we should make the announcement about your engagement to Lorenzo at the same time.'

Ava paused in the middle of scanning the acceptance speech she would read after her father announced his impending abdication and stared at him. 'I disagree.'

'It makes sense to combine the two. It's more efficient.'

Ava's lips pinched together. 'That may be so, but I need to do this my way.'

Her father made a grievous noise that sounded suspiciously like a snort of disgust, but he didn't push it, fussing instead with his military uniform before heading off to the state room where invited guests and the media waited for their arrival.

After double-checking her own outfit—a royal sash pinned diagonally to a satin gown—Ava followed him.

In the past few days they had grown closer than they'd ever been, drawn together by the devastating impact of Baden's actions and a mutual commitment to ensure that he received the best psychiatric care possible. Her father had shown great fortitude in the face of his nephew's betrayal, and Ava wished that she could grant her father this last request of her. But how could she?

Not only did it go against all of her hopes and dreams for herself, but her heart was so heavy she couldn't imagine she'd ever be happy again.

Wasn't it only fair that she worked to get over Wolfe before making the ultimate commitment to another man? Even if that man knew she didn't love him?

But, really, she asked herself, did it matter? Her father's illness had worsened with the stress of everything that had happened, and he was being forced to abdicate. Anders needed an heir… She sighed and came to a stop behind her father's straight figure as he waited for the state room door to be opened. Her pining for unrequited love seemed trivial by comparison.

And Lorenzo was a wonderful man. He would make any woman an excellent husband, and maybe if she committed herself to him the pain of losing Wolfe would start to fade.

'Okay.' She stayed her father with her hand on his arm just before he entered the room. 'Announce it.'

Her father frowned and swiped at the beads of sweat on his brow. Then he nodded. 'You've made me very proud.'

Ava gave a small smile. She hoped her mother had heard that.

Thirty minutes later the large room was buzzing with energy after her father officially announced that Ava would be taking over as Queen in exactly a month's time. Ava's own speech, pledging to uphold and expand on her father's absolute dedication to their country, had been a resounding success. The funny thing was she hadn't once felt nervous or overwhelmed. Either she was more ready to take on this job than she had thought, or all of her nerves had been cauterised when she had walked away from Wolfe.

'And on top of that—' The King waited for the crowd to subside into silence. 'On top of that it is with great pleasure that I also announce—'

'Before you do, Your Majesty, I need a word with your daughter.'

Ava glanced up and gasped as Wolfe strode into the room, the outer door swinging closed behind him. Every head swivelled towards his voice and two of her father's personal guards rushed him—only to fall back when they recognised who he was.

Ava's traitorous heart recognised who he was as well, and started beating heavily in her chest. Her eyes ate him up exactly like that first morning when she had met him as she sat on top of that wall at Château Verne. Only this time he wasn't on a white horse and he wasn't wearing jodhpurs. Instead he stood before her in a business suit and tie that did little to civilise the lethal glint in his golden-brown eyes.

Her father scowled at the interruption and Lorenzo shifted nervously at her other side.

'This had better be good, Wolfe,' her father said.

'It is.' Wolfe's eyes never left hers. 'Ava?'

Ava's heart did a mini-somersault at his commanding tone; shock and surprise that he was standing directly in front of her was making her feel light-headed.

'Surely whatever you have to say to my daughter can wait until after these proceedings are over?' her father said impatiently.

'Not if you're about to announce what I think you are,' Wolfe returned emphatically.

His expression was perfectly urbane but it reminded Ava of the time he had threatened to drag her behind his horse weeks ago. She knew it would be pointless to argue with him in this mood—at least in public. 'It's okay, Father. I'll speak with Monsieur Wolfe in private.'

Lorenzo half rose out of his seat, as if he might object, but one look from Wolfe had him reluctantly subsiding.

'Just tell me this.' Wolfe rounded on her as soon as the footman had closed the door to the small salon she had chosen further down the hall. 'Are you marrying Lorenzo because you love him or because your father wants you to?'

Ava frowned at him. 'Since I know your earlier experiences have given you a very skewed view of how women can be, I'm going to let that slide. But you need to know that question is incredibly insulting to me.'

Wolfe surprised her by shaking his head and laughing. 'Princess, you do have a special way of bringing me back down to size. But the fact that you didn't answer with an emphatic *I love him* gives me hope.'

'Hope about what?'

'Hope that there's still a chance I can convince you to fall in love with me.'

Ava stared at him blankly and then blinked as his words stopped spinning inside her head. 'Why would you want me to do that? You don't even believe in love,' she challenged softly.

A rueful smile formed on his lips. 'I didn't until I met you.'

'You're not making any sense.' Ava didn't dare let her mind head down the track it had veered on to in case the excited beating of her heart was wrong. 'What does that mean?'

It took him three long strides to reach her, and when he did he gripped her fingers in his, his eyes searching hers. 'It means you have opened my eyes to everything that has been missing in my life and why. It means I've been a fool to even think that I could let you walk out of my life.'

He stopped and she watched his throat work as he swallowed, a fleeting moment of nervousness crossing his face.

'It means that I love you, Ava. More than I ever thought possible.'

Ava's mind felt as if it was churning through butter as he said words she'd stopped letting herself imagine would ever fall from his lips. 'Are you serious?'

'About loving you?'

She nodded, lost for words.

Wolfe's lips twisted into a wry smile. 'Absolutely. But I don't blame you for doubting me. I fought my feelings for you the whole way—imagining that they would weaken me, imagining that you would be as flighty and as unpredictable as my mother.'

'I'm not like her, Wolfe,' Ava assured him vehemently. 'I would never abandon my husband. *My child.*'

'I know you wouldn't, baby. You need to know that when I was younger—about twelve or thirteen—and out looking for my brother for the hundredth time, I made a promise to myself that I would never let myself fall in love. That I would never make myself that vulnerable. And until that bright blue-sky morning at Gilles's wedding I've never had cause to reconsider that promise.' He paused, drew her hands up to his lips. 'Then I saw you and...you simply stole the breath from my lungs.'

'You left before I woke up that first morning,' she reminded him.

'That would be one of those foolish moments I was referring to,' he said a little sheepishly. 'And I'm sorry I hurt you. Truthfully, the way you made me feel scared me senseless. Just looking at you makes me burn up with need. When I woke with your head on my shoulder...I admit it—I panicked.'

Ava gave him a lopsided smile. 'I did think it was nice when you fixed my phone.'

'And that was when the trouble really started. After you got the news about your brother you became so withdrawn and I didn't know how to reach you. I tried to tell myself that I didn't want to, but I couldn't stay away from you, Ava. I thought about you constantly.'

'Why didn't you call?' she demanded fiercely.

'Because I didn't *want* to think about you constantly.' He groaned. 'I was still fighting the inevitable at that time...but that's done. Gone.'

'And you don't like talking about the past.'

He loosened his grip on her hands and hauled her into his arms. 'I don't like dwelling on it. But you've shown me that ignoring it doesn't work either. What I want is to learn from it and move forward. I love you, Ava—heart and soul. I want to be with you always. I want to protect you. I want to be the man you turn to when you're busy and… Aw, hell.' He swiped an unsteady hand through his hair. 'When you walked off my plane the other day you took my dead heart with you and made me realise that not only couldn't I live without it, but I didn't want to.'

Ava felt her love for him swell up to the point of overpowering her. 'Oh, Wolfe, I think I've loved you for ever.'

'Thank God.' Wolfe released a pent-up breath and bent to kiss her. 'I think you just made me the happiest man on earth, and there's only one way you could possibly eclipse that.' He reached inside his breast pocket and withdrew a square box. 'It probably doesn't compare to the Crown Jewels in your vault, but I hope you will accept it, baby, as a declaration of just how much you mean to me.'

Ava gasped as she shakily opened the box and saw a ring— a huge navy blue sapphire with two sparkling diamonds on either side.

Wolfe removed it and steadied her hand before slipping it onto her finger. 'Perfect. I knew the colour would match your eyes.'

'Oh, Wolfe.' Ava hugged him tightly, huge shiny tears blurring her vision. 'It's beautiful, and of course I'll accept it, but…' She stopped, suddenly realising the enormity of what he was setting himself up for.

'But what?' His eyes scanned her face. 'If you have a problem I'll fix it.'

'It's not me, Wolfe, it's you.' She gazed at the huge rock on her finger before forcing herself to meet his eyes. 'You probably don't know this yet, but my father has just announced that he'll be abdicating in a month and—oh, *non!*' She squirmed in his arms until he released her enough for her feet to touch the ground once again. 'My father is waiting for me!'

Wolfe buried his face in her hair. 'Wriggling around in my arms like that isn't exactly the quickest way to get back to him. I've missed you,' he admitted huskily.

'And I've missed you. But I have to go to him. You know what he's like. If I don't he'll most likely announce my engagement to Lorenzo without me!'

'He won't.'

'How do you know that? Everyone must be talking. Wondering what is going on.'

'Any fool back there who saw my face knows exactly what's going on. And your father is no fool.'

Talking about her father reminded Ava of her earlier concern and she stilled. 'Wolfe, if you take me on you have to know that your life will change dramatically. You'll have to become a citizen of Anders. You'll have to—'

'Be your back-up person. I get it, Ava. I know what marrying you entails and, frankly, I'd want to marry you if we had to build mud brick houses in the middle of the desert for a living.'

Still she hesitated. 'But what about your business? Your travel? I know if you curb your passions you'll end up unhappy, and I couldn't bear for that to happen.'

'Ava.' He cupped her face in his hands. 'You're not listening—which isn't all that surprising—but…' He laughed as she took a playful swipe at him. 'But you should know by now that I don't do anything without working everything out in advance.'

'So what have you worked out, Monsieur General?'

He gave her the lazy smile of a man who had everything he wanted in life. 'My brother loves running Wolfe Inc far more than I ever did, and I only ever travelled to stop myself from having to think about my life. I don't want to do that any more. And you'll need someone by your side. Just as your father wants.'

Ava finally allowed the smile she'd been holding back to beam up at him, so happy she felt as if her heart was aching with joy. She tightened her arms around his neck. 'You know, in my wildest dreams I imagined love could be just like this.'

Wolfe shook his head. 'My wildest dreams never even gave me a glimpse of this level of happiness. You did that, Ava. You filled a gap in my heart I never even knew existed, and I want you to know that I will be yours for ever.'

Ava gave him a watery smile. She caught the serious undertone to his words and knew that she could trust this man not only with her life but with her heart. Knew that now he had opened himself fully to her he would never let her down. That he would never leave her.

'Good. Because I love you to pieces, James Wolfe, and I will never leave you.'

Wolfe's hungry gaze burned into hers, but just when she thought for sure he was going to lose some of that inimitable control of his he removed his arms from around her waist and clasped her hand with his.

'We need to hurry up and break the news to your father,' he said roughly. 'I've never been a patient man and, as lovely as you look in that dress, it's time you were wearing something else.'

Ava smiled slowly, basking in the glow of Wolfe's unguarded love. 'And do you have something specific in mind?'

'Oh, yeah.' He tugged on her hand and brought her up against him for one brief, soul-deep kiss. 'Me.'

* * * * *

A THRONE FOR
THE TAKING

BY
KATE WALKER

Kate Walker was born in Nottinghamshire but as she grew up in Yorkshire she has always felt that her roots are there. She met her husband at university and originally worked as a children's librarian, but after the birth of her son she returned to her old childhood love of writing. When she's not working she divides her time between her family, their three cats and her interests of embroidery, antiques, film and theatre—and, of course, reading.

You can visit Kate at www.kate-walker.com.

For the class of Fishghuard, February 2012.
Thanks for such a fun and inspiring weekend.

CHAPTER ONE

HE WAS COMING. The sound of footsteps in the corridor outside told her that. Brisk, heavy footsteps, the sound of expensive leather soles on the marble floor.

A big man, moving fast and impatiently towards the room where she had been told to wait for him. A room that was not as she had expected, but then nothing had been as she had expected since she had started out on this campaign, least of all this man she hadn't seen in so long. It had been more than ten years since she had spoken to him, but they would now be coming face to face in less than thirty seconds.

How was she going to handle this?

Ria adjusted her position in the smart leather chair, crossing one leg over the other then, rethinking, moving it back again so that her feet were neatly on the floor, placed precisely together in their elegant black courts, knees closed tight, her blue and green flowered dress stretched sleekly over them. Lifting her hand, she made to smooth back a non-existent wandering strand of dark auburn hair. Her style would be immaculate, she knew. She'd pulled her hair back tightly from her face so that there was nothing loose to get in a mess or distract her. Nothing to look frivolous or even carefree. That was not the image she'd aimed for.

She'd even fretted at the thought that her dress might be a little too casual and relaxed when she'd put it on, but the below knee length of the swirling skirt covered her almost as much as the tailored trousers she'd considered wearing, and the lightweight black linen jacket she'd pulled on over the top added a needed touch of formality that made her feel better.

The room she sat in was sleek and sophisticated with pale wood furniture. Far sleeker and much more luxurious than she had ever anticipated. One of the soft grey walls displayed a set of dramatic photographs, sharply framed. In black and white only, they were the sort of images that had made Alexei Sarova his reputation and his fortune. They were superb, stunning but— Ria frowned as she looked at them. They were bleak and somehow lonely. Photographs of landscapes, places, no people in them at all. He did sometimes photograph people—she knew that from the magazines she had read and the stunning images that had appeared in the articles—but none of those commissions were displayed here.

Outside the door, those determined, heavy footsteps slowed, then halted and she heard the murmur of voices through the thick wood, the deep, gravelly tones making it plain that the speaker was a man.

The man. The one she had come here to meet, to give him the message that might save her country from all-out civil war, and she had vowed that she was not leaving until she had done so. Even if the nerves in her stomach tied themselves into tight, painful knots at the thought and her restless fingers had started to beat an unsettled tattoo on the wooden arm of the chair.

'No!' Ria reproved herself aloud. 'Stop it! Now!'

She brought her nervous hand together with the other one, to clasp them both demurely in her lap, forcing her-

self to wait with every semblance of control and composure, even if the churning of her stomach told her that
this was very far from the case. Too much rested on this
meeting and she wasn't really sure that she could handle it.

Oh, this was ridiculous! Ria drew in a deep, ragged
sigh as she put back her head and stared fixedly at the
white-painted ceiling, fighting for control of her breathing. She should be well able to cope with this. She'd
been trained practically from birth to meet strangers,
talk with them, making polite social chit-chat at court
events. It was what she could do as naturally as breathing while all the time keeping her head up high, her spine
straight so that she looked as good as possible, with first
her nanny's then her father's voice in her ear, telling her
that the reputation of the Escalona family—an offshoot
of the *royal* family—should be the first and foremost
thing in her mind.

She could talk to presidents' wives about their trips
round the glass-making factories, discuss the agricul-
tural output of the vineyards, the farms. She could even,
if she was allowed, converse intelligently on the vital role
of exports, or the mining of eruminum, the new miracle
mineral that had just been discovered in the Trilesian
mountains. Not that she was often asked to do any such
thing. Those important details were usually left to her
grandfather or, until recently, to her second cousin Felix,
the Crown Prince of Mecjoria.

But she had never before had to deal with any mission that meant so much in the way of freedom, both to
her country and herself. That restless hand threatened to
escape her careful control and start its nervous tattoo all
over again at just the thought.

'Do it, then.'

The voice from the corridor sounded sharp and clear

this time, bringing her head up in a rush as she straightened once again in her chair. *Shoulders back, head up...* She could almost hear her father's strict commands as she drew in a long, deep breath to calm herself as she had done on so many other previous occasions.

But this wasn't one of those events. This man wasn't exactly a stranger and polite chit-chat was the last thing she expected to be exchanging with him.

The handle turned as someone grasped it from the other side. Ria tensed, shifted in her chair, half-looked over her shoulder then rethought and turned back again. She didn't want him to think that she was nervous. She had to appear calm, collected, in command of the situation.

Command. The word rang hollowly inside her head. Once she had only to command something and it would be hers. In just a few short months her life had been turned upside down, and in ways that made her status in society the least of her concerns, so that now nothing was as it had ever been before, and the future loomed ahead, dark and dangerous.

But perhaps if she could manage this meeting with some degree of success she could claw back something from the disaster that had overtaken her country—and family. She could hope to put right the wrongs of the past and, on a personal level, save her mother's happiness, her sanity, possibly. And for her father... No, she couldn't go there, not yet. Thoughts of her father would weaken her, drain away the strength she needed to see this through.

'I'll expect a report on my desk by the end of the day.'

The door was opening, swinging wide. The man she had come to see was here, and she had no more time to think.

As he entered the doorway her heart jerked sharply

under her ribcage, taking her breath with it. For the first time she felt suddenly lost, vulnerable without the ever-present security man at her back. All her life he had been there, just waiting and watching in case he was needed. And she had come to rely on him to deal with any awkward situation.

The *once* ever-present security man, she reminded herself. The protection that was no longer there, no longer part of her life or her status here or in her homeland of Mecjoria. She was no longer entitled to such protection. It was the first thing that had been stripped from her and the rest of her family in the upheaval that had followed Felix's unexpected death, and the shocking discovery of her father's scheming in the past. After that, things had changed so fast that she had never had time even to think about the possible repercussions of the changes and to consider them now, with the possible consequences for her own future, made her stomach twist painfully.

'No delays… Good afternoon.'

The abrupt change of subject caught Ria on the hop. She hadn't quite realised that his companion had been dismissed and that he was now in the room, long strides covering the ground so fast that he was halfway towards her before she realised it.

'Good afternoon.'

It was stronger, harsher, much more pointed, and she almost felt as if the words were hitting her in the small of her back. She should turn round, she knew. She needed to face him. But the enormity of the reason why she was here, and the thought of his reaction when she did, made it difficult to move.

'Miss…'

The warning in his tone now kicked her into action, fast. Her head jerked round, the suddenness and abrupt-

ness of the movement jolting her up and out of her seat
so that she came to her feet even as she swung round to
face him. And was glad that she had done so when she
saw the size and the strength of his powerful form. She
had seen pictures of him in the papers, knew that he was
tall, dark and devastating, but in the 3D reality of living, breathing golden-toned flesh, deep ebony eyes and
crisp black hair, he was so much more than she had ever
imagined. His steel-grey suit hugged his impressive form
lovingly, the broad, straight shoulders needing no extra
padding to enhance them. A crisp white shirt, silver and
black tie, turned him into the sleek, sophisticated busi-
nessman who was light-years away from the Alexei she
remembered, the wiry boy with the unkempt mane of hair
who had once been her friend buried under the expensive
tailoring. Snatching in a deep, shocked breath, she could
inhale the tang of some citrus soap or shampoo, the scent
of clean male skin.

'Good afternoon,' she managed and was relieved to
hear that her control over her voice was as strong as she
could have wanted. Perhaps it made it sound a little too
tight, too stiff, but that was surely better than letting the
tremor she knew was just at the bottom of her thoughts
actually affect her tongue. 'Alexei Sarova, I assume.'

He had been moving towards her but her response had
a shocking effect on him.

'You!' he said, the single word thick and dark with
hostility

He stopped dead, then swung round back towards the
door, grabbing at the handle to stop it slotting into the
frame. This was worse than she had expected. She had
known that she would have to work hard to get him to
give her any sort of a hearing, but she hadn't expected
this total rejection.

'Oh—please,' Ria managed. 'Please don't walk out.'

That brought his head round, the black, glittering eyes looking straight into hers, not a flicker of emotion in their polished depths.

'Walk out?'

He shook his dark head and there was actually the faintest hint of a smile on those beautifully sensual lips. But a shiver ran down Ria's spine as she saw the way that that smile was not reflected in his eyes at all. They remained as cold and emotionless as black glass.

'I'm not walking out. You are.'

It was far worse than she had expected. She hadn't really believed that he would recognise her that fast and that easily. Ten years was a long time and they had been little more than children when they had last had any close contact. She knew she was no longer the chubby, awkward girl he had once known. She was inches taller, slimmer, and her hair had darkened so that it was now a rich auburn instead of the nondescript brown of her childhood. So she had expected to have to explain herself to him. But she had thought that he would wait to hear that explanation, had hoped, at least, that he would want to know just why she was here.

'No...' She shook her head. 'No, I'm not.'

Dark eyes flashed in sudden anger and she barely controlled her instinctive shrinking away with an effort. Royal duchesses didn't shrink. Not even ex-royal duchesses.

'No?'

How did he manage to put such cynicism, such hostility into one word?

'I should point out to you that I own this building. I am the one who says who can stay and who should go. And you are going.'

'Don't you want to know why I'm here?'

If she had thrown something into the face of a marble statue, it couldn't have had less effect. Perhaps his stunning features became a little more unyielding, those brilliant eyes even colder, but it was hard to say for sure.

'Not really. In fact, not at all. What I want is you out of here and not coming back.'

No, what he really wanted was for her never to have come here at all, Alexei told himself, coming to a halt in the middle of his office, restless as a caged tiger that had reached the metal bars that held him imprisoned. But the truth was that it wasn't anything physical that kept him captive. It was the memories of the past that now reached out to ensnare him, fastening shackles around his ankles to keep him from getting away.

He had never expected to see her or anyone from Mecjoria ever again. He thought he had moved on; he'd turned his life around, made a new existence for himself and his mother. It had taken years, sadly too many to give his mother the life she deserved as she'd aged, but he'd got there. And now he was wealthier than he'd ever been as a...as a prince, his mind finished for him, even though it was the last thing he wanted. He had no wish to remember anything about his connection to the Mecjorian royal family—or the country itself. He had severed all links with the place—had them severed for him—and he was determined that was the way it was going to stay. He would never have looked back at all if it hadn't been for the sudden and shockingly unexpected appearance of Ria here in this room.

He waited a moment and then pulled the door open again. 'Or do I have to call security?'

Ria's eyebrows rose sharply until they disappeared under her fringe as she turned a cool, green gaze on him.

Suddenly she had become the Grand Duchess she was right before his eyes and he loathed the way that made him feel.

'You'd resort to the heavy gang? That wouldn't look good in the gossip columns. "International playboy needs help to deal with one small female intruder".'

'Small? I would hardly call you small,' he drawled coolly. 'You must have grown—what?—six inches since I saw you last?'

She had grown in other ways too, he acknowledged, admitting to himself the instant and very basic male re-action that had taken him by storm in the first moments he had seen her. Before he had realised just who she was.

He hadn't seen such a stunning woman in years—in his life. Everything that was male in him had responded to the sight of her tall, slender figure, the burnished hair, porcelain skin, long, long legs...

And then he had realised that it was Ria. She had grown up, grown taller, slimmed down. Her face had de-veloped planes and angles where there had once been just firm, round, apple-rosy cheeks. He had loved those cheeks, he admitted to himself. They had been soft and curved, so smooth, that he had loved to pinch them softly, pretending he was teasing but knowing that what he ac-tually wanted was to feel the satin of her skin, stroke it with his fingertips. These days, Ria had cheekbones that looked as if they would slice open any stroking finger, and the rosy cheeks were carefully toned down with skil-ful make-up. The slant of those cheekbones emphasised the jade green of her eyes, and the soft pink curve of her mouth, but it was obvious that any softness in her ap-pearance was turned into a lie by the way she behaved.

In a series of pulsing jolts, like the effect of an electric current pounding into him, he had known stunning attraction and the rush of desire that heated his entire body, the shock of recognition, of disbelief, of frank confusion as to just why she should be here at all. And then, just as the memory of how they had once been together had slid into his mind, she had destroyed it totally, shattering the memory as effectively as if she had taken a heavy metal hammer to it.

That had been when she had looked down her aristocratic nose at him, her expression obviously meant to make him feel less than the dirt beneath her neatly-shod feet. And Ria, who had once been his friend and confidant, Ria who he had just recognised as a sweet girl who had grown into a stunningly sensual woman, had become once more the Ria who together with her father and her family had stuck a knife in his back, ruined his mother's life and cast them out into the wilderness.

'And, as to the gossip columns, I'm sure they'd be much more interested in the scoop of seeing the Grand Duchess Honoria Maria Escalona being forcibly ejected from the offices of Sarova International—and I can just imagine some of the stories they might come up with to explain your expulsion.'

'Not so much of a Grand Duchess any more,' Ria admitted without thinking. 'Not so much of a duchess of any sort.'

'What?'

That brought him up sharp. Just for a second or two blank confusion clouded those amazing eyes and he tilted his head slightly to one side as a puzzled frown drew his brows together. The small, revealing moment caught on something in her heart and twisted painfully.

He had always done that when she had known him before. When they had been children together—well, she had been the child and he a lordly six years older. If he was confused or uncertain that frown had creased the space between his dark brows and his head would angle to the side…

'Lexei—please.' The name slipped from her before she could think. The familiar, affectionate name that she had once been able to use.

But she'd made a fatal mistake. She knew that as soon as the words had left her mouth and his reaction left her in no doubt at all that the one slip of her lips, in the hope of getting a tiny bit closer to him, had had the opposite effect.

His long body stiffened in rejection, that slight tilt of his head turned into a stiff-necked gesture of antagonism as his chin came up, angry, rejecting. His eyes flashed and his mouth tightened, pulling the muscles in his jaw into an uncompromising line.

'No,' he said, hard and rough. 'No. I will not listen to a word you say. Why should I when you and yours turned your back on my mother—on me—and left us to exile and disgrace? My mother *died* in that disgrace. It's not as if anything you have to say is a matter of life or death.'

'Oh, but…'

It could be… The words died on her tongue, burned away in the flare of fury he turned on her, seeming to scorch her skin so painfully.

This was not how she had planned it, but it was obvious that he wasn't prepared to let her lead up to things with a carefully prepared conversation. Hastily she grabbed at her handbag, snapping it open with hands made clumsy by nerves.

'This is for you…' she managed, holding out the sheet of paper she had folded so carefully at the start of her journey. The document she had checked was still there at least once every few minutes on her way here.

His eyes dropped to what she held, expression freezing

into marble stillness as he took in the crest at the head of the sheet of paper, the seal that marked it out for the important document it was.

'You know that your mother needed proof of the legality of her marriage,' she tried and got the briefest, most curt nod possible as his only response, his gaze still fixed on the document she held out.

It was like talking to a statue, he was so stiff, so unmoving, and she found that her tongue was stumbling over itself as she tried to get the words out. If only someone else could have been given this vital duty to carry out. But she had volunteered herself in spite of the fact that the ministers had viewed her with suspicion. A suspicion that was natural, after the way her father had behaved. But they didn't know the half of it. She had only just discovered the truth for herself and hadn't dared to reveal any of it to anyone else. Luckily, the ministers had been convinced that she was the most likely to be successful. Alexei would listen to her, they had said. And besides, with success meaning so much to her personally, to her family, she would be the strongest advocate at this time.

It was a strong irony that all the discipline, the training her father had imposed on her for his own ends, was now to be put to use to try to thwart those ends if she possibly could.

'And for that she needed evidence of the fact that the old king had given his permission for your father—as a member of the royal family—to marry all those years ago, when they first met.'

Why was she repeating all this? He knew every detail as much as she did. After all, it had been his life that had been blasted apart by the scandal that had resulted when it had seemed that his parents' marriage had been declared illegal. Alexei's father and mother had been separated, with him living with his mother in England until he was sixteen, and the fact that her husband was ill—dying of cancer—had brought his mother to Mecjoria in hope of a reconciliation. They hadn't had long and, during what time they had had, Alexei had found the old-fashioned and snobbish aristocracy difficult to deal with, particularly when they had regarded him and his mother as nothing more than commoners who didn't belong at court. His rebellious behaviour had created disapproval, brought him under the disapproving gaze of so many. And too soon, with his father dead, there had been no one to support his mother, or her son, when court conspiracy—a conspiracy Ria had just discovered to her horror of which her father had been an important part—had had her expelled, exiled from the country, taking her son with her.

Then there was her own part in all of it—her own guilty conscience, Ria acknowledged. That was an important part of why she had volunteered to come here today, to bring the news of the discovery of the document…and the rest.

'This is the evidence.'

At last he moved, reached out a hand and took the paper from her. But to her shock he simply glanced swiftly over the text then tossed it aside, dropping it on to his desk without a second glance.

'So?'

The single word seemed to strip all the moisture from her mouth, making her voice cracked and raw as she tried to answer him.

'Don't you see…?' Silly question. Of course he saw, he just wasn't reacting at all as she had expected, as she had been led to believe he would inevitably react. 'This is what you needed back then, this changes everything.

It means that your parents were legally married even in Mecjoria. It makes you legitimate.'

'And that makes me fit to have you come and visit me? Speak to me after all these years?'

The bitterness in his tone made her flinch. Even more so because she knew she deserved it. She'd flung that illegitimacy—that supposed illegitimacy—at him when he had asked for her help. She hadn't known the truth then, but she knew now that she'd done it partly out of hurt and anger too. Hurt and anger that he had turned away from her to become involved in a romantic entanglement with another girl.

A woman, Ria. She could hear his voice through the years. *She's a woman.*

And the implication was that *she* was still a child. Hurt and feeling rejected, she had been the perfect target for her father's story—what she knew now were her father's lies.

'It's not that...' Struggling with her memories, she had to force the words out. 'It's what's *right.*'

She knew how much he'd loathed the label 'bastard'. But more so how he'd hated the way that his mother had been treated because her marriage hadn't been considered legal. So much so that Ria had believed—hoped—that the news she had brought would change everything. She couldn't have been more wrong.

'Right?' he questioned cynically. 'From where I stand it's too little too late. The truth can't help my mother now. And personally I couldn't give a damn what they think of me in Mecjoria any more. But thank you for bringing it to me.'

His tone took the words to a meaning at the far opposite of genuine thankfulness.

There was much more to it than this. The proof of his legitimacy came with so many repercussions, but she had never expected this reaction. Or, rather, this lack of reaction.

'I'm sorry for the way I behaved…' she began, trying a different tack. One that earned her nothing but a cold stare.

'It was ten years ago.' He shrugged powerful shoulders in dismissal of her stumbling apology. 'A lot of water has passed under a lot of bridges since then. And none of it matters any more. I have made my own life and I want nothing more to do with a country that thought my mother and I were not good enough to live there.'

'But…'

There were so many details, so many facts, buzzing inside Ria's head but she didn't dare to let any of them out. Not yet. There was too much riding on them and this man was not prepared to listen to a word she said. If she put one foot wrong he would reject her—and her mission—completely. And she would never get a second chance.

'So now I'd appreciate it if you'd leave. Or I will call security and have you thrown out, and to hell with the paparazzi or the gossip columnists. In fact, perhaps it would be better that way. They could have a field day with what I could tell them.'

Was it a real or an empty threat? And did she dare take the risk of finding out? Not with things the way they were back home, with the country in turmoil, hopes for security and peace depending on her. On a personal level, she feared her mother would break down completely if anything more happened, and she would be back under her father's control herself if she failed. One whiff of scandal in the papers could be so terribly damaging that she shivered just to think of it. The only way she could achieve everything she'd set out to do was to get Alexei on her side—but that was beginning to look increasingly impossible.

'Honoria,' Alexei said dangerously and she didn't need the warning in his tone to have her looking nervously towards the door he still held wide open. The simple fact that he had used her full name was enough on its own. 'Duchess,' he added with a coldly mocking bow.

But she couldn't make her feet move. She couldn't leave. Not with so much unsaid.

CHAPTER TWO

It's not as if it's a matter of life or death, Alexei had declared, the scorn in his voice lashing at her cruelly. But it would be if the situation in Mecjoria wasn't resolved soon; if Ivan took over. The late King Felix might have been petty and mean but he was as nothing when compared to the tyrant who might inherit the throne from him. With a violent effort, Ria controlled the shiver of reaction that threatened her composure.

She hadn't seen Alexei for ten years, but she had had close contact with his distant cousin Ivan in that time. And hadn't enjoyed a moment of it. She'd watched Ivan grow from the sort of small boy who pulled wings off butterflies and kicked cats into a man whose volatile, mean-minded temper was usually only barely under control. He was aggressive, greedy, dangerous for the country—and now, she had learned to her horror, a danger to her personally as a result of her father's machinations. And the only man between them and that possibility was Alexei.

But she knew how much she was asking of him. Especially now, when she knew how he still felt about Mecjoria.

'Please listen!'

But his face was armoured against her, his eyes hooded, and she felt that every look she turned on him, every word she spoke, simply bounced off his thick skin like a pebble off an elephant's hide.

'Please?' he echoed sardonically, his mouth twisting on the word as he turned it into a cruelly derisory echoing of her tone. 'I didn't even realise that you knew that word. Please *what,* Sweetheart?'

'You don't want to know.'

Bleak honesty made her admit it. She could read it in his face, in the cruel opacity of those coal-black eyes. There wasn't the faintest sign of softening in his expression or any of the lines around his nose and mouth. How could he take a gentle word like *'sweetheart'* and turn it into something hateful and vile with just his tone?

'Oh, but I do,' Alexei drawled, folding his arms across his broad chest and lounging back against the wall, one foot hooked round the base of the door so as to keep it open and so making it plain that he was still waiting— expecting her to leave. 'I'd love to know just what you've come looking for.'

'Really?'

Unexpected hope kicked hard in her heart. Had she got this all wrong, read him completely the wrong way round?

'Really,' he echoed sardonically. 'It's fascinating to see the tables turned. Remember how I once asked you for just one thing?'

He'd asked her to help him, and his mother. Asked her to talk to her father, plead with him to at least let them have something to live on, some part of his father's vast fortune that the state had confiscated, leaving Alexei and his mother penniless as well as homeless. And not knowing the truth, not understanding the machinations of the plotters, or how sick his mother actually was, she had seen him as a threat and sided with her father.

'I made a mistake...' she managed. She'd known that

her father was ruthless, ambitious, but she had never really believed that he would lie through his teeth, that he would manipulate an innocent woman and her son.

For the good of the country, Honoria, he had said. And, seeing the outrage Alexei's wayward behaviour had created, she had believed him. Because she had trusted her father. Trusted him and believed in the values of upright behaviour, of loyalty to the crown that he'd insisted on. So she'd believed him when he'd told her how the scandal of Alexei's mother's 'affair' with one of the younger royal sons was creating problems of state. It was only now, years later, that she'd discovered how much further his deception had gone, and how it had involved her.

'What is it, *darling?*' Alexei taunted. 'Not enjoying this?'

She saw the gleam of cruel amusement in his eyes, the fiendish smile curling the corners of the beautiful mouth. Each of them spoke of cold contempt, but together they spelled a callous triumph at the thought of getting her exactly where he wanted her. She knew now that this man would delight in rejecting anything she said, if only to have his revenge on the family that he saw as the ringleaders of his downfall. And who could blame him?

But would he do the same for his country?

'It's no fun having to beg, is it? No fun having to crawl to someone you'd much rather die than even talk to.'

Once more that searing gaze raked over her from the top of her uncharacteristically controlled hair down to the neat, highly polished black shoes. It was a look that took her back ten years, forced her to remember how coldly he had regarded her before he had walked away and out of her life. For good, she had thought then.

'And I should know, angel—I've been there, remember? I've been exactly where you are now—begged, pleaded—and walked away with nothing.'

He might look indolently relaxed and at his ease as he lounged back against the wall, still with those strong arms crossed over the width of his chest, but in reality his position was the taut, expectant posture of a wily, knowing hunter, a predator that was poised, watching and waiting. He only needed his prey—her—to make one move and then he would pounce, hard and fast.

But still she had to try.

'You are wanted back in Mecjoria,' she blurted out in an uneven rush.

She could tell his response even before he opened his mouth. The way that long straight spine stiffened, the tightening of the beautiful lips, the way a muscle in his jaw jerked just once.

'You couldn't have said anything less likely to make me want to know more,' he drawled, dark and slow. 'But you could try to persuade me...'

She could try, but it would have no effect, his tone, his stony expression told her. And she didn't like the thought of just what sort of 'persuasion' could be in his mind. She wasn't prepared to give him that satisfaction.

Calling on every ounce of strength she possessed, stiffening her back, straightening her shoulders, she managed to lift her head high, force her green eyes to meet those icy black ones head-on.

'No thank you,' she managed, her tone pure ice.

Her father would have been proud of her for this at least. She was the Grand Duchess Honoria Maria at her very best. The only daughter of the Chancellor, faced by a troublesome member of the public. The trouble was that after all she had learned about her father's schemes, the way that he had seen her as a way to further his own power, she didn't want to be that woman any more. She had actually hoped that by coming here today she could free herself from the toxic inheritance that came with that title.

'You might get off on that sort of thing, but it certainly does nothing for me.'

If she had hoped that he would look at least a little crestfallen, a touch deflated, then she was doomed to disappointment. There might have been a tiny acknowledgement of her response in his eyes, a gleam that could have been a touch of admiration—or a hint of dark satisfaction from a man who had known all along just how she would respond.

She'd dug herself a hole without him needing to push her into it. But, for now, was discretion the better part of valour? She could let Alexei think that he had won this round at least but it was only one battle, not the whole war. There was too much at stake for that.

'Thank you for your time.'

She couldn't so much as turn a glance in his direction, even though she caught another wave of that citrus scent as he came closer, with the undertones of clean male skin that almost destroyed her hard-won courage. But even as she fought with her reactions he fired another comment at her. One that tightened a slackening resolve, and reminded her just how much the boy she had once known had changed.

'I wish that I could say it had been a pleasure,' he drawled cynically. 'But we both know that that would be a lie.'

'We certainly do,' Ria managed from between lips that felt as if they had turned to wood, they were so stiff and tight.

'So now you'll leave. Give my regards to your father,' Alexei tossed after her.

He couldn't have said anything that was more guaranteed to force her to stay. A battle, not the war, she reminded herself. She wasn't going to let this be the last of it. She couldn't.

He was going to let her go, Alexei told himself. In fact he would be glad to do so even if the thundering response that she had so unexpectedly woken in his body demanded otherwise. He wanted her to walk away, to take with her the remembrance of the family he had hoped to find, a life he had once tried to live, a girl he had once cared for.

'Lexei... Please...'

The echo of her voice, soft and shaken—or so he would have sworn—swirled in his thoughts in spite of his determination to clamp down on the memory, to refuse to let it take root there. Violently he shook his head to try and drive away the sound but it seemed to cling like dark smoke around his thoughts, bringing with it too many memories that he had thought he'd driven far away.

At first she had knocked him mentally off-balance with the news she had brought. The news he had been waiting to hear for so long—half a lifetime, it seemed. The document she had held out to him now lay on his desk, giving him the legitimacy, the position in Mecjoria he had wanted—that he had thought he wanted—but he didn't even spare it a second glance. It was too late. Far, far too late. His mother, to whom this had mattered so much, was dead, and he no longer gave a damn.

But something tugging at the back of his thoughts, an itch of something uncomfortable and unexpected, told him that that wasn't the real truth. There was more to this than just the delivery of that document.

'Not so much of Grand Duchess any more,' Ria had

said to him unexpectedly. *'Not so much of a duchess of any sort.'*

And that was when it struck him. There was something missing. *Someone* missing. Someone he should have noticed was not there from the first moment in the room but he had been so knocked off-balance that he hadn't registered anything beyond the fact that *Ria* was there in his office, waiting for him.

Where was the dark-suited bodyguard? The man who had the knack of blending into the background when necessary but who was alert and ready to move forward at any moment if their patron appeared to be in any difficulty?

There was no one with her now. There had been no one when he had arrived in this room to find her waiting for him. And there should have been.

What the hell was going on?

He couldn't be unaware of the present political situation in Mecjoria. There had been so many reports of marches on the streets, of protest meetings in the square of the capital. Ria's father, the Grand Duke Escalona, High Chancellor of the country, had been seen making impassioned speeches, ardent broadcasts, calling for calm—ordering the people to stay indoors, keep off the streets. But that had been before first the King and then the new heir to the throne had died so unexpectedly. Before the whole question of the succession had come under scrutiny with meetings and conferences and legal debates to call into question just what would happen next. He had paid it as little attention as it deserved in his own mind, but it had been impossible to ignore some of the headlines—like the ones that declared the country was on the brink of revolution.

It was his father's country after all. The place he should have called his home if he hadn't been forced out before he came to settle in any way. Without ever having a chance to get to know the father who had been missing from his life.

'*Lexei... Please...*'

He would have been all right if she hadn't used that name. If she hadn't—deliberately he was sure—turned on him the once warm, affectionate name she had used back in the gentler, more innocent days when he had thought that they were friends. And so whirled him back into memories of a past he'd wanted to forget.

'All right, I'm intrigued.' And that was nothing less than the truth. 'You clearly have something more to say. So—you have ten minutes. Ten minutes in which to tell me the truth about why you're here. What had you appearing in my office unannounced, declaring you were no longer a grand duchess. Is that the truth?'

It seemed it had to be—or at least that something in what he had said had really got to her. She had reacted to his words as if she had been stung violently. Her head had gone back, her green eyes widening in reaction at something. Her soft rose-tinted mouth had opened slightly on a gasp of shock.

A shock that ricocheted through his own frame as a hard kick of some totally primitive sexual hunger hit home low down in his body. Those widened eyes looked stunning and dark against the translucent delicacy of her skin, and that mouth was pure temptation in its half-open state.

His little friend Ria had grown up into a beautiful woman and that unthinkingly primitive reaction to the fact jolted him out of any hope of seeing her just as the girl she had once been. Suddenly he was unable to look at her in any way other than as a man looks at a woman he desires. His own mouth hungered to take those softly parted lips, to taste her, feel her yield to him, surrendering, opening... His heart thudded hard and deep in his chest, making him need to catch his breath as his body tightened in pagan hunger.

'You don't believe me?' she questioned and the un-characteristic hesitation on the word twisted something deep inside him, something he no longer thought existed. Something that it seemed that only this woman could drag up from deep inside him. A woman who had once been the only friend he thought he had and who now had been reincarnated as a woman who heated his blood and turned him on more than he could recall anyone doing in the past months—the past years.

It was like coming awake again after being dead to his senses for years—and it hurt.

'It's not that I don't believe you.'

The fight he was having to control the sensual impulses of his body showed in his voice and he saw the worried, apprehensive look she shot him sideways from under the long, lush lashes. She clearly didn't know which way to take him, a thought that sent a heated rush of satisfaction through his blood. He wanted her off-balance, on edge. That way she might let slip more than her carefully cul-tivated, court training would allow her.

'Merely that I see no reason why you or any member of your family would renounce the royal title that has meant so much to you.'

'We didn't renounce it. It was renounced for us.'

A frown snapped Alexei's black brows together sharply as he focussed even more intently on her face, trying to read what was there.

'And just what does that mean? I've heard nothing of this.'

How had he missed such an important event? The peo-ple he had employed to watch what was happening in

Mecjoria should have been aware of it. They should have investigated and reported back to him.

'It's been kept very quiet—at the moment my father is officially "resting" to recover from illness.'

'When the reality is?'

'That he's under arrest.'

Her voice caught on the word, a soft little hiccup that did disturbing things to the tension at his groin, tightening it a notch or two uncomfortably.

'And is now in the state prison.'

That was the last thing he'd expected and it shocked some of the desire from him, making his head swim slightly at the rush of blood from one part of his body to his head.

'On what charge?' he demanded sharply.

'No charge.' She shook her head, sending her dark hair flying. 'Not as yet—that—that all depends on how things work out.'

'So what the hell did he do wrong?' Gregor had always seemed such a canny player. Someone who knew how best to feather his own nest. So had he got too greedy, made some mistake?

'He—chose the wrong side in the recent inheritance battle. For the throne.'

So that was what was behind this. Alexei might never want to set foot in Mecjoria ever again, but he couldn't be unaware—no one could be unaware—of the struggle that had gone on over the inheritance of the throne once old King Leopold had died. First Leopold's son Marcus had inherited, but only briefly. A savage heart attack had killed him barely months into his reign. Because he had died childless, his nephew Felix should have inherited the crown, but his wild way of life had been his undoing, so that he had died in a high-speed car crash before he had even ascended to the throne. Now there were several factions warring over just who was the legal heir to follow Felix.

'And then when Felix died... My father is currently seen as an enemy—as a threat to the throne.'

She wasn't telling the full truth, Alexei realised. There was something she was holding back, he was sure of it. Something that clouded those amazing eyes, tightened the muscles around her delicate jawline, pulling the pretty mouth tight, though there was no mistaking the quiver of those softly sensual lips.

Lips that he wished to hell he could taste, feel that trembling softness under his own mouth, plunder the moist interior...

'It will all work out in the end.'

Once again his own burning inner feelings made the words sound abrupt, dismissive, and he saw her blink slowly, withdrawing from him. Her head came up, that smooth chin lifting in defiance as she met his stare face-on.

'You can promise that, can you?' Ria asked, her tone appallingly cynical.

And where her unexpected weakness hadn't beaten him now, shockingly, her boldness did. There was a new spark in her eyes, fresh colour in her cheeks. She was once more the proud Grand Duchess Honoria and not the strangely defeated girl who had reached out to something he had thought was long dead inside him. *This* Ria was a challenge; a challenge he welcomed. The sound of his blood was like a roar inside his head, the heated race of his pulse burning along every vein. He had never wanted a woman so much as he wanted her now, and the need was like an ache in every nerve.

'How would you know? You were the one who turned

your back on Mecjoria—haven't even been back once in ten years.'

'Not turned my back,' Alexei growled. 'We weren't given a chance to stay. In fact it was made plain that we were not wanted.'

And who had been behind that? Her father—the very same man who was now, according to her story, locked in a prison cell. Did she expect him to feel sorry for him? To give a damn what might happen to the monster who hadn't even waited to allow him and his mother time to mourn their loss, or even to attend the state funeral, before he had had them escorted to the airport and put on the first plane out of the country?

First making sure that every penny of his father's fortune, every jewel, every tiny personal inheritance, had been taken from them, leaving them with little but the clothes they stood up in, not even the most basic allowance to see them into their new life in exile. Worst of all, Gregor had taken their name from them. The name his mother had been entitled to, and with it her honour, the legality of her marriage into the royal house of Mecjoria. He must have done it deliberately, hiding away the document that showed the old king's permission. The document that Ria had been commissioned to bring here so unexpectedly—because it now suited her father. Was it any wonder that he loathed the man—that he would do anything to bring him down?

But it seemed that Gregor had managed that all on his own.

'And I don't have to be in the country to know what is going on.'

'The papers don't report everything. And certainly not always accurately.'

Something new had clouded those clear eyes and

turned her expression into an intriguing mixture of defiance and uncertainty. There was just the tiniest sheen of moisture under one eye, where a trace of an unexpected tear had escaped the determined control she had been trying to impose on it and slipped out on to her lashes.

Unable to resist the impulse, he reached out and touched her face, letting his fingers rest lightly on the fine skin along the high, slanting cheekbone, wiping away that touch of moisture. The warmth and softness of the contact made his nerves burn, sending stinging arrows of response down into his body. He wanted so much more and yet he wanted to keep things just as they were—for now. It was a struggle not to do more, not to curve his hand around her cheek, cup that defiant little chin against his palm, lift her face towards his so that he could capture her mouth...

And that would ruin things completely. She would react like a scalded cat, he had no doubt. All that silent defiance would return in full force, and she'd swing away from him, repulsing the gesture with a rough shake of her head. She was still too tense, too on edge. But like any nervous cat, with a few moments' careful attention—perhaps a soothing stroke or two—she would soon settle down.

So for now it was enough to watch the storm of emotions that swept over her face. The response that turned those citrine eyes smoky, that darkened and deepened the black of her pupils, making them spread like the flow of ink until they covered almost all of her irises. The way that her mouth opened again to show the tips of small white teeth was a temptation that kicked at his libido, making it hungrier than ever. The clamour in his body urged him to act, to make his move now, when she was at her weakest, but for a little while at least he was enjoying imposing restraint on himself, letting the sensual hunger build—anticipating what might come later—and watching the effect his behaviour had on her.

'So tell me the rest.'

She didn't know if she could go through with this. Ria struggled to find some of the certainty, the conviction of doing the right thing, that had buoyed her up on her journey here, held her in the room in spite of the frantic thudding of her heart. So much depended on what she said now and the possible repercussions of her failure, personal and political, were almost impossible to imagine. The image of her mother, too pale, far too thin, drifting through life like a wraith, with no appetite, no interest in anything slid into her mind. Her days were haunted by fears, her nights plagued by terrifying nightmares.

Her father was the cause of those nightmares. Since the night that the state police had come to arrest him, taking him away in handcuffs, they had never seen him for a moment. But they knew where he was. The state prison doors had slammed closed on him and, unless Ria could find some way of helping him, then behind those locked doors was where he was going to stay. She had wanted to help him—wanted to return him to her mother—and it had been because she had been looking for some way to do that that she had found the hidden documents, the ones that proved Alexei's legitimacy and the others that had revealed the whole truth about what had been going on.

The full, appalling truth.

CHAPTER THREE

IT WAS WHAT she had come here for, Ria reminded herself. To tell him the story that had not yet leaked into the papers. The full details of the archaic inheritance laws that had come into play in the country since the unexpected death of the man they had believed to be the heir to the throne. But that would also mean telling him how those laws involved him, and his reaction just a moment before had made it plain that he harboured no warmth towards the country that had once been his home.

But when he had touched her—the way he still touched her—just that one tiny contact seemed to have broken through the careful, deliberate barriers she had built around herself. It was so long since she had felt that someone sympathised; that someone might be on her side. And the fact that it was someone as strong and forceful—and devastating—as this particular man, the man who had once been a special friend to her, stripped away several much-needed protective layers of skin, leaving her raw and disturbingly vulnerable.

He was so close she couldn't actually judge his expression without lifting her head, tilting it back just a little. And that movement brought her eyes up to clash with his. Suddenly even breathing naturally was impossible as their

gazes locked, the darkness and intensity of his stare closing her throat in the space of a single uneven heartbeat.

In that moment everything that had happened in the
past months rushed up to swamp her mind, taking with
it any hope of rational thought. Except that right now she
needed him. Needed the friend he had once been. So much
about him might have changed: that hard-boned face had
thinned, toughened into that of a stunningly mature male
in his sexual prime; those eyes might now be five inches
above hers where once they had been so much closer to
her own... But they were still the eyes of the friend she
had known. Still the eyes of the one person she had felt
she could confide in and get a sympathetic hearing.

They were the eyes she had once let herself dream of
seeing warm with more than just the easy light of friendship. And the memory of how in the past she had fallen
asleep and into dreams of them being so much more than
friends twisted in her heart with the bitterness of loss.

'Tell me everything.'

'You don't really want that,' she flung at him, gulping
in air so that she could loosen her throat.

'No? Try me.'

Challenge blended with something else in his tone.
And it was that something else that made her heart jerk,
her breath catch.

Was it possible that he really did want to know? That
he might help her? Memories of their past friendship surfaced once again, tugging at her feelings. She was so
lonely, so dragged down by it all, so tired of coping with
everything on her own. So wretched at the thought of
what the future might bring. And here was this man who
had once been the boy she adored, the friend who had let
her offload her troubles on to his shoulders—shoulders

that even then had seemed broad enough to take on the world. They were so much broader, so much stronger now.

Tell me everything, he'd said, and as he spoke the hand that rested against her face moved slightly, the pressure of his fingers softening, his palm curving so that it lay over her cheek, warm and hard and yet gentle all at the same time.

'*The truth,* Ria,' he said and the sound of her name on his lips was her weakness, her undoing.

Unable to stop herself, she turned her face into his hold, inhaling the scent of his skin, pursing her lips to press a small, soft kiss against the warmth of his palm.

Instantly everything changed. Her heart seemed to stop, her breathing stilled. The clean, musky aroma of his body was all around her, the taste of his flesh tangy on her tongue. It was like taking a sip of a fine, smoky brandy, one that intoxicated in a moment, sending fizzing bubbles of electricity along every nerve.

She wanted more. Needed to deepen the contact. Needed it like never before.

The boy who had been her friend had never made her feel like this; never made her pulse race so fast and heavy, her head spin so wildly. In all her adolescent dreams she had never known this feeling of awareness, of hunger. A pulsing, heated adult hunger that grew and sharpened as he moved his hold on her, taking her chin and lifting it so that their eyes clashed and scorched. Something blazed in these black depths, creating a golden glow that had more heat than an inferno and yet was almost—*almost*—under control.

'Ria...' he said again, his tone very different this time, his voice roughening at the edges. He had moved closer somehow, without her noticing, and the warmth of his breath on her skin as he spoke her name sent heated shivers running down her spine, making her toes curl inside her neat, polished shoes.

'Alex...'

But speaking had been a mistake. It made her mouth move against his skin, brought that powerfully sensual taste onto her tongue once again, so that she swallowed convulsively, taking the essence of him into herself in an echo of a much more intimate blending. Immediately it was as if a lighted match had been set to desert-dry brushwood. As if the tiny flicker that had been smouldering deep inside from the moment that she had come face to face with him again in his office had suddenly burst into wild and uncontrollable flame, the force of it moving her forward sharply, close up against him.

She heard his breath hiss in between his teeth in an uncontrolled response that both shocked and thrilled her. The thought that he felt as she did, so much that he was unable to hide his response from her, made her head spin. She could hardly believe that it could be possible, but there was no denying the evidence of the way that his grip tightened on her chin, hard fingers digging into her skin as he lifted her face towards his with a roughness that betrayed the urgency of his feelings.

'Alex...' she tried again, trying to follow the safe, the sensible path and persuade him to stop, but realising as she heard her own voice that she was doing exactly the opposite. The quaver on his name sounded so much more like shaken encouragement.

But a moment later it didn't matter what she said or how she said it. The truth was that she was incapable of any further speech as Alexei's dark head swooped down, his mouth capturing hers in a savage kiss. Hard lips crushed hers, bringing them open to the invasion of his tongue in an intimate dance that made her knees weaken so that she swayed against him, her body melting soft and yielding against the hardness of his.

She heard him mutter something dark and deep in his throat and the next moment she was swung round and up into his arms. Half-walked, half-carried across the room, his mouth never leaving hers, until she was hard up against the wall, its support cold and hard against her back. Both thrilled and shocked by his unexpected response, she shivered under the impact of his powerful form on her, the heat and hardness of him crushed against the cradle of her pelvis. If she had needed any further evidence of the fact that his blood was burning as hot as hers, then it was there in the swollen, powerful erection that was crushed between them.

His mouth was plundering hers, his tongue sweeping into the innermost corners, tasting her, tormenting her. The heated pressure of his hands matched the intimate invasion of his mouth, hot, hard palms skimming over her body, burning through the flowered cotton of her dress, curving over the swell of her hips, cupping her buttocks to pull her closer to him. Ria's blood pounded at her temples, along every nerve. Her breasts prickled and tightened in stinging response, nipples pressing against the soft lace of her bra, hungry for the feel of those wickedly enticing fingers against her flesh.

Unable to stop herself, she nipped sharply at his lower lip, catching it between her teeth and taking his gasp of response into her mouth with the taste of him clear and wild against her lips. Pushed into penitence by his reaction, she let her tongue slide over the damaged skin, soothing the small pressure wounds her teeth had inflicted and sucking the fullness of it to ease away any soreness. But the low growl she heard deep in his throat told her that his reaction had not been one of discomfort. Instead he was encouraging her to take further liberties, crushing her hard against him and letting his hands wander freely over her yearning body.

'Hell, but you're beautiful...'

He muttered the words against her arching throat, his breath warm against her flesh, and she could hardly believe that she was hearing them. Had he truly said beautiful? Was it possible that the man the gossip columns labelled the playboy prince, who had his pick of the sexiest women in the world—socialites, models, actresses— could think her so attractive? Memories of the adolescent dreams she had once indulged in, the yearning crush she had felt for this man surfaced all over again, reminding her of how much she would have given to hear those words back then, years ago. Then all he had ever shown her was a kind, but rather offhand friendship that was light-years away from this carnal hunger that seemed to grip them now.

'Who would have thought that you would grow up like this?'

'It—it's been a long time,' Ria managed to choke out, her throat dry with tension and need. 'I missed...'

But a sudden rush of self-preservation had her catching up the words in shock, clamping her mouth tight shut against what she had almost revealed. The heady rush of sensuality had driven common sense so far from her mind but she needed to grab it back now—and quickly. Alexei was no longer even her friend. He was the man who held her future and that of her country in his hands, even if he didn't know it yet.

In the strong, sensual hands that had been creating such electric pulses of pleasure in her body only a moment before. Pulses she wanted to feel more of. That made her whole body ache with need. But she must deny herself such caresses even though her whole body screamed in protest at the thought of stopping now, here, like this, when every nerve had suddenly come alive and awake in a whole new way. She had to remember why she was here.

'You—you've been missed,' she managed, though her voice shook on the words, betraying the effort she was making to get them out. And then, suddenly aware of how that might sound—that he could interpret it as meaning she was telling him just how much *she* had missed him— she rushed on. 'You've been missed in Mecjoria.'

The sound of that name brought exactly the reaction she feared. She felt the new tension in the long body pressed against hers as he stilled, withdrawing from her immediately, his hands freezing, denying her the shivers of pleasure that had radiated out from his touch.

'I doubt that very much,' he muttered, his voice rough and harsh so that it scraped over her rawly exposed nerves. 'I don't think that could ever be true.'

'Oh, but it is!' Ria protested, forcing herself to go on because this was what she had come here for after all. 'You're missed in Mecjoria—and wanted and needed there.'

'Needed?'

Her heart sank as he pushed himself away from her to stand looking down into her face with icy onyx eyes, all fire, all warmth fading from them in the space of a heart-beat. She had done what she needed to do, turned things back on to the real reason why she was here, so that at last she could tell him just why she had come to find him. But she felt lost and alone, her body suddenly cold and bereft without the heat and power of his surrounding it; her skin, her breasts, her lips cooling sharply as the imprint of his whipcord strength evaporated into the cool of the afternoon air.

She'd lost him again. That much was obvious from one swift glance at his face, seeing the way it had closed off against her, black eyes opaque and expressionless, revealing nothing. His only movement was when his hand went to his throat, tugging at the tie around his neck as if it was choking him. He pulled it loose, flicked open the top button on his shirt, then another, as if just one was not enough. And the restless movement was enough to draw her eyes, make her watch in stunned fascination.

No, that was a mistake—a major mistake. Looking into those deep-set black eyes, she suddenly saw a new light, a darkly burning, disturbing light in their depths, and it warned that there was more to this than anything she might have anticipated already. Memory swung her back to the scene of just moments before. Then, pinned up against the wall with his hands hot on her, she had known exactly what he wanted. And she had been dangerously close to giving it to him, with no thought of her own sanity or safety. Her body still tingled with the aftershocks of that encounter, the taste of him still lingered on her mouth. If she licked her lips she revived the sensation, almost as if he had just kissed her again. And oh, dear heaven, but she wanted him to kiss her again.

'There is no one there who would miss me and as for anyone who might *want* me for any reason whatsoever...'

'Oh, but you're wrong there. You really are.'

But how did she convince him of that? If there was anything that brought home to her how difficult her task was then this office, this building, was it. She didn't need to be told how much Alexei had made his new life here in England. More than a new life, his fortune, his *home*. And it was plain from the way he spoke of Mecjoria that his father's country meant nothing to him. Did she even have the right to ask him to give this up?

She didn't know. But the one thing she was sure of was that she didn't have the right to keep it from him. The decision, whatever it was, had to be his.

'I'll make it easy for you, shall I?' Alexei drawled cynically. 'Twice now you have told me that I am wanted—and needed—in Mecjoria. You have to be lying.'

'No lie. Really.'

'You expect me to believe that I am needed in the country that rejected me as not fit to be even the smallest part of the royal family? Needed by the place that has disowned and ignored me for the past ten years?'

The only response Ria could manage was a sharp, swift nod of her head. She couldn't persuade her voice to work on anything else.

'Then you'll have to explain. Needed as what?'

'As…'

Twice Ria opened her mouth to try to get the words out. Twice she failed, and it was only when Alexei turned his narrow-eyed glare on her and muttered her name as if in threat that she forced herself to speak, bringing it out in a rush.

'As—as their king. You're needed to take the throne of Mecjoria now that Felix is dead.'

CHAPTER FOUR

AS THEIR KING.

The words hit like a blow to the head, making Alexei's thoughts reel. Had he heard right?

You're needed to take the throne of Mecjoria now that Felix is dead.

Whatever else he had expected, it had not been that. She had made it plain that she and her family had suffered some strong reversal of their fortunes in the upheaval that had followed the struggles over the inheritance of the Mecjorian crown. She had come here to ask for help, that much was obvious. Softening him up by producing the proof of his legitimacy first. Perhaps to play on the fact that they had once been friends in order to get him to use his fortune to help, rescue her family. Why else would she be here?

Why else would she have responded to his kisses as she had?

Because even as he had felt her mouth opening under his, the soft curves of her body melting against him, he had known that she was only doing this for her own private reasons.

Known it and hadn't cared. He had let her lead him on in that way because he'd wanted it. No woman had excited him, aroused him so much with a single kiss. And there had been plenty of women. His reputation as a playboy had been well earned, and he had had a lot of fun earning it. At least at the beginning. It was only after Mariette—and Belle—that everything had changed. His mind flinched away from the memory but there was no getting away from the after-effects of that terrible day. His appetites had become jaded; his senses numbed. Nothing seemed to touch him like before. There was no longer the thrill of the chase.

Not that he had to do any chasing. Women practically threw themselves at him and he could have his pick of any of them simply by saying the right word, turning a practised smile in their direction. He was under no illusions; he knew it was his position and wealth that was such a strong part of the attraction. That and the bad-boy reputation that haunted him like a dark shadow. So many women wanted to be the one who tamed him. But not one of them had ever stood a chance. He had enjoyed them, shared their beds, sometimes finding the oblivion he sought in their arms. But not one of them had ever heated his blood, set his pulse racing in burning hunger as this one kiss from the former friend he had once known as a young girl, but who had grown into a stunningly sexual woman.

A woman who, like so many others, had been prepared to use that sexuality to persuade him to give her what she wanted.

But this…

'That's one hell of a bad joke!' He tossed the words at her, saw her flinch from the harshness of his tone and didn't care.

But then something about the way she looked, a widening of those amazing eyes, the sight of white, sharp teeth digging into the rose-tinted softness of her lower lip caught him up short and made him look again, more closely this time. There was more to this than he believed.

'It was a joke, wasn't it?'

A bad, black-humorous joke. One meant to stick a knife in between his ribs with the reminder of just how his father's homeland could never, ever be home to him again. Even if he was the legitimate son of one of their royal family. Disbelief was like an itch in his blood, making him want to pace around the room. Only the determination not to show the way she had rocked his sense of reality kept him still, one hand on the big, carved mantelpiece, the other tightly clenched into a fist inside the pocket of his trousers.

'A very bad joke...*no*...?'

She had shaken her head as he spoke, sending the auburn mane of her hair flying around her face. But it still couldn't conceal the way she had lost even more colour, her skin looking like putty, shocking in contrast to the wide darkness of her eyes and the way that the blush of colour flooded to where she had bitten into her lip again.

'No joke—' she stammered, low and uneven. 'It's not something I'd ever joke about.'

How she wished he would show some sort of reaction, Ria told herself. His stillness and the intent, fixed glare were becoming seriously oppressive.

'But there's no way you can be telling the truth. How would your father benefit from this?'

'My—my father?'

It would have the opposite effect, if only he knew. Her father wouldn't benefit from this, rather he would gain so much more from the back-up plan that would fall into place if Alexei refused the request she had come to him with. But she had promised herself that she would not tell Alexei that; that she would never use the dark reality of her own situation to try to persuade him into the decision she wanted—needed. Her family had committed enough crimes against his in the past. It was going to stop here, no matter what the result.

But she had hesitated too long. That, and her stammering response, had given her away.

'Your father must hope to get exactly what he wants from this.' It was a flat, cruel statement. 'Why else would he send you here?'

How did he manage to stay so still, so stiff, his eyes dark gleaming pools of contempt? He looked like a jewel-eyed cobra, silent, unmoving, just waiting for the moment to strike.

'My father wasn't the one who sent me, but obviously whatever you decide will affect him. And everyone in Mecjoria.'

'And I should care about that because…?'

'Because if you don't then the whole country will fall into chaos. There will be civil unrest, perhaps even revolution. People will be hurt—killed—they'll lose everything.'

The desperation she felt now sounded in her voice but it was clear that it had no effect on that flinty-eyed stare, the cold set of his hard jaw.

'And if you don't take the throne, the only other person who can is Ivan.'

That hit home to him.

She saw his head go back, eyes narrowing sharply at that, and knew the impact her words had had. Only very distantly related, Alexei and Ivan Kolosky had always detested each other. In fact Ivan had once been one of the ringleaders in making Alexei's life hell as he tried to adjust to life at the Mecjorian court, and they had once bonded together against this cousin several times removed

who now was the only other possible heir to the Mecjorian throne.

With one proviso. One that affected her personally in
a way that made her stomach curdle just to think of it.
And she certainly didn't want Alexei to know of it or she
would be putting extra power into his hands. Power she
had no idea just how he would use.

'How would he be next in line to the succession?'

'There are ancient laws about the possible heirs. With
both the old king and Felix gone, they have to look further afield. And with no one who's a direct descendant
left then the net spreads wider—to you.'

'And to Ivan.'

It was throwaway, totally dismissive, and it warned
her of just what was coming. The indifferent shrug of his
shoulders only confirmed it.

'So, problem solved. You already have an heir—one
who will want the throne much more than I ever would.
You wouldn't even need to prove his legitimacy.'

The bitterness that twisted on his tongue made her
wince in discomfort.

'But Ivan isn't the first in line. It's only if you refuse
the crown that he has a claim.' Or if she played her own
part in his succession as her father wanted. The knots in
her stomach tightened painfully at the thought. 'And we
can't let him take the crown!'

That had him turning a narrow-eyed stare on her
shocked and worried face. It was so coldly, bleakly assessing that it made her shift uncomfortably where she
stood. She was afraid that he would see her own fears in
her expression and know that that gave him an advantage
to hold over her.

'We?' he queried cynically. 'Since when was there any
"we" involved in this?'

'You have to consider Mecjoria.'

'I do? I think you'll find that I don't have to do any-thing—or have anything to do with a country that was never a home to me.'

'But you must know all about the eruminium…the min-eral that has been discovered in the mountains,' she ex-plained when he made no response other than a sardonic lift of one black brow that cynically questioned her as-sertion. 'You'll know that it's being mined…'

'An excellent source of wealth for my cousin,' Alexei drawled, lounging back indolently against the wall in a way that expressed his total indifference to everything she said.

'But it's what it could be used for—eruminium can be used to make weapons almost as dangerous as an atomic bomb. Ivan won't care what it's used for—he'll sell the mining rights to anyone for the highest offer.'

Something flickered in the depths of those stunning eyes. But she couldn't be sure whether it was the sort of reaction that might help her or one that displayed exactly the opposite.

'And you actually concede that I might not do just the same?'

'I have to hope that you wouldn't.'

Ria no longer cared if her near-panic showed in her voice. Nothing about this meeting was going as she had thought—as she had hoped. Everyone had told her that all she had to do was to talk with Alexei, get him to lis-ten to reason. He would grab at the position, the crown, they had assured her. How could he not when it offered him the wealth and power he must want?

Anyone who thought that had never seen the man Alexei had become, she told herself, looking at the el-egantly lean and dangerous figure opposite her. It was obvious that Alexei Sarova had everything he wanted right here.

And, worst of all, was any suggestion that his taking the crown would do anything to help her, as her father's daughter, would just provide the death blow to any hope of persuading him to do so. The hatred that burned bone-deep was not going to be easily tossed aside.

'Only hope?' His question seemed to chip away layers of her protective shell, leaving gaping holes where she most needed a shield. 'Well, what else should I have expected?'

There was something that burned in those deep, black eyes that challenged and scoured across her nerves all in the same moment. But there was something else mixed in there too, something she couldn't begin to interpret.

'I can't say for sure, can I? After all, I don't know you.'

'No,' Alexei drawled, another challenge, darker than ever. 'You don't.'

'But I do know that if the problem of the succession isn't solved soon then the whole country will fall into chaos—possibly even revolution. You have to see that.'

'And I see that your father will find it very uncomfortable if that happens. But I don't understand why I need to have any part in helping to deal with it. Your father betrayed mine—his memory—by claiming that his marriage to my mother had never been legal. That was when he wanted someone else to be on the throne—and for himself to have the strongest influence possible.'

The words seemed to strip away a much-needed protective layer of skin, leaving Ria feeling raw and painfully exposed. Deep inside she knew she couldn't defend her father from Alexei's accusations, and the truth was that she didn't want to. In fact, she could add more to the list if she had the chance.

'He destroyed my mother, took everything she had and threw her out of her home, the country.'

And her son with her, Ria acknowledged to herself, wincing inwardly at the cruelly sharp twist at her heart that the memory brought with it. Like everyone else, she'd believed her father's claims. She'd believed that he was loyal to the crown and to the country. She'd trusted him on that, only to find that all the time he had just been feathering his own nest, and planning on using her as his ace card if he could. But that had been before she had discovered that Gregor had held the document of permission all the time. That he had hidden it in order to get Alexei and his mother away from the court. Only now did she realise exactly why.

'But you've done fine for yourself since then.'

'Fine?'

One dark brow lifted in cynical mockery as he echoed her tone with deliberate accuracy.

'If you mean working every hour God sends to earn enough to support my mother and keep her in the way that she needed, give her some comfort and enjoyment when she was desperately ill, then yes, we've done "fine". But that in no way excuses your father for what he has done or puts me under any obligation at all to help him with anything.'

'No—no you're not,' she admitted. 'But don't you think that you might have played some part in what had driven him to push you into exile and kept you there afterwards?'

'And what exactly do you mean by that?'

The silence that greeted her question was appalling, dark and dangerous, bringing her up sharp against what she had said. What she had risked.

Oh, dear heaven, she had really opened her mouth and put both feet right in it there! All she had meant was that it had been his own irresponsible behaviour, the wildness of his ways, that had contributed to her father's reaction against him and his family. But now she had opened a very ugly can of worms, one she could never put the lid back on ever again. Alexei's behaviour at court had been one thing. There had been another, darker scandal that had cast a black shadow over his existence once he had settled in England.

'No—I'm sorry. Obviously...'

'Obviously?' Alexei echoed cynically. 'Obviously you think you know the answer to your question so why ask it?'

'I didn't mean to rake over the past.'

'You would be wise not to—not if you want me to do anything to help your father, because I'll see him in hell first.'

And that cold-blooded declaration was just too much. It wrenched the top off her control, taking her temper with it.

'Well, you'll be right there with him—won't you?' she flung at him. 'After all, what has my father done that compares with letting his baby die?'

It was as if the whole room had frozen over. As if the air had turned to ice, burning in her lungs and making it impossible to breathe. The cold was like a mist before her eyes but even with the swirling haze she could still see the blaze of his eyes, searing through the blurring clouds and scouring over her skin like some brutal laser.

'What indeed?'

She'd gone too far, said too much, and put herself in danger by doing so. Not physical danger because, no matter how darkly furious she knew that Alexei was, she also had a fiercely stubborn conviction that there was no way he would hurt her.

But mentally...that was another matter entirely. And

just the thought of it had her taking several hurried and shaken steps backwards, away from him, putting the width of the polished wooden desk between them for her own safety.

'I wouldn't be too sure of that.' The image of the jewel-eyed serpent was back in Ria's mind as she heard the vicious hiss of his words, felt the flicking sting of their poison. 'There are more ways than one to destroy a child's life.'

That brought her up sharply, blinking in shock and incomprehension as she stared into his dark shuttered face, trying to work out just what he meant. Had he known— or at the very least suspected—just what her father had planned? Was that why he had always been so aggressively hostile to the older man back in Mecjoria, so defiant, rejecting everything the Chancellor had tried to teach him? It was nothing but oppression, bullying, he had declared, and she had always come back with the belief that her father was doing it for their own good, and for the image of the country. At least that was how she had seen it at the time. Now, recognising the side of her father that had shown itself more recently, she was forced to see it in such a very different light, and the sense of betrayal was like acid in her mouth. But had Alexei, with the advantage of extra years, been able to interpret things much more accurately?

Because how could she deny the relevance his words had for her now, coming so close to the secret she had vowed she would keep from him at all costs?

'I didn't mean to rake over the past,' she said hesitantly, trying for appeasement.

'But nevertheless you have done just that.'

Black eyes blazed against skin drawn white across his slashing cheekbones and he slung the words at her like pellets of ice, each one seeming to hit hard and cold on her unprotected skin so that she flinched back, away from them.

'I'm sorry,' she tried but the icy flash of his eyes shrivelled the words on her tongue.

'Why apologise? Doesn't everyone know that I was once a useless, irresponsible drunk? The type of man who left my child alone while I went on a bender? Who drank myself into a stupor so that I didn't even know that my baby daughter had died in her cot?'

'Oh, don't!'

Her hands came up before her sharply in a gesture of defence. She didn't understand why it hurt so much just to hear the words. She'd known about it after all—everyone had. The scandal had exploded into the papers like an atom bomb, shattering lives, destroying what little reputation Alexei might still have had. Most of all it had ripped apart any hope she had clung on to that he might still be the boy she had loved so much—the friend who had once been her support and strength through a difficult, lonely childhood. It had certainly kept her from trying to contact him again when she had been tempted to do just that.

'Don't what?' he parried harshly. 'Don't acknowledge the truth?'

CHAPTER FIVE

HE'D BEEN HOLDING it together until she'd said that, Alexei acknowledged. Until she'd ripped away the protective wall he had built between himself and the dark remembrance of the past. And now the red mist of aching memory had seeped out and flooded his brain, making it impossible to think or to speak rationally.

Belle. One tiny little girl had changed his life and made him pull himself up, haul himself back from the edge of the precipice he had been rushing towards. But not soon enough. He had failed Belle, failed his daughter, and her death would always be on his conscience.

Looking into Ria's face, he could almost swear that he could see the sheen of moisture on those beautiful eyes and found that some inner of stab of jealousy actually twisted deep in his guts. He had never been able to weep for Belle, never been able to fully mourn her loss. He had been too busy trying to deal with the fallout from that tragedy.

But Ria… How could she have tears for a child she had never known, for a baby she had no connection to? He envied her her ease of response, the uncomplicated emotion.

'Why should I deny the facts when the world and his wife know what happened?' he demanded. 'And no one would believe a word that's different.'

'What possible different interpretation could there be?'

Was that what she was looking for? Hoping for? The questions thundered inside Ria's head, shocking her with their force, the bruising power of the need it startled into wakefulness. Was this what she wanted? That he could provide a different explanation for the terrible events of three years before? That he could explain it all away, say it had never happened—or at least that it had never been the way it had been reported? Was this why it tore at her so much, pulling a need she hadn't realised existed out of her heart and forcing her to face it head-on?

If that was it, then she was doomed to disappointment. She knew it as soon as she saw the way his face changed again, the bitter sneer that twisted his beautiful mouth, distorting its sensual softness.

'None, of course,' he drawled so softly that she almost missed it. 'That is unless you can tell me that you believe it could have been any other way. Can you do that, hmm, sweetheart?'

He went even more on to the attack, driving the savage stiletto blade of his cruelty deeper into her heart. And it was all the more devastating because it was still spoken in that dangerously gentle tone.

'Can you find a way to change the past so that the devil is transformed into an angel? A fallen angel, granted, but not the fiend incarnate that the world sees?'

Could she? Her mouth opened but no sound came out because there was no thought inside her head she could voice but the knowledge that what he spoke was the bitter, black truth.

'No...'

'No.'

The corners of his mouth curled up into a smile that

ripped into her heart, it was so strangely gentle and yet so at odds with the fiendish darkness of his eyes.

'Of course. I thought not.'

'If there is any explanation...'

For the sake of their past, the sake of the friend he had once been, she had to try just once more, though without any real hope.

'No. There is no explanation that I want to give you.'

It was a brutal, crushing dismissal, accompanied by a slashing gesture of one hand, cutting her off before she could complete the sentence.

'Nothing that would change a thing. So why don't we accept that as fact and move on?'

'Do we have anywhere to move on to?'

Where could they go from here? He had declared that everything she had heard about him was the truth. He had taken the weak, idealistic image she had once had of him and dashed it viciously to the ground, letting it splinter into tiny, irreparable shards that would never again let her form the picture of a wild but generous-spirited boy who had once been her rock, someone she could turn to when things got too bad to bear.

'I know my father's no saint, but you—you're hateful.'

She was past thinking now, past caring about what she said. Deep inside, where she prayed he would never be able to find it, she knew she was having to face up to the painful bitter truth. And that truth was that when she had found out the reality of what her father had been up to, what he had planned, then she had come running to find Alexei, to find her friend, hoping, believing that he of all people would be there for her, that he would help her. But the reality was that her friend Alexei no longer existed and this cold-eyed monster could be an even more deadly enemy than the cousin she feared so much.

'Not so hateful a moment ago,' Alexei tossed at her. 'Not when you were hungry for my kisses, my touch— for anything I would give you.'

'You took me by surprise!' Ria broke in sharply, knowing she was trying to avoid the image of herself he was showing her.

'And it was only the *surprise* that made you react as you did.'

'What else could there be?' Ria challenged, bringing up her chin as she glared her defiance at him, wanting to deny the cynicism that burned in his words. 'You're not so damn irresistible as you think…'

'Except when I have something that you want. So if I were to kiss you again…'

'No!'

It made her jump, taking a hasty step backwards, banging into the chair and almost sending it flying. The bruise stung sharply but nothing like the feeling inside as she faced the dark mockery in his face and knew that her reaction had only confirmed his worst suspicions.

'You wouldn't…' she tried again.

Her wary protest had his mouth curling at the corners, the sardonic humour more shocking than the cold anger of just moments before. She should have taken that anger as a warning, Ria acknowledged to herself. If anything, that should give her her cue to get out of here—fast. She had tried to persuade him to come back to Mecjoria. Tried to make him see that he was the best—the only—man who could take the throne. Tried and failed. And the worst realisation was the fact that she had miscalculated this so totally. She had thought that she was the best person for this task, but the truth was that she had really been the worst possible one. She had blundered in where she should have feared to tread, raising all the hatred and the anger he had been letting fester for ten long, bitter years and the only thing she could do was to walk out now while she could still hold her head high.

'Oh, but I would.' That dark mockery curled through his words like smoke around a newly extinguished candle, sending shivers of uncomfortable response sliding down her spine. 'And so would you, if you were prepared to be honest and admit it.'

'I wouldn't.'

She was shaking her head desperately even though she knew the vehemence of her response only betrayed her more, dug in deeper into the hole that was opening up around her feet. Impossibly she was actually wishing for the cold-eyed serpent back in place of that wicked smile, the calculated mockery.

'Liar.'

It was soft and deadly, terrifyingly so as he emphasised it with a couple of slow, deliberate steps towards her, and she could feel the colour coming and going in her cheeks as she tried to get a grip on the seesaw of emotions that swung sickeningly up and down inside her. It would be so much easier if her senses weren't on red alert in response to the potently masculine impact of his powerful form, the lean, lithe frame, the powerful chest and arms in contrast to the fine linen of his shirt. Her eyes were fixed on the bronzed skin of his throat and the dark curls of hair exposed by the open neckline. He was so close that she could see the faint shadow on his jaw where the dark growth of stubble was already beginning to appear, and the clean musky aroma of his skin, topped with the tang of some bergamot scent, was tantalising her nostrils.

The memory of that kiss was so sharp in her mind, the scent of his body bringing back to her how it had felt to be enclosed in his arms, feel the strength of muscle, the heat of his skin surrounding her. The trouble was that she did want him to kiss her—that was something she couldn't deny. It was there in the dryness of her mouth, the tightness of her throat so that she could barely breathe, let alone swallow. The heavy thuds of her heart against her ribs were a blend of excited anticipation and a shocking sense of dread. She wanted his kiss, wanted his touch—but she knew just what she would be unleashing if she allowed anything to happen. And she already had far too much to lose to take any extra risks.

'No lie,' she flung at him. 'Not then and not now. I can see I'm wasting my time here.'

'That's one thing we can agree on.'

It was when he swung away from her that she knew every last chance of being heard, or even getting him to give her a single moment's consideration, was over. The hard, straight line of his back was turned to her, taut and powerful as a stone wall against any appeal she might direct towards him. And the way his hands were pushed deep into the pockets of his trousers showed the fierce control he was imposing on himself and the volatile temper she sensed was almost slipping away from him.

'It seems that you're not going to be any use to me so I might as well call it a day.'

'Please do.'

If he stayed turned away, Alexei told himself, then he might just keep his wayward senses under control until she had left. It was shocking to find the way that cold fury warred with an aching burn of lust that held him in its grip, unable to move, unable to think straight.

In the moment that she had stood up and faced him he had known that the rush of hard, hot sensuality of a few moments before had not been a one-off. And that it was not something that was going to go away any time soon.

Something about the woman that Ria had become reached out and caught him in a net of sexual hunger, one that thudded heavily through his body, centring on the hardness between his legs. The fall of the shining darkness of her hair, the gleam of her beautiful almond-shaped eyes, the rose-tinted curve of her lips, shockingly touched with a sexual gleam of moisture where she had slicked her small pink tongue along them, had all woven a sensual spell around him, one he was struggling to free himself from. He could still taste her if he let his tongue touch his own lips, the scent of her skin was on his clothes, topped by that slight spicy floral scent she wore that made him want to press his lips; to her soft flesh, inhale the essence of her as he kissed her all over.

He still did. He still wanted to reach out and haul her into his arms, kiss her, touch her. She was the last person in the world he should feel this way about, the worst person in the world to have any sort of association with, let alone the hot passionate sex his body hungered for. She came with far too much baggage, not the least of which was the connection with Mecjoria, the country that had once been so much a part of his past and had almost destroyed him as a result. Everything about her threatened to drag him back into that past, to enclose him in the memories he hated, imprison him again in all that he had escaped from. Ria might tempt him—hell, the temptation she offered was so strong that he could feel it twining round him, tightening, like great coils of rope, almost impossible to resist—but he was not going to give in to it. It would only drag him back into the past he had barely walked away from, reduce him all over again to the boy he had once been, lonely, needy, and that was not going to happen.

And then she had done it again. She had turned that

look on him. The Grand Duchess Honoria look. It had hit him hard. It was the same look that she'd turned on him ten years before. He didn't know which was the worst, the fact that she still thought she could look at him in that way or the fact that it could still get to him. That she could still make him feel that way. As if all he had done and achieved had never been. As if he was still the Alexei who had hungered for approval and friendship, especially from her. From Ria. His friend.

No longer a friend. That was too innocent a word, and what he felt now was definitely not innocent. Hearing her voice and the way that something—pride? Anger? Defiance?—had hardened it, he knew what he was going to do, even if the roar of heat in his blood made it a struggle to make his body behave as his mind told him he should. Hungry sensuality and coldly rational thought fought an ugly little battle that tightened every muscle, twisted every nerve.

But it was a battle he was determined to win.

'I would appreciate it if you left now.'

It was something of a shock to find that echoes of the training his father had given him before the cancer had stolen even his voice had surfaced from his past to make him impose the sort of control over his tone that turned the formal politeness into an icy-cold distance. She would have had something of the same training so he didn't doubt that she knew exactly what that tone meant.

'But I can't…'

'But you can. You can accept that this is never going to happen—that you have failed. Whoever advised you to come here you should let them know that they sent quite the wrong person to plead their case. They would have done better to send your father—I might actually have listened to him more than I would to you.'

He heard her sharply indrawn breath and almost turned to see the reaction stamped on her face.

Almost. But he caught himself in time. He was not going to subject himself to that sort of temptation ever again.

'So now just go. I have nothing more to say to you, and I never want to see you in my life again.'

Would she fight him on this? Would she try once more to persuade him? Dear God, was he almost tempted by the thought that she might? Fiercely he fixed his gaze on the darkness beyond the window. A darkness in which he could see the faint reflection of her shape, the pale gleam of her skin, the dark pools of her eyes. The silence that followed his words was total, and it dragged on and on, it seemed, stretching over the space of too many heartbeats.

But then at last he saw her head drop slightly, acknowledging defeat. She turned one last look on him, but clearly thought better of even trying to speak as she twisted on her heel and headed for the door, slender back straight, auburn head held high.

It was only as the door swung to behind her, the wood thudding into the frame, that he realised how unconsciously he had used exactly the words that she had thrown at him in their last meeting in Mecjoria ten years before. She had been the one to turn and walk away then too, marching away from him without a backward glance, taking with her the last hope he had had.

Recalling how it had felt then, it was impossible not to remember all he had ever wanted and now could never have—all over again. He had wanted to belong, damn it, he'd tried. He'd thought that when his parents had reconciled that at last he'd found the father, the family, he'd always wanted. But his father's illness had meant that he had never had the time to make a reality out of that dream. It had all crumbled around him.

But this time it had been his own decision to throw it all away. He had had his revenge for the way she and her family had treated him, turning the tables on her completely and reversing the roles they had once had. It should have been what he wanted. It should have provided him with the sort of dark satisfaction that would have made these last ten years of exile and of struggle finally worthwhile. But the troubling thing was the uncomfortable sensation in the pit of his stomach that told him that satisfaction was the furthest thing from what he was feeling. If anything, he felt emptier and hungrier than ever before.

The royal document still lay on his desk where he had dropped it, and for a moment he let himself touch it, resting his fingers on the ornate signature next to the dark-red seal. The signature of his grandfather. King of Mecjoria.

King.

Just four letters of a word but it seemed to explode inside his head. Ria had offered him the chance to return to Mecjoria, not just as himself—but as its king.

It was ironic that Ria claimed to have come here today to ask him to take the crown—to be King of Mecjoria when all that her appearance had done was to bring home to him how totally unsuited he was for any such role. He had failed as a prince, but that had been as nothing when compared to his failure as a father. But she thought that she could persuade him that he was needed in her homeland.

Her homeland. Not his.

But then she had said that the only alternative was for Ivan to be king. What a choice. Poor Mecjoria. To be torn between a bully boy and a man who knew nothing at all about being a royal—let alone running a country. His father's country.

His father must be spinning in his grave at just the thought.

And yet his father had had Ivan sussed even all those years ago. From the corners of his memory came the recollection of a conversation—one of the very rare conversations—he had had with his dying father. Weak, barely able to open his eyes, let alone move, his father had known of the stand-up argument, almost a fight, Alexei had had with Ivan the previous day.

'That boy is trouble,' he had whispered. 'He's dangerous. Watch him—and watch your back when you're with him. Never let him win.'

And this was the man who could take over the throne—unless he stopped him.

Moving to the window, he looked down into the street to see Ria's tall, slim figure emerge from the front of the Sarova building and start to walk away down the street, pausing to cross at the traffic lights. He had wanted her to leave, so why did he now feel as if she was taking with her some essential part of him, something that made him whole?

The part he had once thought that Belle would fill.

'Hell, no.'

He turned away fiercely as the scene before him blurred disturbingly.

Did he really think that Ria would fill that hole in his life? It was just sex. Nothing but the reawakening of his senses that had started from the moment he had walked into the room and set eyes on her. And he had the disturbing feeling that there was only one way to erase the yearning sensations that tormented his body.

The only real satisfaction he could find would be to

have Ria—the Grand Duchess Honoria—in his bed so that he could sate himself in her body and so hope, at last, to erase the bitterness of memories that had been festering for far too long. But he had just destroyed his chances of ever having that happen. He had driven her away, and in that moment he had believed that that was the wisest, the only rational course.

Except of course that rationality had nothing to do with the burning sensuality of his reaction to her, the carnal storm that still pounded through him, even after she had left the room.

Rationality might tell him that walking away from her was the sanest path to take but the bruise of sexual hunger that made his body ache still left no room for sanity or rational thought. This restless, nagging feeling was so much like the way he had felt when he had first come to England, into exile with his mother, a feeling that he had thought he had subdued, even erased completely. One brief meeting with Ria had revived everything he had never wanted to feel ever again, but in the past those feelings had been those of a youth who had not long left boyhood behind. Now he was a grown man, with an experience of life, and Ria was a full-grown woman. He *wanted* Ria as he had never wanted another woman in his life, craved her like a yearning addict needing a fix, and he knew that these feelings would take far more than ten years longer to bury all over again—if, in fact, they could ever be truly buried at all.

He had vowed to himself that he would throw her out of his life and forget about her. Already he was regretting and rethinking that vow, knowing that forgetting her was going to be impossible. He was going to have her—but it had to be on his own terms.

CHAPTER SIX

'YOU MUST HAVE this wrong.'

Coming to a dead halt, Ria stood in the doorway, staring out across the airport tarmac, shaking her head in disbelief. The sleek, elegant jet that stood gleaming in the sunshine was not at all what she had been anticipating and she couldn't imagine why anyone should think that it was there for her.

When she had arrived at the airport for her flight home, she had been feeling more raw and vulnerable than she had ever been in her life. With her one hope gone, the future now stretched ahead of her and her country, dark and oppressive, with no way of rescue or escape unless she took the way her father had planned.

She certainly hadn't expected to be greeted by a man in uniform, swept through the briefest of security checks and delivered out here where the luxurious private jets of the rich, famous and powerful waited for permission to take off to whatever private island or sophisticated resort might be their ultimate destination.

'There really has to be some mistake...' she tried again, coming to an abrupt halt at the foot of the steps up to the plane, as he stood back to let her precede him.

'No mistake.'

The words came from above her, at the top of the steps,

and in spite of the noise of the wind blowing across the tarmac she knew immediately who had spoken.

The open door at the head of the steps was now filled with the tall, powerful figure of Alexei Sarova, the man she had believed she had left behind in London and would never, ever see again. Casually dressed in a loose white shirt and worn denim jeans, his hair blown about in the breeze, his powerful frame still had a heart-stopping impact, an effect that was multiplied a hundred times by his dominant position so high up above her.

'No mistake at all,' he said now, dark eyes locking with hers. 'I asked for you to be brought here.'

'You did? But why?'

'It seemed ridiculous to let you fly cattle class when we are both going to the same place.'

'We are?'

Had she heard right? Was he actually saying that he was flying to Mecjoria? Could he be thinking of agreeing to her request that he claim the throne? The man who had turned his back on her both physically and emotionally.

'We are. So are you going to stand there dithering for much longer or are you going to come up here and take your seat? Everything is ready for take-off but if we don't leave soon we will miss our allocated slot.'

'I'm not going anywhere with you.'

He couldn't have reversed that brutally unyielding decision in the space of less than twenty-four hours, could he? And yet if not then why was he here?

The slightest of adjustments in the way that he stood gave away the hint of a change in his mood—for the worse.

'So it really isn't a matter of life or death that I go to Mecjoria and look into the situation for the accession after all?'

As he echoed the description she'd given him, he managed to put a sardonic note on the words that twisted a knife even more disturbingly in her nerves. She didn't know why this was happening, she only knew that suddenly, for some reason, he seemed prepared to toss her a lifeline, one that she would be the greatest fool in the world to ignore.

'All right!'

Not giving herself any more time to think, Ria pushed herself into action, flinging one foot on to the steps and then the other, grabbing at the rail for support, almost tumbling to the ground at Alexei's feet as she reached the top.

What else could she do? She had spent last night wide awake and restless, going over the scene in his house again and again, berating herself for failing so badly, for driving him further away rather than persuading him round to her side. She had cursed herself for bringing her father into the discussion, seeing the black rage and hatred simply thinking of him had brought into his eyes. She had even reached for her phone a couple of times, wondering if she rang him that he might actually listen, and each time she had dropped it back down again, knowing that the man who had turned his back on her and told her to leave so brutally had no room in his mind or his heart for second thoughts or second chances. Today she'd faced the prospect of going back home knowing that everything was lost, and with no idea how she was going to face the future.

And then suddenly this…

'I don't understand.'

She was gasping as if she'd run a mile rather than just up a short flight of steps, but it was tension and not lack of fitness that caught her round her throat, making it impossible to breathe.

But Alexei was clearly in no mood to offer any explanations. Instead with a bruising grip on her arm he steered her out of the sunlight and into the plane where she blinked hard as her eyes adjusted to the change in light.

Once she would have been the one with access to a private plane. Not for her sole use, or even that of her family, but she had sometimes travelled with a member of the royal family, or accompanying her father in his official role. But it had never been like this. The Mecjorian royal plane had been as old-fashioned and stiffly formal as the regime itself, reflecting the views of the old king. This one was a symphony of cool calm, with pale bronze carpets, wide, soft seats just waiting for someone to sink into their creamy leather cushions. Everything was light and space, and spoke of luxury beyond price; and the impact of it hit like a blow, making her head spin.

Once again that unanswerable question pounded at her thoughts. Just why—*why*—would Alexei want Mecjoria, a small, insignificant, run-down Eastern European country, when he had all this? Why would he even spare a thought for the place or the chaos that would swamp the inhabitants if he refused the throne and let it pass to Ivan?

With his hand still on her arm, the heat of his palm burning through the soft pink cotton of her top and into her skin, the power and strength of his body so close beside her was overwhelming and almost shocking. In spite of the fact that he was so casually dressed, he carried himself with the sort of power that few men could show, making her heart kick hard against her ribs in a lethal combination of physical response and apprehension.

'Take a seat.'

Ria was grateful to sink down into the enveloping comfort of the nearest seat, her legs disturbingly unsteady beneath her. The air seemed suddenly too thick to breathe, the roar of the engines as the pilot prepared the plane for flight too loud in her ears so that she couldn't think straight or do anything other than obey him. She was on her way to Mecjoria and, for his own private reasons, Alexei was with her. That and the powerful thrust of the plane as it set off down the runway was more than enough to cope with at the moment.

'Fasten your seatbelt.'

Alexei was clearly not going to take the trouble to enlighten her on anything—not yet anyway, as he took the seat opposite her, long legs stretched out, crossed at the ankles—and settled himself, ready for take-off.

She was dismissed from his thoughts as he turned his head, focussing his attention through the window to where the green of the grass on the side of the runway was now flashing past at an incredible speed as the plane raced towards take-off. Another couple of minutes and the wheels had left the ground, the jet soaring away from the ground and up into the sky. The impact pushed Ria back into her seat, her head against the rest, her hands clutching the arms of her chair. Unexpectedly, unbelievably, she had another chance and she was going to take it if she possibly could.

But that added a whole new burden of worry to the nervousness she was already feeling. Just for a moment her thoughts reeled. Had she done the right thing coming here? Was she justified in putting her own family, her own personal needs, first like this? It was true that she feared the consequences if Ivan took the crown. She dreaded the thought of what it meant for her personally if she had to follow her father's plans for that event, but how did she know if Alexei would be any better? The memory of the stories of his life in London that had been reported in the papers back home came back to haunt her. There had been one where he had been caught unaware, his hand half-lifted to his face to escape the flash of the camera. But he hadn't been quick enough to conceal the fact that he had obviously been in a fight; that his eye was blackened, his nose bloodied.

And of course there had been his neglect of his poor little daughter. A neglect that he hadn't even tried to deny. Was she right in bringing such a man back to Mecjoria—as its king?

But he was the rightful king. That was the one argument she was totally sure of.

The plane had reached its cruising height and had straightened out of the steep climb but Ria's stomach was still knotted in that unnerving tension that the fast ascent, combined with her own inner turmoil, had created. She had a dreadful feeling of no going back, knowing that she could only go forward—though she had no idea where that might lead.

'Would you like a drink? Something to eat?'

It was perfectly polite, the calm enquiry of a courteous host as a slightly raised hand summoned an attendant who jumped to attention as if she had just been waiting for the signal.

'Some coffee would be nice.' She hadn't been able to eat any breakfast before she left for the airport. 'We do have almost five hours to fill.'

'I don't think you need to worry about filling time on this flight,' Alexei told her. 'We'll have plenty to keep us occupied.'

'We will?' It was sharp and tight with a new rush of nerves.

In contrast, Alexei looked supremely relaxed, lounging back in his seat opposite her as he nodded.

'You have…' he checked the workmanlike heavy watch on his wrist '…four hours to convince me that I should even consider taking up the crown of Mecjoria and allowing myself to be declared king.'

'But I thought—I mean—you're here now. And we're heading for…'

The words shrivelled on her tongue as she looked into the cold darkness of his face and saw that there was nothing there to give her confidence that this was all going to work out right.

'I'm here now,' he agreed soberly, dark eyes hooded and shadowed. 'And we are on a flight path for Mecjoria—for the capital. This plane will land there, if only to let you off so you can go and talk to the courtiers who sent you. But that does not mean that I will disembark as well.'

His tone was flat, emotionless, unyielding, and looking into his eyes was like staring into the icy depth of a deep, deep lake, frozen over with a coating of thick black ice, bleak and impenetrable. He had made one tiny concession and that was all he was going to let her have—unless she could convince him otherwise.

'Our estimated time of arrival is five in the afternoon, Mecjorian time. You have until then to persuade me that I should not just turn round and head home as soon as we have let you disembark.'

He meant it, she had no doubt about that, and a sensation like cold slimy footsteps crept down her back. The thought of being so near yet so far curdled in her stomach. The attendant appeared with her coffee and she took refuge in huddling over the cup as if the warmth from the hot liquid might melt the ice that seemed to have frozen right through to her bones. Just when she had thought she could relax, that Alexei was heading for Mecjoria, and taking her with him to return home—if not in triumph then at least with some hope of success and a more positive future for the country—suddenly he had shown that he had been working on a totally different plan.

It didn't help at all that she was sitting opposite the most devastatingly attractive man she had ever seen in her whole life. Her schoolgirl crush on the adolescent Alexei seemed like froth and bubble compared to the raw, gut-deep sensual impact of his adult self on all that was female inside her. If he so much as moved, her senses sprang to life, heat and moisture pooling between her thighs so that she shifted uncomfortably in her seat, crossing and uncrossing her legs restlessly.

'I told you...'

Another smile was a swift flash on and off, one that put no light in his eyes.

'Tell me again.' It was a command, not a suggestion. 'We have plenty of time.'

It was going to be interesting to see if she came up with exactly the same arguments as she had given him yesterday, Alexei reflected. Arguments that would change his way of life; hell, his whole future if the decision he had come to in the middle of the night was anything to go by. He hadn't been able to sleep and had spent long hours surfing the Internet, researching the situation in Mecjoria even more intensely than usual, finding out as much as he possibly could. There was plenty he already knew. In spite of the mask of indifference he had hidden behind when Ria had confronted him, he had kept a careful eye on all that was happening in his father's homeland ever since he and his mother had been exiled from the place. His research had told him that everything she had said was true, but this time, driven to dig more deeply, he had found there was more to it than that. That there was one vital element to this whole succession business that he had never suspected, and that she had not revealed.

And that was something that changed everything.

Why had she not told him the full truth? What did she have to gain from keeping it from him?

In the seat opposite, Ria stirred slightly, the soft sound of her denim-clad legs sliding across each other setting his senses on red alert in a heartbeat. It was hell to sit here with his body hardening in response to just the thought of her being there, so close and yet so far away. He should never have touched her, never have let the feel of the warm velvet of her skin, the scent of her hair, start off the heavy pulse of hunger that was like a thickness in his blood. It stopped him thinking straight and made him *want.* And wanting was going to have to be put aside for now, for a time at least. He had her just where he wanted her, and he wasn't going to let her get away. But first he was going to make her acknowledge that this was the only way that it could be. The sensual pleasure he anticipated would be one thing. Bringing her to admit that she had nowhere else to go would add a whole new dimension of satisfaction to his revenge on the family that had been responsible for his and his mother's exile from the country where they belonged.

'Persuade me.'

With no other alternative, Ria had to go over it all again. The one thing she didn't do was to mention anything about personal involvement. Deep down inside she knew instinctively that that could only act against her. She knew now how much he hated her family, how he would do anything rather than help them in any way. It was perhaps an hour and a half later that she stopped, drawing in a much-needed breath, reaching for the glass of water that had replaced the coffee of earlier. Gulping down the drink she had left ignored as she focussed totally on the man opposite her, she struggled to ease the discomfort of her parched throat as she waited for his response.

It was a long time coming. A long, uncomfortable time as he subjected her to a burning scrutiny. Like her he reached for his crystal tumbler of iced water but the swallow he took was long, slow and indolently relaxed.

'Very interesting,' he drawled, leaning back in his seat, never taking his eyes off her for a moment. 'But you neglected to explain that the situation is not quite as simple as you made out. There's one more thing I want to know.'

'Anything.' She didn't care if she sounded close to desperate. That was how she felt, so why try to hide it at this delicate stage?

'Anything?' There was a definite challenge in the dark-eyed look he slanted in her direction. 'Then tell me about the marriage.'

'The—the marriage…'

Ria's stomach twisted painfully, her discomfort made all the worse by the way that the plane had suddenly hit a patch of turbulence and lurched violently, dropping frighteningly, down and then back up again.

'Yes, the marriage your father has arranged for you. I am the heir to the throne if the individual positions in the hierarchy—the direct line—are considered. On my own, I have the stronger claim—if I want it.'

There it was again, that note of threat that he might refuse the crown, and leave her stranded without a hope of finding any other way out—as she now suspected he had known all along. How he must have enjoyed watching her perform all over again, knowing all the while that he understood the real truth of her position, the cleft stick she was caught in with little hope of escape.

'But you omitted to point out that it is not just Ivan who also has a distant potential claim to the throne.'

The glass he held was placed on the table with deliberate care. The same control showed as he stood up, big and dark and lean, towering over her and making even the space of the luxurious jet feel confined and restricted in a sudden and shocking way. Forced to raise her head to look up at him, she found that the air in the cabin seemed to have thickened and grown heavier.

'You forgot to say…' His tone made it plain that he didn't think for a moment she had forgotten anything. 'that you and Ivan have a unique connection where the crown is concerned. Individually his claim is so much weaker, but *together* you would be almost unassailable.'

Ria could almost feel the blood draining from her face. She must look like a ghost, and that would show him how perfectly he had hit the mark.

'There is no together!'

His gesture might have been flicking away a fly, it was so scornfully dismissive of her protest.

'Are you saying that none of this is true? That Ivan's claim to the throne is clear and open, with no other help needed—and you won't need him to free your father, restore your family fortunes to the way they used to be?'

He made it sound so mercenary. But then what had she expected from a man who so blatantly despised her and every member of her family?

'No—'

There was no togetherness between Ivan and her. Nothing except the one that had been forced on her, that she would have to accept if Alexei didn't listen to her pleas. The prospect of freedom from the future she dreaded that had seemed to open up before her now seemed to be moving further away with every breath she took. Ria pushed herself to her feet, needing the greater strength of a position facing him on a much better level, her green eyes meeting his head-on.

'I mean, yes, it's true that if I marry him his right to the throne is strengthened…'

'Isn't it *when* you marry him?' Alexei slipped in, cold and deadly. 'I understand that the contract has already been signed.'

By her father. Without any consultation or even her knowledge. She had been used as a pawn in the political bargaining.

'I— How did you find out that?' How could he know about the contract her father had made with Ivan, when she had only become aware of it herself just days before?

'I have my sources.'

He'd been up all night, and he'd called in all his contacts, investigating exactly what was behind this sudden desire of hers to have him as king in Mecjoria. All the time she had been talking yesterday—and again just now—he had sensed she was holding something back, keeping something hidden. He had never expected that it would be this.

Once he had found the real explanation he had been unable to think of anything else. Because this turned everything upside down from the way he'd seen everything at first. He'd been convinced that Ria had brought him the document that proved his parents' marriage valid, and that he was the rightful king, because that would give her— and her family—an advantage if he came to the throne. She was softening him up so that he would release her father, restore the family fortunes…

The discovery of the proposed marriage to Ivan Kolosky made a nonsense out of all that. Even more so because she had never said a word about it.

That marriage would give her everything she wanted—
and more. It would make her Queen of Mecjoria and he
knew that had always been Gregor Escalona's deepest
ambition. The reason why he had insisted on his daughter's immaculate behaviour, training her to be the perfect
young royal, controlling every move, every decision she
made. It was the reason why Gregor had betrayed his father's memory by bringing the legitimacy of his marriage
into question. So why had she even brought the marriage
certificate to him in the first place? And why had she
never mentioned the proposed marriage to Ivan?

Last night he had thought he had decided on a way to
play this that would give him retribution for all that had
happened to him and his mother when they had been
exiled from their home, losing every last penny of the
fortune that should have been theirs, his mother's good
name along with it, but at last it seemed that payback was
within his grasp.

But one more discovery and everything had changed.
There was more on offer now. More than he could ever
have dreamed of. He wanted more. And there was one
way he was sure of getting it.

'So now how about you tell me the real truth?'

He saw the wariness in her eyes, the shadow that
crossed her face, and it made him all the more determined to get to the bottom of all of this.

He'd planned on giving her another chance to give him
the real facts this morning, but the truth was that as soon
as she'd started to speak his concentration had been shot
to pieces. All he could focus on was the way she looked,
with that dark auburn hair pulled back into a pony tail so
that it exposed the fine bone structure of her features, the
brilliance of her eyes. Tiny silver earrings sparkled in her
lobes, seeming to catch the flash of her eyes as she leaned

towards him, elegant hands coming up to emphasise her points. The movement of her mouth fascinated him, the soft rose-tinted curve of her lips moving to emphasise what she had to say, the faint sheen of moisture on them making him want to lean forward and kiss her hard and fierce, plunge his tongue into her open mouth and taste her again as he had done the night before.

She hadn't said anything about Ivan and that made him grit his teeth tight against the questions that needed answers. Now he couldn't look at her without thinking about Ivan—and about her with Ivan. Acid rose in his throat at just the thought of it and the blood heated in his veins, making his heart punch harshly, a pulse throbbing near his temple. The thought of her with anyone else— anyone but him—was too much to take. But with *Ivan*...

And that feeling—that fury of jealousy, the hunger, that sensation of being alive that had been missing in his life for so long—told him so much. It erased the numbness he had been living—existing—with, the deadness that had invaded his world since the loss of first his father, and later the baby daughter he had barely started to get to know. He hadn't felt this way in years and he wanted it back. And he wanted Ria, as the woman who had given sensation back to him.

'That if you can't persuade me to take the throne, then you are tied into a contract to marry Ivan, and so strengthen his claim to the inheritance. Tell me—why not just go with the marriage to Ivan? After all it would make you Queen of Mecjoria.'

'My father might want that, perhaps, but not me!'

But this was what her father had been training her for, the summit of her family's ambitions. And if being queen had been her ambition too then all she had had to do was to leave the marriage document where it was.

'You don't want to be queen?'

'And you want to be king?' she tossed back, earning herself a faint, twisted smile and an ironical inclination of his head in acknowledgement of the hit. But she hadn't spent the past ten years exiled from the country he was now supposed to rule.

'Where was the marriage certificate found?' he demanded now, wanting to get at the truth.

It was a question she didn't want to answer, that much was obvious, and yet he didn't think she was trying to deceive him. Sharp white teeth dug into the softness of her lower lip, and he was suddenly assailed by the impulse to protest at the damage she was doing to the delicate skin. Instead he made himself repeat the question in order to divert his thoughts.

'Where?'

Her delicate chin came up defiantly, gold-green eyes blazing into his.

'My father had it all the time. It was in his safe when I checked in there after he was arrested. My mother begged me to look for something that might help.' Once more her teeth worried at her lip as she obviously had to push herself to go on. 'I also found the contract between him and Ivan then.'

'You hadn't known before?'

He could well believe that of Gregor, conspiring with anyone he could in secret. But would he really sign his daughter's life away without her knowing?

'I knew nothing about it!' There was the tremor of real horror in her voice.

'Your father can't force you into this.'

Her soft mouth twisted into an expression of resignation—or was it bitterness?

'In Mecjoria, royalty—even unimportant royalty like

me—don't expect to marry for love. Dynastic contracts matter so much more than personal feelings. And right now peace is what matters. I meant everything I said about the possible consequences if the succession isn't easy and smooth. If not you, then Ivan is the only logical candidate.'

'But neither of us wants Ivan to take the throne.'

'No, we both know what a disaster that would be.'

The way she rushed to agree with him, the tone in which she did it, scraped roughly across his exposed skin. The mood of calm and control that had come from feeling that he had her just where he wanted her was starting to fray at the edges, coming unravelled with every breath he drew in. Last night she had claimed she'd given him every argument she possessed but she'd kept this vital point carefully back. And hiding that point showed him just how much she had wanted to influence him into agreeing to her plans without ever knowing the full story.

She had only forced herself to come to him because she had no possible alternative. Because her country needed it now that she had proof that he wasn't illegitimate, that he was truly as royal as she was—more. But because she needed it too. Would she have told him about the document if she hadn't also been able to use it to her own advantage? Because she wasn't prepared to sacrifice her own freedom in order to rescue the place herself. She hadn't reckoned on him ever finding out about the proposed union between her family and Ivan's—at least not until it was too late.

'So you will do as I ask? You will take the throne?'

There was a very different mood in the words, with a whole new sparkle in those eyes, a lift to the warm curve of her mouth. She thought she had got what she wanted from him—that she had worked out a way of ensuring an heir to the throne but without her having to tie herself into marriage with the only other candidate for the crown. So that he could live the restricted, controlled life of a royal while she kept her freedom and could live as she pleased.

He felt used, manipulated. But it didn't stop him wanting her.

And wanting her didn't stop him recognising that her father had done a good job in training her up to be a queen—whoever's wife she might be. From acknowledging what an asset she would be as anyone's consort—and it didn't have to be Ivan's. He didn't want her to be Ivan's any more than she did.

'I could be persuaded,' he said slowly.

The light that her smile brought to her eyes almost made him lose his grip on his temper as icy rage swamped him. She thought she was winning and that pushed him dangerously close to the edge. All he wanted was to pull the rug out from under her, let her know that he already had all her secrets and he fully intended to use them to his own advantage.

But there was more pleasure in letting things out bit by bit than in dumping everything on her all at once.

'I will do as you ask,' he said slowly, keeping his eyes locked on her face to enjoy watching her reaction. 'But there are terms.'

CHAPTER SEVEN

'TERMS?' RIA ECHOED the word on a note of pure horror.
'What sort of terms?'

'Terms that you and I need to agree between us. We
need to plan the future.'

'But we have no future…'

She looked so appalled at the thought of any more
time spent with him. She would even refute the flames
that burned between them if she could. It was there in the
darkness that clouded her eyes, the way she was fighting
to deny there was anything between them.

'You think?'

Their eyes clashed, held for a moment. Hers were the
first to drop as she recognised the unyielding challenge
in his.

'What terms?' she asked.

So much of the attack had gone out of her voice, leaving it weakened and deflated. Was it possible that she
suspected what was coming? A dark wave of satisfaction
flooded through his veins.

'I will be king—on the same conditions as it would
have been for Ivan to take the throne.'

It took a moment for her to register just what he had
said, several more to have the words sink in and the meaning behind the flat statement become real. He watched

every change of emotion spill across her face, the way that it tightened the muscles around her mouth and jaw, made her elegant throat contract on a hard swallow. One that he felt echo in his own throat as he fought the urge to press his lips to the pale skin of her neck and follow the movement down.

'But those conditions were only for Ivan...' Ria stammered.

She still hadn't quite realised just what he was talking about. Either that or she didn't want to accept that he could actually mean it.

'It's that or nothing. And I wish you joy being Ivan's wife.'

'And the country?' She'd found some new strength from somewhere, enough to challenge him. 'Are you prepared for the civil unrest that will follow if you walk away now?'

That caught him up sharp. Took him back to the darkness of the night where his memories of his father's dying words had forced him to face the prospect of a future in which the repercussions of his decisions, his actions, reverberated out into the coming days and years with the possibility of guilt and the dreadful responsibility of the wrong choices made in anger. He'd been there once before and it was a hell he had no wish to return to. He'd let someone—not just anyone, he'd let *Belle*—down because of that anger once and even after years the stab of memory, of guilt, was brutal. Was he going to do it again? Let down a whole nation? Thousands of families—hundreds of Belles?

He'd be letting down his father too if he let Ivan take over the throne, ignoring the warning Mikail had given him.

If he stayed angry, that was always the risk. But this,

this was a decision he had made in cold blood. To defeat Ivan. And her father. And to have Ria at his side as his queen and in his bed.

'There is one way to ensure that doesn't happen. And to keep Ivan from the crown at the same time. Believe me, I feel the same as you do at the thought of him ruling Mecjoria.'

She should have expected this, Ria told herself. She knew how much he and Ivan had loathed each other back in the days when they had all lived at the court when the old king had been alive. She should have remembered how the other man had sneered at everything Alexei did, and had made appallingly insulting remarks about his mother—the commoner who had dared to think that she could become a member of the royal family.

A few moments before she had been afraid of the direction in which his thoughts seemed to be heading, but this... Was it possible that he meant that they could work together on this? The thought of doing something with Alexei rather than fighting him for everything made her heart twist on a little judder of excitement. She had hoped to have her friend Alexei back in her life. She had never dreamed it might actually happen.

But did her friend Alexei still exist? Did she want him to? That friend had never made her feel this way. This very adult, very female, very sexual way.

'Exactly what terms are you talking about?' Deep down, she feared she knew but she couldn't believe it.

'I told you. I will accept the throne on the same conditions as would have applied if Ivan was to inherit. The ones your father agreed—and it seems you were prepared to go along with.'

Ria's head went back, her eyes widening. The ice-blooded statement slammed into her mind with the force of a lightning bolt, making her head spin sickeningly. It was like reliving the moment she had found the signed agreement amongst her father's papers, but somehow worse. She had always known her father was an arch manipulator—but Alexei? She'd gone to him with such hope, but now it seemed that she was trapped even more than before. And her own impulsive declaration of just moments before had just entangled her further in this dark spider's web.

'Marriage.' It was dull and flat, the death knell to the hopes she had only just allowed to creep into her mind. 'The terms of that agreement were marriage.'

He didn't respond; didn't even incline his head in any indication of agreement. Just blinked hard, once, and then those black, black eyes were fixed on her face, as unmoving and unyielding as the rest of him.

'You want me to *marry* you?' The words tasted like poison on her tongue. 'Just like that? I won't—I can't!'

'Not what you'd hoped for?' he enquired sardonically, the corners of his mouth curling into a cynical trace of a smile. 'The prospect doesn't appeal as much as being married to Ivan?'

'It doesn't appeal at all.'

The truth was that it was far worse.

She had never had any feeling except of fear and dislike for Ivan. Hadn't once loved him. Had never dreamed of the prospect of a future with him. Hadn't let herself imagine the possibility of loving and being loved by him as she had once dreamed of happening with Alexei.

So now to be proposed to… No, not proposed to— *propositioned*—so coldly, so heartlessly by him tore at her heart until she thought it must be bleeding to death inside.

She didn't want to look at him, couldn't bear to look into his face, and yet she found that she could look nowhere else. Those deep, dark eyes seemed to draw her in; the sculpted beauty of his mouth was a sensual temptation that she fought to resist. Once she'd dreamed of being kissed by those lips. Lying awake in her adolescent bed, she had imagined how it would feel, longed for it to be reality. Last night that dream had come true. She knew now how that mouth kissed, knew how it tasted, and the reality had been as sensually wonderful as she had hoped. It had left her with a hunger to feel those sensual lips on all the other, more intimate parts of her body. But all the time it had been tainted with a poison that threatened to destroy her emotionally.

And once she had dreamed of a marriage proposal from those lips too. But not like this.

'You can't really believe this is possible.'

'Why not? You've already admitted that neither of us wants Ivan on the throne—but if we made a pact to work together we could ensure that never happens, ensure peace for Mecjoria. You say I am the rightful king—you would make a good queen. After all, that was what your father trained you for.'

'I brought you that document because you are the rightful king!'

'And because you didn't want to marry Ivan.'

How could she deny that when it was nothing but the truth?

'My father had delusions of grandeur.' She tried to focus on his face but his powerful features blurred before her eyes. 'That's not the same as tying myself to someone I barely know.'

'You would have agreed to just this with Ivan.' Alexei pushed the point home. 'You said yourself that the royal family doesn't expect to marry for love.'

No, but they could dream of it—and she had dreamed…
Dreams that were now crashing in pieces around her.

'You'd simply be exchanging one political marriage
for another. What if I promise your father's freedom too?'

'You'd do that?' It was something she'd thought she'd
have to give up on, no matter how much her mother had
begged her to plead for Gregor's release.

'For you as my queen—yes, I'd do it. Oh, I don't expect a wedding right here and now—or even one as soon
as we land. I have the proclamation—the accession—to
deal with first.'

He actually sounded as if he thought that he was making some huge concession. The truth was that in his mind,
he *was* making that concession, obviously. He would give
her a breathing space—a short, barely tolerable breathing
space. But the ruthless, cold determination stamped on his
face told her that was all she would get. And it would be
only the barest minimum of time that he would allow her.

'Well, that's a relief!' Shock and horror made her voice
rigid and cold as she fought against showing the real depth
of her feelings. Her shoulders were so tight that they hurt
and her mouth ached with the control she was imposing
on it. 'Do you expect me to thank you?'

'No more than you should expect me to thank you for
cooperating in this.'

'I haven't said yet that I will cooperate!'

'But you will.' It was coldly, cruelly confident. No
room for argument or doubt. 'And you have to admit that
we have far more between us than you would ever have
had with Ivan.'

'I— No!'

She didn't know how she had managed to sit still so
long. She only knew that she couldn't do it now. She
pushed herself to her feet, up and away from him. From

his oppressive closeness, the dangerous warmth of his hard, lean frame, the disturbing scent of his skin that tantalised her senses. She wanted to go further—so much further—but in the cabin there wasn't enough space to run and hide. And at the same time her need to get away warred with a sensual compulsion to turn back into his atmosphere, to throw herself close against him and recapture that wild enticement that had swamped her totally on the previous night.

'Sit down!'

It was pure command, harsh and autocratic, flung at her so hard that she almost felt the words hit her in the back.

It took all her control to turn and face him, bringing her chin up in defiance so as not to let him see the turmoil she was feeling.

'What's this then, Alexei? Practising for when you're king?'

His scowl was dark and dangerous, making her shift uncomfortably where she stood, the movement aggravated by the lurch of the aircraft so that she almost lost her footing. Stubbornly she refused to reach out and grab the back of the nearest seat for support, however much she needed it.

'According to you, I will need all the practice I can get,' he shot back, the ice in his tone taking the temperature in the cabin down ten degrees or more. 'A commoner jumped up from the gutter, with no true nobility to speak of.'

'That was Ivan, not me!' Ria protested.

'Ivan—your prospective husband.'

She knew he was watching for her instinctive shudder but all the same she couldn't hold it back in spite of knowing how much she was giving away.

'But there is some truth in there—so there's another

reason why this marriage will work out,' Alexei continued coldly. 'I can give you the status and the fortune you want...'

Ria opened her mouth in a rush, needing to tell him that she didn't want either. But a swift, brutal glare stopped her mid-breath.

'And you—well you can be the civilising influence I need. You can teach me how to handle the court procedures—the etiquette I'll need to function as king.'

He almost sounded as if he meant it. Was it possible? Could he really be feeling a touch of insecurity here— and being prepared to admit to it? There was no way it seemed possible. But that twist to his mouth tugged on something deep inside her.

'But you grew up at court—for some years at least. You must have learned...'

'The basics, perhaps. But most of it I have forgotten. I didn't exactly see any use for it in the life I'm living now. And, as your father was so determined to point out, I was never really civilised.' The bite of acid in the words seemed to sear into Ria's skin, making her rub her hands down her arms to ease the burning sensation. 'Not quite blue-blooded enough.'

'Well, I'm sure you'll remember it quickly—without any help from me.'

'Ah, but I'm sure I'll pick it up faster with you at my side—as my partner and consort. My wife.'

'I won't do it.' She shook her head violently, sending her hair flying around her face.

Another lurch of the plane, more violent this time, made her stumble. She almost expected to hear the sound of shattering dreams falling to the floor as the movement coincided with the loss of all those hopes she had once had for the word 'wife' coming from this man.

'You can't make me.'

'I won't have to. You've done it to yourself already.'

As Ria watched in stunned disbelief, Alexei seemed to change mood completely, subsiding into his seat again and relaxing back against the soft, buttery leather.

'Let's see now—where shall I begin? Ah yes—the eruminium mines.'

She knew then what was coming, acknowledging an aching sense of despair as she watched him lift one long-fingered hand and tick off his points across it one by one. All the arguments she had ever brought to bear on the subject of his possible accession to the throne, all the reasons she had given why he had to take the crown, to prevent Ivan doing so, to protect the country and to avoid civil unrest. They were now all repeated but turned upside down, twisted back against her, landing sharp as poisoned darts in her bruised soul. Alexei used them to provide evidence of the fact that she had no choice. That she had to do as he demanded or prove herself a liar and a traitor to everything she had held dear.

And break her mother's heart and health—possibly her mind too—if she left her father mouldering in his prison cell, as she had feared she was going to do when she had failed to bring Alexei back with her.

She had no choice. Or, rather, she did have a choice but it was between being trapped into this marriage and honouring the contract her father had made with Ivan. An arranged marriage to a man she loathed and feared. A man who made her skin crawl. Or a cold-blooded union to Alexei who would give her a marriage without love. A marriage with no heart. A marriage of shattered dreams.

'Do I have to go on?' Alexei enquired.

'Don't trouble yourself.' She dripped the sarcasm so

strongly that she fully expected it to form a pool at her feet. 'I think I can guess the rest.'

She couldn't see any way out of it. He had tied her up with her own arguments, left her without a leg to stand on. Looking at him now—at the ice that glazed his eyes, the cold, hard set of his face—the momentary hesitation, if that was what she had seen earlier, now seemed positively laughable. She had to have been imagining things.

'Good, so now we understand each other. I said *sit down,* Ria.' One lean hand pointed to the seat she had vacated.

Fury spiked, making her see sparks before her eyes.

'Don't order me around, Alexei! You don't have the right.'

'Oh, but I do,' he inserted smoothly. 'That is, I do if I am to do as you want. As king I can command and you...'

'You're not king yet.'

'Perhaps not, but we are approaching Mecjoria.' A nod towards the window indicated the way that the deep blue of the sea over which they had been flying had now given way to a wild coastline, a range of mountains. 'Any moment now we will be coming in to land. You should sit down and fasten your seatbelt.'

Was that the quirk of a smile at the corners of his mouth? Knowing she was beaten, Ria forced herself forward, dumping down into the seat with her teeth digging hard into her tongue to hold back the wave of anger that almost escaped her. Focussing her attention on snapping on her seatbelt, she addressed the man opposite with her head still bent.

'I had it wrong earlier, Alexei. You don't need any practice, you have the autocratic tyrant down pat—absolutely perfect. No need for anyone at your side to support you or to instruct you in any of the etiquette needed.'

'Perhaps so.'

His tone was infuriatingly relaxed, disturbingly assured.

'But you know as well as I do that the one way to settle this accession situation once and for all and to bring peace to the country for the future is to have someone with an unassailable right on the throne. Mecjoria rejected me once—what's to stop them doing it again? But you as queen will bring that unassailable right along with you. You can choose to give it to me—or to Ivan.'

Choose. There was the word that hit home, sticking in her throat like a piece of broken glass.

She didn't *have* a choice. She had set out on this mission to make sure that Ivan didn't become king—and that she didn't have to marry him. She'd achieved one aim but only by painting herself into a corner to do it. Alexei would be king, if she married him. She could escape the loveless arranged marriage to Ivan only if she agreed to a different one with Alexei.

Out of the frying pan and into the fire.

The way that the plane swayed and jumped, turning into a new course, and the change in the sound of its engines brought home to her the fact that they were circling, ready to approach the airport and the runway on which the jet would land very soon.

This plane will land there, if only to let you off... Alexei's words came back to haunt her. *But that does not mean that I will disembark as well.*

Marriage to Ivan or marriage to Alexei? She knew which one was better for the country—but right now she was thinking on a very personal level and that made everything so very different. The thought of both marriages made her shudder inside, but with very different responses.

One was a sense of cold horror of being tied to a bully like Ivan. For the other, the instinctive fear she was a prey to blended with a shiver of dangerous, treacherous excitement. The memory of last night and the rush of raw, carnal response that had flooded through her when Alexei had taken her in his arms, when he had kissed her, made it impossible to think beyond how it might feel to know that again.

The marriage would be a pretence but that would be real. She wouldn't be able to hide the hunger she felt or even attempt to disguise it.

'You call that a choice? You know I can't let Ivan take the crown. The results for the country would be so appalling.'

'And how do you know that I will not be as bad?'

She could only stare at him, asking herself the same question and finding no answer for it. She knew about Ivan's alliances with dangerous governments, his profligate habits, his cold nature, but the reality was that she knew nothing about Alexei other than the reports in the papers she had read. But she did know that like her he wanted to make sure Ivan didn't inherit.

'For me or for the country?'

'I thought we had agreed that we were largely irrelevant in this. It is the future of Mecjoria and her people that matters. It isn't personal.'

But he had made it personal with this cold-blooded proposition.

'It certainly isn't personal. It's dynastic necessity, pure and simple.

'You don't need to look as if you're facing imminent execution, Ria,' Alexei continued dryly. 'I'm not a monster. I don't expect you to take your marriage vows as soon as we land. For now all that I ask of you is that you

take your place as my promised bride. My devoted fiancée,' he added pointedly. 'No one must doubt that this is
a real relationship. A whirlwind romance perhaps, but
very definitely real.'

Could the atmosphere in the luxurious cabin get any
colder? Ria asked herself as she swallowed down his statement. Could there be any less emotion in his tone?

A sudden violent jolt, the screech of brakes, the rumble
of tyres on the runway brought her to the realisation that
they were down, had landed and the plane was now taxi-
ing towards the airport building. They had arrived; they
were on Mecjorian soil.

Peering out of the window, she saw the sun-baked
countryside that was familiar, the range of mountains
over in the distance, their tops covered in a coating of
snow. It should have felt like coming home. It was home.
She had only been away for less than a week, one hundred and twenty hours at the most, but it seemed that everything had changed totally. Her life was no longer her
own; her future had taken a totally different path from
the one she had believed it would follow. She had thought
that she would persuade Alexei to take the throne and then
she could quietly retreat into the background, live her life
in private. Now it seemed that instead she was going to
have to be up front and centre.

With Alexei.

Awkwardly she fumbled with her seatbelt, feeling imprisoned, tied down and needing desperately to be free.
But the way her future was going it seemed she would
never be free. She had gone to Alexei in the hope of being
freed from the future that her father had planned for her
but instead she had come up against a man who was even
more ruthless and controlling than Gregor had ever been.

As a result she had jumped out of the frying pan and right into the fire. And she faced the prospect of being burned alive as a result.

CHAPTER EIGHT

'LET ME...'

Alexei had already dispensed with his seatbelt with clinical efficiency and he was standing beside her, his hand reaching out for the awkward buckle on hers. When he bent his head to deal with it the softness of his dark hair brushed against her cheek, caressing her skin and sending shivers of response down her spine. She could smell the citrus shampoo on his hair, the clean scent of his skin, and up this close she could see how already, even at this stage of the day, the dark shadow of the growth of beard marked his cheeks.

Her heart thudded in her throat and she had to sit back and clench her hands into tight fists down at her sides to stop herself from giving in to the urge to reach out and stroke his cheek, feel the contrast between warm satin skin and the rough scrape of hair against her fingertips. Heat flooded every part of her, pooling at the spot just between her legs, so close to where those strong, square-tipped fingers had just completed their task.

Would this instant, shockingly primitive reaction to his nearness make the future he had dictated to her so much easier or so very much harder? She didn't know and with sparks of response flaring in her brain, spots rising in front of her eyes, she couldn't even begin to think of finding a way to answer her own question. She didn't even know if she could get to her feet, the muscles in her legs, even her bones, seeming to have melted in the burn of response that possessed her.

'I can't...' she began but then, afraid of what she might be revealing, swallowed down the admission and changed it to, 'I don't think I can do this. How does a devoted fiancée—your devoted fiancée—behave?'

'You need to ask that? Here...'

Those strong hands came down again, clamping over hers as he straightened up. He hauled her upwards, lifting her to her feet, so fast so roughly that she fell against him, her breasts thrust into the hard, muscled planes of his chest, her face pressed to the lean column of his throat, her senses swimming from immediate sensual overload.

'Of course I need to ask!' Her physical response thickened her tone, making it husky and raw, alien in her own ears. 'I'm not your fiancée—nor am I devoted to you. We have nothing between us.'

'Nothing?' His laughter made it only too plain what he thought of that. 'Lady, if this is nothing...'

His dark head came down fast and hard, those beautiful lips finding hers and clamping tight against her mouth, crushing hers back against her teeth so that she could only gasp in shocked response.

As a kiss it was cold and cruel, more like a punishment than a caress, but appallingly it didn't matter. She didn't care, couldn't think, could only feel. And the feeling that was uppermost in her thoughts, pounding through her body, was a raw hunger, a desperate need for this—and so much more. She would have flung her hands up around his neck, bringing his head down even closer, to deepen and prolong that burning pressure, but the way he still held her prevented that. She couldn't hold back and she crushed her mouth against his, strained her body closer, feeling the heat and hardness of his erection that pushed against the cradle of her pelvis, telling her of his desire and feeding her own until she was swimming on a heated tide of longing, losing herself in him.

The moment when he broke off the kiss, snatched his mouth from hers, dropped her back down on to her feet— feet that she hadn't even been aware had left the floor— was like a brutal slap to her face. His name almost escaped her in a cry of shocked distress but she dragged her hands from his and flung them up and over her mouth to hold back the revealing sound.

'I think that showed you—showed both of us—how this will work. You say you don't know how to do this but it's so easy. I want you...'

Reaching out, he stroked a finger down the side of her cheek, watching intently as in spite of herself she shivered, her eyes closing in instinctive response.

'And I can have you if I want.'

That brought her eyes flying open again to stare, shocked, into his.

'No!'

He ignored her furious protest. 'Because you want me just as much. You responded. More than responded. You know as I do that if we'd been somewhere more private then things would have gone so much further.'

Breathing unevenly, he smoothed a hand over his face, brushed the other down his body to straighten the shirt her actions had creased, pulling it from his trousers at his waist.

'Perhaps it's best that things can't go any further now— before I do something that we'll both regret.'

'You've already done something I regret—something I wish had never happened!'

Was it the fact that it was a lie that made her voice so shrill? Or the way that her body was still struggling with the aftershocks of the reaction his kiss had sparked off in her, sparks fizzing along every nerve, burning up in her blood?

'Really? Then if that's the case, you'll not want this, either.'

She knew what was coming, and the tiny part of her mind that was still rational told her to step back, move away. Fast. But that tiny part was totally submerged in the burning flood of sensual need that swamped common sense, drowning it in the heat of the hunger that still throbbed deep inside. She saw the change in his eyes, the switch from ice to smoky shadows that matched her own mood, and her breath caught in her throat, her lips parting, ready for the very different kiss she knew he planned.

And the kiss she really wanted.

This time it was warm and gentle. It gave instead of taking. His mouth caressed hers, teased, tantalised, tempting it further open to allow the intimate invasion of his tongue. The cool, fresh taste of him was like a powerful aphrodisiac exploding against her lips, totally intoxicating, instantly addictive.

She melted into that kiss, almost swooning against him as the throb of desire took all the strength from her legs, made them feel like damp cotton wool beneath her. And when Alexei's arms came round her it only added to the sensual overload that had her at its mercy. The heat and scent of his body was like the burn of incense in her nostrils making her head swim.

This was the kiss she had always dreamed of, the kiss she had been waiting for all her life. The kiss she had once lain awake imagining long into the night as she felt the awakening of her female sexuality It was a kiss that made her know what it felt like to be a woman.

A woman who had found the man she wanted most in all of the world.

A woman who had discovered the man she…

Oh no! *No, no, no!*

Panic-stricken she froze, jerked back, tore herself away from him. What was she thinking? Where had that come from? How had she let that thought—that terrible, foolish, dangerous thought—creep into her mind?

Was she really so weak that she was allowing her adolescent self to resurface with all her foolish, gullible dreams, the fantasies she had indulged in when she couldn't face reality? The fictions she had created for herself when she had let herself pretend that perhaps one day, Alexei, the boy she had had such a heavyweight crush on, would turn to her and want her as a man would want a woman.

Well, yes, he wanted her now, there was no denying that. And she wanted him. He was right, he could have her if he wanted her. There was no way she was going to be able to resist him if he turned on the true high-octane power of his sensuality, the enticement of the seduction she knew he could channel without trying. But was she going to mistake the white-hot burn of adult sexuality for anything more?

This was the first real experience of true lust she had ever known and it seemed it had the power to burn away some much-needed brain cells, foolishly allowing her to confuse it with real feelings—emotions that her younger, naïve sense had once dreamed of knowing.

'No.'

Alexei had felt her withdrawal and his voice seemed to echo her thoughts, but so much more assuredly, calm and controlled—disturbingly so, considering the fires that had just blazed between them, the sparks that still seemed to sizzle in the air.

'No—we can't take this any further now.'

Shockingly he dropped another kiss on her upturned face. A brief, casual, almost affectionate kiss on her cheek. And the easiness of his response, the light-heartedness of his touch, rocked her even more than her own shattered thoughts of a moment before. They were kisses of certainty, relaxed, almost careless. The kisses of a man who knew that he could get exactly what he wanted—whenever he wanted—so that he didn't have to take too much trouble now.

'Too much to do. A reception committee outside.'

'Really?'

Knocked even more off-balance, Ria twisted on her heel, still within the confines of his arms, and bent slightly to look out the window.

Someone must have radioed ahead, informing the airport authorities—and more—of their planned arrival. And that someone must have announced not just that Alexei's private jet requested permission to land—but that Alexei Joachim Sarova, Crown Prince and future King of Mecjoria, was arriving back in his country, ready to take possession of the throne. There was a fleet of sleek black cars drawn up at the far side of the tarmac, smoked glass, bullet-proof windows, black bodyworks gleaming in the sun. A small Mecjorian flag fluttered on the bonnet of the lead vehicle and someone had rolled out a red carpet across the runway, leading to the bottom of the flight of steps that had now been brought to the door of the plane. A door that a member of the flight crew was hurrying to unlock, to let them out.

'We're here,' Alexei said. 'I'm here. This is what you wanted.'

What she wanted. He was going to make his claim for the throne; and that could only mean that he believed she had agreed to his conditions.

But why shouldn't he think that? Hadn't she given him every indication that she had accepted his terms—welcomed them if her response to his kiss was anything to go by?

After all, what other choice did she have? If she wanted Alexei to take the throne instead of Ivan then she had to go along with what he demanded of her. She had to marry him, become his queen. It was either that or marry Ivan, and the way that her blood ran cold at just the thought was enough to tell her that somewhere along the line she had decided to go along with Alexei's proposal even though she had no recollection of ever rationally doing so. She had no other possible alternative.

Turning back from the window, Alexei looked down into her face, dark eyes probing hers.

'We can make this work, Ria,' he said sombrely. 'Together we can do what's best for Mecjoria.'

Did he read anything else in her face? She would never know, but something made him pause, then go on to add, 'You're right that the royal family doesn't expect to marry for love—and I'm not offering that. I can't love you. I loved once—adored her... Lost her.'

Something darkened his face, his eyes. Something reaching out from the past and coiling round his memory, Ria realised as he went on.

Mariette. He meant Mariette, the dark-haired beauty who had been the mother of his child, who had had a total breakdown when the baby died and had ended up in a psychiatric hospital. Refusing ever to see him again.

'I'll never feel like that again. But as my queen you would be my equal. My consort. And I know you'll be a fine queen. How can you not when your father has trained you for this almost from the moment you were born?'

He must have known how the mention of her father would make her react because he waited as she tried to look away, to look anywhere but into his stunning face. Once again he touched her cheek very softly.

'We'll finish this later.'

It was his total assurance that terrified her. Particularly when she knew she had only herself to blame. Hadn't she practically flung herself into his arms like a sex-starved adolescent who had only been kissed for the very first time?

Well, yes, she wasn't going to deny the desire—the hunger—she felt when he kissed her. But knowing she wanted him was one thing, tying herself to him in the sort of cold-blooded dynastic marriage she had hoped to escape from totally another.

'Later...'

It was all that she could manage as someone knocked on the cabin door and she found herself released so swiftly that she stumbled backwards and away from him. The speed with which he discarded her and turned his attention to other matters, reaching for his jacket, shrugging it on, smoothing a hand over his hair, made her feel like some dirty little secret to be kept hidden away until he had time for her again. He had her cooperation in the bag, he believed, and now he wanted to focus on the reason why he was—why they were both—here.

Reaction setting in made her vision blur, her hands shake, as she collected her own coat and her bag. She couldn't look at Alexei, couldn't bear to see the dark certainty, the satisfaction that she knew must show on his face. She wanted to get out of here, get her feet back down on the ground in more ways than one.

As she reached the door of the plane she was ahead of him. Just a couple of steps but enough. In the doorway at the top of the steps she suddenly realised, all her training kicking in, so that she hesitated, stopped. Reality hit home with the truth of who he now was. Carefully she took that couple of steps back and out of the way.

'Sir,' she said, resisting the urge to drop a curtsey even if only to defy him, to prove that he might have her in a cleft stick, but she wasn't going down without a fight. She was still her own woman and she would hang on to that for as long as she could.

She saw that elegant mouth twitch slightly, curling at the corners in a way that told her he knew only too well what was in her mind and a brief inclination of his head acknowledged everything unspoken that had passed between them. A moment later he was past her, standing in the doorway, looking down at the reception committee waiting for him, before stepping out into the warmth of the evening air.

As he went down the steps to the tarmac with cameras flashing like wild lightning in the distance, warning them of what was to come, what was inevitable now that the prodigal prince had come home, she spotted one moment when he paused, just for the space of a heartbeat, and squared his shoulders like a man accepting his destiny and going to meet his future. He hadn't wanted this, she recalled. He had practically thrown her out of his house when she had first put the proposition to him. Whatever else she might think of him, she could see that unlike Ivan, who wanted the crown for the prestige, the power, and of course the huge wealth that came with it,

Alexei appeared to have totally different reasons for going ahead with this.

Together we can do what's best for Mecjoria.

Whatever else was between them was personal—*this* was for the country's future. And at least on that she and Alexei were in agreement. But it—with her involvement—had taken away his freedom, the life he had lived up to now. His existence would never be the same again, and knowing the position she was in now, with her own freedom given up to secure peace for the country, Ria felt she understood that on a much deeper level than when she had got on a plane here at this same airport to go and try to persuade him to do just this.

So when he paused at the foot of the step, stopping before he actually set foot on Mecjorian land—his country—she spotted it at once. She was there so close behind him that they were almost touching, his sudden hesitation making her almost slam into him from behind. And when he half-turned, dark eyes meeting hers just for a moment, and he held out his hand to her, she moved forward quickly, putting her fingers into his without hesitation or uncertainty. She felt the power of his touch close round her, holding firm and strong, and welcomed it as she walked down beside him, stepping onto Mecjorian soil together.

It was only when she looked back at that moment later, when it was played over and over on national TV, seeing it from the view of the reception committee of government ministers and army top brass lined up beside the red carpet waiting to greet Alexei, that she saw it properly. Saw how clearly it demonstrated that she had made her choice even before she had actually done so rationally within her own thoughts. That she had cast in her lot with Alexei, and without ever saying so had agreed to the future that he had decreed for both of them.

CHAPTER NINE

TOGETHER.

The word seemed to have taken up permanent residence inside Ria's head, mocking her with the memories of the day they had arrived in Mecjoria and the thoughts she had let herself consider then.

Together. She had let herself believe that Alexei had meant that there was a together in all this. That she and Alexei were working to the same ends. That her role as his fiancée might mean that she would actually be by his side, that they could be partners in this.

That he might actually need her just a little bit.

But it seemed that, having announced their engagement and presented her to the court, to the country, as his prospective bride, he had lost interest. There had been the moment when they had set foot on the red carpet, when the army officers, the dignitaries, had moved forward, bowed, saluted, address him as 'Your Majesty' and she had known that this was after all coming true.

Then Alexei had acknowledged their greetings, shaken hands, all the time holding on to hers so tightly that his grip felt like a manacle around her wrist. She had had to move with him; it was either that or create an ugly little scene as she tried to break away. She had to endure the fusillade of camera flashes, the frankly curious and assessing stares of everyone who was there—the ones who knew of her father's fall from grace, his imprisonment, her own loss of any title and status at the court as a result.

And then, at last, just before they headed for the waiting cars, Alexei had finally announced the reason why she was there.

'Gentlemen,' he had said in a voice that carried clear and strong in spite of the wicked breeze that was swirling round them now. 'Let me present to you my fiancée—and future queen—the Grand Duchess Honoria Maria Escalona…'

And with that her place in all this was fixed, settled once and for all. Her title it seemed was restored to her, her place in society reinstated. But she was trapped even more tightly in the web of intrigue and plotting that had created this situation in the first place. The speed and conviction with which it had happened made her head spin.

But once they were back in Mecjoria it seemed that everything she had been anticipating hadn't happened. Nothing might have changed for all the difference it made in her relationship with Alexei. He didn't even seem to want her sexually any more. She had been convinced that he would press home the advantage he'd made it clear he knew he had while they were on the plane. But it appeared that as soon as he had her on his side for the future of Mecjoria and had introduced her as his fiancée, so putting her firmly in the limelight and in the place he wanted her at his side, he seemed to have lost interest.

She had been settled in a beautiful suite in the huge, golden-stoned palace high on the hill above the capital. A far more beautiful and luxurious suite than she had ever enjoyed on her rare visits there in the past. Her clothes, her personal belongings, had been brought from her home and delivered to her room, and she had been left to settle in.

Alone.

Later she had been sent a series of instructions—details of where she was expected to be and when. There were dinners, receptions, public appearances. There had been a whole new wardrobe provided for these events too with visits from top couturiers, fittings for every sort of dress, shoes, jewellery imaginable. She was now dressed more glamorously than ever in life before. But then she was used to this. It was how it had always been with her father. What was different was the way that, once he had let her know where she was to be, Alexei left everything else up to her. Her father had wanted more control than that. For each event she had been given a series of commands disguised as strict guidelines, as to what she was to do, when she was to appear, what she was to wear, the subjects she should read up on in order to be able to talk about. Alexei made no such demands; and she valued the confidence, the trust, he put in her that way.

She had performed her duty at Alexei's side, smiled when she needed to, made polite, careful conversation with everyone she was introduced to, walked with her hand on his arm, eaten the meals put in front of her. She had executed her role of the apparently devoted fiancée to perfection, and then returned to her room.

Alone.

But there had been one special duty that he had entrusted to her. One that he felt that she was the best person in the country to carry out.

'We need to broadcast the story of the discovery of the proof of my parents' marriage,' he told her. 'Everyone is asking questions, making up the most impossible stories.'

Between them, they had come up with a version that came close enough to the truth. A story that involved the missing document being discovered in some long-unopened files. There was no need to detail Ria's father's involvement in it, Alexei had conceded, obviously not wanting his new fiancée's name blackened by any connection with Gregor's plotting.

'You'll be able to get close enough to the truth when you say how you discovered it, and it will explain why you came to England to contact me,' he told her as he escorted her to the TV studios from which she was to broadcast the details the press wanted.

She knew it was all show, just part of the masquerade they were putting on, but all the same she hugged to herself a feeling of delight at the way that Alexei left her to herself to decide what to say and how to say it. She knew he was watching in the background, scrutinising every move she made, but he had trusted her and that was what mattered. And at the end of the interview, when all the cameras were turned off, he had put his hand on her shoulder, drawing her close to drop a kiss on to her cheek.

'Thank you,' he had said quietly, his breath warm on her skin. 'The mention of the way that your visit to London meant we had the chance to renew our friendship from when we were here in Mecjoria all those years ago was inspired. It was just what was needed.'

Ria nodded agreement, swallowing down the way that 'friendship' covered such a multitude of sins. 'And with any luck the romance story will grab the headlines more.'

Her instincts proved right. The 'fairy-tale romance' between the new king and the daughter of one of the oldest families in Mecjoria was what caught the headlines. For every appearance Alexei made on his own, the interest was trebled if the two of them were seen together. The flash and crash of cameras on every occasion was like an assault, and the coverage in every newspaper made it seem as if there was no other subject under the sun.

Alexei hadn't allowed her to make any contact with her family. Her mother might have packed up her clothes for delivery to the castle, and she had included a brief note, just a card, to thank Ria for her success in bringing Alexei to Mecjoria, but that was all. And nothing more was allowed, it seemed. There might be murmurs of curiosity as to where Ria's father could be, but as her mother was known to be ill and had retired to the family's country house to recover it was rarely taken any further than a comment. And when it was, then the next walkabout by the 'fairy tale' couple pushed the query well away from the front page. Her family would be in touch, there would be news about her father, when the time was right, Ria was told.

But when would the time be right?

She had never managed to snatch more than a few moments' conversation with the man she was engaged to and even those were necessarily casual and uncontroversial because of their public setting, with hundreds of listeners in to every word they said, a phalanx of photographers lined up to record their every move. At the end of the day Alexei would smile, give her a kiss on both cheeks, one more on her mouth that their audience was waiting for, and walk away, back to the council rooms or his office, to discuss the next steps in the preparation for the coronation, leaving her alone.

And wanting more.

He might be able to switch off so completely, to concentrate on what mattered most to him—but she couldn't. She spent long, sleepless nights alone in the huge soft bed in the luxurious gold and white room, unable to settle. She was lonely, side-lined—frustrated. It was too painful a reminder of how she had once felt, all those years before, when she had been just an adolescent and she hadn't truly understood what these feelings were, where they came from. Now she was a grown woman, experiencing adult feelings for an adult male, and she knew exactly what they meant.

She wanted him. In every way that a woman wanted a man. She wanted him in her life, in her bed...inside her body. So much so that she ached now just thinking of it. Sighing, Ria tossed and turned, hunger buzzing along her nerves. She had never thought when she had agreed to go and find Alexei, talk to him, that she would open this whole Pandora's Box of memories. She had thought that she could face him as an adult, face down the hurt of past times. That she could persuade him to set her country free from the threats that surrounded it, and put herself on to a new path into the future as a result.

Instead she had thrown herself into a whole new volcano of sensual reaction, taken the lid off a set of feelings that, developed and matured by time, were now too big, too powerful to ever go quietly back into the box no matter how hard she tried.

But had she got it so terribly wrong? Was the truth that he was using her, using the desire she had been unable to hide, to make her do as he said, act in the way that benefitted him most? She had been manoeuvred into this position, playing the role of his fiancée, only to be frozen out on any more personal level. So was she really just a pawn in the game of dynastic chess he had set out to play with the country's future—and with hers? Just a way to cement his position as king or did he want something more from her?

'Oh why do I have to feel this way? Still!'

Turning restlessly on fine linen sheets that suddenly seemed as rough as cheap polyester against her sensitised skin, Ria pummelled her pillow, desperately trying to find a comfortable spot that might help her relax. Outside, the dark of the night was filled with a heavy, oppressive warmth, the low, rumble of thunder circling against the mountains and across the valley towards the castle. The long voile curtains waved in the breeze, as restless and un-settled as her thoughts. But it wasn't the heat outside that made her body burn but the flare of feelings deep inside.

Alexei had declared openly that he would never love her, but she had thought that he had responded to her at least as a woman. That he had wanted her as much as she did him. She had told herself that she wouldn't ask for more. She hadn't thought that she might have to settle for so much less.

Knowing that sleep was impossible, Ria tossed back the bedclothes, swinging her feet to the floor and reach-ing for the pale blue robe that lay at the foot of the bed, a match for the beautiful silk nightdress she was wearing.

When it had been delivered, along with the other new outfits she was expected to wear for her official duties, she had thought that there was perhaps a secret message in the garments. That they were meant for the time when she and Alexei would get together and finish what they had started in London and later on the plane journey here. She had waited six long nights, the pretty blue nightgown had become crumpled with wear. But not any more.

'Six nights is long enough!'

She wasn't going to sit here any longer like some un-wanted spare part. She wasn't thirteen any more, trained to be compliant, doing as her father said.

She didn't even have to do as Alexei said; not unless she wanted to.

Tightening the belt of the blue robe around her waist and pushing her feet into soft white slippers, she marched towards the door and flung it open.

'Madame?'

The instant response, in a quiet, respectful male voice, startled her. She had forgotten that Alexei had warned her of the need for security following the unrest that had resulted from the problems over the accession to the throne. Drawing herself up hastily, she directed a cool gaze at the security officer.

'His Majesty asked to see me.'

'Of course, madame. If you'll just follow me...'

The problem was, Ria acknowledged to herself as he led her down long high-ceilinged corridors, that now she was committed. How would this man react if she suddenly declared that she wasn't going to obey the summons she had claimed after all?

But they had reached their destination before she had time to think things through, her guide stopping by another huge carved wooden door, rapping lightly on it and then standing back with a swift, neat bow.

'Yes?'

The door was yanked open and Alexei stood in the doorway, tall and devastating, more imposing than ever.

He had discarded the dinner jacket he'd had on earlier that evening but he still wore the immaculate white shirt, now pulled open at the throat with his black bow tie, tugged loose and left dangling around his neck. His hair was in ruffled disarray, as if he had been running his hands through it again and again, and he held a crystal tumbler with some clear liquid swirling about at the bottom of it.

'Madame Duchess...'

His voice was dark with cynicism, no warmth of welcome in it.

Without thinking, Ria reverted to the formality of etiquette she had been trained in and dipped into a neat curtsey, holding the blue skirts of her robe out around her as if they were some formal ball gown.

'You asked to see me, sir.'

I did? She could see the question in his eyes, the way the straight black brows snapped together in astonishment, but luckily his sharp jet gaze went to the man behind her and obviously caught on. He nodded and stepped back, opening the door even wider.

'I did, duchess,' he responded with a grave formality that was at odds with the twitch of the corners of his mouth. 'Come in.'

It took all Ria's control to move forward, walk past the security guard and into the room. Just at the last moment she recovered enough composure to turn and switch on a swift, controlled smile.

'Thank you,' she murmured.

Then she was inside and the door was closed behind her, leaving her alone with Alexei.

This suite was larger even than the one she had spent the last week in. Huge rooms, vast windows, decorated in shades of dark green. But now, seeing it with him standing beside her, she couldn't help recalling the building she had seen him in in London. Here, the stiff formality of the décor, the furnishings in the dark heavy wood, made it look as if it had been decorated twenty years or more before. There were no photographs here, she noticed, recalling how those elegant but somehow cold, isolated— lonely—images had hit home the first time she had seen them. In fact there was nothing personal here, nothing of Alexei. Only the new king.

Ria managed another couple of steps into the room, then slowed, stopped, as the full force of the scene outside the door hit home.

'Oh dear heaven…' Even she couldn't tell if her voice

shook with laughter or embarrassment. 'Henri. What he must have thought!'

'And what was that?' Alexei drawled, taking a sip of his drink.

'That you— He must have thought that you had summoned me to your room...'

She couldn't complete the sentence but the dark gleam in Alexei's eyes told her that he had followed her thought processes exactly.

'And would it have been so very terrible if I had? Why should you not be in my room? We are engaged to be married, after all. And from the stories of our romance in the press, everyone will be expecting that we are already lovers.'

The last of his drink was tossed to the back of his throat, swallowed hard. Ria watched every last inch of its progress down the lean bronzed length of his throat, almost to the point where the first evidence of crisp, dark body hair showed at the neck of his white shirt. Compulsively she found herself matching the movement, though her own gulping swallow did nothing to ease the heated dryness of her mouth.

'That being so, they probably wondered why you haven't been here before. So tell me—to what do I owe the honour of this visit?'

What had seemed so totally right when she had been tossing and turning in her bed, her body on fire with longing, now seemed impossible. The restless hunger hadn't eased—if anything, standing here like this so close to the living, breathing reality of her dreams, able to see the gleam of health on the golden skin, the lustre of his black hair, smell the personal scent of his body, made it all so much worse, much more visceral and primitive. But how could she come right out and *say* it?

'Perhaps I feel the way the paparazzi feel…'

His frown revealed his confusion and perhaps a touch of disbelief.

'I want to know more than just what event I'm attending, what dress I'll be wearing. I'm wondering just what I'm doing here—why you have me imprisoned.'

It was the first thing that came to her mind—and the worst, it seemed. Danger flared in his eyes, and the glass he held slammed down on a nearby table.

'Not imprisoned! You are free to come and go as you please.'

'Oh perhaps not like my father, I agree. I'm your fiancée—we're supposed to be getting married but that's almost as much as I know. I need to know just what I'm doing here.'

I need to know what we can do to make this work, she added in her own thoughts but totally lost the nerve to actually say the words aloud.

CHAPTER TEN

'OH COME NOW, Ria,' Alexei mocked. 'You know only too well why you are here. I want you—and you want me. We have only to look at each other and we go up in flames.'

Right now she felt that that was exactly the truth. The moment of cold had vanished and now the surface of her skin seemed to be burning up. When he prowled nearer she had to clench her hands in the skirts of her nightdress and robe, keeping them prisoner and away from the dangerous impulse to reach out and touch him.

'So much so that you haven't even been near me!' she scorned. 'You've sent me jewels—flowers.'

'I thought women liked flowers—and jewellery.'

Ria batted the interruption aside with a wave of her fingers then snatched her hand back again as if stung as skin met skin where it had accidentally brushed his cheek. She could feel the wave of colour rising in her cheeks as she saw the way his eyes darkened in instant response, sending her body temperature rocketing skywards.

'And you look beautiful in that nightdress,' he continued, unrepressed.

'So beautiful that ever since we came back to Mecjoria you have barely spent a day in my company.'

'Are you saying that you've been missing me?' Alexei questioned with sudden softness.

Missing you so badly that it's eating me up inside.

'I am supposed to be your fiancée!' she flung back.

Alexei's slow smile mocked the vehemence of her response.

'And right now you are doing a wonderful job of sounding exactly like the jealous fiancée I would like you to be.'

'Jealous of what—who?'

'Of the time I spend with my new mistresses.'

It took her several moments to realise exactly what he meant. Not real women but the demands of the kingdom, the affairs of state.

'It was inevitable that you would be so occupied in these first days,' she acknowledged. 'You have so much to do. But you were wrong, you know, you didn't need any help.'

She had been impressed at the way he had taken charge since they had returned to Mecjoria. She'd watched him go through all the ceremony, the diplomatic meetings, seen the calm dignity and strength with which he'd conducted himself. He'd handled everyone, from the highest nobility to the ordinary commoner, with grace and ease.

'You've done wonderfully well—never put a foot wrong.'

A slight inclination of his head acknowledged the compliment which had been nothing less than the truth.

'I had a good teacher.'

Now it was her turn to frown. But then her expression changed abruptly as she met his eyes.

'I've done nothing,' she protested.

'The people want to see you,' Alexei countered. 'They love you and so do the press.'

'It's the Romeo and Juliet element—our "romance"—'
She broke off abruptly as he shook his head almost savagely.

'You've been at my side every day. You're a link to the old monarchy and you've lived in Mecjoria all your life. People value that.'

Was he saying that he valued it too? Her heart ached to know the answer to that question.

'Who else could I ask this of other than someone like you?' His hand cupped her cheek, dark eyes looking down into hers in a way that somehow made this so personal between the two of them, not just a matter of state. 'Someone who loves Mecjoria, who belongs here.'

'You belong here now!'

Too late she heard that 'now' fall into a dangerous silence. One that came with too many memories, too much darkness attached to it. And she knew that he felt that way too when his hand fell away, breaking the fragile contact between them.

'I know you never wanted to come back to Mecjoria.'

'Ah, but there you couldn't be more wrong,' Alexei put in sharply. 'Why do you think I was so furious when we got thrown out? Why I hated what had happened to us? This was my father's homeland. I wanted to be accepted here. To belong here. And I grew to love the countryside—the lakes, the mountains.'

His eyes went to the windows where in the daylight those mountains could be seen, rising majestically against the horizon, so high that they were always capped with a layer of snow, even in the summer.

'That was what got me hooked on photography. I wanted to capture the stunning beauty of Alabria. The wildlife in the forests. It was my father who gave me my first camera. That was the one thing I managed to take with me into exile.'

Exile. That single word spoke of so much more. Of love and loss and loneliness. Particularly when she was remembering those photographs on the walls of his office. The ones that had made him his fortune, built his reputation. Their stylised bleakness could not have been in starker contrast to the gentle beauty of the forests and lakes, the animals that had first made him want to capture their images.

'Do you still have that camera?'

He didn't use words to answer her. Instead he gestured to a heavy wooden chest of drawers that stood against the wall. Only now did Ria see the well-worn leather camera case that stood on top of it, its plain and battered appearance at odds with the old-fashioned ornate décor of the rest of the room. Her heart clenched, making her catch her breath.

'Your father would have been proud of you.'

Something in what she had said made his mouth, which had relaxed for a moment, twist tightly, cynically.

'*Now,*' he said roughly. 'He would have felt very differently about the son he had while he was still alive.'

'You didn't exactly get a chance.' Honesty forced her to say it. 'The court is hidebound by archaic rules and protocols. They can take years to learn if you haven't grown up getting used to them. And it was so much worse ten years ago. Even now it's bad enough.'

Alexei's smile was wry, almost boyish, reminding her sharply of so many occasions from the past. 'And have you any idea how many times I've checked you out at some moment this week when I've needed to know exactly what the protocol was?'

'You have?' She had never noticed that. And the fact that he would admit to it stunned her.

'Like I said—I've had a good teacher.'

'I wish I'd done more in the past. I could have helped you then.'

'Your father made sure you had no opportunity for that,' he commented cynically. 'He had his plans for you even then and nothing was going to get in the way. Particularly not some jumped-up commoner from an inconvenient marriage he had thought was long forgotten.'

'You think that even then…?'

She fought against the nausea rising in her throat. It was worse than she thought.

'I know.'

Alexei's nod was like a hammer blow on any hopes that things were not as bad as she had feared. A death blow to the dream that Alexei would not want to take the revenge that he was justified in seeking.

'If it had not been Ivan, it would have been someone else. Whoever offered him the greatest chance at being the power behind the throne.'

'Anyone but you.' It was just a whisper.

'Anyone but me.'

And there it was. The real reason why she was here. What was it people said—don't ask the question if you can't take the answer? She'd asked and so she had only herself to blame if the answer was not what she wanted to hear. And how could she want to hear that her place at Alexei's side, the link to the old monarchy she brought with her, provided the perfect revenge for all that Gregor had ever done to this man, the inheritance he had deprived him of? The father. The homeland.

'Tell me.' Alexei's voice seemed to come from a long way away. 'Could you really have married Ivan?'

Even for the country? She had once thought that she could but now, in the darkness of the night, she couldn't suppress the shudder that shook her at just the thought.

That was why her father was still in jail, Alexei acknowledged privately as he watched the colour drain from her face. All the investigations he had carried out since returning to Mecjoria had only proved even further just what sort of a slippery, devious cold fish Gregor Escalona still was. The man who had plotted his downfall and his mother's ruin would sell his soul to the devil if the price was right. He was not about to let the bastard out of jail until he was sure that he had control of him in other ways. And that control came through Escalona's daughter. With Ria at his side, as his wife, he had an unassailable claim to the throne. Surely even Gregor would think twice about staging a palace revolution when it would harm his daughter?

Though even that was something he still couldn't be sure of. Gregor had always been a cold and neglectful father. That was one of the reasons why Ria had sought out his friendship back in the past. They had been—he'd thought—two lost and lonely youngsters caught in the heartless world of power struggles and conspiracies. The sort of conspiracy in which Gregor had shown himself to be quite prepared to use his daughter to his own advantage. Signing the treaty with Ivan was evidence of that.

Which was why he had to marry Ria—*another* reason why he had to marry her, he admitted. He wasn't going to let Escalona near her until she was truly his wife. Only then could he protect her from being forced to marry Ivan in any counter-revolution to gain the crown. It was the thought of her married to Ivan that had pushed him into the proposal from the start—but now the thought that she might have been pressured into marrying a man she so obviously feared reinforced that already steel-hard resolve to make her his queen.

Whatever else Gregor had done wrong, the way he had raised his daughter had prepared her so well for the role she would fulfil. He had been sure she would be an asset to his claim to the throne and she had proved herself in so many ways.

But of course they weren't married yet. And until they were he wasn't going to let Escalona anywhere near his daughter.

But when an ugly little question was raised inside his head, demanding to know just what made him any different from the bullying father who would have pushed her into a forced marriage without considering her feelings, he was uncomfortably aware of the fact that he didn't have an answer to give, not one that would satisfy even himself.

'And marrying me?' he demanded roughly.

A small flick of her head might have been an answer. It might just as well have been a dismissal of the question as one she refused to answer. Her lips were pressed tight against each other, as if refusing to let any real response out. The problem was the deep gut-instinct that wrenched at him, seeing that. He wanted to lean forward, to stroke his thumb along the line of her mouth, ease those rose-tinted lips apart, cover her mouth with his, taste her, invade the moist warmth.

His heart thudded so hard against his rib cage that he felt sure she must hear it and his body hardened in hunger that made him want to groan aloud. When he had chosen that blue nightdress and robe he had imagined how she might look in it, the pale silk and darker blue lace contrasting with the creamy softness of her skin; the deep vee neckline plunging over the smooth curves of her breasts, the rich tumble of her hair along her shoulders. The reality far overshadowed his imaginings and his senses were even further besieged by the perfume of some floral shampoo as she moved her head, the scent of her skin driving him half-crazy with sexual need.

'That's a *fait accompli*.' Ria's cool voice sliced into his heated imaginings, making him fight to pay attention to what she was actually saying. 'But don't you think our "romance" will be more convincing if we spend more time together—as a man and a woman, not just as king and queen? I appreciate that you have many commitments—duties. Though I would have thought that when those duties were done...'

'You'd have liked me to come to your room, to snatch an hour—maybe less?' he challenged. 'You would have thought that was worth it?'

If he'd gone to her room then he wouldn't have stayed just for an hour, that was the truth. If he'd visited her there once, they would never have emerged until both of them were sated and exhausted. And he would have been totally in her power, sexually enslaved as never before in his life. He wasn't ready to risk that yet. He had the disturbing feeling that it would not be enough. That he would never be free again.

'I would have liked some attention—other than these *gifts!*'

'You don't like presents?'

'Presents are not...'

Ria almost choked on the realisation of what she had been about to say. Presents are not feelings. Presents are not *love*. Just where had that word come from?

Love. She didn't want to think that. She most definitely didn't want to feel that. But, now that the word had slipped into her thoughts, there was no way she was going to get it back into its box.

'Presents are not...?' Alexei prompted when she found her tongue frozen, unable to continue.

'Not important.' She bit the words out.

'A pity.' It actually sounded genuine. 'I had hoped you

would enjoy them. So perhaps I should cancel tomorrow's sessions with the couturier?'

'What would I need *more* dresses for? I have more than—'

'For the Black and White Ball,' Alexei inserted smoothly, cutting her off. There was a new glint in his eyes and his mouth seemed to have softened unexpectedly. 'You didn't think I would go ahead with that?' he asked as he saw the astonishment she couldn't hide. 'It is tradition. And you always wanted to attend such an event.'

She'd told him that when she was thirteen. Ten years ago. And he'd remembered?

'With the masks and everything?'

She couldn't stop the excitement from creeping into her voice. She had always been fascinated by the black and white masked ball that was traditionally held to mark the start of the coronation celebrations. The last time it had happened she had been too young to attend, and the sudden and unexpected death of the new king had come before there had been time to organise it.

'With the masks,' Alexei confirmed.

'I never expected that you of all people would be interested.'

'Me of all people?'

Another mistake. His mood had changed totally, taking with it the lighter atmosphere that had touched the room.

'And why is that, my dear duchess? Did you think that a commoner like me would not be able to cope with a formal ball?'

'I never...' She had been thinking of his wild past, the stories in the papers of long sessions in nightclubs, the images of him emerging, bleary-eyed and dishevelled, in the early hours of the morning. That terrible photo of him battered and bruised, his face bloody. 'I didn't think it would be your sort of thing.'

'I can dance. My father insisted that I had lessons—it's not something I'm likely to forget.'

There was such a wealth of memory in that statement that it woke echoes in Ria's mind.

'Madame Herone?' she questioned, recalling the hours she had spent being drilled in ballroom dancing by the stern disciplinarian.

Alexei nodded, that gleam deepening in the darkness of his eyes.

'I'm surprised we didn't end up having lessons together.'

No, she'd overstepped some mark there, she realised, feeling a painful twist of regret as the warmth faded like an ebbing tide.

'Your father was determined that we should never spend time together.'

She hadn't known that. Had simply believed that the dance lessons, like so many other things, were something that Alexei had rebelled against. How many other stories had she been told that had been just that—lies told to prevent her getting too close to him, getting to know him properly?

'It might have made everything so much more bearable. Do you remember that cane she had?'

Ria shuddered as she remembered how the dance teacher had wielded the cane like a weapon, rapping it sharply and painfully against her pupils' ankles if they made a mistake.

'I used to come out of lessons with my legs a mass of bruises.'

'No Huh-Honoria...' Alexei's tone mimicked the teacher's delivery perfectly, with a strange half-breath before her name. 'On your toes, if you please… And one, two, three—one, two, three…'

He was holding out his arms to Ria as he spoke and she found herself moving into them, picking up the rhythm.

'*One,* two, three…'

The speed was building. She was being swung around, whirled about the room, faster and faster. And she was being held so close, his arm at her back, clamped against the base of her spine, crushing her against him so that she could feel the heat of his body through the fine silk of her nightdress. Not just the heat; crushed this close, she couldn't be unaware of the hardness and power of his erection that spoke of a deeper, more primitive need than the light-hearted dance he had lead her into. Her feet barely seemed to touch the floor, her toes lifting from the carpet as she was steered across the room.

But it wasn't just the speed of the dance or the whirling turns that made her head spin. It was the sensation of being held in his arms, their strength supporting her, the burn of his palm at her back where the nightgown dipped low over her spine. His heartbeat, heavy, powerful, strong just under her cheek, seemed to take her pulse and lift it, make it throb in an unconscious echo of his, her breathing quickening, become shallow.

'One, two, three…'

She would never know if it was an accident or deliberate but at that moment it seemed that his foot caught on the edge of a rug, throwing them off-balance, stumbling, falling. Somehow Alexei twisted so that she landed safely on to the huge soft bed, crushed a heartbeat later by the heavy weight of Alexei's long body.

'Alex!' His name escaped on a rush of air, gasping in a mix of complicated reactions.

With her face buried against the strong column of his

neck, nose against the warm satin of his skin, she could inhale the personal scent of his body, feel the effect of it slide through her like warm smoke. If she just pushed her lips forward a centimetre or less she would taste him, be able to press her tongue against the lean muscles, the heavy pulse.

Above her Alexei went totally still, freezing into an immobility that caught the breath in her throat and held it there, tightly knotted.

'Ria,' he said, rough and raw as if dragged from a painfully sore throat. 'Ria, look at me...'

Half-fearful, half-excited, she made herself look up at him, meeting the gleaming onyx blaze of his eyes and feeling it burning up inside her. His face was set and raw, skin stretched tight across his broad cheekbones where a flash of red stained them darkly. She knew what that meant, knew her own face must bear a similar mark. Her blood was molten in her veins, her heartbeat thundering at her temples so that she couldn't think straight.

'*This* is why I never came to you before now. I knew that if I came to you it would be like this.'

He moved slightly, stroking a warm palm over her exposed skin, shifting against her so that she felt the heated swell of his erection. The heady mix of excitement and hunger drove her to make a soft mewling sound that had him drawing in a raw, unsteady breath.

'I knew that I would never get away again.'

He shook his dark head roughly, closing his eyes against the admission that had been dragged from him. Pushing both hands into the drift of her hair across the pillows, he held her head just so, dark eyes fixing hers, his mouth just a few centimetres of temptation away from her own.

'I didn't want to want you so much—never did. But

there is little point in denying it any more. So now, my duchess, it is decision time. If you are going to say no then say it now—while I can still act on it.'

Bending his head, he took her lips in a kiss that was pure temptation, sliding into a hungry pressure that told its own story. It was barely there then gone again and the moan of disappointment that rose in her throat, the way that her own mouth followed his, trying to snatch back the caress, made it plain that she wanted more. The hands that had been in her hair now slid down the length of her body, one cupping her bottom and pressing her closer against him, the other slipping under the lace-trimmed edge of the blue silk gown, sliding it from her shoulder, baring the creamy skin to his mouth.

The heat of his kiss made her writhe on the dark green covers, and when his teeth grazed her skin in a tender pain another soft cry of response escaped her.

Six restless nights had brought her to his door. Six nights of wakefulness and frustration, six nights of longing and growing need. And every one of those nights was behind her action now. She was hungry, needy, her hands shaking as she pulled at his clothes, wrenching his shirt from the waistband of his trousers, tugging it up so that she had access to the smooth warmth of the skin of his back. With the other hand, she reached up, catching the dangling ends of his unfastened bow tie and holding them together, pulling down on them to draw his head towards her, his mouth imprisoned against her own, his groan escaping from between their joined lips.

She was lost in those kisses, abandoned to his touch. His hands were even more impatient than her own, dispensing with the fine blue silk that covered her with a roughness and a lack of finesse that had the fine material ripping as he tore it away from her. And then his

mouth was on her breast, hot and hungry, kissing, nipping, suckling in a way that brought a moaning response
from her own throat.

'Lexei…' she sobbed, daring at last to use again the affectionate nickname he had once let her call him. 'Lexei…'

A sudden thought seemed to catch him, making him
pause, lift his head.

'You're not…?'

'What? A virgin?' Ria finished for him, the fight she
was having to cope with this abrupt change making her
tone sharp, the words shake on her tongue. 'What—do
you think I spent all these years just waiting, saving myself for you? Don't be silly.'

She might just as well have done, she added in the
privacy of her own thoughts. She had believed herself
in love with Alexei, had had fantasies, dreams in which
he had been the one—her first. So when he had left and
had made it plain that he had never spared a thought for
the former friend he had left behind, when he had been
seen everywhere with the beautiful, glamorous Mariette,
when he had had a baby with the other woman, she had
later flung herself into a relationship at the age of twenty
that she'd known within days had been a major mistake.
And if she had needed any further proof then it was right
here, right now in the storm of feelings breaking over her.
The sort of tempest that no other person had ever been
able to arouse in her.

The nightdress was gone, ripped away and discarded
on the floor, and somehow he had managed to shed his
own clothes, the heat and hair-roughened texture of his
skin a torment of delight against her own sensitised flesh.
And when he combined it with the stinging delight of
his hot mouth closing over one pouting nipple she could

only throw back her head against the pillows and choke his name out loud.

When he threw a leg over hers, pushing her thighs apart, opening her to him, she went with him willingly, arching up to meet him, to encourage him, to welcome him. With her face muffled against his throat she slid her hands down to his buttocks and pressed hard, urging him on.

'Ria...' Her name was rough and thick on his tongue, revealing that if she was on the brink of losing control then he was right there with her all the way. His mouth was at one breast, his hands teasing the other, tugging at her nipple, drawing it tighter, and she thought that she might lose the little that was left of her consciousness as she felt her head swim with the sensual pleasure that was burning up inside her.

The moment that he eased himself inside her had her holding her breath, abandoning herself, yielding herself up to him. The slow slide of his body into hers was like that teenage dream come true but harder, hotter, so much more than she had ever been able to imagine in her fantasies. It went beyond any experience that she could have ever thought was possible.

She was so close to the edge already that there was barely time to breathe between this moment of intense connection and the pulse of something new, something hot and hungry and demanding as he moved within her, and she lifted herself to meet his thrusts, gasping her delight as they took her higher, higher...soaring into the heavens, it seemed.

A moment later she was lost. Sensations stormed every inch of her body, assaulting every nerve, her mind whirling in the delirium of ecstasy. She froze with her body arched up to his, her internal muscles clamping around him so that she caught his choking cry of release as he too let go and abandoned himself to the tidal wave of pleasure, losing himself in the oblivion of fulfilment.

The storm of sensual ecstasy that had exploded inside Alexei's head took a long time to recede. Even then, it was impossible to move, impossible to think. His heart thundered against his ribs and it seemed his breathing would never get back under control. But at long last the red-hot tide receded, his blood cooled, his mind was his own again. With Ria's soft warmth curled up close beside him, her face buried against his chest, her hair spilling across his arms, he knew a powerful sense of satisfaction, of the closest thing to contentment he had known in a long time.

A contentment that was shattered in the moment that the first rational thought invaded his mind like a shaft of ice.

What the hell had he done?

He had known that he had kept away from Ria for a reason. The reason being that he didn't trust his own control when he was with her. He wanted her but, after the bitter lesson he had learned in the past, he had vowed that never again would he risk sleeping with any woman without contraception. But the moment Ria had been in his arms, the heat of the hunger he had felt as she lay underneath him, open to him, giving to him, had taken all his ability to think and shattered it. He hadn't even had a brain cell working that had thought of protection or consequences or the future. Only here and now and what was happening between them.

In a lifetime of wild, reckless, foolish mistakes, he might just have made the worst possible one ever.

CHAPTER ELEVEN

RIA STARED AT her reflection in the mirror and tried to recognise herself in the woman she saw there. The change wasn't just physical, though the groomed, elegant person who looked back at her was so far from any previous image of herself she had ever seen. There was so much more to it than that. And that meant that she found it hard to look herself in the eye, harder to admit to what she was seeing there.

Her dress was perfection, the sort of dress she might have imagined in her dreams. A narrow, strapless column of white silk, it had tiny crystals stitched into the material so that the effect when she moved was like a fall of stars. Her hair was swept into an elegant half-up, half-down style with the rich glowing strands falling over the creamy skin of her shoulders and partway down her back.

Growing up, she had always dreamed about one day being able to attend the black and white masked ball. She had also dreamed of falling in love, of marrying and living her own happy ever after. And the biggest part of that dream had been loving just one man.

Loving Alexei Sarova.

Well, she had done just that. She'd given him her heart as a child, but now she'd fallen in love with him for real, as an adult woman, and there was no going back. But the dream she had longed for had turned into a total, bitter nightmare as more and more of it came true. Because there was no happy ever after. Now here she was, about to attend the ball that people were calling the event of the decade. She would be expected to put on her public face, stand at Alexei's side, dance with him, smile—always smile!—and never let anyone see just how bruised and crushed her heart actually was.

Least of all Alexei himself.

Alexei, who had made it so plain that he desired her— in a physical sense at least. Who had acknowledged that he wanted her at his side, as his queen, his consort, but only in a dynastic marriage. She would be deceiving herself if she even allowed the hope of anything more to creep into her mind. Nothing had changed since the night she had gone to Alexei's room.

Well, yes, one thing had changed. And that was that she no longer lay awake, alone in her bed, in an agony of sexual hunger and frustration. She shared Alexei's room, Alexei's bed, every night and the passionate fire that had burned through them both that first time showed no signs of dimming. If anything, it had grown wilder, fiercer, stronger, with every night that passed. Though after that one heated coming together Alexei had always been meticulous, even dogmatic, about using the contraception they had both forgotten in the heat of the moment the first time.

But there was more to life than their searing sexual connection. There were the days to get through as well. The rest of the time it was business as usual, the demands of the throne taking so much time, so much energy. She woke every morning to find that the space beside her where Alexei had lain was cold and empty, revealing how he had been up so much earlier and how long he had been gone. Spending time with those 'new mistresses', the affairs of state that absorbed him so completely.

He had nothing else to offer her. No emotion, no caring, no...

Choking up inside on the last word, Ria swung away from the mirror, unable to meet her own eyes.

I can't love you. I loved once—adored her... Lost her.

No love. That was the word she was avoiding. The word she was running away from. The one that had no place in Alexei's life but that had taken over her existence completely.

The acid of unshed tears burned at the back of her eyes as she remembered that morning, when Alexei had been up early and dressing as usual while she still dozed. She had tried to lie still, not speaking a word, but in the end it had proved impossible. He had been heading towards the door when she had been unable to hold back any longer.

'When will you be back?'

She knew the words were a mistake as soon as she let them pass her lips, digging her teeth down painfully into her tongue as if she could hold them back. But too late. The stiffness of that long, straight spine, the set of his shoulders under the impeccably tailored steel-grey silk suit, told its own story without words.

'I have a full day.' It was flat, unemotional. 'But we will be together this evening. For the ball.'

Tonight the Black and White Ball would mark the culmination of all the ceremonial that led up to Alexei's accession to the throne. After tonight there would be the coronation itself.

And then their wedding.

On their wedding day he had said he would release her father. That move would mean that the balance of her mother's mind would be restored, possibly even her life would be saved when she had her husband back at her side. But wouldn't the dark hand of the past still reach out and touch the present, overshadowing it?

'Alexei. Are you sure you should release my father?'

He had started to move away again but that brought him up short, stilling totally.

'I thought that was what you wanted.'

'For my mother, yes. I'd give anything to see her happy and healthy again. And no matter what he is, she loves my father. But won't Gregor still be a threat? To Mecjoria. To you.'

To us, she wanted to add but it was a step too far.

'Why do you think I haven't let your father out already?'

When had he turned, swinging round to face her? She didn't think she had actually seen him move, but suddenly she was looking into his face, drawn into sculpted lines, hard and carved as a marble statue.

'Do you really think I would want him to have any more chances to bully you?'

Bully *her?* It was the last thing she had been expecting. She had thought that Alexei had left her father in prison out of revenge. That he had wanted to show he had control over the other man as Gregor had once had control over his future. She had never dreamed that he might actually be doing this to protect her.

'I'd like to see him try. I came to you because you are the king Mecjoria needs and everything I've seen just proves I was right in that. If he saw you now—saw how you've handled things—even my father would have to think again.'

'He'd have hated the walkabout.'

He was thinking of the events of the day before, when she and Alexei had opened a brand-new children's hospital here in the capital. The official part of the ceremony had been over in less than an hour, but the crush of people waiting to see them had shouted and called their names until Alexei had totally discarded the protocol and planning that had set the timetable for the day and launched into a spontaneous walkabout, shaking hands, talking, smiling. She doubted if she had ever seen him smile so much. He'd even…

A sudden memory of the day came back to haunt her.

A little boy had been pushed to the front of the crowd, a slightly bent and dented bunch of flowers in his hand. He'd tugged on Alexei's trousers, drawing the response he'd needed. And Alexei had turned, crouching down beside him, his attention totally focussed on the one small person. Totally at ease, he had lifted the child up, balancing him against his hip as he'd turned to face Ria.

'You have an admirer,' he'd said. 'And he wants to give his flowers to the princess.'

'Not protocol…' Her voice broke the last word into two disjointed syllables as she struggled with the memory. 'Not at all what I was trained for.' Her smile said how little she cared. 'But it was the right thing for the day.'

'And the future.'

Alexei wished he could express just what that reception had meant to him. Those smiling faces, the cheers, the flowers, the hands thrust forward to take his, the women wanting to press kisses on his cheek. His mouth had ached with smiling, his fingers raw from clasping so many other hands. So many times he had been told he was the image of his father; so many people had said 'welcome back'. If he turned or glanced out of the corner of his eyes, Ria had been at his side as she had been so many times and with her support he had actually felt free…

'It felt like coming home.'

'You are home. This is where you belong.'

But where did she belong? The question hit him like a blow in the face. She had been at his side but had that been from choice? What would she do if she was left free to follow her own destiny, without being trapped into linking it with his? The thought of how he had ensnared her, how he had manipulated her into his life, into his bed, was like the sting of a whip on his soul.

No—he hadn't manipulated her into his bed. She had come to him. When they had reached the palace he had tried to keep his distance from her, wanting to give her time to consider her position, but she had broken through the walls he had built around himself and just appeared at his door. Walking into his room as if she belonged there.

And that was how he wanted it. Wanted her warm and willing as she had been all night and every night since then. So much so that his body still pulsed at the memory, the burn of hunger not subdued even by the ache of appeasement.

But surely something that burned so white hot inevitably risked burning itself out? How long would this last and when it did end what did they have to put in its place? He had told himself that this was the only way to keep her safe. To marry her for now and then later—when it no longer mattered—he would let her go.

When it no longer mattered? How could it no longer matter? He had come alive, had lived in a new degree of intensity in the past weeks. How could something that felt this way ever fade into nothingness?

But would he ever be justified in keeping her here with him like this? He might call her father a bully but wasn't he trapping her into marriage just as much as Gregor had wanted to do? She had never wanted to be queen, just as he had never wanted to be king. Together they had built a way to take Mecjoria into a peaceful and prosperous future. But would that be enough to create their own futures?

If it wasn't then he'd have to set her free. But not yet. He couldn't let her go yet.

'We make a good team. But I'm not a monster—I won't force you to stay in this marriage for ever.'

The abrupt change of subject caught Ria unaware. One moment she had felt that they had moved to a new understanding, then this had come out of nowhere. Just as she had thought they had been celebrating a new beginning, it seemed that Alexei had already been thinking of the prospect of an end. She supposed she should have expected it. But the real horror was in the way he said it, as if he was offering her something worthwhile. Something that he believed she wanted.

'We could set a limit on the time it has to last,' Alexei stated flatly. 'Two years—three.'

Not a life sentence, then. She should feel relieved. Three weeks ago that was what she would have felt. It would have been a relief to her then to know that she hadn't signed her life away in this heartless marriage of convenience. But relief was not the emotion flooding through her now at the thought of a very limited future with this man. The terrible, tearing sense of loss threatened to rip her heart to pieces. She felt the blood drain down from her cheeks and she was sure that she must look as if she had seen a ghost. The ghost of her hopes and dreams. Dreams she had barely yet acknowledged to herself existed.

'I would give you a generous divorce settlement, of course.'

'Of course,' Ria echoed cynically. 'Once you have been king for a decent amount of time.'

'For which I will have you to thank.'

Again there was the sting of knowing that he meant it as a compliment. Because really he hadn't needed her in the end.

'You've won your own place in the hearts of the country. Surely you could see that yesterday?'

'Your help has been invaluable.' He was addressing her like he was at a public meeting. As if she was one of the ministers of state he had been spending so much time with of late. 'I knew you would make a perfect queen.'

'But only for a strictly limited time.' It was impossible to keep the bitterness from her voice. 'So perhaps we'd better really discuss the precise terms of this arrangement before we go any further? I'm to—what…?'

Sitting up in bed pulling the covers up around her because she felt too vulnerable otherwise, she checked off the points on the fingers of one hand.

'To be your fiancée, create the image of that fairy-tale romance, appear at your side in public, warm your bed in private. Marry you—provide you with an heir… No?'

His reaction had startled her. Shocked her. It was as if a sheet of ice had come down into the room, cutting them off from each other and freezing all the air in the room.

An heir. Of course she had known that was a touchy subject. But that had been when she had been concentrating on the future of Mecjoria. Now she had let herself think about his past, about the way he had fathered a child already, only to neglect the tiny girl who had died so tragically. He hadn't even tried to deny it when she had raised the accusation.

Why should I deny the facts when the world and his wife know what happened? And no one would believe a word that's different. The memory of the bitter words made her flinch inside, her stomach lurching nauseously.

An heir. Alexei felt as if someone had reached inside

his heart and ripped away the dressing he had thought he had slapped on there to protect it, revealing a wound that hadn't really healed but was still raw and vulnerable. A wound that he had been trying to ignore ever since that night that Ria had come to his room. The night that he had thoughtlessly made love to her without using a condom, breaking the number-one rule by which he'd lived his life since Belle had died.

And now this. Now with that one short word she had forced him to face what he had been pushing to the back of his mind, focussing his attention on the duties of being a king—the public duties—while ignoring the one private element that would always be there, needing to be considered for the future.

Ria had put her finger unerringly on it, dragged it out of the darkened corner to which he'd confined it, brought it kicking and screaming into the light—and it couldn't have come at a worse time.

He'd slept badly. Dark dreams had plagued his night. And it was with Ria's words that he had understood why. Yesterday had been a triumph. He knew there was no other word for it. But then there had been the small boy who had wanted his attention.

His heart kicked hard as he remembered the tug on his trousers, barely at calf level. He'd looked down into a pair of wide blue eyes, seen the curly fair hair, the gap-toothed grin. The impulse to pick the child up had been instant and spontaneous. The feel of that strong, compact little body in his arms had been nothing at all like the tiny, fragile speck of life that Belle had been but in a way that had been so much worse. It had hit home so hard with all the might-have-beens that he'd struggled with, forced him to look down into the dark chasm that he'd thought he'd put a lid on once and for all. The chasm he knew he was going to have to open up again someday or fail in his duty to Mecjoria.

Because how could he be a true king if he left the country without an heir for the future? That would mean that all this—that Ria's sacrifice—would be for nothing. The country needed an heir. Poor child with him as its father. But with Ria as its mother...

But how could he ever hope to follow through his resolution to let Ria go if he had made her pregnant?

'This will be a real marriage. In all possible ways. Of course.' It was flat and unemotional, the dangerous truth hidden behind blanked-off eyes. 'What else had you expected? That was what would have happened with Ivan. Wasn't it?'

Ria swallowed hard in an attempt to ease her painfully dry throat. Yes, it had been one of the conditions of the arranged marriage, how could it not have been? Which had been exactly why she had been so desperate to get out of that arrangement. To get away from the horror of being tied to a man she didn't love; to keep her freedom. Only, it seemed, to lose it all over again with the terms that Alexei was tossing out to her.

'And we do at least have huge chemistry between us. Come on Ria, admit it...' he added when he saw her eyes widen, heard the swift intake of breath she was unable to hold back. His eyes went to the other side of the bed in which she still lay, drawing attention to the crumpled pillows, the wildly disordered sheets. 'There is a real flame between us. You know, you've felt it.'

It was more than a flame. It was a raging inferno. She didn't need the state of the bed to remind her of how it was. Remembering last night and the way she had gone up in flames in his arms, the wildfire that his kisses had sent raging through her, she had to admit that there was no way she could deny this. Her whole body still throbbed with the aftermath of their shared passion and the heat he had stirred in her blood through the night had burned so hard that she almost imagined that the sheets would scorch where she touched them.

His implication was that this would make it easier to have that 'real marriage'. To create that much-needed heir. It could have done just that. It should have; it really should.

She wanted Alexei so very much. Being with Alexei, making love with him, was her dream come true. The fantasy she had let herself indulge in in her teens, as she fell in love with him with all the strength of her young, foolish, naïve heart.

But that was also what made the thought of this so terrible. To have been tied into an arranged marriage with Ivan would have been bad enough. But then only her body and her mind would have been involved. Not like with Alexei. With Alexei there was the risk to her heart—her soul.

Because she also knew, when she faced the truth, that there was no way she was making love with Alex every night. He was simply having sex, giving in to that flame he had said burned between them. Throw a child—his child—into the mix and she was done for. It would be lethal emotionally, totally destructive.

'It will be a real marriage—with everything that entails. As king, it will be my duty to have an heir, so naturally...'

'Naturally...' Ria choked, earning herself a cold, flashing sideways look from those deep, dark eyes.

Any child they created together would be so much more than that—at least to her. But that thought caught and twisted her nerves at the prospect of exposing a child to the toxic mix of hunger and distrust that their marriage would be. The temporary marriage that he had insisted

was all it was going to be. It made her stomach clench
in nausea, pushing bitter words from her uncontrolled
mouth.

'Another child for you to neglect?'

She flung it at him, hard and sharp, her own bitterly
divided feelings tightening her voice and putting into it
more venom than she actually felt. The truth was that she
didn't even know if she really felt that bitterness or not.
She didn't even know what she should be feeling.

'Another child that might…'

She couldn't say the word. It might only have three
letters in it, but 'die' had to be one of the most terrible
words in the world.

'I would not neglect her.'

Alexei's eyes had turned translucent, like molten steel,
and yet cold as frost in the same dark moment. Ria felt
a terrible sense of wrong twist deep inside. There was
something here that she didn't understand. Something
she couldn't put her finger on and the danger in his expression, in his tone, warned her that she was somehow
treading on very thin ice.

'This child would not be neglected,' he continued, each
word snapped out, cold and brittle. 'It would be too important, too—'

He choked off the word, leaving her wondering just
what he had been about to say. Too significant? Too essential to his plans for the future? His role as king?

'He or she would be cared for, treasured, watched over
every moment of its days.'

'Because they would be the heir that you need so much.'

'Because I would have you to be its mother—to take
care of it.'

How could something so quietly stated have the force
of a deadly assault?

'So that is my future role as you see it? As a brood mare first, and then a nursemaid to your *heir*.'

Something new blazed in those molten eyes, colder and harder than she would have believed possible. She couldn't imagine what she had said to put it there. After all she had simply agreed with what he had declared he wanted from her, making it plain that they both knew where they stood.

'You don't value that role?' he demanded, low and harsh. 'You think Ivan would have offered you anything else?'

'I think that you and Ivan are two of a kind. That you would both use me—use anyone without a second thought—to get what you wanted. Well, don't worry—I'll do my duty.' She laced the word with venom and actually saw him wince away from her attack, his eyes hooded and hidden. 'After all, you've probably achieved all you ever wanted already.'

'Achieved what?' His dark brows snapped together in a hard line. 'What the hell are you talking about?'

'Well, we've made lo—had sex—what, a dozen times now? And you have been scrupulous about using contraceptives—each time but one! I could well be pregnant already with the heir you need. Another nine months and the baby will be born—you'll be crowned king, settled on the throne, and have everything you want. And I'll be free to leave.'

She tried to make it sound airy, careless, but the misery she felt only succeeded in making it seem cold and hard, ruinously so. Alexei obviously took her at her word.

'And you could do that, could you? You could leave your child? Hand it over to be brought up as a prince or princess, the heir to the throne?

He sounded harsh, brutally critical. How dared he?

How dared *he* imply that she would abandon her child when he had neglected his baby in that heartless way?

'No, I could never do that—but then you knew that already! You can guarantee that I will never leave, as long as I have a child to care for. That's how you know that you have me trapped so completely.'

She had never seen him look so, white, so totally bloodless, his skin drawn so tight across his cheekbones that she almost felt they might slice it wide open, leaving a gaping wound. His jaw clenched too, a muscle jerking hard against the control he was forcing over it, and for a moment she flinched inside, wondering just what he was going to come back at her with.

But no such retort ever came. Instead, after a moment seeming frozen into ice, Alexei was suddenly jerked into movement, as his phone on the side table buzzed in timed warning of an upcoming event.

'Duty calls,' he said curtly, and that was all.

A moment later he was gone, snatching up his phone on his way out the door. And when that slammed behind him she was left, stark naked and with only a sheet to cover her, unable to run after him for fear of encountering the ever-watchful Henri or someone else who had taken over today's particular shift.

Not that she had the emotional strength to even try. The war of words might have been physical blows for the effect they had had on her. She could only lie back and stare at the ceiling as the words replayed over in her head, burning tears rolling down her cheeks to soak into the pillow behind her head.

CHAPTER TWELVE

FINDING THAT SHE was still staring blankly at her reflection in the mirror, not having moved for who knew how long, Ria blinked hard, trying to clear her thoughts and failing completely. The truth was that she was emotionally involved in this relationship and so she would be emotionally committed to the marriage. And that was why it would hurt so badly to be confined to the sidelines of Alexei's life. She could be his temporary queen of convenience, his bed mate, the mother of his child, but in his heart she would be nothing.

Ria's hand went to the sparkling diamond necklace that encircled her throat, fingering the brilliant gems as she recalled the way that the ornate jewels and the matching earrings had been delivered to her room earlier that evening.

Wear these for me tonight, the note that accompanied them had said in Alexei's firm, slashing handwriting.

Ria's fingers tightened on the necklace so convulsively that the delicate design was in danger of snapping under her grip. Alexei certainly no longer needed help with his position as king. He was issuing orders left, right and centre. She was strongly tempted to take the damn thing off and...

You don't like presents? Alexei's words came back to her, stilling the impulsive gesture. Remembering them from this distance, she couldn't be sure whether she had really heard the trace of—of what? Defensiveness? Uncertainty?—she had thought she had caught behind the mockery the first time. *I thought women liked flowers— and jewellery.*

Well, not this woman! Ria told him in the privacy of her thoughts. Not when she wanted so much more.

But going down that path was a weakness she couldn't afford. It came too close to dreams she could never have. It even, damn it, brought tears to burn at the back of her eyes. Fiercely she blinked them away, knowing she didn't have time to do any repair job on the make-up that a beautician had applied not an hour before. She would have to hope that the ornate silk mask, edged with sparkling crystals and pearls, would conceal the truth of the way she was feeling.

Swinging away from the mirror, Ria paced restlessly about the room, struggling to control her raw and unsettled breathing. She stumbled for a moment awkwardly when her toe caught on something on the floor, almost tripping her up. Glancing down, she saw that what she had trodden on. A man's wallet. Elderly, its worn brown leather partly hidden under a chair, it looked out of place in the elegant cream and gold room.

It must be Alexei's, she realised, recalling how he had visited her here the day before, his tie tugged loose, his shirt sleeves rolled up, his jacket off and slung over his shoulder as soon as he had escaped from his formal duties of the day. He had tossed the jacket on to the chair as he had gathered her to him and kissed her hard and, as always happened, his touch had ignited the flames between them so that in the space of a couple of heartbeats they had fallen on to the bed, oblivious to everything else. The wallet must have slipped from his pocket then.

Picking it up, she couldn't resist the impulse to flick it open, examine the contents. There was nothing unexpected in there—some credit cards, a few banknotes—but then one thing caught her attention, the corner of a photograph tucked into the back section. Curiosity stinging at her, she pulled it out carefully and felt the room swing wildly round her as she took in what it was.

A small print of a photograph. A tiny baby, barely a few weeks old, with dark, dark eyes and a wild fuzz of black hair on her small head. There was only one person it could be. Sweet little Isabelle, Alexei's baby daughter. The child who had been born as a result of such scandal and disgrace and who had only lived for a few short weeks, dying alone and neglected by her drunken father.

But that was where something caught on a raw exposed corner of Ria's nerves, making her heart jerk hard and sharp in reaction, and she had to close her eyes against the sensation. But when she opened them again, the photo in her hand was still there. Still clutched between her fingers.

Still telling the same story.

She had seen enough of Alexei's photographs in the magazines or the press, in his offices and again in his home. She knew the stylised, stark style he favoured, the careful framing, the deliberate focus. And this photograph had none of those. It was a quick, candid snap, snatched in a moment of spontaneity to capture the first flicker of a smile on the tiny girl's face. He had grabbed for his camera, and as a result he had captured something so truly special.

Not just an image of his little girl's first smile. But also a picture of his daughter snapped, with love, by her doting daddy.

Memory rushed over her like a thick black wave. The memory of a small boy held in strong male arms, totally secure, totally confident, a wilting bunch of flowers in one rather grubby hand, the fingers of the other tangling and twisting in Alexei's hair. The image of Alexei's face that morning when she had accused him of neglecting his baby. Even worse, there was the echo of those terrible, harsh words on that day in London.

Why should I deny the facts when the world and his wife know what happened? And no one would believe a word that's different.

How differently she heard those words now, catching the burn of bitterness, something close to despair that, focussed only on her own needs and plans, she had failed to notice that first time. And, knowing that, her stomach quailed and tied itself into knots at the thought of having to face Alexei again tonight.

'Ria...'

As if called up by her thoughts, there was a knock at the door. Alexei? What was he doing here?

He was standing on the landing so tall and elegant in the beautifully tailored evening clothes, the immaculate white shirt, the plain black silk mask across the upper part of his face, polished jet eyes gleaming through the slits in the fine material. This was Alexei the king, no longer her childhood friend but a man grown to full adulthood and ready to accept his destiny. He was the ruler Mecjoria needed, strong, powerful and in control. And he was her lover. Heat pooled low in her body at just the thought. Ria actually felt her legs weaken, her hand going out to his for support.

'You look wonderful.'

Alexei's dark gaze slid over her body, taking in every inch of the dress that the designer had created for her. The white silk clung to the curves of her breasts and hips in a way that dried his throat in sexual need, leaving him hot and hard in the space between one heartbeat and the next. He could never get enough of this woman, and the carnal thoughts she inspired had turned his brain molten, had tormented him through the day so that he barely had the strength to focus on what he was doing. The white mask gave her an other-worldly appearance, like a character at a Venetian carnival, with its ornate design, the eye pieces edged with pearls and sparkling crystals, drawing attention to the mossy green of her eyes fringed by impossibly thick and long dark lashes.

'You don't scrub up so badly yourself. Madame Herone would be proud of you.'

Was that a trace of uncertain laughter in her voice? The eyes that met his looked unusually, almost suspiciously bright. Her hand, impossibly delicate where it was enclosed in his, held on rather too tight.

The strapless design of her dress exposed the long, beautiful line of her throat, the creamy curve of her shoulders. Only hours ago, in the growing light of dawn, he had kissed his way down that smooth skin, lingering at the point where her pulse now beat at the base of her neck, before moving lower, to the delicious temptation of her breasts. He could almost still taste her rose-tinted nipples against his tongue and his lower body was so hard and tight that it was painful.

This was the way he had felt all week. He had resented the official duties, the diplomatic meetings and governmental debates that had taken so much time away from what he really wanted, from this woman who possessed his body, obsessed his mind. When he was with her he could think of nothing else. And when he was away from her all he could think about was getting back to her and being alone with her, of burying himself in the glorious temptation of her body. He knew she felt that way too—

the long hot nights they had spent together had made it plain that she wanted him every bit as much as he lusted after her. She had been as hungry as he had been, taking every kiss, every caress he offered, opening herself to him and welcoming him into her body as often as he could wish—reaching for him in the middle of the night to encourage him into even more sensual possession when he had thought that she was exhausted and could take no more.

But he couldn't think that way any more. He couldn't let himself think at all or he would back out of this right now. He had done all the thinking he needed to do and, with the memory of the scene in his bedroom that morning, had come to his decision. The only decision he believed was possible. He couldn't live with himself if he went any other way.

And now he had to tell Ria what was going to happen.

'We need to talk.'

Could there be any more ominous line in the whole of the English language? Ria questioned as she made herself step backwards to let him into the room.

'But we said we would meet downstairs, in one of the anterooms, ready to go into the ballroom together.'

'I know we did—but this has to be sorted out before we go down. Before anything else.'

Which was guaranteed to make her throat clench tighter, her lungs constrict, making it hard to breathe. Unthinkingly she lifted her hand to wave some air into her face, remembering only what she held when she saw Alexei's eyes focus sharply on the photograph.

'Belle…'

If she had any doubts left then they evaporated in the

burn of his expression, the shadows of pain that darkened his voice. Ria took a slow deep breath. She owed him this.

'The stories they told about that—you didn't do it. You couldn't have done it.'

He'd dropped her hand, reached out and took the small snapshot, holding it carefully as if afraid it might disintegrate.

'Cot death, they called it. But if someone had been there…'

'But wasn't Mariette?'

'Oh, she was there but she wasn't any help to anyone. Mariette had problems. Depression—drink—drugs.' His voice was low and flat, all emotion ironed out. 'We'd had a savage row. She told me to get out. I planned on getting drunk but I couldn't get rid of the fear that there was something wrong. I had to go back—but Mariette's door was locked against me and she wouldn't answer no matter how much I knocked and shouted. Eventually I had to break the door down—and found a scene of horror inside. Mariette was in a drug-fuelled stupor and Belle had died in her cradle.' His breath caught hard in his throat and he had to force the words out.

Ria hadn't been aware of moving forward, coming closer, but now she realised that she was so very close to him and, reaching out, she took his hand again, but the other way round this time, feeling his fingers curl around hers, hold her tightly.

'But everyone thought— You took the blame.' Incredulity made her voice shake.

Alexei's shrug was weary, dismissive.

'Because you loved her?'

'No, not Mariette.' He was shaking his head before her words were out. 'We'd run our course long before, but we stayed together for the baby's sake.'

Reaching up, he pulled the mask away from his face and let it drop, the lines around his nose and eyes seeming to be more dramatically etched as they were exposed to the light.

'My shoulders are broad enough. And Mariette had demons of her own to fight. She never wanted to be pregnant, and when she found she was she wanted to have an abortion. I persuaded her not to. She hated every minute of it, and I think she suffered from post-natal depression after Belle arrived. She ended up having a complete breakdown and had to be hospitalised. The last thing she needed was a horde of paparazzi hounding her, accusing her...'

For a moment he paused, his head going back, dark eyes looking deep into hers.

'She'd already cracked completely and lashed out when I tried to see her.'

His twisted smile tore at her heart. Could it get any worse? In her mind's eye, Ria was seeing the notorious photo of Alexei, bruised and bloodied. She had assumed—everyone had assumed—that he had been in a fight. But now she could see that those scratches had been scored into his skin by long, feminine nails.

'And I had plenty of my own scandals to live down. But...' His eyes went to the photo in his hand. 'I adored that little girl.'

'I know you did.'

'You believe me?'

Ria nodded mutely, tears clogging her throat. 'You're not capable of anything like they accused you of.'

Just for a moment Alexei rested his forehead against hers and closed his eyes.

'Thank you.'

I can't love you. I loved once—adored her... Lost her.

And it was little Belle, the baby daughter, who had

stolen his heart. If she hadn't seen that photograph she would know it now from the rawness in his voice, the darkness of his eyes. Oh dear heaven, if only she could ever hope to see that look when he thought of her. But he had confided the truth to her. Would she be totally blind, totally foolish to allow herself to hope that that meant he felt more for her than just his convenient, dynastic bride-to-be? Ria couldn't suppress the wild, skittering jump of her heart at the thought.

Downstairs, in the main hall of the castle, the huge golden gong sounded to announce the fact that it was almost time for the ball to start. Another few minutes and they would be expected to go down, ready to make their ceremonial entry. As always, the demands of state were intruding into their private moments. Obviously Alexei thought so too because he lifted his head, raked both his hands through the crisp darkness of his hair.

'You said we needed to talk.' She didn't know if she wanted to push him into saying whatever he had come to tell her. Only that right now she couldn't bear to leave it hanging unsaid for a moment longer.

'We do.'

He had always known that this was going to be hard and the conversation they had just had, the trust she had honoured him with, would only make things so much worse. But he also knew that it was the only way he could do things. The way she was looking at him, eyes bright behind that white satin mask, was going to destroy him if he didn't get things out in the open—fast.

But if ever there was a time that he owed someone the truth then it was now.

'This isn't going to work.'

He could see her recoil, eyes closing, the hand she had put on his snatched away abruptly.

'What isn't working?'

'Everything. The engagement—the marriage—you as my queen. Everything.'

'But I don't understand.' He was giving her what he knew she wanted but she wasn't making things easy for him. 'We've already announced the engagement. To-night…'

'I know. Tonight we are supposed to face the court, the nobility and every last one of the foreign diplomats in the country. Tonight is to mark the first step on to the final public stage of this whole damn king business.'

Tonight they would face the world as a royal couple— the future of the country. The potential royal family. And that was where one great big problem lay. A problem that had grown deeper and darker since this morning. Could he and this woman, this gorgeous, sexy woman, ever be more than the passionate lovers they had been in the past weeks? Could they ever become a *family?*

Family. That was the word that showed him what he wanted most and why he could not ever allow himself to think of letting this continue.

He had always wanted a family. The family he'd hoped to find when they had first come to Mecjoria. The one that had been denied him when his father had died and all that had followed. That was why he had begged Mariette not to have the abortion she'd wanted. Why he'd fallen in love with his little daughter from the moment the doctors had first put her in his arms just after the birth. Memories of Belle and all that he'd lost with her were like a dark bruise on his thoughts. The accusations Ria had flung at him this morning had brought those terrible memories rushing back, so that he hadn't been able to stay and face them down. And even now, when he knew she understood—more so *because* she'd understood—he knew he couldn't keep her trapped with him, not like this. She deserved so much better.

The accusation of trapping her that she'd flung at him was so appallingly justified, and the thought stuck in his throat, made acid burn in his stomach. He'd pushed her into a situation that took all her options, any trace of choice away from her. What made him think that she would want marriage to him any more than she would want to become Ivan's bride? It was true that the country benefited from the arranged marriage but, hell and damnation, he could have handled it so much better.

Did he really want a bride who looked so tense whenever they were alone—unless they were in bed together? A queen who held herself so stiffly that she looked as if she might break into a thousand brittle pieces if he touched her? A woman who, like his own mother, had been used as just a pawn in the power games of court? He had forced Mariette into a situation that she didn't want, and the end result had been a total tragedy. He could not do that to Ria.

'Tell me one thing.' He had to hear it from her own lips. 'Would you have agreed to marry me if I hadn't made it a condition of my accepting the throne?'

'I…' She swallowed down the rest of her answer but he didn't need it. Her hesitation, the way her eyes dodged away from his, told their own story. If he followed this path any longer he was no better—in fact, worse—than her father. He would be using her for his own ends, keeping her a prisoner when she wanted so desperately to fly free.

'I can't ask this of you.'

'You didn't ask,' Ria flung at him. 'You commanded.'

Was that weak, shaken voice really her own? Once again she had retreated behind false flippancy to disguise the way she was really feeling. The way that her life, the future she had thought was hers, had crumbled around her, the dreams she had just allowed herself to let into her mind evaporating in the blink of an eye. But she had let them linger for a moment and the bite of loss was all the more agonising because of that.

Reject that! Please. Argue with me, she begged him in her thoughts. But Alexei was nodding his head, taking her word as truth.

'And you had no choice but to agree. Well, I'm giving you that choice now. I never should have asked you to marry me. I don't need you to validate my position as king. The engagement is off—it should never have happened. You're free to go.'

'Free…'

The room swung round her violently, her eyes blurring, her breath escaping in a wild, shaken gasp. If this was freedom then she wanted none of it.

'Tonight? Right here and now?'

How did he manage to make the most appalling things sound as if he was giving her exactly what she wanted? Their eyes came together, burnished black clashing with clouded jade, and the ruthless conviction in his totally defeated her. She was dismissed, discarded, just like that.

'But what about…?'

In the hallway the gong sounded once again, summoning them. The sound made Alexei shake his head, his eyes closing briefly.

'How could I have been so bloody stupid?' He groaned. 'I'm sorry, Ria. I had meant to talk to you after the ball, but…' His eyes dropped to the photograph of Belle he still held in his hand. 'Things knocked me off-balance. Now everyone is here.'

'Why?'

It was the one thing she could hold on to. The one thing

that had registered in the storm of misery that assailed her. Alexei had decided that he didn't need to marry her—that he didn't want to marry her. *He didn't want her.* And there was no way she could fight back against that.

'Sorry for what?' Somehow she forced herself to ask it. 'Why did you plan to tell me *after* the ball?'

His expression was almost gentle and if it hadn't been for the bleakness of his eyes she might almost have believed that he was the Alexei of ten years before. The Alexei she had first fallen in love with.

'Because it was your dream,' he stated flatly. 'You always wanted to attend the Black and White Ball.' Just for a second, shockingly, the corner of his mouth quirked up into something that was almost a smile. 'You even trained for long hours with Madam Herone just for it. I wanted this to be for you.'

'But the engagement?' She didn't know how she had found the strength to speak. She wasn't even sure how she was managing to stay upright, except that she couldn't give in. She couldn't just collapse into the pathetic, despondent little heap that she felt she had become since he had declared he no longer wanted to marry her.

'After the ball, we would announce that you had changed your mind about marrying me.'

That she had changed her mind. He had thought of everything. But at least he would have left her with some pride by making it seem that she was the one who had ended their relationship. Not that she had been jilted, as she had just been. And for years he had remembered how much she had wanted to go to the ball, and had planned to give her that at least.

It wasn't much, not compared with the lifetime, the love, she had dreamed of. But it was all she was going to get. And, weak and foolish as she was, she knew in her heart that she was going to reach for it. For one last evening with Alexei. For one last night, this Cinderella was going to the ball with the man she loved.

Drawing on every ounce of her strength, she straightened her spine.

'You've obviously thought it all through. We'll do that, then.' She hoped she sounded calm, convincing. If he was giving her her freedom, then she could give him his. She wouldn't beg or cling. If her father had ever taught her anything worthwhile then it was dignity, even in defeat.

Below them they heard the third and final sound of the gong that preceded their arrival in the ballroom. It was now or never.

'Let's go.'

The journey down the wide, sweeping stairs seemed to take a lifetime. Alexei had offered her his arm for support and she managed to force herself to take it, knowing that the stinging film of tears she would not allow herself to shed blurred her vision and made her steps uncertain without his support. And if just having this one last chance to touch him, to hold on to his strength, was a personal indulgence, then that was her private business. An indulgence that she was never going to admit to anyone but keep hidden in the secrecy of her thoughts, stored up against the time when this was no longer possible and memories of how it had felt to be so close to him, to look into his beloved face, were all she had left.

At the bottom of the staircase the Lord Chamberlain was waiting, saying nothing, but the look of carefully controlled concern on his face told them that the world of ceremony and court appearances had already been delayed for long enough.

'Sir…'

Alexei's hand came up, commanding silence.

'I know. We're coming.'

Reaching out, he took Ria's fingers again, folding his own around them as he nodded his head in the direction of the huge doors to the ballroom. The glittering chandeliers and gold-decorated walls were hidden behind the huge double doors, but the buzz of a thousand conversations, the sound of so many feet moving on the polished floor, gave away the fact that their arrival was expected and waited for with huge anticipation.

'Duty calls. Are you sure you want to go through with this?' he murmured.

'Do we have any choice? Right now Mecjoria is what matters,' she managed to assure him, keeping her head high, her eyes now wide and dry.

'Then let's do this.'

They took a step forward, another. Two footmen stepped forward to take hold of the large metal handles, one on each side of the door.

And then, totally unexpectedly, Alexei stopped, looked straight into her face.

'You really are a queen,' he told her, low, husky and intent.

It was meant as a compliment, she knew, and her smile in reply was slow and tinged with the regret that was eating her alive.

'Just not your queen,' she managed, wishing that it was not the truth and knowing that all the wishing in the world would never ease away the agony of loss that was tearing her up inside.

As she spoke the big doors swung open and the buzz of talk and noise rose to a crescendo of excitement. Alexei took her hand in his as they walked forward into the ballroom, putting on the act of the fairy-tale couple for one last time.

CHAPTER THIRTEEN

UNDER ANY OTHER circumstances, it would have been a magical night.

Everything that Ria had ever imagined or dreamed about the Black and White Ball had come true, and most of it had been beyond her wildest imaginings. The huge ballroom was beautifully decorated, the lights from a dozen brilliant crystal chandeliers sparkling over the array of elegant men and women, all dressed, as the convention for the night demanded, in the most stylish variations on the purely monochrome theme of dress. They might be confined to black and white but the fabulous couture gowns, the brilliant jewels and, most of all, the stunningly decorated masks meant that everyone looked so different, so amazing, creating a stunning image in the room as a whole. One that was reflected over and over in the huge mirrored walls.

There was food and wine, glorious, delicious food for all she knew. But none of it passed her lips, and she barely drank a thing. She was strung tight as a wire on the atmosphere, the sensations of actually being here, like this. With Alexei. But at the same time those sensations were sharpened devastatingly by the terrible undercurrent of powerful emotion, the icy burn of pain that came from knowing that the man beside her was the love of her life, her reason for breathing, but that when this night was over he was expecting her to go, walk out of his life for ever.

From the moment they had walked into the room, and paused at the top of the short flight of steps that lead down the highly polished floor, all eyes had been on them. Just their appearance had triggered off a blinding fusillade of camera flashes that made her head spin and had her clutching at Alexei's arm for support. For long minutes afterwards she was still blinking to clear away the spots in her vision and bring her gaze back into focus properly. And he was there, at her side, silently supporting her, seeming to know instinctively just when she was able to see again clearly, when she could stand on her own two feet and turn her attention to the crowds of statesmen, dignitaries and nobility who thronged the room.

That was when Alexei carefully eased his way away from her side, resting his hand on hers just once as he turned her towards another group of guests. A faint inclination of his head, the touch of his hand at the base of her spine, spoke volumes without words. For this one night, still his fiancée, officially soon to be his queen, she should mix with their guests, socialise, talk with them. And he knew she could do it. Knew he didn't have to stay with her. Instead he headed off in the opposite direction, working the room. And the bittersweet rush of pride at the thought that he knew she wouldn't let him down helped Ria's feet move, warmed her smile when all the time she was feeling broken and dead inside.

She had no idea how much time had passed when they met up again. Only that he came to find her just at the point she had started to flag. When her mouth was beginning to ache with smiling, when her fund of small talk was beginning to dry up. Just when she felt she'd had enough, suddenly he was there by her side.

'Dance with me,' he said softly, and she turned to him, feeling as she gave him her hand and he lead her out on to the dance floor that, for her, the evening had really just truly begun.

With his arms round her, warm and strong, his strength supporting her, the scent of his skin in her nostrils, she barely felt as if her feet were on the ground any longer. She was all talked out, unable to find any words to say to him. But Alexei didn't appear to need conversation; seemed instead, like her, to be content to remain in their own silent bubble.

She had wanted to be here so much. Had dreamed of being here in so many ways—at the Black and White Ball, at the start of a new reign for the country, with the succession secured, with Mecjoria safe. With Ivan kept from the throne and Alexei, a strong, honest, powerful ruler, in his place. Here with the man she loved.

And that was when her thoughts stumbled to a halt. Where her mind seemed to blow a fuse and she could go no further, could not get past the thought of how much she loved this man. How much she wanted to be in his arms, and stay there for ever. At this moment she felt that she wouldn't even ask for his love in return. Just to stay with him, love him would be enough.

But already the clock was ticking towards the end of the convenient engagement Alexei had decided he no longer needed. Like Cinderella, she had until midnight before all the magic in her life disappeared and she found she was once more back in reality, all her dreams shattered around her. Already, an hour or more of the last remaining precious time she had with Alexei had passed and try as she might she couldn't hold back a single minute of the little that was left.

'Enjoying yourself?'

Alexei asked the question strangely stiffly, his breath warm against her ear, her cheek pressed close to his. She could only nod silently in answer, not daring to look up into his face, meet his eyes through the black silk mask. It would destroy her if she did. She would shatter into tiny pieces right here on the polished floor.

Enjoying yourself! Alexei couldn't believe he had been stupid enough to ask the inane question. The same one that he had asked a dozen, a hundred, times already that evening. It was the sort of polite, formal small talk that he used to put people at their ease, to make them feel that he had noticed them, that he appreciated the fact that they were there. It was for the Mecjorian nobility, the foreign dignitaries, the press even.

It was not for Ria. Not for this woman who he now held in his arms for perhaps the last time and who, at the end of this evening, would walk out of his life and into her own future—totally free for the first time ever.

Because how could he not notice Ria when she looked so stunningly beautiful, when she was all his private sensual fantasies come at once? How could he not appreciate what she was, who she was, when she had been there with him, always at his side, always offering her support through the long weeks since she had come to him with the news that he was king? Because it was right.

That was why he had known tonight that he had only one way forward. That, like Ria, he had to do what was right. Right for her, even if everything that was in him ached in protest at the thought. He had forced her into the marriage that he had believed would bring him the satisfaction he craved. It had brought him all that satisfaction—and more. So much more. But to keep her in such a marriage would be like chaining up some beautiful, exotic wild creature.

She would die in captivity. And he couldn't bear to see that happen to her. So tonight he was setting her free.

But first he would have just a few more hours to dance with her, hold her, maybe even kiss her. In spite of himself, he let his arms tighten round her, drew her soft warmth closer, inhaled the perfume of her skin against his. The bittersweet delight of it made his body burn in a hunger that he knew would have him lying awake through the night, and many more long, empty nights when this was done. He had until midnight. A few more hours to pretend that she was still his.

His! The lie cut terribly deep. The truth was that Ria had never been his. And that was why tonight had been inevitable, right from the start. But everything that was in him rebelled at the thought.

He couldn't do it. He couldn't let her go.

Ria was so lost in her thoughts, in the deep sensual awareness of being held so close to Alexei that at first the flurry of interest was just like a blur at the edge of her consciousness. She heard the buzz of sound as if it was that of a swarm of bees somewhere far distant, on the horizon but coming closer, growing louder, with every second.

Uncharacteristically, Alexei's smooth steps in the waltz stumbled slightly, hesitated, slowed. She heard him mutter a low toned, dark, fierce curse, the furious, 'Too early. Too damn early,' and suddenly the whole dance was stuttering to a halt as the murmur around them grew, as if that swarm of bees was coming closer, dangerously so.

'Escalona…'

On a sense of shock she heard her own name muttered over and over again. But once or twice it came with an addition that startled her, shocked her into stillness, bringing her head up and round.

'It's Gregor Escalona. And his wife.'

Beside her Alexei had stilled, his powerful body freezing in shock and rejection. She could almost feel the pulse of anger along the length of his frame. It was there in the tightening of the hand that held hers, the extra pressure of the one now clamped against her spine, the delicate dancer's hold replaced by something that felt disturbingly like imprisonment, a fierce control that shocked and upset her.

'Alexei…' she began, her use of his name clashing with the way he said hers.

'Ria…'

It shocked her because it sounded so rough, so ominous it made her heart thump nervously. Instinctively she wrenched herself out of his constraining hold, swivelling round against the pressure of his hands. Her vision blurring in disbelief, she could only stand and stare as she tried to take in the impossible reality of what she saw.

'*Mum!* And—and—'

And her father.

Her father who had just made his way into the room and was now standing at the top of the steps, her mother beside him. He looked paler, thinner, diminished somehow, though nothing like as pale and wan as Elizabetta who was holding onto his arm for grim death, and seeming dangerously close to collapsing in a heap on the floor if she loosened her grip. It couldn't be real; it was impossible. Her father was still locked away in the state prison, his freedom dependent on her marriage to Alexei…

But there wasn't going to be a marriage any more.

'Ria.'

Alexei's hands were on her shoulders, straining to turn her round, working against the instinctive resistance she put up. She couldn't believe what was happening. Why this was happening? Why they were there?

'Ria, look at me!'

One hand had come up in a slashing gesture to silence the orchestra and the whole room was suddenly still and frozen. In the quiet, the note of command was enough to take the strength from her. Her shoulders slumped and she found herself swung back again to face him, trapped in the sudden circles of isolation that had formed round them as every one of the other dancers froze, silently watching.

She had only a moment to look up into his dark, shuttered face, see the glare of fury he directed at her father, before he moved again suddenly, stunning her by going down on one knee right there in front of her. In front of the whole crowded ballroom.

Alexei—don't. She tried to open her mouth to say the words but nothing would come out. She knew just what was coming and she couldn't bear it. Couldn't cope with this. Not now; not like this.

Please, not like this...

She wanted to run but Alexei's grip tightened around it, holding her still. But what held her stiller was the deep, dark gaze that clashed with hers from behind the black silk mask.

'Ria, I didn't do this right last time. I want to do it properly now. I want your family—all the country—to know that I want you to be my queen. I don't want to be king without you at my side.'

'No...' She tried again but her voice was only a thin thread of sound, buried under the buzz of curiosity, the murmurs of incredulity and interest that came from their audience who were clearly hanging on to every word.

'Ria—will you marry me?'

Was the room really swinging round her, lurching nauseously, or was that just the rush of shock and panic to her head? She could see that her parents had been prevented from moving forward, the security guard putting a restraining hand on her father's arm, her mother stopping at his side though her eyes were fixed on her daughter's face. She saw the stunned, astonished, the frankly curious expressions on the faces of those around them, expressions that even the concealing masks could not disguise. And there, at her feet, was Alexei...

Alexei, the man she loved and whose proposal she would have so loved to hear—if only he had meant it. But not like this! Only this evening he had told her that he didn't want to marry her, that he was breaking off their engagement, that it was over. So this...

So this could only be some cold-blooded political statement. A statement of power in front of every dignitary, every statesman at the ball.

The conditions were that I would free your father when you became my wife. Call it a wedding day gift from me.

Oh, why did she have to remember that? But it had to be what was behind it—the need to show the world, the court and her father, that Alexei was the one with the power. That he was totally in control.

Here she was, with the whole court hanging on her every word, with her parents looking on. The freedom—temporary, surely—her father was enjoying hit home to her how easily Alexei could change everything, order everything with a flick of his head just as he had silenced the orchestra just moments before.

He had presented her with an ultimatum. Accept his proposal, here in the most public place possible, or everything he held over her would fall into place in the most appalling way.

She had thought that she couldn't face a future without him in it. But how could she ever have a future with a man who would force her hand in this way? Who would go to these lengths to emphasise the power he had over her?

'I can't!' she gasped, tasting the salt of her own tears sliding into her mouth as she flung the words into the silence, not daring to look into Alexei's face to see the effect they had as they landed. 'I won't marry you! And you can't make me!'

CHAPTER FOURTEEN

I won't marry you!

The words seared through Alexei's thoughts, burning an agonising trail behind them.

I won't marry you! And you can't make me!

'Make you?'

Alexei got slowly to his feet, his eyes still fixed on her indignant face, the way that her proud head was held so high, the green eyes flashing wild defiance into his. The stunned silence around him reflected his own shock and confusion, taking it and multiplying it inside his head.

He had been so sure. So convinced that at last he was on the right track with Ria. He knew he had pushed too hard, forced her into the position as his fiancée because he wanted her so much. And as a result she had felt bullied, trapped.

So he had come up with what had seemed like the perfect plan. To let her go, set her free. He had even arranged for her father to be liberated as a symbol of everything he wanted for her. But at the last minute he had known he couldn't go through with it. And something about her tonight, a new delicacy, a touch of melancholy, had given him a foolish, wild hope. He had known that he had to try.

He'd hoped a fresh proposal—one at the event that she had always longed to attend—might have some magic in it. But, if the truth were told, it had had the exact oppo-site effect of the one he had been looking for.

She had frozen, all colour leaching from her face, star-ing at him as if he had suddenly turned into a hissing, spitting poisonous snake right before her eyes.

'How the hell…?' he began but she shook her head wildly, loosening the elegant hair style so that locks of it tumbled down around her face. He could see how her eyes shone, the quiver of her lips that seemed to speak of some powerful emotion only just held in check, but every inch of her slender body was tight with defiance—and rejection.

'You may be king,' she declared, focussing on him so tightly that it seemed as if there was no one in the room but the two of them. 'And perhaps you can order people around—order their lives around for the fun of it! But you can't control people's hearts. You can't dictate the way I think—the way I feel! You can't force me to—'

But that was too much to take.

'Force? What force have I used?'

But she wasn't listening, launched on her stream of thoughts, flinging her fury into his face without a hint of restraint or hesitation.

'You might be able to command that I do as you say and I will have to obey you with a "yes, Your Royal High-ness. Anything you say, Your Majesty".'

Her elegant frame dipped in the most flawless—and most sarcastic—curtsey ever delivered. That was, unless you remembered the one she had given him on the night she had come to his room, when the blue silk nightgown had billowed out at her feet, forming a perfect pool of silk on the floor around her. Alexei's groin tightened at the memory of where that had led but he had to fight the impulse, knowing that it would distract him too much.

And he didn't need any distractions, not if he was to work out just where everything had gone wrong—and think of some way to put it right.

'You can even make me marry you—but you can't command my heart. You can't force me to love you!'

Love.

Things might have moved rather faster than he had intended, the careful plan he'd decided on rushed and confused at the last moment, but he could swear that he had never said anything about... Why would she mention love? Why would it even be in her thoughts unless...?

'Who the hell said anything about love?'

Her only response was a swift, startled widening of her eyes, the sudden sharp biting down of her teeth onto the softness of her bottom lip in a way that made him wince in instinctive sympathy.

They couldn't talk like this, not with every ear in the place tuned to what they were saying, hanging on to every word. For a second he considered grabbing hold of Ria's hand, taking her out of here—on to the terrace, into the garden—but one glance into her face had him reconsidering. She would fight him all the way, he knew that, and they had already created enough of a fever of interest to be the talk of the country for several years or more.

'Everyone out of here.' His hand came up to brush off the murmurs of concern. 'Now.'

He might get used to this king business after all, Alexei reflected as everyone obeyed his order, moving out of the room at his command. Even though they all hurried to obey him, it still took far longer than he had anticipated to empty the room and shut the doors behind them. It seemed an age before he was alone with Ria, and she was itching to get out of here; he could see that in her eyes, in the uneasy way she moved from one foot to another, nervous as a restive horse.

But she had stayed, and he had to pin his hopes on that.

What the devil was he going to say that didn't make her throw up her head and run? There was only one place to start. One word that was fixed inside his head, immovable and clear.

'Love?' he said, still unable to believe that he had heard her right. 'Did you say love?'

Had she? Oh dear heaven had she actually made the biggest mistake ever and come out with it just like that—in front of everyone here? Ria could feel the colour flood up into her face, sweeping under her mask, and then swiftly ebb away again as she heard her own voice sounding inside her head.

'You can't make me love you!' She flashed it at him in desperate defiance, fearful that he might take advantage of it, use it against her.

But somehow he didn't look quite how she expected. There was none of the anger, none of the coldness of rejection, nothing of the withdrawal she had thought she would see in his face if she ever admitted to the way she was feeling.

'I wouldn't even try,' he said and his voice was strangely low, almost soft. 'You're right, love can't be forced. It can only be given.'

Was she supposed to find an answer to that? She tried, she really did, but nothing came to mind. Her brain was just great, big empty space, with no thoughts forming anywhere.

'But you did try to force it.'

'Is that what you thought I was doing?'

He raked both hands through his hair, pushing it into appealing disorder. The movement knocked the mask sideways slightly. And, as he had done earlier in her room, he snatched it off and tossed it to the ground.

'I thought I was proposing. Let's face it, I never really *asked* you to marry me—we just agreed on terms.'

We didn't exactly agree, Ria was about to say, but something caught on her tongue, stopping her from getting the words out. She was looking again at that shockingly unexpected proposal. The sudden silence, the gaping crowds, and Alexei on his knee before her.

The man who had been so convinced that Mecjoria wouldn't want him, that the nobility would reject him as they had once done ten years before, had taken the risk of proposing all over again, of opening himself up in front of everyone here tonight. He'd risked his image, his pride, his dignity—and what had she done? She had thrown the proposal right back in his face.

'I tried to set you free tonight. I knew I couldn't tie you to a marriage to me in the way that it was going to be. I couldn't trap you like that, cage you—force you into sacrificing yourself for the country. I had to let you go, no matter how much I wanted you to stay. I had no right to impose those terms—any terms on you at all.'

'But you reinforced those terms so clearly here tonight.'

'Did I?' Alexei questioned softly. His eyes were deep pools in his drawn face. She couldn't look away if she tried. But she didn't want to try.

'My father...'

'Your father was here tonight as a free man. Did you see any chains?' he questioned sharply. 'Any armed escort?'

'No.' She had to acknowledge that. 'Then why?'

'I wanted to give your family back to you. I know what it feels like to be without a family.'

It had happened to him twice, Ria remembered. When

he had been brought to Mecjoria, supposedly to spend the rest of his life with his father and mother reunited at last, only to have his father die suddenly and shockingly and then to have his parents' marriage thrown into question so that he was rejected by the rest of the royal family. Again when he had had his own family, with Mariette and baby Belle. That too had ended in tragedy.

But he had talked of setting her free, and he'd wanted to give her family back to her. None of this meant what she had believed at first.

'I'm not sure that my father deserves your clemency,' she said carefully. 'He has schemed against you—plotted…'

'Oh, I'll be keeping a very close eye on him from now on,' Alexei assured her. 'For one thing I never want you to have to deal with him again. If he tries to interfere in your life then he will have to answer to me. Though I know you'll be able to stand up to him for yourself from now on. And I think the fear that he might have lost your mother will be punishment enough. Love can do that to you.'

Love? That word again.

'I should know,' Alexei went on.

I loved once—adored her… Lost her.

'Belle…'

Alexei nodded sombrely, his eyes still fixed on her face so that she could read his feelings in his expression. And those thoughts made her heart contract on a wave of painful hope. Because the look on his face now as he looked at her was the same as when he had stared down at the little snapshot of Belle, the person he had loved most in all the world.

'It broke my heart to lose her. I never thought I'd feel that way again—about anyone. But this morning when you said that I'd trapped you, I knew I was risking losing you when I forced you into marriage.'

'For the good of the country and because you wanted me.'

She could risk saying that much. Did she dare to take it any further? He had wanted to set her free. Surely that was the act of a man who…

'And I wanted you every bit as much.' Her voice jumped and cracked as she forced herself to add more. 'I always have. I still do.'

Alexei lifted his hands, cupping her face in both of them, his lips just a breath away from hers.

'Forgive me for tonight. I tried to let you go, but I couldn't. But I thought it was worth one last try to show you that I love you and to…'

'Alexei.' Ria's hand came up to press against his mouth, stilling the rest of his words. She didn't need to hear any more. 'You love me?'

He nodded his dark head, his intent gaze never leaving hers.

'I love you. With all my heart—the heart I thought was dead when I lost little Belle. But you've brought it back to life again. You've brought me back to life. But I don't want to trap you. I don't want you here if it's not where you want to be. I'll set you free if that's what you truly want but—'

Once more she stopped his words, but this time with a wildly joyful kiss that crushed them back inside his mouth.

'That's not what I want,' she whispered against his lips. 'What I want—all I want—is right here, right now. In you.'

He closed his eyes in response to her words and she felt him draw in a deep, deep breath of release and acceptance.

'I love you,' she told him, needing to say the words, glorying in the freedom of being able to speak them out loud at last.

'And I love you. More than I can say.'

She didn't doubt it. She couldn't. She could hear it reverberate in his deep tones, in the faint tremble of the hands that held her face. It was there in his eyes, in the set of his mouth, etched into every strong muscle of his face. This was the only truth, the absolute truth. And it made her heart sing in pure joy.

'Can we start again, please?' she whispered, making each word into a kiss against his mouth. 'And if that proposal is still open...'

'It is.' It was just a sigh.

'Then I accept—freely and gladly—and lovingly. I'd be so happy to marry you and stay with you for the rest of my life.'

She was gathered up into his arms, clamped so close against his chest that she could hear the heavy, hungry pounding of his heart and knew it was beating for her. The kiss he gave her made her senses swim, her legs lose all strength so that she clung to him urgently, needing him, loving him, and knowing deep in her soul that he would always be there for her now and in the future.

It was some time before a noise from outside reminded them that everyone who had come here to attend the ball was still waiting. A thousand people, waiting to discover just what her reply had been to his proposal. Glancing towards the door, Alexei looked deep into her face and smiled rather ruefully.

'Our guests are getting impatient. We should let them in again. Let them share in our celebrations.

'But,' he added as Ria nodded her agreement, 'This will be the official celebration. The time for our private celebration will come later. I promise you that I'll make it very, very special.'

And the depth of his tone, the way he still held her close, reluctant to let go even for a moment, told Ria that it was a promise not just for tonight but for the rest of their lives together.

* * * * *

PRINCESS IN THE IRON MASK

BY
VICTORIA PARKER

Victoria Parker's first love was a dashing, heroic fox named Robin Hood. Then came the powerful, suave Mr Darcy, Lady Chatterley's rugged lover. . .and the list goes on. Thinking she must be an unfaithful sort of girl, but ever the optimist, she relentlessly pursued her Mr Literary Right and eventually found him lying between the cool, crisp sheets of a Mills & Boon. Her obsession was born.

If only real life was just as easy. . .

Alas, against the advice of her beloved English teacher to cultivate her writer's muse, she chased the corporate dream and acquired various uninspiring job titles *and* a flesh-and-blood hero before she surrendered to that persistent voice and penned her first romance. It turns out creating havoc for feisty heroines and devilish heroes truly *is* the best job in the world.

Victoria now lives out her own happy-ever-after in the north-east of England, with her alpha exec and their two children—a masterly charmer in the making and, apparently, the next Disney Princess. Believing sleep is highly overrated, she often writes until three a.m., ignores the housework (much to her husband's dismay), and still loves nothing more than getting cosy with a romance novel. In her spare time she enjoys dabbling with interior design, discovering far-flung destinations and getting into mischief with her rather wonderful extended family.

This is Victoria's stunning debut—we hope you love it as much as we do!

Many thanks to my good friend Vicky, for all her patience and generosity in answering my questions about her son's fight against JDMS and how the rare adolescent skin condition has affected their lives. Together, they were a huge inspiration—not only for this book, but for the way in which the power of love can protect and heal, inside and out.

For Nina and my family—thank you for sharing the smiles and hugging away the blues on my path to publication. Without your love and enduring support reaching for the stars would still be light years away. I hope you enjoy my debut.

And finally I dedicate this book to the amazingly talented Michelle Styles. You taught me to have faith in my writing voice and inspired me to believe. Without your unwavering conviction Lucas and Claudia's love story would never have been told. So this, my dear friend, is for you. . .

CHAPTER ONE

'*Lucas, my friend, I have a favour to ask of you.*'

Favour?

Lucas Garcia had survived some of the worst conditions known to man, therefore a *favour* in his eyes involved hand grenades, automatic rifles or the calming of troubled waters on an international scale. What it unequivocally did *not* suggest was flying to London to retrieve a wayward snit of a girl, who disrespected the wishes of her father and showed no concern for her family or the country she'd been born to!

Anger blended with a tinge of discomfort in his gut as he took shelter beneath the green-striped awning of a coffee shop on Regent Square. Although summer approached, rain fell in heavy sheets, pooling at his designer-clad feet. Cold and inhospitable, the damp seeped through the wool of his Savile Row attire to lick at his skin.

'*Dios,* this city is miserable,' he muttered, scanning the wide glass entrance of ChemTech, London's foremost biomedical research centre, as he awaited the arrival of his current mission.

Claudia Thyssen.

'*Bring her home, Lucas. Only you can succeed where others have failed.*'

He was honoured by such high regard, and during his three years as Head of National Security for Arunthia he *had* successfully executed every order without question, standing by his moral code to honour, protect and obey. But this…

'I write. I appeal. Yet she ignores my every plea.'

Lucas flexed his neck to relieve the coil that had been tightening there ever since he'd left the office of his crowned employer two days ago.

What kind of person turned her back on her heritage, her birthright? Who would give up the luxurious warmth and beautiful lush landscape of Arunthia for a perilous city built of glass and thriving on iniquity?

As soon as the thought formed the answer came stumbling out of a traditional black London cab, weighed down with enough paperwork to make a significant dent in the Amazonian rainforest. Smothered in a long grey Mac, with her slender feet encased in nondescript black pumps, she blended into the dour backdrop seamlessly. Yet his avid gaze lingered on the wide belt cinching her small waist, enhancing the full curve of her breasts. Her dark hair was scraped back, gathered at her nape in a large lump, yet Lucas could almost feel it lustrously thick and heavy in his hands. Hideous spectacles covered a vast proportion of her oval face. But that didn't stop his imagination roaming with the possible colour of her eyes.

Princess Claudine Marysse Thyssen Verbault.

Hunched under the punishing thrash of rain, with the elegant sweep of her nape exposed, she seemed...vulnerable. Swallowing hard, he could almost taste her flurried panic as she grappled with her purse, fighting against the clock to be on time for a meeting he'd ensured would never take place.

Lucas ground his heels into the cement—*stand down, Garcia*—and stemmed the impulse to rush to her aid, erase her panicked expression. Instead he called upon years of training, focused on doing his job and concluded that her appearance was neither his care nor his concern.

Flipping back one charcoal cuff, he glanced at his Swiss platinum watch. With a jet on standby he'd estimated a four-hour turnaround, and frankly it was all the time he was willing to spare.

Taking one last look at the reluctant royal as she stormed

through a deluge of puddles, bedraggled and unkempt, Lucas stroked his jaw in contemplation.

Trained in warfare, and adept at finding the enemy's weak spot, he *should* be confident this assignment would be a stroll on the beach. After all, she was a biochemist—he'd captured mass murderers in half the time. Still…

'Oh, my God, no.' Claudia Thyssen glanced at the wall clock, swaying on her feet as she stood at the entrance to her lab. Her. Very. Empty. Lab. Instinctively she reached for the doorframe and gripped so hard a dull ache infected her wrist.

On any other day she would have been grateful for the isolation. So it was rather ironic that when she needed a room full of heavy pockets to fund her research the place was as deserted as an office on Christmas Day.

Her face crumpled under the sting of frustration burning her throat.

She was too late. Twenty minutes late, to be precise. Unable to avoid a visit to the children's ward at St Andrew's, where she'd been collating data for weeks, she hadn't banked on a monsoon and the entire city shuddering to a standstill.

It had taken her days to psyche herself up for this visit. *Long* days, considering she'd prepped through the night. Even her walk today came with a rattle, courtesy of a bottle and a half of stress-relieving tablets. But through it all she'd managed to convince herself that twenty minutes of spine-snapping social networking would be worth it.

Hot and wet, a single teardrop slipped down her cheek, and each framed article covering the walls—announcing her as a top biochemist in her field—blurred into insignificance. Because she was mere weeks away from a cure for JDMS— a childhood condition close to her heart—and her budget had careened into the red. Now fifteen months of development and testing would scream to a juddering halt. And the fault was hers alone.

Before the habitual thrash of self-loathing crippled her legs, she commanded her body to move and stumbled through the sterile white room, throwing the contents of her arms atop the stainless steel workbench. Shrugging out of her coat, she let the sodden material fall to the floor in a soft splat and collapsed onto one high-backed stool. Ripping the glasses from her face, she hurled them across the table and buried her head in ice-cold hands.

'Could this day get any worse?'

'Excuse me, miss…?'

Claudia bolted upright, swivelled, and nigh on toppled off her perch.

'Who are you?' Slamming a hand over her riotously thudding heart, she slid off the plastic seat and righted her footing before the mere sight of the man, almost filling the doorway, all but knocked her flat on her back. Hand uneasy, she brushed at her lab coat until the damp cotton fell past her knees in a comforting cloak. 'And how on earth did you get in here?'

She was surprised the floors hadn't shaken as he'd walked in. In fact it was quite possible they had. Because Claudia felt as if she were in the centre of a snowglobe, being shaken up and down by an almighty fist.

Of course it was just shock at the unexpected interruption, blending with the disastrous events of the morning. It had absolutely *nothing* to do with the drop-dead gorgeous specimen in front of her. Claudia had never been stirred by a man, let alone shaken.

Strikingly handsome, smothered in bronzed skin and topped with wavy dark hair, he stood well over six feet tall. Dressed to kill in a dark grey tailored suit and a white shirt with a large spread collar, he exuded indomitable strength and authority. But it was the silk crimson tie—such a stark contrast—wrapped around his throat and tied in a huge Windsor knot that screamed blatant self-assurance. Her stomach curled. Whether with fear or envy she couldn't be sure.

'Apologies for the intrusion. You left the door open when you came in just now,' he said, in a firm yet slightly accented drawl that shimmied down her spine, dusting over her sensitised flesh like the fluff of a dandelion blowing in the breeze.

Gooseflesh peppered her skin and she glanced down at her soggy lab coat, convinced her strange reaction was nothing more than the effect of rotten British weather.

With a deep, fortifying breath, she raised her gaze to meet his. Perfectly able to look a giraffe in the eye, she felt a frisson of heat burst through her veins at the mere act of looking up to a man. Yet the chilling disdain on his face told her she was wasting vital body heat and energy reserves.

Who on earth did he think he was? Coming into *her* lab and looking at her as if she'd ruined his day?

'You shouldn't be in here,' she said, her tone high, her equilibrium shot.

Claudia had not only ruined the day for thousands of children, she'd gambled with their entire future, their health and happiness. Unless she could think of a way to reschedule the meeting. Oh, God, why had they left so soon? Twenty minutes wasn't so long, and—

Her brain darted in three different directions. 'Wait a minute. Are you here for the budget meeting?'

Maybe he was one of the money men. Claudia could appeal to his better nature. If he had one. Because the customised perfection of his appearance couldn't entirely disguise a nature that surely bordered on the very edges of civilised.

His jaw ticked as he shook his head, the action popping her ballooning optimism.

'My name is Lucas Garcia,' he said, striding forward a pace and announcing his name as a gladiator entering the ring would: fiercely and exuding pride. With the face of a god—intense deep-set eyes the colour of midnight, high slashing cheekbones and an angular jaw—he seemed cast from the finest bronze. Beautiful, yet strangely cold.

A stinging shiver attacked her unsuspecting flesh and she wondered if there was a dry lab coat in the room next door. 'Well, Mr Garcia, I think you've lost your way.'

An arrogant smile tilted his mouth. 'I assure you, I lose nothing.'

Oh, she believed him. His mere presence pilfered the very air. She was also sure Lucas Garcia wouldn't have just lost the chance of three and half million pounds.

An unseen hand gripped her heart. What was the point of her life if she couldn't save others from what she'd gone through? Oh, she realised most of the children she met had families who cared for them, loved them—unlike Claudia, who'd been abandoned at twelve years old. But they still had to suffer the pain, the pity. The bewildering sense of shame. As with most childhood diseases, when adolescence gave way to adulthood the side effects waned. But she knew firsthand that was altogether too late to erase the emotional scars etched deep in the soul.

Eyes closing under the weight of fatigue, she inhaled deeply. She was so close to success she could taste musky victory on the tip of her tongue. Or was that his glorious woodsy scent? Good grief—she was losing it.

'I need to speak with you on a matter of urgency,' he said, the deep cadence of his voice ricocheting off the white-tiled walls.

God, that voice… 'Have we met before?' There was something vaguely familiar about him.

'No,' he said, standing with his feet slightly apart, hands behind his back, just inside the doorway.

Claudia suppressed an impulse to stand to attention. He was the most commanding man she'd ever seen. Almost military-like. Not that she had much to compare him to. One of the downfalls of self-imposed exile: she didn't get out much. The upside was that she rarely broke out in hives and she didn't get close to anyone. Claudia had no one and that was exactly how she liked it. No touching of her body mind or soul and there'd be no tears.

'I'm extremely busy, Mr Garcia,' she said, tugging at the cuffs of her coat, covering her wrists. 'If you don't mind…'

The words evaporated from her tongue as she caught the searing intensity in his blue eyes as he followed her every move, a frown creasing his brow.

Her stomach hollowed. *Stop fidgeting and he'll stop staring!* 'What exactly is it you want?'

'May I come in?' he asked, moving closer.

The word no was eclipsed from her mind as his body loomed impossibly larger. Within two seconds self-preservation kicked in and she edged her way around the desk to ensure a three-foot metal barricade. *Back off, handsome.*

Showing some degree of intelligence under all that ripped muscle, he paused mid stride, then devoured her face as if his eyes were starved. After he'd looked his fill their gazes caught…held. Claudia stared, mesmerised, as black pools swelled, virtually erasing the blue of his irises.

Pulse skyrocketing, the heavy beat echoed through her skull. After a few tense moments she blinked, trying to disconnect and sever the pull, unsure of what was happening. But no matter how hard she tried things just seemed to get worse: the temperature in the room soared and her spine melted into her pelvis under the scorching intensity.

'Why are you staring at me?' she whispered.

'You look like…' He blinked rapidly, his face morphing into a mixture of amazement and disgust as if he couldn't quite make up his mind what he was feeling or thinking.

The past slammed into her and she stumbled back a step. She'd seen that look on too many faces as they'd stared at her juvenile muscle-fatigued body, ravaged by skin rashes as unsightly as they were unfair. Yet the most destroying memory of all was the black-hearted response from her own flesh and blood.

Oh, God, why was she thinking about that now?

'What?' she asked, reaching behind her to pat the desk, searching for her glasses.

Lips twisting, almost cruel, he said, 'You look like your mother.'

Her hand stilled together with her heartbeat.

The glass door, the stark overhead lighting—all seemed to implode, raining shards of glass to perforate her carefully controlled, sanitised world.

Such a fool. So preoccupied with work. So pathetically enraptured by this man. She'd missed the signs staring her in the face.

His name. His deep, devastating voice. His fierce, powerful demeanour.

'My parents sent you,' Claudia breathed in a tremulous whisper.

No, no, *no*. She couldn't go back to Arunthia. Not now. Maybe never. It was a place she was only willing to visit in her imagination during moments of agonising loneliness. If only to reassure herself she was better off on her own.

'Yes,' he said, with a cool remoteness that made her shudder and remember all at once. For her childhood years had been made up of her parents' haughty detachment and hostile impatience.

It was their impatience that had condemned her, because Claudia had been an enigma no doctor could diagnose. Their detachment had sentenced her to extradition because she was an embarrassment—she'd been swept off to England, placed under the care of tutors, governesses and an army of paediatric specialists while her so-called loving parents forgot she'd ever existed.

They had betrayed her in the most unforgivable way.

The ache in her chest crawled up her throat and she squeezed her eyes shut.

It didn't take a brainiac to decipher their message. This man said it all. They wanted something and this time they were deadly serious. *Just fight, Claudia. You've done it before and you can do it again.*

She just wasn't entirely sure she had the strength.

Exhaustion pulsed through her weak leg muscles and her hand shot out to grip the edge of the desk as she begged her body to stand tall. *Come on, Claudia, fight. They don't need you. They didn't want the imperfect child you were. Don't give them the chance to hurt you again.*

Memories gushed like a riptide, flooding her psyche with such speed they threatened to break through the dam and obliterate her every defence.

Within the blink of an eye Claudia's day veered from bad to apocalyptic.

Lucas recognised shock when he saw it, and for the first time in his adult life the same emotion coursed through his veins, hot and unfathomable. While it blanched her exquisite flawless face, and widened her huge cat-like amber eyes, it completely severed his vocal cords from his brain.

Sans hideous spectacles, with wispy damp ebony curls framing her oval face, Claudia Thyssen was much like her mother. But where Marysse Verbault was strength personified, her daughter appeared almost…frail. The sight of her bending forward, her small hand pushing into her flat stomach, resurrected a dark tonnage of guilt that sat on his chest like an armoured tank.

Vulnerable. Undoubtedly timid. Traits he associated with the cold sweat of nightmares.

Yet his internal reaction to this woman was the complete opposite of chilling. The instant thrash of desire was so strong it knifed him in the gut.

She radiated supreme intellect, and Lucas would be the first to admit he preferred his women to be like uncomplicated candy. Covered from neck to calf in a frumpy lab coat, Claudia was more geek than glamour puss. So why did the mere sight of her raise his body temperature, thicken his blood?

Lucas frowned as his lethargic pulse slowed his every reaction and his mentally prepared speech drifted to the melamine floor in tatters.

Dios, why the bland exterior? She was the most beautiful

woman he had ever seen. Even the Queen's striking beauty paled in comparison to her second-born.

'Well, Mr Garcia,' she said, her voice firming together with her backbone, until she stood at her full height and he was almost bowled over by her stature and regal bearing. 'If my parents sent you, no doubt you have a message for me.' Her tone—now cold enough to reawaken the memory of frostbite—delivered the final blow. 'Consider it delivered.'

And if that wasn't a sharp swift kick out through the door, he didn't know what was.

What the...?

Realisation hit him square between the eyes, easing the tightness in his chest. Her façade was an illusion. An ingenious cloaking device to ensure she was hidden within a society who knew nothing of her real identity. For her resemblance to the Verbault line was astounding.

Grateful for the reminder of the real reason he was here, and of how beauty was only skin-deep, Lucas clenched his fists until spears of pain lanced up his forearms. Needing the dull ache winding through his body to regain control.

'You would be correct on the first count,' he said. 'Your parents have many things to say to you.' They were so anxious they had written countless letters over the last two months, begging for her return to Arunthia. Letters she had ignored. 'But this time, I assure you, their words will be spoken.'

Had she honestly thought she could ignore her family for ever? He'd been astounded to learn of her defiance. Such blatant disregard for her parents and the country of her birth.

The woman had no honour.

Treading lightly, as if flirting with a minefield, Lucas considered his next move. 'My apologies, Your Royal Highness.' No matter what he thought of her character she was above him in station, and he purposefully used her title, intent on her reaction. Her pale face remained impassive, which only served to prove his point. 'As I mentioned, my name is Lucas Garcia and I am the Head of National Security for Arunthia.'

'Congratulations. I'm very happy for you,' she drawled, raising one perfect dark brow.

Mesmerised, he watched the residual skittishness fade to be replaced with an emotion bordering on acerbity.

Twenty-four hours ago this was the woman he'd expected. *This* he could deal with.

'Your sentiment is appreciated,' he said, his silky tone forced for maximum impact.

Claudia focused those stunning eyes on him, her full mouth a moue as she sized him up. Lucas returned her glare, caught in an odd battle of wills, determined not to give an inch. It would be exceptionally easy to stand and look at her all day. If it were a power-play she desired he'd be a worthy opponent.

'How *are* my doting parents?' she asked overly sweetly, veering away, breaking the spell.

Before satisfaction could swell his gut, she began to shuffle around the table, shifting files from one place to another as she scoured the surface.

'King Henri and Queen Marysse wish to see you,' he said, somewhat distracted, his curiosity mounting as she searched the desk.

With a breathy little satisfied sigh that quite frankly belonged in the bedroom she reached over a paper mountain. Her lab coat moulded to her curvaceous bottom, the hem riding upward, giving Lucas a tantalising glimpse of sculpted ankles and sleek, toned calves. Swallowing hard, he whipped his gaze back up, just in time to see her pushing those huge ugly spectacles up her nose.

Swaying between the need to rip them back off or glue them in place, he cursed under his breath. *Dios,* he was not meant to feel anything. And the only thing he needed from *her* was to damn well comply.

'Well, I've no wish to see them,' she said.

Lucas kept his tone modulated, easy. 'That is unfortunate. They desire your hasty return to Arunthia. I have been commissioned to escort you home.'

She slammed her hands onto lush, rounded hips and her eyes fired darts full of ire. 'Mr Garcia, I'm not an express shipment. If it's haste you desire the door is directly behind you. Furthermore, if I wanted a vacation in Arunthia I'm quite capable of getting there myself. I don't require an escort.'

Lucas hitched a brow. He knew exactly what she required. A damn good—

'More importantly, I can't leave England right now.'

'Do you not wish to see your family? Reacquaint yourself with the country of your birth?' he asked, trying a little guilt on for size.

'Not particularly,' she replied, a hint of pink dusting her sculpted cheekbones.

Was she lying or embarrassed by her callous disregard? The notion began to appease him—until her arms fell listlessly to her sides and she bit down hard on her bottom lip. A drop of blood pooled on the plump surface and she sucked the flesh. Grimaced.

Miss Verbault was either into self-punishment or underneath her chosen façade lay an emotional maelstrom. Lucas decided to go on the first theory. If she had any conscience she would have returned home months ago.

'If they're that desperate to see me, why aren't they here?'

'Unfortunately they are incapacitated at present.'

'They usually *are* incapacitated, Mr Garcia,' she said, rubbing her brow with the tips of her fingers.

His head reared. 'Naturally. They do rule a small country. Something I'm sure is a time-consuming vocation.' What did she want? Weekly trips? How narrow-minded could one person be?

'Oh, I've noticed. For twenty-eight years, believe me, I've noticed,' she said, now rubbing harder, almost punishing. As very well she should.

Any other woman would be overjoyed to have even a small taste of the privileged life she rejected. To be royalty and live in pure luxury was, for most, an impossible dream. *Dios,* for some, placing food upon the table or returning to their loved ones at all was an impossible dream.

The woman was a conundrum. *You're not here to crack the code, Garcia. Just do your job and get the hell out.*

Lucas flexed his neck and battled on. He hadn't forged his way through the ranks by falling at the first hurdle or being a passive negotiator. Then again, he was adept at dealing with *men*. Not tall, striking, obstinate females.

Ordering his voice to remain civil, Lucas persisted. 'Regardless of their responsibilities, they look forward to your visit.'

A heavy sigh poured from her mouth. 'Oh, I'm sure. The question is, what do they want from me?'

A growl rumbled up his chest. 'They merely want to see their daughter.' He avoided the topic of an Anniversary Ball, celebrating her parents' fifty years of marriage, as had been suggested. Apparently she was uncomfortable at such gatherings. It was more likely she couldn't bear to leave her precious lab. Even Lucas could see it was the personal white fortress of an ice maiden.

'I'll arrange a conference call,' she said.

'In. Person.'

She snorted. Actually snorted. The most unladylike sound he'd ever heard. *Dios,* he'd met camels with more grace.

'I don't think so.' Turning back to the desk, she began to stack files. Then unstack them. Yanking at the cuffs of her lab coat every so often. His eyes narrowed on her small wrists. She was either cold or the habit was a nervous tic.

'Why now? Their timing is impeccable.'

'You *seem* to be an intelligent woman. Did you honestly think you could ignore your family for ever?' Could she not have mustered the decency to return one note from over half a dozen letters?

'Hoped would be more like it.' She swivelled on her heels to face him. 'I'm sorry, Mr Garcia, but your journey has been wasted. I've no intention of leaving here, with you or anyone.'

Crossing her arms tightly over her chest, she stood mutinous. His eyes dipped of their own accord, his pulse hitting one-fifty at the sight. Her pose had tightened the shapeless lab coat, offering him a hint of her rounded hip, cinching her small waist and enhancing the lush fullness of her breasts.

Blood hot as Arunthian lava seared through his veins.

'I'm afraid you have no choice,' he bit out, furious at his inappropriate physical reaction. 'Responsibility and duty outweigh personal desires.'

Claudia's luscious mouth dropped open and a fleeting image of those full lips pressing into his chest gave him momentary pause. His imagination flamed and he could practically feel her softness sliding against his strength. The heaviness of her breasts as he cupped the soft globes.

Primal lust hit with devastating impact. Sweat trickled down his spine. Torrid heat surged south. His groin pulsed once, twice, and hardened within seconds. Holy…

Lucas flexed his neck until he heard a soft click. What the hell was wrong with him? *Nothing that an hour with a woman wouldn't fix.* Any woman bar this one. Preferably a blonde. With blue eyes.

Dios, when was the last time he'd engaged in no-strings self-indulgence? Months? *Years?* No wonder he was in such a damn state. Working night and day had obviously begun to take its toll.

Claudia's sudden laughter crashed into his train of thought. A dark, hollow sound designed to chill the air.

'How wonderfully droll. I live in a free country, Mr Garcia, what are you going to do? Carry me out of here?' Laughter died on her tongue as her hand snaked up her chest to curl around her delicate throat.

The temptation to replace her hand with his made his palms itch. To caress or throttle—he'd yet to decide.

The air crackled with sweltry tension and Lucas raised one dark brow…

Claudia took a tentative step back. 'You wouldn't dare.'

No, he wouldn't, but she didn't know that. *Dios,* he was no animal. Although he'd witnessed many in his lifetime.

Suddenly his thoughts locked as his brain malfunctioned and an image flashed in his mind's eye. Nostrils flaring, he hauled air into his lungs and shut down the defect.

He searched for a retort. 'I would far rather you walked.'

She shook her head slowly. 'Not going to happen. Listen, just tell them I'll think about it, okay?'

Lucas smiled, although he imagined it was more of a smirk. What she asked of him was not only unthinkable but impossible. He was *not* going home empty-handed.

'I have to finish my work, Mr Garcia.'

Ah. He'd wondered how long it would take before she dropped the topic of her profession into the equation. The obvious chink in her armour.

'It's *very* important,' she said.

So was the country she belonged to. Lucas glanced around her workspace, troubled by the stark environment. After spending ten minutes under the harsh flood of lighting he already felt like a lab rat.

Control began to slip once more and he closed his eyes, breathed deeply…only to inhale a strange blend of clinical sanitation and elements of her work. Bleached cleanliness punched his gut, gripped and twisted with a hard fist. Sweat bubbled on his upper lip and he turned to pace, exorcising the demons. How could she stand being cooped in this cage? The violent need to escape pumped pure adrenaline through his system, and he clamped his jaw hard enough to crack a molar.

Shrugging off the discomfort, disgusted at his own weakness, he veered towards her. 'You may live in a free country but you were born to another and you have responsibilities to uphold. You will always have your work. But right now your family needs to take precedence. Three weeks at the most and then you may return. That is all they ask of you.'

'All they *ask?*' she flared. 'Why should I do *anything* for them?'

Lucas scrubbed at his nape, smacked with the need to butt his head against a brick wall. 'Your selfishness is astounding. Do you not feel one iota—?'

'I have responsibilities here, Mr Garcia. Petri dishes full of them,' she said, her arm outstretched, pointing to a wall where a bank of shelves held a legion of chemical equipment, jars and small plastic dishes of what looked like goop.

He raised a dark brow in her direction, only to be faced with one ink-smudged palm. The slight quiver of her long fingers betrayed her heightened state of anxiety.

'I don't expect *you* to understand what I do here,' she said waspishly and somewhat degradingly.

Lucas allowed the insult to slide, since he understood perfectly what her job entailed. If she thought him beneath her level of intelligence he was not only unperturbed—for it would be a cold day in hell before he valued the opinion of one so selfish and irresponsible—but his apparent ignorance would only serve to work in his favour later on. While he understood her motivations, her priorities were clearly misaligned.

'So,' she said, tearing her spectacles off her face, flaying him with amber fire. 'You can stop pacing like a caged animal, trying to figure out your next move. I've seen them all and I'm immune.'

Lucas clenched his teeth to avoid his jaw dropping to the floor. Incredible! She fought as a warrior. He'd never seen anything like it. Or felt anything like it. Because his entire body seethed with the need to haul her into his arms and kiss her pert, insolent mouth.

He scoured her face. Flawless apricot skin, huge distinctive amber eyes begging him for something he couldn't place. Understanding? Or to be left in peace?

Lucas could give her neither.

Failure was not in his vocabulary. He'd built his life, its very foundations, on honour, duty and protection. Not even an act of providence would steer him off his chosen path. Nor the most beautiful self-centred woman he'd ever laid eyes on.

Damage limitation was futile.

It was time to change tactics and up the pressure.

Because, come nightfall, Claudia *would* be returning to Arunthia.

CHAPTER TWO

IT MIGHT HAVE been nanny number four who'd told her not to play with fire, Claudia reflected as she took a tentative step back. But for the life of her she couldn't remember the woman who had screamed the warning *never* to provoke animals. Such a shame she hadn't listened and taken the same diligent approach to her safety as she had to her reading materials.

Standing no more than five feet away, Lucas locked his fierce blue eyes on her. Blatant intent slashed colour on his high chiselled cheekbones and her heart thumped against her ribcage. Without a doubt he would throw her over his shoulder and haul her out of here given half the chance.

Ignoring the ridiculous frisson of excitement *that* thought evoked, she focused on what was quickly becoming one of the most surreal days of her life.

Lucas, this dark, devastating brute, was by moral nature a carbon copy of her parents. Only thinking of their beloved country, of duty and responsibility. Uncaring of Claudia's desires or, more importantly, her needs.

Why should she do anything for them? What had they ever done for her, apart from abandoning her in a foreign country? Twelve years old and so sick she could barely walk. So unsightly they'd secreted her away. The loss of everything and everyone she'd ever known had soaked her pillow at night. So frightened. So very alone.

Throat swelling with the sting of past hurts, she swerved

back to the workbench and fumbled with the paper disarray for fear he'd see too much.

'I would like you to leave, Mr Garcia,' she said, the sheet in her hand quivering as violently as her voice. *Please just go.*

'You ask me the impossible, Your Royal Highness,' he replied in that delicious tone that licked at her senses like a hungry cat. Which only made her hate him even more.

She slapped the paper atop the stainless steel and braced her arms on the squared edge.

Trust her parents to send in the big guns. Lucas Garcia was proving to be as immovable as Big Ben, and she could hear the tick, tick of the clock. *Don't be ridiculous. They've sent for you before. You can get rid of this guy just as easily.*

Their last threat had been the abolition of her living funds. 'Go ahead,' she'd told them, and promptly moved out of her swanky three-bedroom apartment on the banks of the River Thames. The bluff had backfired spectacularly, because the vast space lay empty to this day. But she loved her kitsch one-bed studio because it was hers alone, flying the flag of her hard-won independence.

Stiffening her spine, she turned in time to see Lucas finger his over-long hair back from his forehead and her insides liquefied. Must be a chemical reaction linked to irate frustration.

'And please don't call me, Your Royal whatever. I know perfectly well what you're doing. Your tactics won't work with me.'

'Regardless of your preference, that *is* your title,' he said, his voice toughened like steel, brow etched with exasperation. 'When will you acknowledge the fact and behave accordingly?'

'*Behave?* I've always been the upstanding daughter, Mr Garcia. I work hard and, more importantly, I make no ripples that will reach Arunthian shores to embarrass or disgrace.' An implausible feat for Claudia, but he didn't need to know that.

The dark glower he fired her way said he was far from impressed.

'And I have two sisters,' she said, suppressing any girlhood nostalgia and focusing instead on the little she'd gleaned of

them by searching their names on the internet. Just to see if
they were well…happy. If the thousands of glamorous photographs and articles were anything to go by they were more than
well. They were true royalty in every way. 'My parents don't
need me.' Which was just as well because the mere notion of
life at the palace, evermore in the public eye, made her skin
crawl as if the venom of a scorpion pulsed through her veins.

'Good grief, I'm as far away from being a princess as you
are from being Prince Charming!'

Lucas coughed around a closed fist, then uncurled his long
fingers to stroke his jaw. 'I've noticed,' he said, searching her
face as if looking for an answer to the question hovering in
the air.

Why? Let him come to his own conclusions, she mused.
Claudia owed him nothing.

In thinking mode his face almost softened, and for the first
time she noticed beautiful long thick lashes surrounded eyes
so dark, so intense, they glittered like sapphires.

'Then how would you like to be addressed?' he asked.

Claudia frowned, blinking over and over, scrolling through
the past few minutes of conversation, slightly disturbed by his
silky intonation.

'Just Claudia is fine,' she said warily.

'Very well, *Just Claudia.*'

Oh. My. Giddy. Aunt. Something hot and sultry splashed
through her midsection. His accent thickened when he said
her name. His full mouth formed a perfect O as if he'd kissed
it past his lips: *Cllowtia.*

Kissed it past his lips?

She gave her head a quick shake. Twenty minutes in his
company and she'd lost hundreds of brain cells, waxing po-
etical. This was what happened when a romance novel thrust
itself into her hands during a spontaneous visit to the charity
bookshop at St Andrews.

Claudia preferred to base her life on facts and scientific
evidence.

And the fact was Lucas Garcia wouldn't give her a second glance if he passed her in the street. The idea of mutual attraction was laughable. She wasn't only socially inept but also the strangest-looking creature on earth. They were quite literally worlds apart. Or they would be as soon as she got rid of him.

From the way his long blunt fingers trailed down the lapel of his charcoal single-breasted jacket and deftly unpopped the button, it didn't look as if he felt the need to go any time soon.

Mid-exasperated sigh, the air locked in her throat as he rolled his broad shoulders, revealing a wide panel of crisp white shirt stretched taut over his rock-solid physique, and strolled over to where her qualifications hung on the wall, filling the white expanse.

'I understand you are a biochemist?'

Claudia's eyes narrowed on his fluid gait, lithe for a man of his stature, and her traitorous mind imagined all kinds. 'Mmm-hmm.' Oh, lovely—she couldn't even speak, her mouth was so dry.

'What exactly does your work involve?'

Was he really that interested? She gave a little huff. Of course he was interested. It was his job to be interested.

'At the moment I'm studying a childhood auto-immune disease and developing drugs to reduce the side-effects—along with a cure, of course.' Claudia just had to think of a child suffering from the same condition and her life made a strange kind of sense. She was here for a purpose. One that didn't include sitting around looking impossibly pretty, cutting ribbons at galas and chatting to foreign dignitaries.

Lucas paused before the largest frame. Her second Masters. 'You feel strongly about your work.' Reaching up, he straightened the gilt-framed plaque with tensile fingers and ran the tip of his index finger across the black lettering of her name.

The gesture was so unexpected, so intimate, it felt like a physical touch.

Without conscious thought she reached up and brushed her lips in a continuous circular motion, wondering what his too-large hands would feel like against her skin—rough and purposeful or seductively thrilling?

'The strength of my dedication is unimaginable, Mr Garcia,' she said softly, her hand plunging to her side.

Because suddenly, like the instant flare of a Bunsen, it occurred to her that he couldn't possibly understand her avoidance of going home. *Your selfishness is astounding.* In his opinion she was being awkward and highly unreasonable. Having no idea why the notion weighed so heavy on her heart, she wanted to explain. Would she see pity in his beautifully fierce gaze or scorn because she'd yet to overcome the lingering effects?

'That is quite understandable in the circumstances,' he said, with a cool sincerity that snuffed out her burning desire to elucidate.

Was he saying he already knew?

'This condition that you study?' he went on. 'JDMS?'

'Juvenile Dermatomyositis. I'm surprised you've heard of it. It's not a particularly common affliction.' Hence it was a constant fight to keep money rolling her way. Fingers of suspicion stroked her throat, curling like a noose around her neck. 'Did my parents tell you?'

'No.'

One word—sharp as a scalpel and just as ominous.

Claudia frowned. Was he deliberately being evasive?

Having reached the far corner, Lucas unclasped his hands and began to swivel on his heels. Before he made the full turn she braced her weight against the edge of the desk, clenched her fists, determined not to fidget and calling upon years of practice in the art of facial indifference.

Despite all her efforts her eyes still flared at the indomitable calculating expression on his face.

'Like you, I take my position seriously, Claudia. I would not be doing my job correctly if I stumbled into a situation without all the relevant facts to hand.'

Meaning he'd pulled her files. Not full medical—he wouldn't

have had the authority—so his information would be brief. 'So you understand my reasons?'

'I understand perfectly,' he said, his voice weighted with dark power.

A sinking sensation tugged at her limbs and she pushed her spine into the blunt edge of the bench.

'What I cannot comprehend is your reluctance to travel home. As far as I can tell, you are using your job as a convenient excuse. Luckily I had been forewarned of any possible obstacles.'

Panic pounded at her heart and Claudia bit her inner cheek to prevent an untimely sniping retort.

'With that in mind,' he continued, 'my first port of call this morning was with your manager. A Mr Ryan Tate.'

Her stomach lurched so violently her wheat-bran flakes threatened to reappear. But that didn't stop her brain firing synapses faster than the speed of light.

'That's how you gained access to this floor,' she whispered.

'Correct.'

'How dare you…?' Her voice cracked, failing her miserably. 'How dare you intrude on my life this way? What was discussed at this meeting?'

Lucas flexed his neck, his unease a palpable thing, but Claudia was far too busy stemming hysteria to take comfort from the sight.

'I enquired if you were free to take annual leave,' he said. 'The answer was yes.'

Oh…

'I asked him if there was anything standing in the way of your returning home immediately. The answer was yes. You have five days to secure additional funding before the work on your project is terminated.'

My…

'I questioned if there was anything I could do to relieve the time pressure and pave the way for your return home. The answer was yes.'

God.

She'd underestimated him. Badly.

Directing her voice to match the cool detachment in his face, she said, 'When you arrived I asked if you were here in connection with the budget meeting. While you didn't lie outright, you deliberately withheld facts which would have a profound effect on me. Why?'

'I had hoped we would come to an understanding without the need for—'

'Blackmail? Coercion?' she cried, her entire body trembling with panic and frustration.

Forget cool detachment. He was icily cruel—from his glacial blue stare to the hard line of his mouth.

'This is not personal, Claudia.'

'You've just made it personal, Lucas!' God, she had to control herself. Tears stung like tiny daggers but she swallowed every one even as they sliced at her throat. She refused to cry in front of this man.

For the first time his eyes flicked away from her. 'Do you or do you not require funding to complete your work?'

'If you've discussed this with Tate, then you already know I do.'

'Then consider it a favour for a favour,' he said amiably, his gaze returning, eyes narrowed on her face.

'A *favour?* What was the outcome of this meeting?' Stupid, stupid question—but she needed him to say the words before she gave up all hope.

'I informed Mr Tate that I would certainly consider providing the additional three point five million pounds of necessary funding if certain conditions were met. By you.'

'You… You…' The lab swirled before her eyes, gaining speed as if she were in the centre of a whirlwind. No. *No.* She was *not* going back. 'I'll find another way to get the money,' she said, desperation blurring her mind. *Don't be stupid, Claudia. You need the money. Take the money. You just asked yourself what your parents have ever done for you…let them do this.*

But at what cost? Her heart? Her hard-won independence and the little pride she had left? 'I will not be bought.'

The sides of his face pulsed as he clenched his jaw. 'Then I shall withdraw the offer. You can go to Ryan Tate and explain your actions. Neither of you will find such a large sum of money within the next few days. I guarantee it. So tell me,' he said, drawing it out, encompassing the room with one sweep of his hand, 'just how important *is* your work, Claudia?'

Stomach cramping, she forced her heels into the ground to stop her body from doubling over.

The man was heartless. He knew how important her research was to her. Knew of her personal connection. And still he was nigh on blackmailing her! No, he was using her weakness against her. Bizarrely, instead of hatred she felt utter disappointment. In both of them. Why in Lucas she had no idea. But in herself it was the heart-pumping, blood-fizzing desire that brought her such misery. So there ended her life lesson on physical attraction. She couldn't even trust her body to decipher the good from the bad. Then again, her body had let her down since she was ten years old.

'What exactly are these conditions?' she asked, proud of her unwavering voice.

'Three weeks' leave. Effective from nine this morning. Coupled with your return to Arunthia.'

Claudia shook her head slowly. 'Have you no conscience?'

Whether it was his words—spoken like an automaton, as if he were programmed—or his face—a picture of haughty detachment—her heart was torn wide open.

'I have a duty, Claudia. As do you. The choice is yours.'

CHAPTER THREE

DON'T YOU DARE crumble in front of this man, Claudia. Don't you dare.

An hour ago she'd prayed for a miracle and, as if the gods were playing tricks on her, they'd sent a warrior hell-bent on her destruction. The stronghold she kept on her emotions teetered precariously and her bones throbbed with the effort to stand tall.

Three weeks in exchange for three and a half million pounds.

Breathing in and out, slow and even, she locked her knees so tightly, a sharp pain shot up her thighs. But it was nothing compared to the blood dripping from her heart.

Lucas, the blackmailing beast, stood in the centre of the room, a dark lock of his hair falling over his brow in bad-boy disarray. Tall and gladiator-strong, he waited patiently—no doubt for a sign of her surrender. If she didn't loathe him so much she would melt at the sheer sight of him. He'd played her since the moment he'd arrived.

'Choice?' she said, and thank God her voice didn't falter. 'My so-called choice is either to follow you or lose my job, Mr Garcia. I'm fairly certain my refusal to comply with your conditions would land me in the unemployment line.' Oh, she could beg Ryan Tate to give her time to find the money elsewhere, but it would be a useless pursuit. There was a reason he was known as a hard-ass among her colleagues. Ryan Tate would question her sanity. Tell her to swallow her damn pride and think of the bigger picture. Don't look a gift horse in the mouth and all that. 'Then again, you knew that, *Lucas*, didn't you?' she said bitterly.

His throat convulsed and after a few seconds he relaxed his stance and rolled his broad shoulders. The fact that he didn't answer made her madder still.

'Who on earth do you think you are?' she said, her control slipping a notch. 'You went to Tate's office without even consulting me. Is this what I have to look forward to? A life of being coerced, controlled and dictated to?'

A light flashed in his intense stare before his face contorted with stunned incredulity. 'Since when does three weeks equate to a lifetime?'

It might seem a measly three weeks to him, but what would they demand after that? It didn't bear thinking about. 'Since you've given me a taste of the new regime!'

Lucas scrubbed his palm over his mouth, his chest heaving. 'Claudia,' he growled, his hand dropping into a large fist by his side, 'I am attempting to do my job, but your obdurate attitude leaves me with few options. Instead of focusing on *how* this happened, why not take some pleasure from what you will benefit from. Three and a half million pounds, to be precise.'

'But at what cost to *me?*' she asked. Then immediately bit her lip when the words echoed through the room.

'Three weeks of your time. It is nothing,' he said, with a savage slash of his hand.

A pitiful laugh broke through her thick throat. How wrong he was. Lucas had no idea of the personal price she'd pay. He was oblivious to her inner turmoil. But that didn't excuse his behaviour in her eyes. She was dedicated to *her* job, but did she go around blackmailing people? No.

'You speak of the strength of your dedication. Your work taking priority. Yet if that were true the money would make your decision in an instant. Or,' he continued, his mouth twisting, 'is it a case of you using your job as a convenient excuse?'

'No!' she cried.

Lucas's head reared at her outburst and she winced inwardly.

'No,' she tried again—softer, quieter. But it was altogether too late. The hitch to his brow told her so. And to some extent he was right.

When the effects of her illness had waned in her late teens her parents had visited once, maybe twice. Other times they'd sent messengers, and for years she'd declined everything from a short vacation to a simple dinner on her own turf, using her work as an excuse. Avoiding her own parents because they'd hurt her, betrayed her, cast her aside. When she'd needed them the most. If she took the money this day she would be giving them the power to destroy her all over again. *But you can keep your distance, Claudia. You're adept at doing just that.*

Three weeks of God knew what, in exchange for her funding.

Taking short ragged breaths to ease the pain in her lungs, she squeezed her eyes shut. In the space of two seconds her mind began its attack, assaulting her with a multitude of visions and images.

Arunthia—a world in which she'd been deemed unworthy and dispensable.

St Andrew's Hospital—where she could make a real difference. And—*oh, God*—the children trying to smile through the pain, the misery. If she lost her job work on their case would scream to a halt. Claudia was their advocate. They needed her. Could she ever look at them in the face again, knowing she could have helped if only she'd faced her past?

Pain cracked through her mind and her eyes pinged open. Lucas was staring, his eyes curiously hot and heavy, fixed on her mouth where she tore at her bottom lip. Gooseflesh pimpled every inch of her skin and she shuddered ferociously. Why did he have to stare at her so much? It was as unnerving as it was confusing. Made her want to reach up. Touch. Check her skin. Bury her face in her hands. Hide. But she couldn't. Wouldn't.

As if he'd caught himself, he scrubbed his hands over his

face and combed his glorious hair back from his brow with long
blunt fingers. Heat flushed through her core and her breasts
grew strangely heavy. She stroked her clavicle and felt the burn
sear her palm. *Oh, great.* Her body wasn't complying with the
new hate programme.

'Accompany me to Arunthia, Claudia,' he said, in a per-
suasive drawl that made her quiver. How was she meant to
stay sane with a man who made her spontaneously combust?
'Despite what you think, I understand your desire to crack the
elusive code of an illness that must've been difficult for you,
but surely you can continue to work from home during your
stay? With your family's support?'

Support? She almost choked. The very last thing she would
ever get from her parents was support.

Lucas's gaze dropped to her hands and she realised she was
tugging at her cuffs with the tips of her fingers. Again. Her
stomach nose-dived to the floor. His eyes were like fidget-
seeking missiles. She couldn't think straight around him. Instead of controlling her habits, which she usually managed to
hide unerringly, she kept being distracted by *him*. Her attention constantly snagged on his long, powerful legs, his huge,
masculine hands, his utterly contemptuous handsome-as-sin
face. And no matter how hard she tried her traitorous mind kept
imagining things—like those big hands touching her in all the
places she felt warm and sensitive. Kissing her. Caressing her.

Heat slapped her cheeks. This had to stop!

Her life was crumbling before her eyes—her career, her
life's work, slipping through her fingers like grains of salt—
and all she could think about was being kissed. If that wasn't
bad enough, she wanted the man who'd plotted her destruction to do it! She was seriously beginning to question her mental faculties.

Panic fired a shot of adrenaline down her spine, surging
to every extremity. Her feet were the first to move and she
swerved around the desk, walking towards the door with no

forethought to her destination. But getting away from Lucas sounded like paradise.

Before she made it past he bolted forward, one hand out-stretched, reaching for her. 'Claudia. *Dios!* Stop. Do not walk away from me,' he growled. 'We are not done.'

Oh, God. She flinched, jerked backwards, and almost lost her footing. 'Oh...' Steely hands closed around her upper arms, steadying her, and she scrunched her eyes shut, unable to look at his face for fear of what she might see. Pity? Or, worse still, disgust?

Through two layers she could feel the heat of his palms, and the power of his grip fired a blaze of sorcery through her bloodstream. His breath tickled over her face and the scent of warm strong coffee wafted over her, making her crave a caf-feine fix. As soon as she regained her balance his hands fell away and Claudia yearned for them to come back. Which was crazy for all kinds of reasons.

The noise of his throat clearing told her he'd moved back a pace or three, and Claudia opened one eye to check. Sure enough, he stood a few feet away, fists clenched, eyes rag-ing with a storm. Darkness tainted his tone. 'Where are you going, Claudia?'

Somewhat safer, she opened her other eye and practically ran towards the door. 'I have to see Ryan Tate,' she murmured, grateful for the excuse that flashed into her brain.

'What?' His thunderous voice became a distant blur as she swerved into the corridor. She imagined him standing there, his gorgeous blue eyes glittering with ire, his fists balled to stop himself from wrapping them around her throat.

'Claudia, wait!' he hollered. 'We need to finish this. *Now!*'

'Go to hell, Lucas.'

She kept on walking, blinded by a mind-fog, and within minutes, oblivious as to how she descended three floors, she was standing in front of Ryan Tate's door, her fist hovering over the solid oak panel.

And then she saw it. The violent tremble in the hand poised

in front of her. Then she felt it. The pain searing up her legs, crippling her entire body. Quickly she turned and leaned against the wall before her knees surrendered. Tipping her head back, the beige paint a glorious pillow, she closed her eyes and swallowed hard.

Come on Claudia, get a grip, she mouthed silently. *Three weeks. Three and a half million pounds. Keep your distance. Stay away from Lucas the Devastating. You can do this.*

She just had to remain strong and self-reliant. Always self-reliant.

You don't get close, you don't get hurt. Breathe, Claudia, breathe.

Time ticked by, the trembling subsided, and the pain dulled to its usual ache. Finally able to stand tall, she inhaled a lung full of fortifying air, lifted her chin, raised her hand to knock once, twice…and walked through Ryan Tate's door.

'Claudia, my girl. Good news, aye?'

After years of honing her brave face, Claudia slipped behind her iron mask and smiled.

Sweat pierced the base of his spine as Lucas stalked the lab, focusing on breathing and formulating a new plan. As long as it involved getting out of this white box he'd be slightly mollified. Claudia might prefer her small hideaway, but he required vast open space to feel alive.

It hadn't escaped him that when the prickly Princess had been in the room he'd been less aware of the enclosure. *Probably because you only had eyes for her.* Lucas growled, satisfying himself that it was more a case of distraction.

Was she pleading with Tate to give her more time to find the money elsewhere? *Dios* she was the most awkward, feisty, self-centred, gorgeous woman he'd ever met.

She also despised him with a passion. The disgust in her eyes had almost floored him. Only a fool would have walked in here without the necessary weapons at his disposal. God knew he'd have preferred to reach some kind of compromise, but she was recklessly tenacious and ignoble at best.

Yet as soon as he'd revealed his tactical strategy his stomach had ached as if she'd punched him in the guts. How did she manage to unearth emotion from him? He knew she selfishly pursued her own agenda. Knew she'd given him no choice but to push her. It was bewildering. Unnerving. Inappropriate and unwelcome. For Lucas had buried his emotions twenty years ago, and that, he thought, hardening his heart, was the way they must stay.

Glancing down at his hands, he curled his fingers into his palms. He could still feel her; he'd swear it. Warm, toned, yet lusciously soft. And her scent—*Dios*, she smelled of summer. Warm notes of vanilla blossom and honey. Up close she was impossibly more beautiful, and as he'd held her he'd willed her to open her eyes. But the hate had still been there and she could not bear to look at him. Which was good—great, fantastic. Being likable was not in his job description. Getting her home, however, was.

'Why are you still here?'

His stomach flinched but he managed to become fixated on her fascinating collection of test tubes. It was her voice: snippily sexy beyond belief. Why a schoolmarm tone should flick his switch he'd never know. He'd never had a teacher in his life. Children from the slums were not afforded such privileges. No books, no paper nor pens to draw with. Only walls stained with tobacco, bloodied fists and a penknife beyond decay.

'A trip to hell was unappealing,' he replied thickly, knowingly. He'd been there plenty of times, after all. 'And, with the greatest will in the world, I cannot deliver a package I do not have in my possession.'

'Quite.'

Lucas swivelled on his heels in time to see her arch one dark brow, her eyes firing with newfound determination. And his chest seized with such force his lungs pinched with deprivation.

'You knew I'd come back, didn't you?' she asked.

'Let's just say I had faith you would come to your senses.' While she'd virtually admitted that she used her work as a shield to hide from her parents, he believed she loved her job. If he could admire her for anything, it was the strength of her dedication. What he struggled to comprehend was why she couldn't extend that devotion to her role in Arunthia. He wanted to ask her, to try to understand. But the longer he stood here, skirting quicksand, the more entrenched he became.

Pouting her luscious lips, she canted her head like an inquisitive meerkat. 'I can't work out whether you're extremely diplomatic or downright arrogant.'

'I shall leave that for you to decide.'

She walked farther into the room, snatched a pair of spectacles from a plastic tub on the bench, and pushed them up her pert nose. With steel in her spine, her head high in a model-type pose, Lucas was smacked with a vision: Claudia Verbault, strutting down a catwalk, wearing a ruffled blouse and a tweed skirt, sucking on a pencil. Seductively intellectual.

Blood pooled in his groin and his mouth turned as dry as Arunthian dirt. He had to drench his lips with moisture in order to speak.

'I have a jet on stand-by. We'll leave the country within two hours.' Lucas could have her home within five and his job would be done. In future he'd only have to see her at state functions. By then, having appeased his newfound sexual appetite, he'd be able to look at her without imagining her naked. For he knew her body would be sublime. Soft and pliable to his steel and strength, and tall enough to be the perfect fit.

'Rather presumptuous of you, isn't it?' she said.

Madre de Dios! Had he said that out loud? Lucas focused on her bent head as she slid the files lying on her desk into a large briefcase, one on top of the other.

He cleared his throat of pure want. 'What is?'

'To assume I'm leaving with you.'

The tightness in his neck drained down his spine. 'Apologies, *Just Claudia.*'

Her hand stilled, and from his sideways vantage point he watched one eyelid shutter while she inhaled deeply, her breasts rising with life, pinky rouge blooming up her cheeks.

Did he affect her? The notion sucker-punched him straight in the solar plexus.

Her gentle touch forgotten, she began to ram two or three more files into the case, pushing until the bag was fit to burst. Maybe she was imagining it was his head. Oh, he certainly affected her. With annoyance rather than sexual attraction. Instead of relief he felt ridiculously irked.

How typical that the one woman in the world he could never have was a nemesis he instinctively wanted to devour.

'So. What is your decision?' He already knew it, but if she wanted to put up the pretence of a fight he would humour her. For now.

Kid gloves were his current choice of weapon.

'I'm coming with you.'

His lips curved.

'But not today.'

They flattened faster than a bomb detonation site.

'What?'

'I need three days,' she said, adamant.

'Impossible.' He wouldn't last two days without assaulting her gorgeous mouth.

Lucas worked to his own schedule, but just the thought of spending time near that sensational body while his stomach churned with a noxious mixture of frustration and fury ratcheted his deadline up into the red zone.

'Delaying the inevitable is not only a foolhardy display of awkwardness on your part but a waste of time.'

'Not for me. I need to go back to my apartment and pack. I have a personal matter to attend to, and most of all I need time to think,' she said, tucking a wayward curl around the delicate shell of her ear.

'Think?' What did she need to think about? How many lab coats to pack? 'I have no time to spare.' Lucas blinked. Wait a minute... Personal matter? *Dios,* he'd never thought of that. And why did it make him feel like punching the wall?

'Tough. Find time. Because I'm not going anywhere today.' There it was again—that surge of heat when she used that sexy, stern voice.

And there *she* was, being selfish again. Why did he keep forgetting what kind of person she was? 'Claudia, I cannot stay in London. I have to work.'

'Oh, *really?*' she said, yanking the case off the table and almost toppling over as it fell to the floor with a thud. 'Well, now you know how I feel. I'm being dragged away from mine for three weeks. I'm sure you can afford to take three days.'

His nostrils flared. 'My terms—'

'Lucas,' she said, attempting to disguise her rude interruption with an untried honeyed tone that made his skin prickle, 'you will quickly come to realise I forget nothing. Your terms are—and I quote—three weeks' leave, effective from nine this morning. Coupled with my return to Arunthia. On no occasion did you state a day of departure.'

Dios! Lucas seethed. She was impossible. 'It is almost noon. You have eight hours.' Let it not be said that he couldn't compromise.

Arms crossed tight, her full breasts were pushed upwards to stretch the stiff cotton and she canted her hip in a sexy pose. The ten-bell alarm siren going off in his head almost rendered him deaf. Almost.

'Two days,' she bartered.

Lucas ground his jaw. 'Twenty-four hours. Final offer.' He was crazy. Certifiable. A day of Claudia would tip him over the edge of reason to plummet headlong into insanity. He did not negotiate. *Ever.* People obeyed him. Always.

She smiled. It might have been small and somewhat triumphant, but she actually smiled at him.

Lucas felt his eye twitch.

'Done,' she said, all smug sweetness.

God help him if she ever put her heart and soul into it. Because Lucas had an uneasy feeling it would be him that would be 'done'.

'Fine,' he snapped, his abnormal behaviour pushing his soaring anger levels from dangerous to critical.

He only prayed her apartment on the Thames had separate floors. Or at least a fifty-foot distance between bedrooms. Fighting with bloodthirsty night demons would be child's play in comparison to the blistering temptation that would be down the hall.

Lucas didn't look happy, Claudia mused. Waves of dark fury poured from his tight shoulders, much like the rain streaming in rivulets down the black bodywork of his Aston Martin Vanquish.

The engine of his Aston Martin Vanquish roared like a sleek panther as he revved his displeasure, and she wiggled on the cream cowhide in an attempt to cover her quivering reaction. She'd never thought of a car as arousing before. Well, she'd never thought of *anything* as arousing before. Today seemed to be a day for firsts. Even the heady smell of leather and damp clothing couldn't douse the warm, woodsy scent of Lucas lingering in the air.

With the exception of his barking request for her to enter her address into the sat nav, their drive to her apartment had been deadly silent. Now, parked at the kerb, she was desperate to be away from his fiercely primal aura. She was so tired she no longer had the strength to argue, and her legs throbbed so viciously she'd be lucky if she made it inside the building, let alone up the stairs.

'Erm…thanks for the lift, Mr Garcia. Unless the gods grace me with a reprieve, I'll see you tomorrow.' Without further ado, she yanked hard on the door handle. After a third *kerthunk,* she surrendered, directing her voice to be sweet. 'Could you open the door, *pleeease?*'

'Claudia,' he growled, nostrils flaring, his chest heaving with barely suppressed anger. Staring out of his window at the three-storey townhouse where she lived on the second floor, he twisted his long fingers around the dark wood steering wheel. Maybe he was imagining it was her neck. 'Have you ever once acknowledged who you *actually* are?'

'Who I am?' she asked wearily, not entirely sure what he was getting at and unable to summon the energy to care.

'Yes, Claudia,' he said slowly, as if speaking to a child. 'A member of the Arunthian Royal Family.'

Never. 'Not really. Can I go now?' She gave the handle another tug. *Kerthunk.* A long sigh poured from her lungs.

'How long have you lived in this…this place?' The way he said *place,* as if the word was rat poison on his tongue, was like taking a grater to her nerves. Without bothering to look out of the window, her mind's eye recalled a picture of the tired frontage of this Victorian townhouse on a less than stellar street. What was he getting into a funk about? *He* didn't have to live here.

Claudia bit her tongue and thumped her head off the rest. 'Oh, about eighteen months, I think.' She slept most nights in the lab—more for convenience than because of the emptiness that shrouded her body when she lay between cold damp sheets, she was sure—but she kept that titbit to herself.

Lucas continued to fume, steam blowing from his nose as he stared out of the front windscreen. 'You could've been abducted fifty times over,' he growled, and she lifted her head from the buttery soft leather to see him scrub his face with rough hands. 'Burgled, raped, assaulted,' he went on. 'What the *hell* were you thinking, Claudia?'

Pushing down on the froth of fury bubbling up her throat, she pursed her lips. He'd turned from blackmailer to overprotective bore!

'You're overreacting, Mr Garcia,' she said calmly. 'This is a decent area and I have an excellent alarm system. Anyway, who would look at…?' The words died on her tongue as she realised how pitiful she would sound if she said *me.* She knew she wasn't pretty, and she'd given up wishing she looked like one of her famed-for-their-beauty sisters long ago. Right now, faced with the most astoundingly handsome man she'd ever seen, she couldn't face the prospect of his sympathy or his averment.

'Who would look at *what?*'

For the first time in thirty minutes he turned to look at her. The intensity in his sapphire blues acted like a laser beam and, as if locked on target, she couldn't tear her gaze away.

Choosing her words carefully, she said, 'Who would look twice at a normal person? The problems start when people appear moneyed and pampered. I bring no attention to myself. No one would give me a second glance.'

Jaw dropping open, Lucas slowly shook his head incredulously. 'And what if your cover was blown?'

'I would move. Can I go now?'

'No. You *cannot* go now,' he said fiercely, and her hackles prickled. 'Why are you not living in the *security-enhanced* apartment on the Thames?'

Claudia stiffened and finally managed to wrench her gaze away. 'How do you know about—?' She held up her hand in a stop sign. 'Forget I said that. I needed to be closer to work.' A half-truth, but that was all he was getting. It was seriously unnerving to know someone had files detailing her life events. She imagined it read like a chronological disaster essay.

'You gave it up?' he asked, his brows almost hitting his hairline. 'To live *here?*'

For some reason she actually followed his finger, which unsurprisingly pointed to her flat. 'Yes,' she said simply.

'*Dios,* Claudia!' His hands lifted as if pleading for patience from the heavens. 'How can an intelligent woman be so unthinking?'

A ball of fury began to swirl in her stomach, and no matter how hard she sucked in air the motion picked up pace like a cyclone. 'Now, just wait a minute—'

'You have no regard for your safety. None,' he said with a slash of his hands. 'I have seen safer streets in the slums.

Well, I will tell you this right now. We are not staying here. *Comprende?*'

Her mouth shaping for a scathing retort along the lines of *It's none of your damn business,* she felt his words loop round her skull like a broken record. Her hand crept up to her throat, where her pulse jumped erratically. 'What do you mean, *we?*'

'From the time you agreed to the terms to the time we arrive at the Arunthian palace you are under *my* protection,' he grated, seemingly not entirely happy with the prospect.

Well, neither was she!

'Next time you barter with me, Claudia, you'd better think twice about the consequences. For the next twenty-four hours we are stuck together. Whether you like it or not.'

Oh, God. As Shakespeare might say, she'd been hoist with her own petard.

'Clearly you don't,' she said. She felt sick. She felt dizzy. Was it physically possible to strangle yourself?

'I have better things to do than babysit a self-centred, senseless, se... *Arrrrggh.*' With a frustrated roar, he pushed open the car door and launched himself from the bucket seat. Before he'd even slammed it shut she yanked on the handle to follow him. And finally the rotten thing worked!

'Whoa—wait a minute,' she said, veering round the front bonnet, sloshing in puddles. Freezing water seeped into her shoes, while the rain lashed down to drench her hair and pummel her skin. Vision blurring, she pushed her glasses on top of her head, visor-like. 'Where I live has *nothing* to do with you.' By the time she'd caught up to him he was pacing back and forth on the walkway in his usual caged predator manner. 'You barge into my life and proceed to conduct some sort of military operation. And now you're going on like an interfering, dictatorial knave!'

Suddenly he stopped and turned on his heels to face her. 'Do you have an aversion to authority, Claudia? Is that what this is? You don't like being told what to do?'

The grey silken weave of his sartorial suit darkened to almost black as huge rain droplets seeped through his clothing. His over-long hair was already dripping, plastered to his smooth forehead and the high slash of his cheekbones. And—*oh, my*—the sight of him, wet and dishevelled, flooded her core with heat. Like this he was far more powerful and dangerous to her equilibrium. He looked roguish, gloriously untamed.

Her heart thumping so hard she could hear her pulse echo in her ears, she had to scroll back to remember what he'd said. *Oh, yeah. The brute.*

'No, actually, I don't. Do you think it's right to force someone against their every wish? To blackmail in order to do your job?' Something dark flashed in his eyes but she was too far gone to care. 'And because I dare to put up some sort of fight you deem me selfish and irresponsible. Do you have *any* feelings?'

'I am not paid to feel,' he ground out, taking a step closer towards her.

'It's a good job, 'cos you'd be broke,' she replied, taking a step back.

Lucas pinched the bridge of his nose with his thumb and forefinger. 'You are the most provoking woman I have ever met.'

A mere two feet away, Claudia could feel the heat radiating from his broad torso. Oh, God, she had to get away from him before she did something seriously stupid. Like smooth her hands up his soaked shirt. 'You know what, Lucas? You can sleep in your posh car for all I care. Frankly, I've been more comfortable on the 271 bus from Highgate. I'm staying here.'

Before he could say another word she bolted sideways. Only to be blocked by a one-arm barricade.

'Over my dead body,' he growled, corralling her back towards the car.

'That could be arranged,' she said, suddenly breathless.

Rain poured down her face, her throat, to trickle down the inside of her collar. That was why she shuddered so hard. It had nothing to do with the fact that Lucas was inching towards her with lethal intent.

'You are coming with me. From now on I am in charge.'

'Well, you can just rid yourself of *that* illusion. You'll never be in charge of me!'

Suddenly her back connected with the car in a wet slap and she felt the engine thunder and roar with its need to unleash power. The vibration shot up her spine and then pinballed back down her vertebrae, surging for every extremity until she felt like a pulsing livewire.

'You know what, Claudia?'

It was his hot, heavy tone more than his words that caught her attention, and she jerked up to catch the feral gleam in his eyes.

'Wha...what?'

Water streamed down his brow, dripped off his nose and lingered on his darkening jaw as she hung on his every word. After swiping his face with deft hands he shook his head, like a dog shedding its bath, to send even more rain showering over her.

Hot and sultry liquid pooled in her abdomen and she pushed against the cool metal to stop herself from sliding into a heap at his feet. The awesome sight of him was distressing enough, but for some reason Claudia wished he were utterly naked. Well, not totally. Maybe just his top half. So she could take a peek. *Oh, God,* what was happening to her?

'I am beginning to think I've handled you all wrong,' he said, licking his lips hungrily. 'I have been a negotiator,' he said, holding up one finger. 'Waste of time and effort.'

Her eyes were glued to his sensual mouth, mesmerised by the way his wet lips moved as he spoke. He had great teeth.

'I have tried to appeal to your better nature,' he continued, holding two fingers up. 'However, I'm not at all sure you have one.'

'Hey, that's not fair—'

He silenced her with two warm fingers and her cool flesh

sizzled on contact. It took every ounce of self-control to stop herself licking. Nibbling.

'I have even tried kid gloves and allowing you to barter for extra time. And look where that has brought us. To a hovel in one of the scummiest areas I have ever had the displeasure to visit.'

Lucas dragged his fingers over her mouth, the pressure curling her bottom lip and tugging her eyelids shut. 'This is a nice area. You're just a snob,' she breathed.

'I should have hauled you out of that lab hours ago,' he said, his volume lower, his tone silkier. 'Straight onto a plane and straight home to Arunthia. This is what I get for being considerate.'

Oh, he *had* to be joking!

Her eyes flew open. He was staring at her mouth, following her tongue as it licked her lips over and over in basic instinct. The fresh taste of Mother Nature blended with bittersweet anticipation. 'You're an animal. A…a beast.'

'You know what else, *Just Claudia?* I think there's only one way to shut you up.'

Bracing his hands against the car on either side of her, he leaned forward, eyes glittering.

Oooh, my. Her heart kicked into overdrive. Her blood fizzed through her veins. A strange bearing down in her abdomen forced her to clench her insides, the slight twitch making her core spasm with liquid fever.

Lucas's body heat burned through her wet clothing and she trembled so violently that her words—'You wouldn't dare…'—came out more like a plea.

Hitching a dark, sexy brow, he murmured. 'Ah, Claudia, didn't anyone ever tell you never to provoke an animal?'

CHAPTER FOUR

ANIMAL.

The word assaulted his brain, fighting to break through the heady maelstrom of anger and high-octane sexual desire. Blinking rapidly, every shuttering of his eyes brought another aspect of their surroundings into sharper relief.

London. Unsafe. Protect.

They were soaked to the skin. Claudia's grey Mac moulded to the swell of her full, high breasts with every shivery breath she took. Minuscule drops of rain beaded on her long lashes like black diamonds, and as her eyes fluttered the rare gems lost their precarious hold and trickled down her beautiful face.

She slowly opened her eyes and focused on his mouth. She rose on her toes and her breasts grazed up his chest. His groin hardened to titanium as the moisture sizzled on his skin.

Dios, what was she doing? More to the point, what was *he* doing? She made him lose his mind, his self-control, and at this rate he would be *sans* all honour by Monday next.

Retreat, Garcia. Retreat. Now!

She stilled, flicked her big amber eyes up to his, and what he saw nearly shocked his heart into cardiac arrest. Fear. She was scared. Of *him*.

Animal.

'No.' *Never.*

This was his idea of protection? Crowding her against the side of a car in the sheeting rain?

'Apologies, Your Royal Highness,' he said, pushing off the car and taking three large paces back.

'Don't call me that,' she whispered.

A deep V creased her brow as she searched his face, then took a keen interest in her feet. If it were anyone else he would think she was disappointed but, *Dios,* the fear.

He had to remember who she was, even if she didn't quite grasp the fact. Why the hell was she living in this cesspool? For the sake of a twenty-minute taxi-ride to work? No, he doubted it. But now was not the time to cause further animosity. He needed her to listen and obey him. If she could just do as she was told for five minutes things would get a hell of a lot easier.

'Claudia, get in the car. I need to get you dry. Away from this place.'

'I don't mind being wet. I love the rain. So pure and clean.' Chin lifting, she tipped her face skyward. 'I can't remember the last time I did this.'

His eyes traced the graceful line of her throat and his heart thumped back to life. The abysmal weather had failed to diminish the colour of her lustrous gold-toned skin—her Arunthian heritage.

'I am very glad,' he murmured, his fingers howling to stroke her silken cheek. Claudia's face plummeted back to his and he realised he must have spoken out loud. *Damn.* 'I do not think delivering you home with a bout of pneumonia would go in my favour.'

Her lips curved ruefully. 'Of course.' She stood tall, swiped her forehead with the back of her hand to brush tendrils of hair from her temple, and glanced up to the building behind him. 'I can go and change, but I haven't got anything for you, I'm afraid.'

The tense muscle in his shoulders eased as she inadvertently gave away her lack of live-in-lover status. Of course that didn't mean she was single. And collating all the facts was his job, was it not?

'My clothing is of no consequence.' Compared to being

caked in three months' worth of dirt sweat and blood, a little water was exiguous. 'Please—lead the way.'

She swung her gaze back to him, eyes wide. 'I can manage perfectly well myself. Just give me five minutes—'

'No. I will accompany you. You'll need more than five minutes to pack. Then we'll spend the night in the Thames apartment.'

Her eyes grew impossibly larger. 'We can't do that.'

'Why not?'

'Well…because it's empty.'

He groaned, long and low, clenching his fists to stop himself from giving her a damn good shake. 'And your post? Letters? They are forwarded…yes?'

She nibbled on her plump bottom lip. 'No. Come to think of it, I haven't picked them up for months. I've been so busy.'

Dios, little wonder her father's letters had gained no reply. But why warmth rushed through him at the realisation he had no idea.

'No matter. I will extend my stay at the Astoria. We'll stay there for the night.'

'I don't want to stay there.' Tugging at her cuffs, she tossed her head in an aggravating lofty flounce. 'I can just stay here.'

Head snapping upright, he gave her *The Look*. The look designed to command hundreds of soldiers and stop assassins in their tracks.

And what did she do? Rolled her amber eyes!

'Fine,' she said. 'But for heaven's sake don't use that look on me again. It will never work.' She caught a yawn in her small fist. 'I'm just so tired I can barely think straight, let alone argue with you.'

She looked past tired, but he had no intention of taking the blame for her ferocious work ethic or any other night-time activities she indulged in.

'This is progress indeed. Keys?' he said, palm outstretched.

She dug into her pocket, rummaging. Out came a tissue, a

pencil, a small notepad. All of which she stuffed in her free hand. 'I know I picked them up. I *know* I did.'

Raking his hair back from his face, he took a moment to rein in his anxiety. And in that instant an arrow of ice speared up his nape and his head snapped upright.

Traffic weaved around his parked car—a black hatchback, a red coupe—and beyond, on the opposite side of the street, there was a small Italian restaurant, a run-down clothes store, a church. And, parked directly in front, a large white pick-up.

'Get in the car.'

'What?' she said, delving into her other pocket.

'Now!'

'Do you have to be so impatient? I'm telling you the rotten key is in here somewhere.'

Lucas gripped her arm, ignored the pocket paraphernalia clattering to the pavement, marched her round the car, opened the door and pushed her inside.

'Lucas, really,' she said, poking her head out. 'What is *wrong* with you?'

Palm flat on top of her head, he pressed her back into the car, slammed the door, ate the tarmac in five quick paces and folded his frame into the seat beside her. 'Buckle up.'

'No. I need to go inside,' she said, exasperated, pointing at the red brick façade of her grotty flat. 'I don't have any—'

'Claudia, I do not care what you want. We are being watched, and I need to get you out of here.'

'*Watched?*' she repeated, in a high-pitched squeak as her hand crept up her chest and wrapped around the base of her throat. 'But that's impossible. No one knows me.'

Yesterday that might have been true, but when the Arunthian King disclosed his intent to gather the royal family for the event of the decade things changed. Lucas had known that. Which was why he'd flown into a military base. Why he hadn't ordered chauffeur-driven cars. When the King's three daughters were dotted around the globe, and in particular when one had been missing for well over a decade, interest was ripe.

Claudia was spoken of in hushed tones, and in all his years working for the King he'd never been told her exact whereabouts. Until now. He didn't envy her the scrutiny she'd be placed under when they returned. Only the best guards would be selected to watch over her, and Lucas would ensure he chose men with eyes in the back of their heads—for she was nothing but reckless obstinacy.

His mind flitting through the options, he took one last glance at the white pick-up truck.

'Unless…' she said.

Lucas pulled out into the lane of traffic, feeling her eyes burning into the side of his face. He knew what was coming—could feel the initial flare of her wrath. Perversely, it began to stoke the fires he'd managed to douse.

'Oh, my God,' she said, elbows bent, fingers pressing into her temples like one of those telepaths harnessing their brain power. 'You know what, Lucas? I've known of your existence for three hours and already my life has gone to the dogs. There's only one reason for someone to take a sudden interest in me. *You've* blown my cover!'

Lucas slapped the indicator and gripped the steering wheel until his knuckles ached. *Dios,* how had this happened? For the first time in his career he'd failed to do his job. First by almost kissing her and second by putting her in jeopardy. Within five seconds of their meeting he'd lost control of his carnal appetites and his instincts were sloth-like. How long had the pick-up truck been standing there? While he, the Head of Security, had had her hard up against a car, ready to devour her mouth and anything else he could reach.

'I cannot see how,' he said, vexed as he attempted to find an explanation for this strange phenomenon. 'Do you think me so inept I would announce my arrival in the country to the press?'

'How do I know if you're any good at your job? So far I've been blackmailed, shouted at and suffered a good soaking.'

Good point.

From the corner of his eye he watched her yank her glasses

from atop her head and rub the lenses on her coat. Her sodden coat.

'Great. Now I don't even have a tissue because you—' She took a deep breath and tossed the thick frames into the footwell. 'Anyway, how do you know...?' He heard her audible gulp. 'That they were press.'

'I only suspect,' he said, knowing his hunch was enough. It always had been. Apart from that one time. When he'd lost everything. When he'd been ruled by emotion—something that would never, *ever* happen again. Emotion made you sloppy. Careless.

Lucas ignored the crucifying scratch of his conscience, warning him of the similarities to his current predicament. This was different. *This* was a dire case of sexual chemistry messing with his head.

'Well, forgive me if I don't share in your suspicions. You could be overreacting. There are hundreds of vans in London. Thousands, in fact. No one has ever given me a second glance.'

'*Dios,* Claudia, that's because no one knows who you are. You are hidden well in London and you purposely dress in camouflage.'

'I don't purposely dress in anything. I dress for comfort and my personal taste.'

He snorted, and was about to tell her that against all evidence to the contrary he was not a stupid man when he glanced in his rearview mirror.

'Push your spine into the seat and look straight ahead. I need to lose my *suspicious overreaction* and take some swift turns.'

'Oh, good grief. Could this day get any worse?' she said, her fingers curling around the leather lip of the seat alongside her slender thighs.

Sí. He could have kissed her.

And if that thought wasn't bad enough, they lost the van within three minutes only to get snarled up in traffic—while Claudia caught yawn after yawn in her small fist.

'You need sleep,' he said, frowning at the dark smudges beneath her eyes. 'You look ill.'

'Why, thank you, Lucas,' she said, voice dripping with sarcasm. 'Just what I wanted to hear.'

In his peripheral vision he watched her rub the outer flesh of her thighs for the third time and his foul mood ratcheted up a notch. Why did his brain insist on informing him of every damn move she made?

'Next you'll tell me we're still being *followed*.'

Why didn't she believe him? Never had his word been questioned. The knock to his honour gave his tone extra bite. 'No. You may rest.'

Lucas determinedly switched off, focused on changing gear and lowering his pulse. Soon enough he pulled into the private rear entrance of the Astoria and watched daylight being eclipsed by the metal security doors until only a thin sliver remained. Extinguishing the engine, he glanced over at Claudia. Her head was cushioned by the soft leather padded wing, her eyes were closed, breathing steady and even. In peace, her beauty was breathtaking.

Eyes trailing down her body, his guts twisted at the sight of damp cloth sticking to her skin, outlining her lush curves.

'Claudia?' he said—loud enough to wake the dead. Otherwise he'd have no choice but to touch her, and while his body was willing and able his mind rejected the idea immediately.

The problem was, where Claudia was concerned his body seemed to rule. Why else would he be in this imbroglio in the first place? He should have her ensconced in the jet by now, halfway to Arunthia. Perfectly dry and unruffled.

Unfortunately it seemed his reluctant royal was dead to the world.

'Dios.' Lucas thrust open his door and launched himself to his feet, adrenaline pumping through his body and making him hard all over.

Barking orders to the security guard to clear his path, he

scooped her into his arms and strode through the darkened corridors, ordering his body not to feel. Not to react.

Damn impossible when she curled into his arms, snuggled against his damp chest, laid her head on his broad shoulder and grabbed fistfuls of his white shirt. Heat shot down his spine, pooled in his groin, and by the time he reached the penthouse his heart was thumping a twenty-man stampede that had nothing to do with exertion.

The guard opened the door to the penthouse and Lucas marched to the enormous bed, laid her down and backed the *hell* away.

'Sir? Do you need any further assistance?'

Lucas scrubbed his jaw. 'Clothes. She needs something dry to sleep in.' Why hadn't he thought of this? What did women sleep in apart from their skin? Gorgeous honey-gold skin... His throat turned thick as molasses along with his blood, and against a direct order his eyes toppled back to the bed.

'We have a concession downstairs, sir. I could ask one of the assistants to help?'

He nodded, heard the man exit the room with a decisive click and reached for his mobile phone. He was determined to find the man who'd followed them, and soon, but first... *Dios,* she was in serious danger of becoming ill.

Claudia was curling her long body into a foetal position on the gold coverlet, and he was smacked with that hint of vulnerability once more. His mind latched onto another woman at another time. Defenceless. Frail. Unprotected. By him.

Lucas clenched his stomach to stop the pain ripping his abdomen clean in half, reached for the plateau he visited in the dead of night and banished the memory.

Gritting his teeth, he focused on Claudia, curled his hand round her soft upper arm and gently tugged her onto her back. The sight of her stretching sinuously against the satin was one adrenaline shot to his groin too many. Cursing, he began to pop her coat buttons from top to bottom, peeling away the layers, trying his utmost to stay disconnected, yet unable to deny the tremor of his fingers.

Then, *gracias a Dios,* she murmured and began to stir, turning on her side.

'Claudia? Wake up. I need you to take off your clothes.'

'Okay,' she murmured sleepily, as she rolled back on her side and buried her face in the palm of her hand.

'No. No! Do not sleep. Not yet.'

That did it. She opened her eyes. Blinked. Stretched again. Writhed her centrefold body like the she-devil she was. Then bolted upright. 'Where am I?'

'In my hotel suite. You may sleep, but first you need to undress,' he said, his already tentative hold on control fraying at the image of her undressing in front of him. *For* him.

Her face scrunching in a strangely pretty grimace, she twisted her legs, folding them underneath her. 'Ugh, I feel horrid,' she said, absorbing her surroundings, her eyes wide as they flew to his. 'How did I get up here?'

'I carried you. In slumber you bring new meaning to the adage sleeping like the dead.'

Cheeks pinkening, she swung her legs over the edge of the bed, her eyes riveted to his chest. 'Oh, I know. Comes from sleeping in the noisiest places.' At his quizzical glance she elaborated. 'In a hospital full of children with paper-thin walls. Still, I'm surprised you managed it.'

'Are you?' Was it his imagination or did she fixate on his chest a little too long?

'No, not really. You're huge.'

Her voice was husky but he managed to put that down to thirst. The alternative was a treacherous road to travel down.

'I'd bet good money you're the only man on the planet who could manage it, though.'

Plenty of his men could—not that he'd ever allow it. The thought unearthed a foreign sensation in his guts. 'You are far from heavy, Claudia. I have carried twice your weight on my back for days on end.'

'Why on earth would you do that?'

Thuds began to pound at his temples. 'Up,' he ordered, amazed that he'd told her that. Frankly astounded that he'd divulged one iota of his past. *Dios,* he needed to get rid of her. 'I've decided that we should return to Arunthia today.'

But she wasn't listening. Something had occurred in her fierce brain. 'Oh, of course. How silly of me. I saw it straight away too. You're military. Or ex-military at least.'

She attempted to stand but fell straight back onto her rear. A curvaceous bottom now imprinted on his forearm—lush and firm.

A groan rumbled up his chest but he managed to stall it halfway up his windpipe.

'And, by the way, you can forget leaving today. You promised me twenty-four hours, Mr Garcia.'

She stood then, unfolding to her full height: a phoenix rising from the flames.

'I was under the impression I was dealing with a man of his word.' *Ouch.*

'I'm not leaving until tomorrow. I have business to attend to in London, tomorrow morning, and I'll be there. Fire, flood or obnoxious control-freak notwithstanding.'

Lucas fumed from the inside out. 'There is every chance we will be followed again.' He'd make sure they were not, but he had no intention of making her feel comfortable. She should be concerned for her safety, dammit. She was in for a rude awakening back at home.

'*If* we were followed. I'll chance it.'

'Still you continue to doubt my word.' What could possibly be so important for her to even risk it?

She met his eyes, tore on her lip. And he knew. It must be a man. The thought struck a knife to his heart. Dragged him back into the darkness. Why did women do this to themselves? Jeopardise their life for a man?

'You may be willing to chance it but I am not,' he said, hard enough to ram the point into the next millennium. 'You have ten seconds to tell me what or who is so important. Then I promise you, Claudia, the decision will be mine.'

Her stunned mouth worked. 'But…you gave me your word.'

Lucas moved in, slowly biting out each syllable. 'I will break it in a heartbeat if your safety is in question.'

She slumped back onto the bed and stared up at him. 'You mean it.'

'I am *deadly* serious.' He'd had enough. Of her blasé attitude. Of the constant spike of his pulse. Of the fact that he'd forgone his word of honour for her protection as a result of her sheer obstinacy. Of everything *Claudia*. 'You have less than five seconds.'

Her eyes widened.

'Four.'

'I have to see someone,' she said, her words rushing out as she covered her heart with the palm of her hand.

'Not enough. Three.'

'I promised, okay? I can't just disappear. You've smashed into my life with the delicacy of a ten-ton brick. I have to see her before I leave.'

'Two. Her?' he asked, slightly mollified by the sex of this person.

'Bailey…she would be devastated. This is a huge deal to me, Lucas. *Please*.'

Clenching his fists, he eased back. Maybe if she hadn't been looking up to him, with those heart-achingly beautiful eyes pleading. Maybe if he hadn't seen the effort it had taken her.

Tamping down on the emotion flickering inside him, he motioned towards the bathroom door with a jerk of his head. 'If you can manage a hot shower, there is a robe on the back of the door. Then we will eat and you may sleep.'

Her entire body wilted. 'I *may?*' she said, a smile quivering about her lips.

Lucas imagined it was half pleasure that he'd granted her

leeway and half indignation that he was calling the shots. She had spunk. He'd give her that.

'*Sí*. You *may*.'

Claudia closed the bathroom door, turned and slumped against the solid oak.

'That man is killing me softly,' she whispered. He was so stern his icy orders could freeze a running tap mid-flow, yet he'd agreed to let her visit Bailey *and* carried her from the car. Although she imagined in that instance he'd acted on automatic, and the experience had been as pleasurable for him as being tear-gassed.

Groaning, Claudia pushed away from the door and began to unpeel her sticky clothes from her skin. After kicking off her shoes, she wriggled out of her tights and panties, glancing around the huge plush bathroom.

A black clawfoot tub sat on cream tiles luxuriously warm under her now bare feet. Walking over to the shower, she unbuttoned her lab coat with one hand and turned the shower dial with the other, until steam began to pour over the glass wall—shaped in a slinky S—and filled the room, blissfully warming every inch of skin she unveiled.

Shallow twin basins took up one wall and, unsnapping her bra, she walked over to peek inside the huge complimentary basket, wrinkling her nose at the visual feast. God only knew what products were in there. Before she got a decent look she was snagged on her condensation-hazy reflection in the wide mirror above the ceramic bowls.

'Oh, lovely!' Colour high, clumps of dark-brown hair hanging about her face, huge puffy bags under her eyes: she looked like a human panda bear. Was it any wonder Lucas looked at her as if she were half-mad? She certainly acted half-mad around him.

Grimacing, she closed her eyes, and her mind drifted to a close-up of Lucas, towering above her, as she was plastered to his car. Who was the woman who'd reached up for his kiss? So sure she'd been. So *wrong* she'd been. He'd been furious, attempting to show her who was boss. A man like Lucas wouldn't be interested in her. His women would be lithe, glamorous, *über*-confident. Everything Claudia wasn't.

Sadness crept into her chest until each breath ached and she gently rubbed her wrist, her eyes wavering on the basket. He might not fancy her, but she didn't have to look a fright in front of him, did she? Snagging a bottle of shampoo, she dipped into the shower. The hot splash of water firmed her resolve. She had twenty-four hours to get her head on straight, visit Bailey and fly home to face her parents for the first time in years.

Suddenly it didn't matter what Lucas thought of her. What mattered was that her mask didn't slip in front of him. In front of any of them. Staying strong, she had more chance of getting back to London, with her body, mind and soul untouched.

So when she strode out of the bathroom twenty minutes later, a towel wrapped turban-like around her head and cloaked in a huge white robe, she was armed and ready. Sort of. As long as she ignored the scent of Lucas seeping through the thick cotton, infusing her extreme nakedness with what she imagined a lover's caress would feel like.

Bedroom empty, she took a deep breath and strode through the open doorway into a lavish Victorian-style living area— and stopped dead.

Lucas stood with his back to her, looking out of the wide expanse of windows offering a spectacular view of the fading Thames skyline. A dark blue shirt clung to his broad shoulders, stretching tight as he bent at the waist and reached down. Claudia couldn't care less what was on the floor. Her eyes were riveted to the small of his back leading to a very tight butt. *Wow.* Her vision began to swim; maybe she had brain fever.

She heard him firing orders like soft bullets. Strangely subdued, she couldn't make out the words, but the low growl of his voice made her insides quake. The base of her stomach fluttered and a honeyed whimper floated past her ears.

Brow furrowing, she wrenched her gaze towards the door,

only to be faced with…a *woman?* A woman failing miserably at hiding her own response: cheeks overly pink, finger stroking her small cleavage as she checked out Lucas for herself.

Claudia stifled the impulse to tell the impeccably dressed blonde to get out. 'Can I help you?'

Three things happened. Lucas whipped around. The blonde dropped a coat hanger to the floor. And Claudia fisted the lapels of her gown together at the base of her throat, suddenly wishing she'd kept her mouth shut and left the way she'd come. Given her current panda bear appearance, being faced with a sultry cat was more than she could take.

'Ah, Claudia. *Finally,*' Lucas said. 'This is Jessica from the concession downstairs. She has clothes for you.'

Not a chance. 'Can't we just send my clothes to be cleaned?'

A muscle ticked along his jaw and he set stride towards her. She stiffened, bracing herself.

'Give us five minutes,' he said to the blonde, who nodded and then disappeared into another room.

'Doesn't she know where the door is?'

'This is not the time for your awkwardness,' he growled for her ears only, so close she shuddered.

Determined not to look at him, she kept her eyes fixed on the clothes rail. 'How is it awkward not to want new clothes?' God, how ungrateful she sounded. She couldn't remember the last time anyone had thought of her needs—was too used to fighting for them herself. 'I do appreciate the gesture, Lucas, but…' The rail sagged beneath the weight of tens of hangers adorned with a colourful array of every garment imaginable. She swallowed. Hard.

'You wish to wear a lab coat on your journey home?' he asked, exasperation hardening his voice.

'Maybe I could pop back to my flat later? I just want my own things.'

'*Dios,* Claudia, give it up,' he snapped. 'I doubt there is anything suitable in that place. There is no need to hide here. I know who you are.'

Her head jerked so quickly a spasm catapulted up her neck. Standing no more than a foot away he looked furious. 'What are you talking about?'

'I understand the need for dour camouflage while you are in London. But from this moment on everyone you meet will know exactly who you are. I will make sure of it.'

She blinked. Took a step back. Then another. Why did her heart shrivel in her chest because he thought her appearance dour?

His brow etched into a deep V, the skin around his eyes crinkling, he scoured her face. Claudia looked back to the rail and crushed the hurt before he could witness it.

'Fine,' she said, proud of her unwavering voice. 'One outfit.' Truth be told she had little choice in the matter. It was clear she wouldn't be permitted to return home, and surely there was *something* among this glut that wasn't…skimpy.

Lucas cleared his throat. 'Do you wish to sleep in that robe?' he asked, a little softer, silkier, while his eyes slid down her body in a bold visual caress, as if he craved to see her extreme nakedness beneath. *As if.*

'Sleep in it?' Hardly. Not with *his* woodsy scent lingering on every fibre. 'I think not. And do me a favour and stop staring at me. I realise I'm not your standard issue—'

A knock at the door severed her tongue. Both their heads turned in the same direction.

'Why do I suddenly feel like I'm standing in the middle of King's Cross Station?' Butt naked!

She adhered her feet to the floor in case she edged closer to Lucas. She'd never needed anyone and she didn't need him now.

A pause. Two raps. And a beat. A pattern, she realised. 'Forget King's Cross. I'm in the Arunthian Intelligence Agency.'

'Enter,' Lucas barked, his lips twitching, and Claudia stepped back a pace when another incredible hunk strode through the gap.

'Good grief. Your brother?'

Lucas coughed into his fist. 'One of my men. Armande. And I do not believe we are alike.'

The man—Armande—bowed in front of her. 'Your Royal Highness.' He straightened to resemble a ramrod and nodded at Lucas. 'Sir.'

'No, you're right. He seems too nice,' she whispered, so only Lucas could hear.

Lucas had ordered clothes. Been thoughtful. Agreed to let her see Bailey. Carried her from the car. Cared for her. He needn't have done that, she realised. He could have woken her up. Ordered her to walk.

She shivered from the top of her turbanned head to the tips of her toes just thinking about his big strong arms embracing her, holding her tight, snug against his chest. Wasn't it just typical that she'd slept the entire time? She wanted a replay.

Unmindful, her eyes sought his. He was staring at her mouth again, at where she gnawed at the flesh of her lip with her front teeth. Then he looked to Armande...back to her...and his jaw set rigid.

'Armande is in charge for now,' he said, strangely ill-tempered. 'I have something to take care of.'

'*What?*' Turning her back on Armande, she instinctively latched onto Lucas's forearm. 'You're leaving me? With...with *him?*'

He frowned, flicked his attention to her white-knuckled grip. 'You'll be perfectly safe.'

'Are you coming back?' She did *not* sound needy—definitely not. She sounded inquisitive.

'*Sí.* Of course.'

How many times had she heard that? Too many. Yet for some reason she believed him. Who in their right mind would coerce her into going to Arunthia only to abandon her before the flight?

She slackened her hold, feeling like a total idiot. 'Fine. I'm going to bed anyway.'

'One hour,' he declared, before dipping his head discreetly towards her ear.

Stomach fizzing, she clenched her lower abdomen and sucked her tender bottom lip. His breath tickled down the sensitive skin of her neck, his husky murmur igniting each tiny fizzy bubble until it exploded inside her.

'Try to behave yourself, *Just Claudia.*'

CHAPTER FIVE

'ALONE?' LUCAS SAID, satisfied with his controlled volume as he lowered the morning newspaper to the breakfast table and sent Claudia *The Look*.

Dark insolent brows arched in his direction before she sipped pure orange juice between her ripe lips. A direct order from God couldn't have stopped him from watching her slender throat convulse, her pink tongue snake out to lick the pith sticking to her perfect bow. The newspaper crumpled in his fist as heat snaked through his veins, making his pulse spike.

'Yes, Lucas. I want to go alone.'

He cleared his throat. 'Impossible. I will accompany you or you will not go. End of discussion.'

Keeping his paper lowered, he waited for her reaction, but the ice maiden had risen with the morning sun.

Dressed in a sharp, fitted black suit, her hair tied back punishingly into a twisted knot, she looked a world away from the dowdy lab rat of yesterday. Still, every inch of her skin was covered, the only break in the black a fawn shirt, stroking her decolletage. Satin, he mused, eyeing the way the expensive fabric rippled around her neck. Today she had an untouchable, regal aura—one he was extremely grateful for.

'Why are you staring at me? Do I look *dour* this morning?'

Lucas jerked his eyes back to her face. Had he just imagined her wounded tone? With his limited experience of the female sex outside the sheets he felt unsure how to proceed. *Unsure? Dios,* he felt something close to panic claw down his chest. Never had he been asked to comment on a woman's appearance.

Lucas snapped the paper shut and laid it on the table beside his empty coffee cup. 'Not at all. I was just thinking how smart you look.'

'Smart?' she repeated, deadpan, tapping her pencil off her front teeth, popping the end into her mouth and nibbling it.

He shifted in his seat. '*Sí.* Appropriate for your arrival in Arunthia.'

'I'm not there yet,' she said, no more happy with his comment than he was.

Damn. He should have told her she was beautiful. How he itched to untie her hair, to caress her long, sultry curls.

As it was, the memory of a hard floor against his back and a walking centrefold in the cushy bed thirty feet away would haunt him for days. By four a.m. he'd done six hundred sit-ups, cleaned his gun, had three showers and interviewed the man in the white pick-up. Armande had hauled the bastard into the adjoining suite at midnight. A shifty Arunthian reporter whom Lucas had despised on sight. One who wouldn't be returning to his home country for some time. Not as long as Claudia was there.

The reminder brought him back to her comment. She wasn't in Arunthia. *Yet.*

'Our flight is at three p.m. You have plenty of time to make your visit. Accompanied,' he tagged on, unwilling to be moved on the point.

Tearing at a slice of wholemeal toast, she chewed with vigour and speared him with arrows of contempt.

Good. She hated him. As long as he kept that look on her face they'd make it home without another hitch. Problem was Lucas had an uneasy notion that Claudia was about to produce a hitch the size of Mount Vesuvius.

* * *

'There is something wrong with you?' asked Lucas, with a harshness that made Claudia's skin bristle.

Sliding her eyes over the vast entrance of St Andrew's Hospital, she knotted her fingers atop her lap.

What? Was he concerned that he'd have to take damaged goods through Security in Arunthia? Claudia would laugh if the chord didn't strike through to the very heart of her. How many times had she dreamed of being perfect, being cured, just so her parents would come back for her? Days, months, years spent waiting, her naïve heart still hoping.

Throat thick, pain smashing into her forehead, she rubbed her brow with an unsteady hand. Why couldn't she forget? Why couldn't she just get over it and move on?

'Claudia? Answer me!'

She turned to look at a scowling Lucas in the seat beside her, hating the instant fire in her belly just one look ignited. 'No, Lucas, there is nothing wrong with me. Apart from the insane urge to strangle you.' The man was driving her to Valium.

Scowl diminishing, a smile played about his lips. 'The feeling is entirely mutual, *princesa*. So, tell me, why are we here?'

'I sometimes work here and—'

He snorted, relief easing the two little lines he got when he frowned. 'I should have known.'

'Actually, on this occasion it isn't about work. I was about to say I met someone here. Bailey, remember? So if you'll excuse me—'

'Wait,' he said, grasping her wrist.

Whether it was the hundred volts ripping up her arm or the fact he'd touched her wrist, she wasn't sure, but she twisted her arm, writhing from his hold. 'Please don't touch me there.'

Lucas instantly let go and held up his hand. 'I would not hurt you, Claudia,' he said, voice gruff, his brows low over intense eyes brimming with…*pain?* Oh, no. *No!*

'Of course you wouldn't.' No thought, no hesitation, she

reached over, lightly grazing his fist where it now curled on his hard thigh. His skin was so warm. So perfect. 'I know that.'

'*Bueno.* Good,' he said, his chest visibly easing.

Yes, he was hard—but in a warrior-like way. Good fighting against evil.

And that one thought…the mere possibility that he might have faced evil…coupled with that one agonised look derailed her pride, her every defence. 'I'm just really funny about my wrists. That's all. And when…' *When you touch me I feel alive. For the first time in my life. And it scares me.*

Those beautiful sapphire eyes flicked down to where her fingers still smoothed over his flesh and his hand slowly began to stiffen as if repelled.

Hurt kissed her heart and she snatched her hand back. 'Anyway, I need to go inside.'

Lucas reached for the door handle. '*Sí.* We will go,' he said, fierce, dominating, as if the moment had never happened.

The change in him was so swift it took her a moment to gather her wits. '*We?* No, Lucas. That's not acceptable.'

She wouldn't put Bailey through a meeting with a stranger. She remembered all too well the pity. The staring. The crushing silence that seemed to stretch the air so thin she could barely breathe. The powerful desire for them to leave followed by the stomach-wrenching emptiness of the room. And just as unforgettable was the palpable unease of others. It wasn't fair on Lucas either.

'Claudia, you are in my protection,' he ground out.

'For once will you stop thinking about your bloody job and give me an hour's peace before my life is obliterated? I need to see someone. In private. Can't you understand that?'

Lucas tore his gaze from the grim scenery and narrowed his eyes on her. 'You feel deeply for this person?'

'Yes. Just an hour. Please?'

The shutters slammed down over his face. 'One hour. I will wait.'

'Thank you.'

'In Reception.'

'*Reception?* People are sure to ask questions as soon as they clap eyes on you. You're hardly inconspicuous.'

He shrugged those broad muscular shoulders. 'Tough.'

'God, you're the most arrogant louse I've ever met.' And to think she'd just told him something she'd never told another soul just to make him feel better.

Pushing her glasses up her nose, she yanked her bag from the floor as the car door opened before her. And there stood Lucas.

'How…? You know something? You're the human equivalent of a silencer.'

He flashed her a killer half-smile. 'One hour, *Just Claudia*.'

Lucas paced the reception area, his size twelves wearing holes in the thin matting, and yanked back the cuff of his jacket to check his watch. Again. One hour, seven minutes, thirty-six seconds.

Dios, he abhorred hospitals: the thick air of grief sliding down his throat, the dread, the notion that control had been handed to God and Lucas would pay the price.

Teeth bared, he let out a low growl. Where the hell *was* she? And who was this Bailey person? A lover? She'd intimated a female, but he knew women lied under the dense weight of desperation.

Anger swirled, black and heavy in his gut, as well as some indefinable emotion he was loath to name. The suspicion sparked a flare of unease in him. Was she safe? The shock of it suddenly engulfed him and acted like an almighty trigger.

He strode towards the curved reception desk, set like a barricade, denying all further access to the floors beyond. Her private business was no concern of his but, *Dios,* one hour was one hour, and if something happened to her…

After flashing a smile to the emaciated blonde, some extreme lash-fluttering, flaunting his government credentials and name-dropping his right-royal-pain-in-the-ass, she directed him to floor seven and one Bailey Michaels.

Adrenaline surged to every extremity until he felt hard—armed and ready to take on the world as he stalked towards the lift, then bypassed it for the stairs, needing to run off some excess energy, throwing open the doors to the seventh floor a minute later.

Three things happened simultaneously to punch the air from his lungs. The musical sound of children's voices floated past his ears. The colourful images of cartoon characters painted on vast glass plates drew his eyes. And the scent of strong disinfectant speared up his nose to assault his mind.

Stomach revolting, he stiffened his abs to prevent his six-egg omelette from making a reappearance. Twenty years vanished and he was back in the halls of hell.

His hand shot out to grip the wooden ledge framing a window. His thoughts fractured. His vision blurred. Air was imprisoned in his chest. *Get up, boy. I'm not done. Get the hell up!* Glancing down at his hands, he grimaced as blood dripped from his fingers to splash into a dark red puddle at his feet.

Get it together, Garcia. Stand to attention. Now!

Breathe. He needed to breathe. Dragging in oxygen, he infused his spine with steel and reached for the plateau between consciousness and serenity. In and out, slow and even. His mind's eyes gradually turned black, his heartbeat slowed, and a voice filtered through the murky haze.

'...and then the brave dark knight took out his sword and fought the dragon with all his might. Past the castle walls, past fire and flame, through the walls of men he charged to find her. Up the stairs to the turret where she lay in a deep sleep waiting for his kiss...'

Claudia?

His eyes sprang open and Lucas scanned the hallway for the direction of her voice, moved stealthily towards an open door.

'Oh, and she was so beautiful. With long golden hair, just

like yours, and big blue eyes the colour of the Arunthian ocean…'

'Like mine?' a little voice asked.

'Just like yours.'

'No one would want to kiss *me,*' came the little voice.

'Oh, the dark knight would want a kiss. But you'd have to be older. Like the Princess. And when you're older your eyes won't be sore any more and your wrists will be just like mine. See?'

Lucas surveyed the small room, knowing he shouldn't be intruding—that it was, as Claudia had said, private. And Bailey sounded very much like a young girl. Not a man. The rapid flush of relief was because she was safe, he was sure.

Claudia was perched on the edge of a small bed, blocking his view of the patient. Her jacket was gone, the sleeves of her shirt rolled high as she twisted her arm this way and that, seemingly allowing the girl to inspect her wrists. He remembered all the times she'd tugged at her clothes, and earlier when he'd grabbed her.

Stiffening his limbs, he fought the emotional throb of his body.

'I wouldn't want to kiss a boy anyway,' Bailey said. 'Clara in Bay Four said it's like eating custard. I hate custard.'

'Custard?' Claudia repeated, and Lucas could hear the smile in her voice. He wished she wasn't turned away from him so he could see the widening of her lush mouth for himself.

'But maybe my dad would come…'

'I know, darling,' Claudia said softly, the affection in her voice strong, the rich, melodic tone unfamiliar to him. Yet somehow it had the power to unearth a long-buried memory and create a strange surge of longing. 'I know,' she repeated. 'Look what I brought for you.'

Claudia bent from the waist, reaching into her bag on the floor, and his attention snapped to the child. *Dios…*

He stepped to the side in an instant, before she caught sight of him, unwilling to frighten her. His size tended to do just that and she was immensely frail. *Frail?* She was tiny.

'Who's that man, Claudia?' the girl asked.

Damn. Lucas schooled his features, flexed his neck and re-laxed his big body in an attempt to become as unthreatening as he possibly could. Then he turned to the open doorway, al-most filling the narrow gap.

'Good morning,' he said.

The girl, Bailey, gaped openly, and Claudia shot to her feet. 'Lucas. What are you doing here? Can't I have one hour's peace?'

'*Sí,*' he said. 'Except it now happens to be one hour and twenty-three minutes.' He turned to Bailey. 'May I come in?'

'No,' Claudia said.

'Okay,' Bailey said.

'Since this is your room, *señorita,* I shall take your answer,' he said to the young girl, and was rewarded with a small ten-tative smile. One that lifted the heavy bruising from around her eyes and sent a fresh burst of emotion through his system.

Claudia fisted her small hands as if she wanted to punch him into next week, and stepped toward the bed in an entirely protective move. What the hell did she think he would do?

As he approached the bed Claudia moved closer still, prac-tically smothering his view. And, like a warning flare illumi-nating the sky, light dawned. She was not only protecting the child, she was *hiding* her.

He tossed Claudia a quizzical look and she volleyed with a silent plea, mouthed, 'Do not stare.'

Anger screamed through his innards, blending with affront, and he ground his jaw fiercely to prevent it pouring from his mouth. He'd always prided himself on being unreadable—he'd been trained by the best, after all—but the chastised look on Claudia's face told him he'd failed to hide his fury in this in-stance. And he was inordinately pleased.

In one sweeping glance he'd gained several key pieces that made up the Princess Claudine Verbault conundrum. *And when you're older...your wrists will be just like mine...*she'd said. This girl had the same condition that Claudia had suffered from in her youth. Lucas was looking at the past.

At enflamed wrists and elbows, painfully sore skin. At puffy eyes and purplish branding that spoke of bone-deep lethargy. And the way she barely moved from the bed, wincing as she tried to straighten her legs, told him she suffered serious muscle fatigue. Tiny hands tugged at the white sheet to drape over her slight frame. Hiding.

Pain banked in his chest. Through it all, the girl was very pretty, and he could see glimpses of the beautiful woman she would become. A woman who would replace the white sheet with a dour wardrobe.

Madre de Dios. His gut ached.

While he'd read brief notes on the illness, seeing it, looking at it for himself, was something else entirely. Much like visiting a bombsite—knowing the damage was already done, hoping for the best, but witnessing devastation that left soldiers numb for hours.

Clearing his thick, tight throat, he looked towards Claudia. 'Would you like to make the introductions?'

Her deep amber eyes bored through his skull and he returned her glare, caught in that odd battle of wills that so often ensnared them. Not once had he lost the fight, and this time the stakes were gravely higher.

Soon enough she blinked, then stepped to the side. 'Bailey, this is Lucas. Lucas, this is my friend Bailey.'

Lucas tore his gaze from Claudia, knowing full well that he shouldn't be here. That with every passing second he was becoming more embroiled with the mysterious Arunthian Princess. It wasn't his job to consider her past, present or her future. Getting her home was his remit. His obligation. His mission. His promise to the King.

Pausing for a second, he weighed the risk. Looked at the expectant child, the hopeful softening of Claudia's beautiful face.

'*Buenos días,* Bailey,' he said, with a quick bow that pinked her cheeks. 'I am honoured to meet you.'

* * *

Claudia tried to pick her jaw up off the floor and only just managed when Lucas raised one dark brow in her direction. Clearly he had no idea of the in-topics for girly conversation, because small talk slipped in a steady decline and he kept looking to Claudia for direction. And each time he did something warm and delicious unfurled inside her.

Oh, God, he was utterly wonderful. Which was great for Bailey, disastrous for her. She wanted to hate him. For barging into her life, stripping away her independence. For taking her away from Bailey and throwing her to the wolves.

He was the oddest mixture of man. Arrogant. Infuriating. Thoughtful.

'We have to leave now, Bailey,' she said, her heart breaking in two. 'I won't be able to visit for a few weeks, but I'll be back.'

Claudia stared into her big blue eyes, willing her to believe. Because she knew exactly how she felt. One sentence—*I'll be back*—had the power to plague you with excitement for hours and then crush your heart when no one came.

Bailey tried for a smile and Claudia's throat stung under a seething fire.

'I'll be back. I promise,' Claudia said, making a cross on her breast with the tip of her finger. 'And I'll bring you a present. The most beautiful gift you've ever seen. And I'll write,' she said, her voice laced with desperation, her hands trembling, her chest quaking. 'We can e-mail, just like I showed you.'

Claudia grabbed her jacket from the back of the chair, silently chanting. *Three weeks. Then you'll have the money to finish what you started. You'll be back to hold her hand every day. Just three weeks.*

Blinded by the need for air, Claudia stormed down the hall and stopped dead at the double doors leading to the stairwell, opposite the gaping steel mouth of the lift. Seven flights of stairs might be nothing to Action-Man, but she didn't have a hope of making them.

'Claudia?'

'Don't speak. Don't be nice, please.' She'd break. She'd crumble. And no way was she doing that in front of this man.

Lucas eyed the steel box with something close to contempt and Claudia laughed. The hollow sound echoed off the green-flecked walls. He couldn't even bear to get in the lift with her. And, my God, it hurt. Why did she persecute herself like this? Wishing, dreaming of things she could never have.

Turning, palms flat, she pushed through the double doors and begged her legs to stay strong, keep her upright.

'Claudia, slow down.'

Step, step, step went her feet. The heavy thud of Lucas came behind her. Bearing upon her. Closing in. 'Where do you get off, telling me what to do?' she muttered, her breath short and raspy, her feet now pounding down the stairs.

'Claudia, I understand—'

His voice verged on the consoling, and the hint of pity unleashed the storm raging inside her. 'You had no right. No right coming up there!'

'We are on a strict time limit,' he said harshly, while the thud, thud of his shoes became louder, echoing off the walls and drubbing her temples.

Don't you dare fall, Claudia. Don't you dare.

'Oh, please,' she said. 'You've just wasted twenty minutes talking. If…if time was so important to you…you would've ordered me out of that room instantly.'

'*Dios,* Claudia, slow down. You will fall. I realise you are anxious—'

'Anxious?' she said, stumbling when the first flight broke for a landing and a human blur jumped from the sky and landed dead in front of her. *Too close. Too close.* Taking a step back, she winced as pain shot up her calf and continued to vent, 'Do you know how many people will visit her while I'm gone? *Do* you?'

He said nothing, just looked at her with a grim expression that made her feel even worse. For God's sake, he wasn't even breathing hard. While she rasped and heaved as if she'd endured a triathlon.

'Her mother died when Bailey fell ill and her father works on an oil rig. If she's lucky he'll come by once during his leave.' More family visits than Claudia had ever had, but that was between her and her parents. 'But why am I telling you this, Lucas? I forgot. You don't feel, right? How can you possibly know what I feel like right now?'

Her back slapped against the wall but this time he kept his distance. Though from the lines scoring his handsome face it seemed to cost him.

'I do not. But I can see leaving her torments you. So many things make sense to me now, but you will be back. You have other responsibilities, Claudia.'

'Oh, Lucas, shove your royal responsibilities where the sun doesn't shine, will you?'

He massaged the bridge of his nose with his thumb and forefinger. He did that a lot, she realised.

'So elegant. So refined.'

'What are you? My elocutionist? I had one of those once. The woman lasted three days.'

'I am not surprised. I imagine you scared her off.'

'Probably. *You* try being a European princess dropped in a London hospital and surrounded by children who talk of apples and pears when all you want to know is where the stairs are.'

He frowned. 'Apples?'

'And pears. So, you see, her version of helping was a bit like yours. Unwanted.'

Frightened, alone, she'd been drowning in a river of intolerance, bitterness towards the elite, so she'd done the only thing she could to survive. Shunned her aristocratic birthright. Not that she'd cared. She would have done anything to forget who she truly was. And now they wanted her back. A woman who didn't exist.

'You are hurting. If it makes you feel any better hit me. Hard. But *do not* give up. Courage, Claudia.'

Closing the gap, he reached up and brushed the hair from her brow, the slight scrape making her shiver. She had no idea what possessed her. Maybe it was the sympathy in his eyes—God, she hated that. But she hit him. Just once. Her small fist connected to his shoulder with a soft thump. Not even hard. Her heart wasn't in it, she realised. It was too busy breaking.

Throat stinging, eyes shuttering, her legs gave way. And he was there, scooping her into his arms, lifting her close, laying her against his broad, muscular chest and walking down the stairs as if she weighed nothing more than a test strip. And in that moment she'd never despised herself more.

Twisting, she pushed against his chest. 'Put me down. I don't need you to carry me.' She didn't need anyone. Least of all him.

'Be still.' His bark reverberated off the walls. 'And in future I suggest you give more thought to your body than your pride and take the lift when your legs ache.'

'What are you? A telepath?' The fight slowly drained from her body. 'God, I hate you right now,' she whispered, even as she laid her head against his carved shoulder. He was so strong…so annoying…so everything.

'*Bueno.* That is good,' he said, his voice dropping to a low, somewhat soothing husky rumble.

As he embraced her so tightly Claudia tried to remember if anyone had ever held her close. No. Never. Not even when she was a little girl. And it felt…wonderful.

Her body grew lax, her breathing steadied and his luxurious sandalwood scent enveloped her in a cashmere blanket. His heart thumped beneath her cheek, lulling. Claudia wrapped her arms about his neck, snuggled against him, burrowing, suddenly desperate to absorb his strength. Had she ever felt so safe in her life? It would be oh-so-easy to need him. And oh-so-stupid even to contemplate it.

On instinct she brushed her nose up the column of his throat to his unyielding jaw, the rasp of morning growth tickling the tip. A shiver racked through her core, so addictive she did it again. Blood rushed through her head, drowning out sound, but she felt his chest rumble in a little quake before he swayed slightly on his feet.

'Claudia,' he said, his voice tight, throaty, as if he needed a drink.

She needed something, but water was the last thing on her mind. She felt extraordinary. An incredible blend of fizzy excitement and drugging anxiousness.

Summoning the courage to lift her head, she looked up, felt his breath trickle over her face, so close. Her mouth was mere inches away from his lips. 'Lucas?'

He had a mystifying glint in his eyes, pupils dilated, heavy. Hot. 'Do not do that, Claudia. I cannot—'

'Why not?' she whispered, moving a little closer...

Then *leap* went her heart when, in one deft move, he sank his fingers beneath the loose twist at her nape and whisked his arm from under her thighs until she slid down his hard body onto her feet. With his free hand he brushed a stray curl from her eyes so she could see him properly, or maybe so *he* could see all of her. And all the while his fingers tightened in her hair, sending tides of sensation flooding down her spine in one glorious wave after another.

'So brave,' he said, eyes glittering like two rare sapphires. Was it pity she could see lurking in the depths? *Please, no*—anything but that.

His body grew as taut as his jaw and she fancied he fought some inner battle. One she lost when he slackened his hold, sending her stomach plunging to the floor. *No.* Claudia grabbed a handful of his shirt to stay upright, to bring him back...

A groan tore up his throat and with one tug—*oh, yes*—his mouth was on hers. Soft, yet achingly hard, scorching her lips until she burst into flames.

Alive. She'd never felt so alive. Her entire body shook with an excitement so intense it blanked all thought of self-preservation.

His kiss was blatant and intense as he bowed her in a delicate arch, caged by the unyielding steel frame of his awesome body. Firm, smooth lips moved over hers, back and forth so skilfully she quickly cottoned on to his rhythm and skill, earning a wickedly thrilling growl. The touch of his tongue sliding against her lower lip, flicking to the corner, was a call to surrender and she opened for him with a high-pitched moan, laying siege to his delicious assault.

Eyes closed, fingers flaring on his shoulders, she plastered herself against him. The crush of her heavy breasts, the flick of his velvet tongue against hers, set off a chemical reaction: heat surged through her veins, the deafening rush of blood sped past her ears. A hot splash of liquid melted her core—awakening her body in a way she'd never dreamed of. Never known existed. And all she could think was more, *more*.

Her fingers skimmed the broad contours of his shoulders, followed the column of his neck and slid under his ears…into his hair.

Lucas groaned long and low, tightening his hold, one hand on her nape, the other still at her waist, until she felt precious, wanted.

Desired.

The seductive pull of his mouth became pure exhilaration as she felt his hands wander, as if he craved to learn her shape—curving over her hips, slinking into her waist. And when his thumbs brushed the underside of her breasts…*oh, my*.

No fantasy had ever lived up to this. Even when she'd lain in bed the previous night, knowing Lucas was so close in the room next door, dreaming he'd kiss her awake, imagining the hard press of his weight on top of her.

As if caught in between a dream and reality she ground her pelvis against him—instinctive, wanting—and revelled in the thick hard ridge digging into her stomach. The thought of that part of him inside her drove a soft pleading moan past her lips.

Lucas stilled, his mouth fused with hers. His breath, warm and wet, slipped past her parted lips. 'Claudia?' Gruff, yet undoubtedly perturbed, his voice doused the flames of desire and she rocked back on her heels.

'*Dios,*' he muttered, scooping her back up against his chest. 'I need to get you out of here.'

She said nothing, just buried her hot face in his shoulder, trying not to touch, twisting her fingers together in the deep well between her stomach and his. Her brain was in a complete state of confusion. Why had he kissed her? What on earth had possessed her to kiss *him*? One minute she'd been ranting like some despicable idiot and the next… Heart breaking, she'd craved a distraction—that was all. Maybe comfort. There wasn't anything pathetic about that, was there?

Oh, God.

Any lingering warmth froze solid in her veins as he opened the door and reality closed in.

Daylight stroked her eyelids. London's midday crush filtered through her ears and Lucas's scent was replaced with smoggy car fumes and greasy bacon from the van permanently stationed in the hospital car park. The mingling aromas were enough to plunge her farther into reality, and her heart crumpled when she realised what she'd allowed Lucas to see. Her. Pathetic and needy. Vulnerable. The girl she'd buried long ago.

'Are you able to stand?' he asked.

'Of course,' she said, sliding down his body to her feet. The sensation reminded her, made her voice hitch. 'Thank you.'

He raked an irritable hand round the back of his neck. 'Claudia, about what just happened…'

He averted his gaze to some place over her left shoulder. But not before she caught the glimpse of uneasy regret.

Claudia closed her eyes. It was worse than she'd thought.

Sharing a student flat at university had taught her to close her ears to wanton chatter. But she wasn't tone deaf or completely ignorant about sex. She'd heard of a pity lay, and she guessed she'd just experienced the pity-kiss equivalent. The thought made her feel physically sick. Yes, she'd felt him, hard and amazing against her stomach, but how many times had she seen classmates hop from one bed to another regardless of attraction? Sex was sex to men, as long as it resulted in a high-octane pay-off.

'I should not have done it,' he bit out, anger slashing across his cheeks.

'You're right. You shouldn't. Not for the reasons you did.'

His brow crunched, his mouth shaping for speech, and she couldn't bear to hear any more excuses. This was humiliating enough.

'Don't worry about it, Lucas. It meant nothing, right?' She shrugged in an attempt to lighten the mood.

'Right.'

'We'll just go on like it never happened.'

Painfully aware he was starting to read her like a kindergarten book, she didn't appreciate the way he scanned her face. The notion made her reach for a curveball and throw it out there. 'I just thought—what the hell? I'll try it.'

A stunned light flashed in his intense stare. *'Qué?'*

'Kissing,' she said, her heart lifting as she warmed to the idea. The *last* thing she needed was Lucas thinking she had designs on him. 'It was better than I thought.'

He blinked.

She smiled.

'That,' he said, pointing back to the hospital, still blinking wide eyes, 'was the first time you've been...*kissed?*'

'Yes.'

It took a few seconds for him to absorb that tasty little snippit, his jaw falling off its hinges in the process. As embarrassing as never-been-kissed was to admit, it was a far better alternative to the undoubted ego-boost that she fancied the pants off him.

And then her scurrilous mind darted in yet another direction, spawning her need to be the very best. At everything.

'So tell me, just so I know for the future, did I do it right?'

A sound spluttered from his lips—something between a cough and a growl. *'Sí,'* he said vaguely. Too vaguely for her liking.

He was just being a gentleman. She didn't like being under par. As a person she fed off success. On an intellectual level, that was. Until now.

She rubbed her fingertips across the plump flesh of her lips. Had she been too soft? Too hard? Too wet? Maybe she hadn't opened her mouth enough. It had been perfectly delicious to her, but…

Oh, heavens. He was staring at her mouth.

She stilled.

His eyes shot up to hers: liquid ozone, dark and intense. 'And was it as you'd hoped?'

Stifling a smile, she went for light, airy. 'Oh, it was fine. Nothing like custard.'

CHAPTER SIX

NEVER BEEN KISSED.

Lucas sat in the plush lounge area of the jet, coffee sliding over his tongue, scorching the erotic blend of Claudia from his mouth. Lowering the cup to the table, he glanced covertly across the cabin to where she'd finally settled—curled into a deep swivel bucket seat, her long legs dangling over the side.

She was buried in work. Fierce concentration marred the silky skin of her brow as she pushed her glasses up her nose and scribbled another note in her book.

Did I do it right?

Lucas scrubbed his hands over his face. Trust Claudia to pour every ounce of delectable effort into her first kiss and succeed in blowing his mind.

What the hell had he been thinking, kissing her in the first place? He hadn't been thinking. Not with the correct head anyway. With one forbidden touch he'd lost control. *Dios,* he should never have laid a finger on her. But she'd been aching, hurting. The pain in her eyes had thrown him.

Practically across the corridor.

Holding her—her scent a warm shroud, her flesh heating his blood, her touch a sensual deluge—resistance had become futile.

And if he thought Claudia had been lost in the moment she'd soon murdered the notion, squashing his ego like a bug underfoot. No, no, *no*—she'd just wanted to *try* it! *Madre de*

Dios, what was he? One of her experiments? And his kiss apparently was *fine.* She'd used the most insipid word in the universe. To describe him. While he'd sunk deeper into the abyss with every tentative stroke of her tongue.

If one kiss could devour his body and mind, what kind of destruction could she cause with her clothes off? He was a man who preferred a predictable low-level and controllable response to a woman. Yet he was hard just thinking about sinking into her sensational body—as ludicrous and impossible as it was.

Jacket discarded, she still wore the fawn silk shirt and figure-hugging trousers of earlier, and he swallowed around a bullet-clogged barrel. His hands were imprinted with her flesh, firm and lush, and his eyes dipped to her breasts, remembering the heavy weight of their perfection.

Catching a groan halfway up his throat, Lucas tore his eyes away, tension building in his chest as he became more resentful of her powerful allure. Not only was she his current mission, he lived his life free of encumbrance and always would. To be in thrall to his desires, to any kind of emotion, was like begging for an assassin's bullet: it made you weak. So he worked, he fought for everything he believed in—justice, honour, duty— the only way he knew how. Hollow to the core.

Claudia—any woman, for that matter—deserved far more than an empty shell of a man.

Lost in thought, he mechanically ate lunch. Claudia declined anything bar a glass of sparkling water, and the silence stretched to breaking point.

Until the smack and skid of a glossy magazine on the table in front of him broke through the lull.

'What...?' She took a deep breath. 'What is this, Lucas?'

Hands flat to the table, Claudia leaned forward, and he ordered his eyes not to dip to the gaping V of her shirt and the heaving swell of smooth golden skin. Skin he could kiss and lick and suck for hours, until the woman forgot her own name and begged him to—

'A magazine,' he said, as fierce as the erection pushing against his zipper.

'Funny how you've never bothered to tell me the real reason my parents want me back.'

He shifted slightly, grateful for the mention of her parents. His promise. Her duty. 'They wish to see you. That is the true reason.'

'No. They want to showcase their perfect family to the world for the event of the decade.' Her trembling fingers curled into fists in front of him, and a quiver seeped through her voice. 'A party, Lucas?'

'What is so bad about a party?'

'They want a princess and I'm no longer that person. I can't be what they want. You told me—'

'You can be anyone you want to be. I have seen enough versions of Claudia in the past twenty-four hours to convince me of that.'

The ice maiden, the seductive intellectual, a Mother Teresa, and glimpses of a vulnerability that cut him to the core. Not forgetting the scientist who wanted scoring on a kiss. *Dios, little wonder he didn't know what he was about in her company. She did *not* make sense.

His stomach dipped in time with the plane. 'Buckle up, Princess.'

She scrambled onto the seat beside him, her fraying temper visibly morphing into sheer panic. 'Could we circle a few more times?'

Her fingers fumbled with the metal buckle and after a few seconds he pushed her hands away and clicked it shut.

'No, we cannot. What is wrong with you?'

Amber eyes locked on his. 'I'm not too good with people.'

'*Qué?* Do I look stupid to you, Claudia? Within ten minutes of our meeting you were chewing my head off, and you were perfectly at ease with Armande and Bailey.'

'I've known Bailey for months. She's a child. And how

would you know how I was with Armande? You left me! So much for your personal protection.'

Indignity was a slap in his face. 'I was dealing with the rep—' He broke off. She didn't need to know about the reporter. He still had a hard time believing he could have been so negligent. This was what she did to him. Threw him so far off course it was like navigating the jungle without a compass.

'Reporter?' Her hand curled up her chest to wrap around her throat, where her pulse beat erratically. 'The man outside my flat? You found him?'

'*Sí*. Not a figment of my imagination after all.'

She sucked her bottom lip into her mouth. 'Did he take pictures?'

'Yes. I destroyed them.'

Her eyes turned stormy, frantic. 'This is what it's going to be like. I'm going to be watched. Stared at. Photographed. Basically put under the microscope.' Her words trailed to a panicked whisper.

A coil of unease snaked through his guts. *That* was the problem, he realised. Without camouflage, with her identity known, she couldn't hide. Neither from the paparazzi nor in a ballroom full to bursting with people.

Bracing himself for landing, he waited for the inevitable crash.

'I can't do it, Lucas. I'm sorry,' she said, shaking her head, her amber eyes brimming with tears. Tears that tore at his heart. 'You have to turn this plane around and take me home.'

Lucas rejected the imminent threat of a memory ready to suck him under. 'Impossible. I cannot. It is too late.'

He had to get her home. Her true home. Not some dingy flat in central London. She needed to be with her family, surrounded by the dense, protective barrier of the palace walls. Where she could finally do her duty and take responsibility for that part of her life.

Long fingers gripped his forearm, bit into his flesh, frenzied…wild. 'You can do anything you want to, Lucas. I know that now.'

'No, I—' He broke off, steely dread making his limbs feel heavy as he sank down, down, suffocating under the sudden image of another time, another place, another woman. Begging him to hide her, desperate fear in her eyes for what was to come.

A woman who hid from the world while vulnerability ruled her every waking moment.

The truth slammed into him.

This was the real Claudia Verbault. She too hid her tender vulnerabilities, her secrets from the world—just as his mother had. A woman who'd needed him. A woman he'd failed.

'Please. I'm begging you, Lucas. Take me home.'

Claudia was way past the point of no return. Lucas had been so distracting she'd never even given herself time to consider what arriving in Arunthia would feel like. Now she knew. It felt as if the world was about to quake, slash open to form a gigantic crater and swallow her whole.

Buried deep, her memories began to scramble to the surface, hitting her with one deft punch after another.

It was quite possible that at the back of her mind she'd hoped her parents wanted to see her again so desperately they would do anything. Like send a towering brute to give her three and a half million pounds to make her happy. She was such a fool. They wanted Claudine the Princess, and she was anything but. She wasn't ready. Nowhere near ready. She wanted to go home and wrap herself in a warm cocoon. To think of work— the only thing she knew, the only thing she was good at. To be alone and safe. Just for a little while longer.

The ache in her stomach was another deep, dark hollow that seemed to engulf her very soul.

Yes, Lucas had been right about the reporter, and from the look on his face there was more to that story than he was telling her. Were people so interested in her? *Please, no.* She couldn't cope with that kind of intrusion.

Lucas was staring at her, thunderclouds brewing in his dark eyes. Then he blinked and vanquished the storm. '*Dios,* you are trembling. Claudia, all will be well. Your family will be there for you.'

A mirthless laugh burst from her searing throat. Her parents offering her *support?* 'Oh, Lucas, you have no idea.'

He frowned. 'So tell me.'

How could she? He worked for the crown. She could sense he respected her parents. Admired them. And deep down she knew Lucas would take their side. She might as well dig compassion out of a stone.

'I've been away from here so long,' she said, trying to think of a way to explain past the insistent throb in her head.

Smack went the wheels against the tarmac and Claudia rocked back in her seat. *Oh, God. Think, Claudia, think.*

The wings kicked up, the jet slowed and horror stung the back of her retinas at the sight before her. 'Oh, no.' She gripped his arm tighter, her fingertips digging through dense muscle. Hordes. What looked like thousands of flesh-eaters, hauling huge great cameras. Ready to pounce. 'No photographs.'

Lucas glanced at the pack, seemingly unaffected. While she felt wild, miserable, attacked.

'I can't do this. I'm sorry. Truly. Blame everything on me. Tell them I'm selfish and unreasonable and you tried everything.'

Cupping her face, Lucas looked into her eyes. 'Calm yourself. A car will pull up at the bottom of the steps. Let them see the beautiful Princess has returned home. Hold your head high.'

'No. They'll follow us…' She blinked at a flash. A memory. A noose wrapped around her heart tugged, choking the life out of her. How had she forgotten about that? 'Like before…' The car. The plink and flash of cameras. Her mother. The screaming. 'I think I'm going to throw up.'

His expression grew dark and as taut as the fingers cradling her face. 'Before?'

Throat burning, she gave a little shake of her head. Unwilling, unable to go back, revisit.

After a few beats he sighed. 'They cannot pass the enclosure. We will not be followed.' His voice turned fierce, indomitable. 'I promise you. I am here. You are safe. I will not let anything happen to you.'

Claudia closed her eyes. God, she wanted his lips on hers. He made her forget everything. Lucas made her feel safe.

Her eyes snapped open. 'And what happens when you drop me off at the palace and leave me there?'

Hands sliding from her cheeks, his gaze drifted to some place over her right shoulder. So strange that he was still right in front of her and yet it was as if he'd physically left. Leaving a numb sensation climbing up her spine. Because wasn't that always the way?

'You will have the best guards,' he said, his powerful voice blazing with conviction, an oath written in blood. 'I swear it.'

Everything inside her rebelled. 'No. I want you. Only you. *You* brought me here.' And he could damn well stick with her.

Reticence engulfed him, sharpening the air. 'Very well,' he said, his hand fisting against the tabletop as if the very idea was anathema to him. 'I will be in charge of your full security.' His gaze flicked back to hers. 'Yes?'

She slouched back into her seat. 'Yes. Okay. I'll stay with you.'

'What?' he said, his thunderous voice caroming around the cabin.

'That's the deal. Surely you have a house…a spare room?'

'You cannot be serious!'

'Deadly,' she said, switching off her pride button—a surprisingly easy feat when she considered the alternative. 'You take me with you or you turn this plane around.'

'Dios, Claudia, it is not appropriate. Have you lost your

mind?' he asked, incredulity contorting his features as if he was staring at a scary mad person.

It was a look that made her falter. *Was* she crazy? To ask for shelter under his roof. Yearning for his touch the way she did?

But after four hours cooped up on a plane she'd had time to put their kiss to rest. Clearly Lucas wasn't interested, and in three weeks she would have her life back. That was all she wanted. Her freedom. Until then she needed to feel safe. And, without knowing how or why, she trusted him with her life.

'We've just spent the last two days together,' she said. 'Was that appropriate?'

'*Sí.* We were in a different country. And your father expects you at the palace.'

'Just tell him I'm awkward and selfish and I need a little time. Nothing but the truth. Right?'

'Right.'

His eyes plummeted to her mouth and she watched them ignite, flare into a sapphire blaze. An answering heat unfurled deep down in her core even as she told herself he was simply vexed with her.

His words, the way he ground them out, confirmed her suspicions. 'The answer is still no. What you ask is impossible.'

Claudia lurched as the jet came to a dead stop. Reeled at the sight of a world long forgotten. Glanced at the harsh Mediterranean sun bouncing off the asphalt. Grappled with her shirtsleeves, pulling at the soft silk, desperate to be covered. 'What you asked of me yesterday morning was impossible in my mind, Lucas,' she said, the pit of despair gaping wider. 'Yet here I am. So, you see, nothing is impossible.'

From the corner of her eye she watched him flex his neck, his wide chest heave.

'We cannot always have what we desire, Claudia,' he bit out.

'Fine.' She pinned her spine to the seat and pulled the cord on her belt to cinch the black strap nice and tight. 'Refuel and take me home. Your mission is unaccomplished. Because I'm not getting off this plane.'

He raked his hands through his gorgeous sable hair and the silence stretched to a thick oppression. One she couldn't seem to breathe through.

One of the male flight attendants swerved towards them and Lucas hollered, 'Go the hell away.' So loud Claudia flinched.

Waiting until the attendant had darted towards the cockpit and disappeared from sight, she turned back to Lucas. 'Are you angry with me?' Stupid question when she was hyper-aware of the dark power emanating from his body, pulsing through the air, humming over her skin. Perversely, she'd never felt so protected in her entire life.

'Goddamn furious. You play a dangerous game with me, Claudia. I make the rules. *Comprende?*'

Oh, she understood perfectly. 'So tell me the new rules and I'll obey. Every single one.'

CHAPTER SEVEN

'Wow. Being Head of Security must pay well.'

With the exception of Marianne, his housekeeper, Lucas had never had a woman in his home before. Now he knew why. It was a complete invasion of privacy and entirely too distracting. He'd rather camp with twenty men than one of Claudia.

'Glass. Everywhere. I suddenly feel like a goldfish swimming around an enormous bowl,' she said, with a quick tug on the sleeves of her jacket.

Ah, yes, Lucas mused, his mouth twisting. She preferred walls of steel to match the walls she'd built up inside herself. At first he'd thought the vulnerability was her cloak. He'd been wrong. It was her inner core. Everything was designed to fight off intruders like some high-tech alarm system. Together with her high intellect, it was unsurprising no one had managed to breach it.

Standing in the centre of the hundred-foot open-plan living area, he watched her absorb his life, the pit of his stomach weighted with lead. This was a mistake. He knew it. He didn't want her here. Didn't want any woman here. Especially not her. But what choice did he have? Dragging her to the palace would have been more barbaric than even he was capable of. And the panic, the terror, the vulnerability in her eyes—*Dios,* it got to him every time. At least here she was safe. From what haunting demons he had no idea. But he intended to find out.

'The view is the most spectacular I've ever seen,' she said, awe lending her voice a creamy note. She moved up close to the wide plate glass, looking towards the ocean, and sunlight gilded her in an angelic aura. He knew then she'd been in the dark too long.

She trailed her fingers along the polished black top of his baby grand and he could feel those very tips branding his skin, setting his blood on fire.

'I'm not sure what I expected,' she said, slowing to examine an original masterpiece taking centre stage on one of the few internal walls. 'Beautiful brush strokes. I'm sure the National Gallery has one of these.'

With a tilt of her head she bestowed upon him her profile. The soft curve of her lip told him she knew all too well the value of the painting. But purchasing the portrait hadn't been about money or investment or even the artist. It had everything to do with the subject.

'What did you expect?' he asked, unsure why he even cared for her opinion.

Swivelling on her low heels to face him, she gave a small smile, lifted at one side in a kind of embarrassment. 'Probably some Americanised version of a bachelor pad. Huge TV, empty pizza boxes and…' Colour warmed her cheeks rose-gold.

'And?'

'I was going to say a stash of *Playboy* magazines, but for all I know you have a girlfriend.' Biting her lip, she lifted one foot, bent her ankle and scratched her opposite calf with the black peeptoe. 'Which, come to think of it, is something I should've asked before I ki—'

Jumping in before the image engulfed him, he bit out, 'I do not get involved with women, Claudia.' He laid his commitment-free card face-up. For both their sakes. Lucas would *not* kiss her under this roof. Because if he did he would never stop.

Claudia pursed her lips, canted her head. 'At all?'

'No. Like you, I live for my work. I have neither the time nor the inclination for relationships.'

He had one-hour-stands with women who knew the rules.

Claudia wouldn't know what to do with a rulebook if it smacked her on the head—something that made him doubly wary of their current predicament.

'Something else we have in common, then,' she said.

'I cannot think of any possible "something else".'

'You value your privacy. You don't talk much about yourself.'

'It is not necessary in my job.' He was being sharp—overly so. But he needed her to understand. Just because she'd managed to wrangle herself a bed under his roof it didn't mean she could burrow into his life. And to stop her from doing just that, Lucas was determined to focus on hers. When she finally decamped he'd make damn sure she held her head high, without the need for any of her façades.

'Our agreement was one week. Seven days and seven nights you may stay. Your father was quite willing to allow you time to acclimatise.' The relief in Henri's voice had said it all. She was on Arunthian soil and that was what mattered. Lucas's secluded estate rivalled Fort Knox, so they would be free from prying eyes.

No, the real problem was standing directly in front of him. One finger swirling around her pout, one hip tilted in that sexy pose that made his blood roar. *Dios*...

Hoping she would retire and leave him with some measure of peace, he said, 'First thing tomorrow we visit your parents, and during the remaining time I will reintroduce you to your country.'

Eyes widening, her mouth worked. 'Tomorrow?'

'*Sí.* And then I will show you your *real* home.' Once she became captivated by her heritage and discerned her true import the desire to do her duty would come, he was sure.

If what she said was true and she was uncomfortable around people he needed to fix it. Otherwise, come the end of the week, they would be back to square one and there was no way she could stay here for *three* weeks. He would go grey. And insane. The sooner she was confident in her abilities the sooner she would be gone from his life.

Gone. Ignoring the sharp blade driving through his gut, he forged on. He had to tear down her defences one by one, vanquish every fear. It was his job, he told himself, despite the claw at his conscience saying otherwise.

'Firstly, do *not* concern yourself with the paparazzi or your personal safety. There was a time when Arunthia was plagued with villainy and the crime rate was high. Too high,' he said, keeping his voice steady, betraying none of the emotion warring inside. 'But not any more.'

Dark brows rose above stunned amber eyes. 'Not since you took over, you mean?'

'*Exactamente.* Welcome home, *Just Claudia.*'

The *whoop, whoop* of rotorblades echoed the thump of her anxious heart as they flew over the famed hunting grounds of her childhood residence. And when Arunthe Palace burst into view—standing atop a gigantic rock in dramatic cliff-edge splendour—it was as if the helicopter had been torn open beneath her feet and she was freefalling to earth.

Cream stone-walls, fanciful turrets with conical slate roofs, large spiralling towers firing into the sky like fireworks—a Disney-esque vision that was merely an illusion, a fairytale. For no happy endings could arise from this world of chilling austerity.

Despite all the years of fighting for her freedom she was finally here. Her parents had sent King Kong for Fay Wray and she'd never had a chance. And some sixth sense ran like a river of screams beneath her skin, warning her that now she'd returned she would never escape. *Nonsense, Claudia. Breathe.*

The military helicoptor touched down and she ordered her legs to stand tall, stay strong, even as she reached for her iron mask, admitting, if only to herself, that she would have done anything for Lucas to take her hand and hold it tightly in his.

So she could absorb his awesome strength. *No, Claudia. Self-reliant. Always self-reliant.*

By the time they were ushered into her mother's apartment, her stomach was alive with seething nausea, and the sickly scent of lavender hit her just as hard as the sight of Marysse Verbault.

Dressed in an elegant buttery skirt suit and a black chiffon blouse, with not one hair escaping her coiffed dark pleat, she oozed class and sophistication. Claudia pinched her fingers to stop herself from smoothing her own rumpled *'dour'* appearance or tugging on the threadbare hem of her sleeve.

Then that voice—so cool, so calm—stroked her soul with fingers of ice. 'Claudine. Finally. Let me look at you.'

A bolt of indignation shot down her spine and pinned her in place. At one time this woman hadn't been able to bear to look at her. To touch her. Yet now her mother clasped her upper arms and Claudia foraged for the bravura to lock onto the amber eyes that were so like her own. Not only that, for one cataclysmic beat of her heart Claudia imagined her mother wanted to embrace her, and one tiny part of her—the little girl she had once been—wanted that so much. Craved to know she was wanted for herself, loved in some small way. But her mother merely examined every inch of her face, as if to check her daughter was well—well enough to parade in front of thousands.

'I am very happy to see to you, Claudine. Look, Henri, our daughter is finally home.'

Resisting the urge to argue that *London* was her home, she waited for his words…then flinched when his imperious voice caromed around the room.

'It is about time. Good job, Lucas.'

Claudia perfected a smile that cracked her heart and looked across the opulent expanse of the room to where Henri Verbault stood with Lucas in front of a large, ornate cherrywood desk, papers in hand. Age had amplified his autocratic demeanour even as his greying hair softened the contours of his face.

'Good morning, Father.'

'*Buenos días,* Claudine.' Steel-grey determined eyes held hers, turning liquid with something like relief. Relief that she was well, or relief that she was back to pay her dues? Who knew? He turned his attention back to Lucas, her dismissal loud and true.

'Sit down. Take tea.'

Her mother's voice warmed just a touch as she perched on the edge of a Gustavian carver chair, one leg demurely tucked behind the other. And with one last longing look at the door Claudia eased down onto the gold-striped sofa opposite.

Staff came and went, and there was no mistaking the questions in their eyes as they surreptitiously glanced her way. The need to reach up, touch her face just to check, was so all-consuming, she trembled with the power of it. So she folded her hands atop her lap, so tightly her fingers wept. She could feel Lucas's intense gaze—was he thinking the same as her mother? The same as everyone in this room? That she didn't belong. That she looked out of place.

Suddenly her mother's voice smashed through the thin veneer. 'The ball is Saturday next, Claudine. I shall arrange for a selection of gowns to be delivered.'

Mask rigid, her mind screamed. *You can dress me up like a china doll but lavish fripperies can never veil the woman I am inside.* A woman as far away from being a princess as her mother was from having a heart.

Did she feel anything? Claudia wondered. Had this picture of perfection felt anything the day she'd said Claudia wasn't beautiful any more? The day Claudia's nightmares had been born, and the horror that had finally sentenced her to extradition? Maybe her mother didn't remember the terrible things she'd said, done. But Claudia would. Until the end of time.

'Then, once you are settled and back at the palace,' her mother continued. 'we can discuss the future.'

Slam went her defences as they locked into place and her

head jerked upright. Future? Her future was in London, where she'd built her life. 'I have three weeks' leave, Mother. That is all.'

'Let us not place time restrictions on ourselves. Now you are home it is important we get to know each other once again.'

Once again? She doubted if her mother even remembered her first steps, never mind her favourite book.

'And we have a couple of weeks to do so,' Claudia said, her tone sharp, slicing through the room. She'd fought for years and she was *never* giving up her freedom.

Unfazed, her mother went on. 'Andalina also returns tomorrow, from New York, and Luciana flies in from Singapore the day after. It will be nice for you girls to come together.' Her voice was laced with...*pleasure?* 'Show our country a united front.'

Claudia crushed her lips. Oh, of course. The reason she'd been torn away from her job saving lives and curing pain was to play happy families. Yes, she wanted to see her sisters again, but how could she possibly compare to their scandalous, famed-for-their-beauty presence?

She couldn't. It was impossible. She almost told her mother so. But then that red river of screaming returned to sluice beneath her skin. Because she could hear Lucas making his excuses to her father, declaring his intention to leave. And she knew.

Lucas was leaving her here. Either he didn't want her with him or... Oh, God, had her father insisted she stay here?

'Your Royal Highness?'

And there it was. Her title. Not *Just Claudia*.

Discreetly she inhaled a fortifying breath, perfected serenity and looked up to where Lucas stood beside her, an enigmatic hardness to his gorgeous face. Every delicious atom of his being oozed military man dominance—his duty to king and country was in his every powerful step. Her heart throbbed.

Her mind yelled. *Don't do this, Lucas. Please don't break your word to me. Not you.*

Intense sapphire eyes bored into hers. 'Come. It is time to leave.'

Lucas kept his stride short as they walked across the court-yard to the helipad. Not an easy feat for a man with extra-long legs, but he sensed Claudia was at the very edge of her limits. Even with her damn façade in place. *Dios,* his vision of a heart-warming reunion had just been exploded with a double-barrelled shotgun.

The sound of her feet scoring asphalt, as if she were about to trip in her haste, was a kick to his protective gut and he snagged Claudia's arm, tugging her into a darkened corridor leading to the armoury.

'Breathe, Claudia.' Grasping her shoulders, he manoeuvred her to lean against the stone wall…then backed the hell away. Before he hauled her into his arms. The situation was already complex enough. But, *Dios,* she wanted him to. He knew from the way her eyes devoured his wide shoulders, his chest, even as she wrapped her own delicate hands around her body.

He clenched his fists so hard a spear of pain lanced up his forearms. 'Why are you running?'

'I'm not running anywhere,' she said, still breathless. 'We're leaving…aren't we?'

Lucas thrust his fingers through his hair. '*Sí.* After you calm down, speak to me.'

Closing her eyes, she gently banged her head on the stone wall—once, twice. 'God, Lucas, what do you want from me. I came, didn't I? Just like you wanted.'

'No, just as your parents wanted.' Yet there had been no embrace. No words of joy. Only duty. While he understood duty took priority over all else, pure empathy had torn through him as he'd watched her encounter such insouciance. After all she'd been through.

A humourless laugh slipped from her lips. 'Oh, yes—except they want someone who doesn't exist.'

Lucas frowned. 'Explain this to me.'

'I can't be what they want,' she said, her voice pitching with frustration. 'Do I look like a princess of the realm to you? No. What if I embarrass them in front of the world? Make some pithy remark to the King of Salzerre? Look ridiculous in some frou-frou dress with no sleeves—?'

'Look at me,' he demanded.

When she did not obey he slid his fingers up her jaw, cupped her face and tilted it to look at him. He felt himself almost drowning in her amber eyes. Eyes that were now brimming with hurt.

'No more excuses. You must believe in yourself. In what you are capable of. As I do.'

'You...you do?'

'*Sí.* Of course. Do you know what your people call you, Claudia? The Lost Princesa. How right they are—for still you are lost. When I saw Bailey I knew. You hide. You need to break free. Show them who you truly are inside. The rest will come.'

He could feel her pulse thrumming against the ball of his hand, her throat convulse.

'Being back here—' Her voice cracked on a whisper. 'I'm twelve years old again. So sick. So cold.'

A giant fist punched him in the guts. 'You have bad memories of being here.' It made perfect sense, but there was more, he knew. Problem was, he was treading perilously close to quicksand. For her relationship with her parents, however awkward and frigid, was none of his business. Still, he was unwilling to watch her fall or unveil another damn façade.

'You are sick no more, Claudia. While I am angry as hell that life has dealt you such a card, you have found your way. You have become an accomplished, intelligent woman in your own right. Be proud of this.' With his thumbs he drew small circles on her soft cheeks, luring her in to believe him. Fighting the craving to kiss the sadness from her lips. 'Be proud of your brave heart.'

'I don't feel brave,' she whispered. 'I feel lost. I know my role back home. I know my job. Here—I'm not one of them. I don't know how to be.'

Lucas pulled back, his hands slipping from her face to rake around the back of his neck. 'And do you think I did?' he asked, aggravated by the tightness in his voice, yet determined to show her he understood. 'I was not born to this world, Claudia. Far from it.'

Her lips parted on an indrawn breath. 'But you're perfectly at ease here.'

'*Sí*. I too had to learn. And I found honour in doing so.' He'd found more than honour. He'd found a way of life. One that had saved him from the dark side. Given him the strength to move on, to fight. 'Fear has no place in your heart right now.'

Eyes firing with the first spark of that spirit he craved, she said, 'I'm not scared. I—' Her brow creased as she bit her lip. 'Maybe I am. A little. But you said so yourself. I look *dour*. I can't be elegant like *her*. Like my sisters. It's impossible.'

Lucas raised one brow and gave her The Look. 'And where is the woman who told me only yesterday that nothing is impossible?'

Lips curving sweetly, sadly, she said, 'I have no idea.'

'Then let us find her.'

CHAPTER EIGHT

THE NEXT MORNING, Claudia feast her eyes upon the orange groves lining the driveway leading from Lucas's estate to the open road and nestled closer to the car door, depressing the window button with the tip of her finger.

An intoxicating sweet scent drifted up her nose, filling her lungs until she never wanted to exhale.

'I'd forgotten,' she said. 'The amazing smell of orange blossom.'

It seemed to cling to her senses, stir something deep inside her…something long forgotten. A surreal feeling of peace washed over her—a sensation that didn't make any sense.

'It is heavier during spring when the trees are in full bloom. More decadent, I think.'

Lucas's deep masculine voice overwhelmed her and made her headier still, her pulse skipping.

Tilting her head to peek skyward through the large gap in the blackened window, she closed her eyes, basking in the morning sun, wondering about the kind of man who proclaimed he didn't feel and yet used the word *decadent. The same man who is sheltering you from the storm.* But that, she told herself, was Lucas doing his job. Keeping her in Arunthia to fulfil her duty. A role which had once again kept her eyes wide through the night. But when the dawn had come so had her vow. If Lucas believed she could pull it off and play princess for the night she would give it her best shot. If only to prove to herself that she could. That she wasn't shackled by the past.

Heavenly rays stroked through the clusters of fruit, the light speckling over her face. Shadows came and went, during which time she could just make out the tiny white flowers clinging to the bulbous dewy fruit.

'Are they still Arunthia's main export?'

'Yes. Although as a country we are now richer from other timely investments. Mango, grapes, olives—that kind of thing.' Leather creaked as he shifted on the seat beside her. 'You are too hot, Claudia.'

'I know,' she said, tugging at the neckline of her long-sleeved tunic.

'Close the window and the air-con will cool you.'

'I need something cooler to wear.'

Black was no good in this horrid heat. And close proximity to Lucas didn't help. If she hadn't been distinctly uncomfortable in her own skin before she was now.

'I have already made an appointment for you at the boutique in town.'

A moan slipped past her lips. Why, oh, why had she agreed to this? *Come on, Claudia. We're talking clothes, not strains of cholera.*

'Afterwards we will take a stroll. Today is market day, I believe.'

Another moan. 'Don't feel the need to ease me in gently, will you, Lucas? This isn't one of your military operations. At least allow me time to feel comfortable in full regalia before a full inspection.'

'Dream on, Claudia.'

Was he smiling? She didn't dare look in case she melted.

'The people will see you and you will dig deep for that inner radiance and that beautiful smile of yours.'

She blinked. The scenery shuttered in and out of view. That was the second time he'd put her name and the word beautiful into one sentence. Wait a minute… *Inner radiance?* Was he high? Unable to resist looking at him for a second longer, she twisted at the waist and braced herself for the habitual hormone overload. It didn't work. Utter waste of energy.

Absorbing eighty percent of the oxygen and encompassing ninety-five percent of the space, Lucas was a modern-day gladiator. Leaning pensively on his wrist as he took particular interest in the opposite side of the road.

With a quick glance to check that the privacy glass between themselves and Armande was firmly in place, she snapped back to him, 'I think you need your eyes tested, Lucas.'

Fist dropping to his lap, he turned and speared her with his don't-mess-with-me look. 'It is you who needs an eye-test, Claudia. Maybe then you would not wear reading glasses for long distance.'

She gawped. Outright glared at him. 'You're beginning to scare me, do you know that?'

He smiled. The brute actually smiled. And—oh, boy—her stomach flipped, then fluttered as if filled with white blossom bobbing on a breeze. It was a lopsided sinful smile that was loaded with bad-boy charisma. Just a hint of straight pearly teeth and a dimple in one cheek. Licking her lips, she'd swear she could taste that gorgeous mouth of his.

'A shield, in whatever form, only hides so much,' he said, before shifting on his hip and reaching up to where her glasses sat visor-like atop her head. 'You do not need them for visiting, for shopping, for the breathtaking scenery or as a hairband.'

His husky voice… The slide of his fingers, abrasive on her scalp…

'Do not deny people the pleasure of seeing your amber fire.'
Amber fire?

'How do you do it?' she asked, a little breathless, a whole lot stunned. 'You soak in every nuance. It's really intimidating. Am I so easy to read?'

'No. You have many layers and they are proving hard to strip away.'

Strip? She wished to God he'd strip her right now—or take

off his own clothes. She wasn't picky. Against all logic she wanted to touch him. With one kiss he'd given her a taste of undiluted desire and like a potent drug she craved another shot.

Thought vanished as he pulled her glasses free and the light scrape of his fingers brushed across her cheek. She focused on his eyes. Rich dark blue, hot and intense, pupils dilated.

Claudia held onto the moment and the past forty-eight hours disappeared. She could feel him surrounding her—hard and fiercely passionate. The seductive pull of his mouth. What would his mouth feel like on her neck? Her breasts? Her stomach? What would he feel like deep like inside her?

Something hot and sultry splashed through her midsection and she gripped the edge of the buttery leather seat with one hand and squeezed her thighs together. *Oh, God,* what was happening to her?

Lucas broke the connection and closed the arms of her glasses in on themselves. Bereft, Claudia watched him plop the frames into the cubbyhole lining the door, delve into the inside pocket of his suave black jacket and pull out a platinum-encased pen. Lowering his eyes to the small table in front of him, where a sheaf of papers lay, he began to scrawl his signature, his long fingers stroking the silver column.

Visions—vividly sensual and achingly explicit—poured into her mind. Where they came from she had no idea, but she couldn't seem to stop them. Clenching her insides, she wriggled to ease the damp sensation between her legs and pulled at the small window button to douse the sweet bouquet of nature. Only to be ensnared in a whirlwind of musk-drenched pheromones.

Vision blurring, she squeezed her eyes shut. 'How far?'

'Ten minutes,' he said, in a growl she'd come to recognise as Lucas being unhappy with her. 'Nine.'

He was on a countdown. Nine minutes? Heavens above, she'd be a puddle in the footwell by then. She rubbed her brow, felt the moisture coat her fingertips and tore at the high neck of her tunic.

Lucas reached for the control panel between them and lowered the temperature in the car by four degrees. He might as well have hiked it up, because the sight of his long thick fingers stroking the controls detonated the nuclear bomb in the pit of her stomach and she began to literally quake.

'Are you car-sick?' he asked.

Sick? She was sick in the head. This had to stop! Frantic, she dug deep to unearth hate and came up blank. When had that happened? Yesterday, when he'd swept her away from the palace? Or when he'd slanted that hot hard mouth over hers? Or had it been when he'd been so damn wonderful with Bailey?

'Claudia, did you hear me?'

'Sick. Yes. Terribly.'

Okay no hate. What else did she have? Well, for starters, he didn't want her. Wasn't it mortifying enough that one kiss had put him off? And she didn't even know him! While he was stripping her bare—somehow with all her clothes still intact—she still had no idea who he was.

Lucas lowered the privacy glass to speak to Armande. 'I will tell him to pull over.'

Claudia gripped his arm, tugged. 'No. Not that kind of sick. Just…' She flicked her shoulder, scrambling for a word. Any word. 'Nervous. Just nervous. Carry on. Honest.' The more time they spent in this car, the more chance she had of making a fool of herself.

Up went the glass partition, yet his searching eyes never left her face. Since she'd moved to grab him they were too close, but she couldn't seem to let go—just luxuriated in the touch of fine wool and hot steel beneath. Colour scored his cheeks and she watched, mesmerised, as his throat convulsed, a muscle ticked his jaw.

'*Dios,* I cannot continue travelling in these confined spaces with you. It is agony.'

There it was. It shouldn't hurt. But it really, really did.

She snatched her hand away. 'Agony. Right.' While she was

burning up, ready to spontaneously combust, he abhorred their close proximity.

Slamming the table upright with one hand, he shoved the papers in his briefcase with the other. Breath short, his chest began to heave, and his amazing blue eyes speared an arrow of heat straight to her core. '*Dios,* your brain is addled. And I am running out of ideas on how to convince you.'

'Convince me of what?'

'That you were not born to hide!'

'Hide? You're not making sense.' And why was he always so angry with her?

'Tell me, what do you feel like right now? In here?' he said, punching his own rock-hard stomach. 'Truthfully, Claudia,' he growled in warning.

On fire. A tight fusion of energy cells clustered into a fiery ball—sparking, fighting to explode. As if she had the worst stomach ache on earth. Or was it the best stomach ache on earth? Regardless, if she moved one muscle and rubbed down *there,* where her knickers were so wet, she'd seriously…

'Agony,' she said, the word slipping out before she had a chance to stop it.

'*Sí.* Agony. As do I.'

Her eyes slid to where the expensive weave of his suit pulled tight around his thick thighs and groin. He couldn't possibly…

'Oh,' she said a little shakily as her insides grew heavier still.

Tucking one of his fingers under her chin, he raised her head until their eyes met. 'You are clueless, Claudia. You think I could devour you like that and feel nothing?'

'I just thought…maybe you kiss everyone like that.'

His chin dipped as his eyebrows shot skyward. 'I appreciate your confidence in my abilities.'

'And you pulled away. In fact you pushed me away!'

'*Sí,'* he said, ripping his finger from her chin so quickly her head bobbed. 'For my own damn sanity and your honour. Before I took you against the wall.'

'Oh? It was good, then?' she asked, trying to quell the initial elation and excitement until she knew for sure.

Facing front, he thrust his fingers through his hair and clawed down his face. 'And now I finally see what has been staring me in the face. Tell me, when you look in the mirror, what do you see?'

Shaking her head, she inched backwards. But given the space deprivation she didn't make much progress.

'Exactly,' he said, turning back to face her. 'You do not like what you see.'

She tore at her lip. Why was he persecuting her like this? In truth she couldn't remember the last time she'd peered at her reflection—except for in the en-suite bedroom in Lucas's penthouse. Because she loathed every flaw. Wondered if every slight shade variation on her skin was her imagination or a sign of something to come.

His eyes darkened to the colour of midnight. 'Why? I ask myself. When you are the most beautiful woman I have ever seen.'

Stupefied, she parted her lips as a war erupted inside her—her mind tripping over disbelief, her heart squeezing at his earnest words. Because she knew he wouldn't lie. 'Oh…'

Lucas snorted. 'Suddenly you have lost your internal dictionary. It seems I have found another way to shut you up. I shall remember this.'

'I preferred the other way,' she said, remembering the way he'd backed her up against the car outside her flat. She'd been right! He'd been going to kiss her. She wanted him to. Right. Now.

He laughed without a speck of humour. 'Do not even think about it.'

'Well, why not? If I want to and you want to… Couldn't we just…?' She wanted him to kiss her again so desperately she smothered her lips in moisture. Maybe if he touched her, put his hands on her breasts, they wouldn't ache so much.

'No. *No.* And do not look at me in that way!'

'I'm not,' she said, before his words registered. 'What way?'

'With those slumberous eyes and that sexy mouth. I—' He groaned and flung himself back into the seat.

She had a sexy mouth? 'So where's the problem in that?'

'The problem with that, Claudia, is that along with your beauty I see a woman who I am forbidden to touch—and no,' he said, palm facing her in a stop sign, 'I am *not* only talking about my position at the palace. I am talking about my life. My rules. Did you not listen to a word I said yesterday? I have *sex*. Pure and simple.'

'Really?' It sounded kind of exciting to her. She'd never done anything exciting in her whole life. If just the idea exploded some of those fiery cells inside her, imagine what thrilling ecstasy she would experience if they actually did it. Although she guessed excitement was the improper response, because Lucas had seemingly caught the stimulated pitch in her tone and grim contempt slashed across his face.

'It is just sex, Claudia. Meaningless. A short diversion with women I do not know. Woman who comprehend that I will leave and never, *ever* come back.'

When he said it like that, so cold and detached, she felt a shiver swarm across the base of her spine. He left. But didn't everyone? Of course they did. Except this time *she* would be leaving. After this trip she'd never see him again. She knew that. And surely the hollow pang she felt inside her at that thought was only because Lucas kept distracting her at breakfast.

'*Sí*. Now you understand,' he said, somewhat relieved.

Yes, clearly he used women. But surely they used him too? For pleasure? What was so wrong about that? Now she knew the attraction was reciprocated it was her chance to experiment with her body, explore all these new and fantastic sensations. When his lips touched hers she forgot everything. The past. What was to come. And, in truth, she wanted to experience being desired, wanted. Just once in her life. She'd never trust another man as long as she lived.

'I am hard, unfeeling,' he bit out. 'I am not a man to become attached to. *Comprende?*'

Claudia began to wonder who exactly he was trying to convince here. She nodded. 'I'm not deaf, Lucas, I understand perfectly.'

Good grief, the last thing she wanted was to become *attached* to the man. Apart from the fact he was emotionally void, he lived in a different country. She was going home in three weeks—back to her life, to London, to Bailey. And she might trust him with her life but she'd never trust him with her heart. Claudia knew the price of loving, of needing. Inevitable heartbreak.

'*Bueno,*' he said, giving her a searching look, not entirely convinced. 'Good.'

'You just have sex. You don't get involved. You walk away,' she said, warming more to the idea with every passing second even as her body was shaking itself apart with adrenaline. No emotions. The thrill of undiscovered excitement. One taste of passion: a memory to last her a lifetime. And, more importantly, *Claudia* would be the one to walk away. 'And you find me b...beautiful, right?'

He blinked, worked his mouth round the word. 'Yes.'

'That's okay, then. Because I just want sex too.'

A stunned light flashed in his intent stare. '*Madre de Dios!*' he said, raising his hands as if praying to the heavens for patience.

'I do.'

'*Sí?* Well,' he said, with caustic bite, 'we both know that oftentimes your sense of self-preservation is severely lacking.'

'But I—'

'No, Claudia. No buts. It is impossible.'

The slash of his hand acted like a zipper across her lips.

Slumping back onto the leather seat, she fastened her eyes on the view. Watched the flashing images of small stucco homes as the car sped through the outskirts of town—everything a blur.

Maybe she hadn't handled that so well. Obviously he thought she'd want more than he could give. So she had to convince Lucas that beyond this visit and her obligation to play princess for the night of the ball she was *Just Claudia*. And *Just Claudia* wanted exactly the same thing he did. No commitment. No messy entanglements. Just sex.

The question was: how did she convince him of that?

A blast of trepidation evaporated the moisture on her nape as she remembered who she was—gauche, fidgety and, to use one of Lucas's words, *clueless* in the art of all things sexual.

Her stomach hit the leather with a disheartened thump.

Lucas's women were no doubt the opposite of her in every way—glamorous spelk-like things who knew what they were about. Knew how to lure, to seduce. She wouldn't know where to start. And how could *she* possibly satisfy a veritable god of war and passion? It was the most ridiculous idea she'd ever thought up. So why did it also feel like the most wonderful?

Risking another look at him, she bit her inner cheek.

Fingers curved over his mouth, he stared into the distance, his other hand clenching and releasing where it lay on his thick thigh. One look and that wicked, salacious torrent doused some of her unease. She brushed her hair from her face with the back of her unsteady hand and straightened in her seat.

Fear has no place in your heart right now.

She could do this. Absolutely. He was worth it. She wanted a taste of passion. Just once in her life. And she trusted him. It was perfect.

She could do this.

After all, had he not told her she was capable of anything she put her mind to?

CHAPTER NINE

THAT'S OKAY, THEN. Because I just want sex too.

Lucas scratched his name along the bottom of another LGAS contract, no doubt scoring the wood beneath, then flexed his neck, rolling the stiffness from his shoulders.

Dios, the woman was going to be the death of him. And, although she'd seemed to accept his 'impossible' decree in the car, he could not shake the sense that he was staring down the barrel of a gun.

'I'm done. We can go, if you're ready.'

Claudia's soft voice, a tad apprehensive, drifted from somewhere over his left shoulder.

'*Sí.* One moment.' Feet flat to the floor, he pushed his chair back from the small table where he'd set up a temporary office in the corner of the boutique. Twisting at the waist, he bent double and wedged the papers back into his briefcase on the floor.

The click-click of heels on parquet snagged his attention and his gaze darted to a pair of... He swallowed. A pair of sexy-as-hell black peeptoe heels, adorned with a diamond and sapphire-encrusted brooch just above small toes.

A tsunami thundering through town couldn't have stopped his eyes from doing a slow glissade over sculpted ankles, up over sleek honey-gold skin that sheathed the sexiest pair of calves he'd ever seen...until they disappeared at the knee beneath the flirty edges of a sapphire-blue pleated skirt. No, he amended, his heart thumping in his chest, it was a dress, skimming the lush flare of her hips, cinching the small span of her waist with a black silk sash. At the full curve of her lush breast his eyes lingered, just a beat, before rising to the slash neck and floating down the length of her arms to stop at her wrists

His pulse spiked so hard a shaft of pain shot across his chest

A delicate throat-clearing made him blink. He was half out of his seat, staring like some doe-eyed recruit, for God's sake.

Lucas bolted upright. The chair hit the floor with a thud and his eyes careened into Claudia's.

'Do I look okay?' she asked, head canted, sucking provocatively on her lower lip, her brow creased in an endearingly nervous little frown.

'*Sí,*' he said, searching for the right words, cursing himself that he was ill equipped to do her justice. *You look beautiful* wasn't quite right, because nothing on earth was as beautiful as her face. Sophisticated? Or just downright knee-knockingly gorgeous? In the end he settled for the absolute truth, knowing she needed to hear it. 'Words fail me, Princesa.'

One corner of her delectable mouth lifted. 'That's good, right?'

Shrugging, he made his reply lazy, despite the magnitude of its importance. For it was extraordinary to believe a woman of such beauty disliked her own reflection. Believed she was imperfect in any way. When in reality the only thing she lacked was self-confidence. Well, not today. '*Sí*. Very, *very* good. It is also unheard of.'

Her smile blazed to killer proportions before she gnawed her lip and slowly, warily, closed the distance between them.

'Claudia?' he growled, not liking where this was going. Or possibly liking it too much.

Being assailed with her vanilla-drenched scent doubled the dose of want and he stiffened from top to toe as she curled her fingers round the lapel of his jacket, tugged...rose on her tiptoes and dropped a delicate kiss on his cheek, whispering, 'Thank you...' against the sensitive skin on the underside of his ear.

A shudder racked down his spine and he fisted his hands to stop himself from hauling her close. Instead he watched her long nimble fingers stroke down the lapel of his jacket—an innocent touch he swore he could feel against his bare skin—then turn on her kitten-heels towards the door, hips swaying with a natural hypnotic rhythm that distorted his vision.

'Lucas, are you coming?'

No, unfortunately not. Although if she kept touching him…

What the hell was she thinking, kissing him like that? When he'd already told her no! *Dios,* maybe he was over-analysing what could have been a simple thank-you.

Discarding his unease, he snatched his briefcase from the floor and strode towards her. 'Give your bags to Armande and we'll walk through town.'

The assistants scurried over with an armful of bags, a pair of large sunglasses and a black hat trimmed with the same blue of her dress. Claudia eased the hat atop her head and slowly pushed the glasses up her nose.

'Camouflage, Claudia?' Although he had to admit she looked stunning. Like the front cover spread of some glossy American magazine.

'Baby steps, Lucas.'

He didn't bother telling her she was wasting her time.

As predicted, flying under the radar had become a distant memory, because every pair of eyes swung in Claudia's direction and locked on target as they sauntered down the main avenue—his favourite part of the old town.

Blossom trees lined the road, branches heavy with a full show of colour, and the light breeze wafted tiny pink and cream petals in every direction to settle on the cobbles beneath their feet.

'Now I know what it feels like to be a cell on a slide,' she said, tugging on the sleeves of her dress in that habitual way that drove him *loco,* before inching closer as if needing to absorb his strength.

'Let them see the Lost Princess has returned.'

'Is that why they're staring so much?' she asked, her honey-eyed voice tainted with amazement. With a discreet jerk of her head she motioned up ahead. 'Even him?'

Pausing mid-stride, Lucas looked up to see a young hotshot sitting on one of the stone benches lining the street, leering at Claudia with blatant lust.

Locking a growl in his chest, he curved his arm around her small waist, protectively, and steered her past, ignoring the slow burn up his arm. It was untenable to realise the ramifications of her illness.

'Has it never occurred to you that after you recovered from your illness people would look at you for an entirely different reason? Men would stare because they were enthralled? Women would stare with envy?'

'N...no,' she said, stunned, and breathless as she sidled closer still. 'Not once.'

Dios, little wonder there had been no men in her life. 'Well, now you know,' he said, dropping his arm as if she were a grenade. Before he nigh on detonated.

'As for the rest—remember you are a mystery to them.'

On cue, a small girl tentatively approached Claudia, all long blonde curls and sweet smiles as she curtsied and bestowed upon her a small posy of lilacs from behind her back.

Claudia blinked as if the child were an apparition, then bent at the waist until they were at eye level. In the same rich-with-affection tone she used with Bailey—the one that made a strange yearning pour through his soul—she said, 'How beautiful you are. I shall treasure them, for they are the first flowers I've ever been given. Thank you.'

A wild torrent of feeling flooded down his chest. How could that be? Had her parents never sent her flowers? Even on her birthday? Claudia turned to him, her forehead nipped, as if trying to suppress the power of her emotions. And a memory slammed into him, making the world tilt on its axis. His mind flickered...

There he was. His ninth birthday. His mother—so soft, so

sad—trying to smile through the pain of a broken jaw. A small box wrapped in her favourite blue headscarf. A car—a toy Ferrari. The brightest shade of red he'd ever seen. His throat closed, his heart bleeding, when he realised the exorbitant price she had paid. *Dios. Breathe, Garcia. Breathe.*

'Lucas?' Claudia's voice, rich with affection, tainted with concern, drifted on the sweet-scented air and he fisted his hands to stop himself reaching out, hauling her to him, burying his face in her neck, breathing her in.

'Are you okay?'

'*Sí,*' he said, slamming the door on the past. 'Do you like your gift?'

She tried for a smile. One that cut him to the core.

'Arunthia holds its royal family close to its heart. And your career has made you very popular with the people.'

'I didn't think...' Her husky voice cracked.

'That you were so important?' he asked incredulously.

With a little shake of her head, she tore at her lower lip. 'That I would matter at all.'

Jaw slack, Lucas floundered at the severe lack of her self-worth. 'Well, you are of high import, Claudia. So let them be awed by you. Enjoy it.'

A small huff burst from her lips. '*Enjoy it?*' she repeated, her mood lifting, firing her back into motion to resume their walk. 'That's a bit of a stretch, Lucas. Two days ago I lived in a lab. And, before you say another word, *you* don't care much for attention either. Every time someone bows in your direction I can hear your molars crack.'

His teeth ached just thinking about it. 'Because it is not appropriate.'

'Seems to me you're a local hero, Lucas,' she said, nudging his arm with her elbow, a small smile playing about her lips. '*Enjoy it.*'

A growl rumbled up his chest. 'They are grateful, and I must allow them to show their respect. I have no desire to revel in success when I was merely doing my job and improving the kingdom.' Even then he'd had his own agenda. No one would suffer in filth and violence as his mother had. Not as long as he lived.

A cluster of tables from a café spilled onto the pathway dead ahead and Claudia slid her arm through his, leaning close until he felt the full crush of her breast against his arm.

Lucas ground his jaw. His breathing grew short. 'Let us go back to the car. Down this side street.' Nice. Quiet. Space.

Except the tall stucco buildings seemed to curve inward and Claudia did *not* let go of his arm. Just curled in tighter. And, impossible as it seemed, the silence rang through his head like a ten-bell siren.

'Lucas—earlier, when you—' Coming to a dead stop, she tilted the brim of her hat as she lifted her gaze to a window display, licked her lips. When he finally tore his eyes from that gorgeous mouth he followed her viewpoint to—

Holy...

'Let us move on,' he said, trying to pull her away before his imagination provided him with a view of Claudia dressed in such a thing. But it was much like tugging on the reins of a stubborn horse.

Pressing the tip of one finger against her pout, she focused her gaze, moved a little nearer to the glass plate. 'Do men like that kind of thing?'

Throat thick, he scratched out, 'No...'

'It's pretty, don't you think?'

'No.' Sexy, yes. Seductive, certainly. Erotic, absolutely. *Pretty?* 'Definitely not.'

'Maybe the white one, then?' she said, pointing to a poster of a woman in a tight ivory basque and stockings.

'I know little of these things, but I imagine that ensemble is more suited to a wedding night,' he ground out, attempting another tug, desperation fuelling his force.

Claudia simply let go. And the loss of heat did strange things to his mind-set.

'Oh. I'll never need one of those, then. I couldn't think of anything worse.'

Lucas blinked, scrolled back through the conversation. 'Worse than a wedding night?'

'Getting married.'

She shuddered. Actually shuddered. Why were they suddenly talking about marriage?

Thuds began to pound at his temples. An army of ants began to crawl across his nape.

'I'm married to my job and I always will be. I don't want commitment. I've fought for my freedom and I'm keeping it.'

Lucas's eyes narrowed. 'Every woman wants to get married, Claudia. Surely every little princess dreams of Prince Charming?'

She laughed—mocking, dry. 'I promise you, I've slept through many a dream and Prince Charming has never taken a leading role yet.' With the tip of one unsteady finger she hooked the bridge of her sunglasses and slid them halfway down her nose. 'Do you want to know who has?' she asked, shooting him a look.

On the brink of being coy, that look morphed into something so catastrophically loaded he felt the bullet ricochet to his groin.

Madre de Dios!

'No, I do not,' he said. 'Dreams are private things.' If she ever found out what he did to her in his dreams she would faint dead away.

First kisses equalled purity, and so long as he had breath left in his body she was remaining as pure as new-fallen snow. Whether she liked it or not. Whether she wanted sex or not. And sex, he realised, was exactly what she had on her mind.

Dios, how could he possibly have sex with Claudia? The suggestion was absurd. There were two types of women in the world: those you could slake your carnal appetites on and come away feeling empty and those you made love to. He'd never made love in his life. He wouldn't know how. And Claudia was one of those women. Claudia who wanted sex!

'I've had enough of going slow and talking nonsense. Come,' he said, placing his hand at the base of her spine and giving her a good push.

What she needed was a damn chastity belt. Lucas had a sneaking suspicion he had initiated her into the realms of passion, and the thought of someone else touching her made his fists clench, ready and armed to physically hurt. And just the notion that he might be capable of unwarranted violence…

'You know, Lucas, it occurred to me earlier I know nothing about your personal life,' she said, breaking through his thoughts with the delicacy of a sledgehammer.

'I do not have one,' he said, stiffening against the black twist in his guts.

'Do your parents live nearby?'

'*Sí.* In the graveyard.' Ordering his body not to react—even as sweat trickled down his spine—he kept to the basics. Information anyone would know should she dig for dirt.

Feet faltering, she stroked her palm over her heart while her eyes brimmed with empathy. 'I'm so sorry, Lucas.'

Ignoring the dart of annoyance, he shrugged. 'It is the way it is.'

She smiled ruefully. Knowingly. 'Do you miss them?'

'Ah, Claudia, such a tender soul. I was too young. I do not remember if there was anything to miss.' Years he'd managed to erase must remain in the past. For he knew if the floodgates opened he would surely drown.

Even now, standing here in the town his mother had loved, the town he'd rebuilt, those gates rattled on their hinges and water seeped through the cracks, whispering of hunger so deep his stomach would twist. Walls so thin he could hear every scream, every tear. Blood so thick it clotted his hair.

'Oh, Lucas.'

Something snapped inside him. 'Your sympathy is wasted

on me, Princesa,' he said, with satiric bite. 'Save it for children who deserve it.'

He wanted the fiery spark of her temper—craved it. But the little fool just looked up at him, so damn exquisite, as if she understood. She understood nothing.

For a woman who'd been through so much heartache she was astoundingly naïve. Living in her own little bubble. Which made him beyond resolute to protect her from herself. From him.

She had no idea who he really was, what he was capable of. For he too had walked on the dark side. Yet she wanted him with an incredulous passion that now seemed to ooze from her pores, fashioning her with a warm sensual glow.

Bewitching. Precious.

A warning flare—fierce, deadly accurate—discharged in his mind. Lucas had to keep his distance. No more enclosed spaces. No more touching. No more talking in hushed tones or primed glances that made his body seize with a need so fierce he shook with it.

Ignoring the knife-blade to his chest, he faced facts.

He had to kill her feelings dead.

CHAPTER TEN

CLAUDIA LOUNGED ON heaps of velvet cushions atop her bed and pressed 'send' on her latest e-mail to Bailey. The news that the little girl's father was back from the rigs had been the only moment of bliss in an otherwise wretched three days. Days of awkward lunches with her mother. Days since her gauche attempt at seducing Lucas had failed miserably and he'd plonked a barrier the size of the Great Wall of China between them.

If he walked into a room where she was he walked straight back out again. A seemingly impossible feat in a glasshouse, but he always managed to find some place to go. No doubt his office, which was always locked, or the kitchen, which actually boasted walls.

If he didn't have a two-million-pound painting hanging on one of them she would think he couldn't afford plaster divisions at all. Not for the first time she pondered how he was as rich as Croesus. Unless you were the President of the United States no government official could live like this. If he'd ever speak to her in more than one disgustingly polite syllable she would ask him.

Closing her eyes, she banged her head on the silk cushioned headboard. It wasn't that she missed the man—heavens, no—but at home she worked such long hours and here she was just…plain *bored*. So he didn't want to sleep with her? Fine. His version of agony was obviously in a different league to hers. But did that mean they couldn't talk? God, she missed that. And, truly, what was the harm in taking pleasure from his company while she was here?

Swinging her legs off the bed, she surged to her feet. She was going to find the gorgeous brute, act completely normal and convince him to have dinner with her tonight.

Grabbing one of the boutique bags from the floor, she up-ended the contents atop the bed. And groaned aloud at the final laugh at her expense as something slipped from between layers of frothy tissue paper. A swathe of black satin and lace that she swatted to the floor. *'C'est la vie, negligée.'* Then she lifted a coffee-coloured splash of Lycra from the pile and braced her chest for a panic attack.

Bikini.

The beach. Sand, sun, sea and sensitive skin. Just the thought made her pores prickle and her nails beg to scratch but, honestly, she needed air. She could never remember needing air before. Then again, she'd never lived with a prime specimen of six-foot-plus virile male before. And maybe, a little voice whispered, he would offer to take her down to the beach.

After donning the frighteningly tiny scrap and a sheer mocha cover-up, avoiding every mirror in the room, she padded down the stairs, heading for his office…when she rocked back on her heels. The door to his off-limits space was swung wide, the dark-wood-lined expanse human-free.

'Lucas?'

Only the sound of metal clanging against wood drifted from deeper inside. Without conscious thought she followed the noise through his office, across the plush ivory carpet towards another door at the far side. Several steps led down to another room and, barefoot, she crept down, coming to a dead stop on the last wooden plinth.

She gasped, eyes wide. So *this* was where he hung out. Another vast expanse, with one wall lined with aluminium cases, locked and bolted to within an inch of their life. A shiver scuttled through her as she envisaged their contents, yet it wasn't fear for herself that tore through her—it was fear for Lucas.

Being in the military must have placed him in serious danger over the years, and her throat caught fire just thinking about it. Had he ever been hurt? Her stomach ached at the very thought.

Biting hard on her lip, she let her gaze meander to heavy boxing bags hanging from the ceiling, to state-of-the-art gym equipment, the sight of which made her veins throb in an entirely different way and then turn even thicker, even hotter, as she spotted the man himself. He was working his awesome half-naked body so punishingly her heart cracked in two. Why did he do this to himself?

Claudia counted the powerhouse thrusts of his torso up and down, press-up after press-up. The temperature in the room spiked. Her body dissolved in a long, slow melt. She lost count at the two hundred mark as sweat poured off his honed frame, running in rivulets down his temples, trailing over the indentation of his spine as his muscles flexed and bunched.

Oh, my, he was divine.

Snag went her gaze on his left shoulder, where black ink stroked his flesh with the Arunthian crest.

Her molten core spasmed so hard a moan catapulted up her throat. Palm slapped over her mouth, she backed up the stairs. She shouldn't be in here. He'd expressly told her that his office was off-limits. And being someone who hated to be stared at, who loathed the violation of privacy, she was bang out of order watching him at all.

Claudia hit the hallway and ran down the stairs. Suddenly the cool waters of the ocean had never sounded so good. She wouldn't be gone for long.

Lucas would never know.

What was this? The Bermuda triangle?

Fresh from the shower, and after searching the house for over seven minutes, Lucas hurtled back up the stairs, two steps at a time.

'Claudia!'

Had she finally had enough and ordered Armande to take

her back to the palace? It wouldn't surprise him, and in reality he should be pleased. And he *was,* he told himself. But, dammit, she should have told him she was leaving. Just so he knew she was safe. *That* was the reason for the maelstrom of emotion clattering in his chest. Had to be.

Palm flat, he pushed her bedroom door wide, eyes assaulted by the sight before him. *Dios,* the woman was messy. But surely if all her clothes and feminine junk were strewn over every surface she hadn't left him.

Ignoring the warm flush inside, he turned his back on the chaos and strode down the hall to his office. He would ring Armande and see if his right-royal-pain-in-the-ass had asked him for one of her *favours.* The more distant Lucas became, the more she became pally with his second-in-command. And there came another emotion altogether.

Lucas scrubbed his nape. Five days she'd been living under his roof, and already the hair at his temples had turned grey.

Passing the window by his desk, a light flickered in his brain and he turned, looked out onto the private cove. And the air rushed from his lungs....

Dios, the woman was going to be the death of him.

There she was, flirting with the ocean, sheathed in a long-sleeved filmy top that stopped halfway down her thighs. He raked his gaze over her sleek toned legs. Made-for-sex legs. Long enough for her to wrap them around his waist, hook her ankles behind his back and draw him into his hot, tight, wet heat.

Lust punched his groin, the impact jolting him forward. Bracing his hands against the glass pane, he crunched his abs in an effort to stop the blood rushing from every extremity. It didn't help. Not one iota. Watching her play was not in his remit. Her safety, however, was.

Her feet sloshed through the foamy crush as she danced and skipped along the water's edge, using her toes as tiny shovels and kicking the sand high in the air.

With a shake of his head Lucas smiled. For the first time

since they'd met she appeared carefree. Almost happy. It suited her. Elevated her beauty in a way he'd never thought possible.

She faltered, faced the vast expanse of water looking out to sea—and that tiny action made his fingers ball into fists against the glass.

'Do not even think about it, Claudia,' he said, unclenching one hand and stretching for the keypad that operated the high security doors. His hand froze in mid-air as she took a step back, then another, heading back to shore, fingering the hem of her sheer tunic.

Lucas shuttered his eyes against the view, suddenly filled with the notion that he was becoming a voyeur, but his eyes weren't playing the gentleman and opened regardless.

Her fingers still toyed with the hem, as if uncertain, then began to lift the material up her thighs until he could see the low-cut edge of her bikini as it scooped the cheeks of her heart-shaped bottom.

A growl rumbled up his chest. They were like shorts—far sexier than any skimpy triangle he'd ever seen litter a beach. Demure, yet sensual. Head twisting, she looked left and right, as if checking her privacy, then whipped the top clean off her body and tossed it to the sand behind her.

Swallowing hard, he traced the flare of her hips, the small indentation of her waist. *Back off, Garcia. Turn away.*

One of her arms rose, bent at the elbow and pulled a stick—no…a pencil from the huge bun atop her head. His heart stalled for one, two, three beats as her glorious dark bitter-chocolate locks tumbled down her back in a heavy swathe of curls. Falling, falling until they swished around the base of her spine.

Lucas groaned, pushed off the glass, turned…then snapped his head upright. The sudden question of *why* she was stripping darted through his brain and sent his heart into cardiac arrest. Again.

'No. Do not. I warned you,' he said, reaching for the keypad again to unlock the security alarm on the sliding doors, keeping one eye on her as she tentatively stepped out to sea.

His heart slammed against his ribcage. 'You unthinking, senseless…' He punched in the code, eyes darting back and forth from the panel to her. Back to the panel.

Red.

Dios, what was wrong with him?

He tried once more, wondering if the damn thing had jammed, and calculated the time and distance to run through the house. No contest. One more try.

His fingers flew across the pad.

Red.

'Dammit.'

She was thigh-deep, almost at the ledge, and his hands were goddamn trembling.

Sloppy, Garcia, very sloppy.

He closed his eyes, breathed deep, found the higher plain he often visited in the dead of night. Focused on the pad once more. Punched the code a little slower, more controlled.

Green.

Grabbing the lever handle, he pulled the heavy door wide enough to slide his frame through the gap. Then he gripped the steel rail surrounding the terrace with one hand and launched over the side to drop twelve feet down onto the sand, ignoring the shard of pain slicing through his foot.

Lungs tight, he ran for the shoreline. 'Claudia, do not go any further!'

But the closer he got the more he could see she was nowhere near the sheer drop. Yet.

'Claudia!' He hit the water, feet pounding, the sand sucking at his loafers. 'Damn woman,' he muttered, lifting one foot to yank off his shoe, then the other, and throwing them over his shoulder. 'Claudia!' he repeated, closing the distance.

She spun around, her eyes…*alight?* A huge smile illuminated her face. Curls bobbed, caressing her smooth, honeyed shoulders.

'Lucas, look!' she said. 'Fish.'

Bending forward, she pointed to her feet with both forefingers, ramping her cleavage to a lush slit, and his vision blurred.

'I'm in the sea and I can feel squillions of teeny fish tickling my legs. It's amazing.'

She hopped, breasts bouncing, and desire slammed into him with the force of a tidal wave—which did *not* help his current state of mind

'Fish! *Madre de Dios—fish,* Claudia!' he said, balling his hands before he hauled her into his arms, because the need to touch her was so violent he quaked with it. 'What the hell are you doing all the way out here? I told you the sea was off-limits!'

Eerily slowly she straightened, narrowed her eyes, and folded her arms across her taut stomach—the action bunched those incredible breasts above her bikini top, making them threaten to spill over.

'No, you didn't. You told me—and these were your exact words—"No swimming in the sea, *Cllowtia. Comprende?* There is a ledge beyond which a fierce undercurrent could suck you under." That is what you said.'

His chest heaved, '*Sí.* That is exactly what I said.'

'So I'm paddling.'

'Paddling is also forbidden!'

'*Forbidden?*' she yelled, arms dropping to her sides, hands fisting for a fight, her tone as angry as her gorgeous face. 'What do want me to do, Lucas? Stay in the house while you ignore me or bark instructions as to where I'm going next. Don't I obey your every command? Well, I've had it. It's driving me crazy!'

Getting turned on even more by her temper was probably a bad sign, he thought. 'Quiet and solitude never bothered you in London!'

She seemed to think about that. 'That was then. And I was working. Really, Lucas, don't you think you're overreacting?'

'No.' Although he had to admit from his office she'd seemed a lot farther away.

'For God's sake, can't you forget about your blasted job for one minute?' she hollered.

'My *job?*'

'You aren't going to deprive the country of an apparent national treasure by letting me paddle! And... Oh!'

She scrunched her nose in that cute way she did sometimes.

Cute? Dios, he was losing the plot. She was senseless and selfish and— Wasn't she?

'Ow!' she said, wincing as she looked down. Lifted her foot.

Before she could blink, he shot forward, grabbed her waist and lifted her clean out of the water. 'What is it?'

Her hands clamped on his shoulders, fingers digging into his flesh, and either he pulled or she jumped, because the next thing he knew her breasts were crushed against his chest and her legs were wrapped tight around his waist, hooking at the small of his back.

Madre de Dios!

'Something was getting a bit too friendly,' she said, a little tremble in her voice.

'*Sí.* I do not blame them,' he muttered, distracted by the feel of the soft skin sheathing her decadent curves. *Bad, bad idea, Garcia.* The only thing missing from his earlier erotic fantasy was his carbon-steel erection sliding inside of her. 'You are killing me, Claudia.'

Cupping her delicious derrière, Lucas took all her weight and her fingers slackened their death grip on his shoulders— trusting him, knowing he wouldn't allow her to fall. Such a small thing, but it made his heart stutter and the need to pull her tighter into his body was a ferocious claw. To hold her, just this once, with her glorious hair falling over his bare forearms, a soft and silky caress.

One of her hands slipped off his shoulder, smoothed down his chest, lay over his breast.

'Your heart feels like it's going to burst through your skin,' she said, her voice awed.

'It might,' he breathed, watching her face heat as she stared at his open collar.

With her free hand she tiptoed her fingers to the base of his throat…stroked up his neck and over his jaw, leaving a blazing trail in her wake. And when she slipped her finger between his lips he couldn't resist licking the blunt tip and lightly sucking on her salty flesh.

Fire ignited her amber gaze and through two layers he could feel her pert nipples rub his chest, the erotic graze making him groan long and low.

'This is insane. I have to put you down.' Before he came in his damn boxers. 'Are you hurt?'

'Agony,' she murmured. 'Can't possibly walk.'

His lips twitched. He knew full well they were not discussing her foot, and he turned back towards the house, heading for shore. Which was torture in itself, because with every step the tip of his erection rubbed her moist core.

Dios…

Claudia wrapped her arms around his shoulders. Hung on tight as if she never wanted to let go. Thrust her fingers into the hair at his nape and nuzzled the skin beneath his ear.

'No,' he growled, a shudder racking his big frame.

So of course she did it again, quick learner that she was, and he could feel her lips curve into a wicked smile.

'You haven't shaved,' she whispered. 'I love the rough scrape against my lips. I want to know what it feels like in other places.'

He groaned as the heat built to inferno proportions. 'No, you do not.'

As if to prove him wrong she ground her pelvis against him and Lucas gritted his teeth…he was going to lose it any damn second.

A tiny moan from deep in the back of her throat goaded him…tearing at his precarious hold. And when the hot sand seared his feet Lucas loosened his grip and allowed her to slide down his body. The friction severed the final thread, and he slanted his mouth over hers and kissed her with the full crush of his pent-up desire.

Finally.

Her lips, soft and pliant, felt like heaven, and the last few days and nights of sexual tension drained from his neck, trickled down his vertebrae to pool with more heat in his groin.

Dios, if he were any harder he'd be dead. But still he hauled her closer, pressing her tight against his body and glorying in the sensation of her lush curves surrendering.

Just one kiss, he told himself, needing to assuage the fear that still clung to his brain. One kiss. No more, he bargained. He traced the line of her mouth to be let in—a quick flick to the corner, a soft slide along her lower lip and she parted instantly.

Blood roared through his head, drowning out all caution, and he drove his hands into the thick fall of her hair, holding her head still as his tongue took hers in a wild dance of pleasure. Slip-slide, intense and erotic. All he could think was more…*more.*

Dios, he could kiss her for hours, days, months… 'Claudia,' he said, taking a breath before he suffocated. 'Push me away.'

She cupped his jaw, her fingertips dangerously close to the underside of his ears, and nipped at his lips. 'Make love to me, Lucas.'

His heart crashed against his ribcage. 'No.' Impossible. He closed his eyes. Touched his forehead to hers. 'You need to keep yourself for…'

'I told you—I'm married to my job, just as you are.'

He knew it. Bone-deep, he knew she was right. She was trying while she was here, but as soon as the green light shone she'd be gone.

'I heard you the first time,' he said, tightening his grip on the small span of her waist to grind against her. The delicious abrasion made them moan in unison—an erotic, mind-blowing sound that rent the air.

'Oh, good. Finally we're on the same page. I want you so much, Lucas.'

'Untouched,' he murmured, forcing himself to pull back, needing distance. To breathe. To think.

'Mmm-hmm. And I want you to touch me. Make love to me.'

A fist of panic hit him in the chest. 'I thought you wanted sex.'

'What's the difference?' she asked, dropping lush, moist kisses along his jaw.

She'd never know what the difference was—not if he could help it. Claudia might not want commitment, but she was not some quick, easy lay. The mere thought made his guts twist, made him suddenly unsure if he was capable of being the man she needed.

Slightly distracted by the pulse pounding in his trousers, and the sight of her toned flat stomach leading to the curve of her femininity, it took a huge amount of effort for him to think. 'You should not be so willing to part with your purity for a man like me.'

Slivers of molten anger lit her eyes. 'What man is that, Lucas? The country's hero? My protector?'

'Claudia, you do not know me.' He might be all of those things to her right now, but if she knew the dark truth of his dangerous past—

'I know enough,' she whispered, fisting his hair, tugging gently, kissing his mouth with the moist crush of her lips. 'There's only one man in the world who I want…who I trust. And that man is you.'

Lucas bowed his head. Trust. She trusted him. And he'd never wanted anything more than to taste her. To show her.

Watching the rapid rise and fall of her chest, he stroked up her midriff, ran his thumb along the underside of her breast and felt her stomach spasm beneath his palm. Desperate to see her every reaction, he gazed into her eyes while he cupped one heavy breast, taking the weight, thumbing the tight nipple poking through the Lycra.

'Oh…' Her dark lashes fluttered.

Her legs gave way and Lucas tightened his hold on her waist. *Dios,* she was so responsive. But what if he hurt her?

'Look me in the eye and tell me you don't want to make love to me,' she said. 'If you can, I'll leave. Tonight.'

Everything inside him rebelled. His voice turned thick, pained. 'You know I cannot say that, *querida.*'

'*Exactamente,*' she whispered, her gorgeous Arunthian accent heavy. '*Bésame.* Kiss me until we can't breathe. Take the agony away. Please, Lucas.'

She opened her mouth and sank her teeth delicately, deliciously into his bottom lip. And he gave up the fight, uncaring of tomorrow, just knowing he needed her, needed this explosion of passion to take him to the edge of the abyss and throw him over the other side.

CHAPTER ELEVEN

CLAUDIA BASKED IN the taste of his wild desperation as Lucas carried her swiftly through the dusk-drenched house, never leaving her mouth.

When they finally reached his bedroom he slowly ended the kiss and oh-so-languidly let her slide down his body until her feet hit the luxuriously thick wool carpet. As he stepped backwards a cool sweep of air dashed over her body and she shivered, the thought of him changing his mind a deep, dark hollow in her soul.

Risking a look at him, she felt the chill evaporate in an instant when, with a sexy smile, he tugged the shirt from his waistband and tore it from his torso, making her insides dissolve into a potent liquid heat.

She'd seen him earlier, of course, but up close he epitomised a modern-day gladiator. Smooth cast-bronze skin stretched taut over military-honed dominating muscle, and his hard pecs flexed as he unsnapped the button of his trousers.

Her breath was now coming in short pants and she swallowed hard. Told herself to look away while he undressed. But she was desperate to watch him, see him. In all his spectacular glory.

The expensive cut of black cloth parted excruciatingly slowly, as if to tease, and she couldn't help the smile toying about her lips. Lucas loaded with bad-boy charisma gave her a swift sharp thrill that made her want to come out and play.

Reaching behind her, she gripped the bikini catch and then stilled—heart thumping against her ribs—wondering if Lucas would like what he saw. Oh, she hadn't thought of that, and she felt the heat leach from her face. But she *was* in a bikini, and really there wasn't much left to uncover, right? And she'd felt his hardness, tasted his passion on her tongue. Now was not the time to torture herself with visions of his other women. He was Claudia's. For now. She didn't need to hide from him. And the hunger to satisfy him, prove she was worth the effort so he'd never regret making love to her, overwhelmed any lingering doubt.

Claudia unsnapped the clasp, rolled her shoulders and watched the coffee-coloured splash drift to the floor at his feet. After a bracing heartbeat she looked up to his face, saw the fierce need in his sapphire eyes and felt a delicious river of satisfaction pour down her spine.

He slowly peeled the material back from his ripped stomach, shucked his trousers to the floor in one deft move, taking his hipsters with them. So self-assured, so brazen, and—*oh, my*—he had every right to be. Not that she had anything to compare except what she'd seen in art—much, *much* smaller—but, hey, intellect told her they would fit together. They had to or she'd die.

Then he cupped her face in his hands, traced the full curve of her lips, the arcs of her cheeks with his thumbs. 'We go slow. I need to know if I…' His throat convulsed. 'If I hurt you.'

Heart-shatteringly wonderful—that was what he was. She wondered if her inexperience was what bothered him the most. It made her even more determined to relax, to make it good for him. 'You won't.'

Lucas lowered his mouth and kissed her hungrily. She melted into his arms, loving the feel of his fevered skin, touching as much of him as she could and brushing up against his hardness. She squirmed, needing him to hurry, to do something to relieve the clenching knot of tension building in her stomach.

'More,' she said against his mouth.

'Slow,' he murmured back.

She groaned as his lips slid from hers, already missing the wild tangle of his tongue, and sucked at her lower lip, wanting, needing, to taste him again.

'*Dios,* you are incredible,' he said, tracing hot, wet, exciting kisses down her throat. And when he reached the spot, just *there,* where her neck met her shoulder, and grazed her with his teeth, nibbled, her stomach spasmed on a rush of heat.

'Oh, Lucas. I…'

She sank her fingers into his hair, twisted, holding on, pulling him into her tighter.

One of his big warm hands cupped her breast, squeezed gently, thumbed her nipple and that was it—her legs crumpled beneath her.

In one swift move Lucas swept her up and laid her upon the bed. '*Querida,* you are so responsive,' he said, his voice pained. 'The smallest touch sets you ablaze.'

'*Your* touch, Lucas,' she whispered, needing him to understand. Only him. There would only ever be him. 'Could you do something about that?'

He chuckled, crawled over her, and braced his arms above her head. 'I know exactly what you need.'

'I'm so glad,' she said, smiling up at him, drinking him in.

Lowering himself to his elbows, his face inches from hers, he swept the hair away from her brow. 'Your glorious hair against my sheets. *Dios,* you are so beautiful, Claudia.'

Her heart cracked wide open at the pure masculine appreciation slashing across his handsome face and she tugged him down for another of his scorching kisses, exulting in the feeling of being wanted, desired.

She writhed on the sumptuous covers as he trailed his lips down her neck, his hand following the curve of her waist, gripping so possessively she shivered.

That same hand curved around her ribs, scooped her breast and—*oh, my*—the sensation of him taking its weight, lapping at her pebbled nipple, before taking the peak into his hot wet mouth to suck gently made her cry out. The high-pitched sound flooded the room, mingling with his hoarse groan.

When he nipped at her wet nipple, teeth sharp yet gentle, she lost control. 'Oh, yes…' She jerked her hips, wanting, needing him to touch her. *There.* 'More.' But the brute didn't seem to care. He merely redirected his attention to her other breast, laving it, taking her higher still.

She phased in and out, the need in her belly curling tighter, more urgent, until she was tangling her fingers in his hair, raking her nails down his wide muscular shoulders.

Lucas tore his mouth away. 'I need to see you. All of you,' he said, sounding a little more desperate, and she revelled in the sudden infusion of female power as he shuffled down the bed, hooked his fingers in her shorts and eased the material down over her hips.

She gripped the satin covers, fisting the cool material in her hands, raised her legs, one and then the other, to help him, squeezing her eyes shut. Oh, God, what was he thinking?

'Open for me, angel,' he said, voice thick.

Angel? Oh, why did that make her feel special? As if she was the only woman he wanted. Could ever want. She shouldn't think like that, but this was a dream and she never wanted to wake up.

Lucas stroked up her thigh, stilled…

Hauling in some much needed bravery, she opened her eyes, saw the look of unadulterated desire slashing his cheekbones crimson. His hair tumbled over his brow as he looked down at the very heart of her and stroked the soft skin of her inner thigh.

Reflexive, audacious, her legs fell wide.

'You are so perfect. Untouched. I need to taste you,' he said, lowering his head.

Her pulse skittered through her veins. 'Er, Lucas?'

'Quiet, *querida,* let me show you.'

One touch of his tongue against her folds and she vaulted off the bed, quivered… Then he took one long, leisurely lick and a cry tore from her throat, filling the room with her passion. He kept on kissing, sucking gently, until the world was spinning and she grappled for safe ground.

Eyes shut, her body arched. She found his head and pushed him deeper, pulled, unsure whether she wanted him to stop or keep going, because she was careening towards something and— 'Lucas, I…need…'

'Let go for me,' he said, before easing one finger inside her and ghosting his thumb over her clitoris…once, twice.

Tension spiralled in her core, winding tighter and tighter as her insides clenched around his finger.

'Ohhh, my G—' She lost her grip, cried out, gasping for breath, her body quaking as the coil unravelled so fast ecstasy shot though her core and lights exploded behind her eyes.

Delirium, she realised, took a while to recover from, but when she eventually came round she prised her eyes open to find Lucas braced above her, palms flat to the bed, a purely masculine, ego-drenched smile across his gorgeous face.

'Better?'

'Amazing,' she whispered, feeling heat scorch her cheeks.

'I've never seen anything so damn sexy as when you come.'

His voice, coarse and needy, gave her the courage to touch him, just as she'd dreamed of.

She stroked his shoulders, down his arms, smoothing her palms over his chest. 'I adore your big hard body, Lucas. Just looking at you makes my stomach flip.'

He smiled with that heart-stopping rogue charm she loved so much and dipped his head, kissed her. The taste of herself exploded on her tongue as she devoured the essence of their mingled passion, until everything began to blur around the edges and heat began to build up again. As if the last twenty minutes had never happened. She'd never felt so alive. So gloriously alive.

As his tongue flicked hers, her fingers became daring and she reached down to touch him. *There.*

A groan rumbled up his chest, 'Careful, *cariña,* or this will not last. I feel like my head is going to explode. Both of them.'

She laughed—happy, carefree, a sound she didn't recognise.

Emboldened, she curled her hand around his satin and steel shaft, dusted her thumb over the taut velvet tip, over and over, just as he had with her.

'Enough,' he growled, jerking from her grasp.

With her eyes locked on his she brought her thumb to her mouth and licked the moisture, tasting his unique blend of salty virility—just as he had with her.

'*Dios,*' he said, falling on top of her, plundering her mouth until everything spiralled out of control.

Patience evaporated in the searing heat of their entwined bodies. Skin on skin. Their mouths ravenous. Hands stroking everywhere they could reach.

'Wait—protection,' he breathed, pulling away.

'I'm covered,' she said, tugging him right back. She'd thought of that. She wasn't that naïve.

He threw her a questioning look.

'Women's stuff,' she said, reaching up to smooth the crease from his brow. 'Don't stop. Please. I want to feel you inside me.'

'Ah, Claudia, such passion.' He kissed her softly, cupped her breast, squeezed gently. And the heat surged back—greedy, heady, intense.

Lucas manoeuvred until he was settled snugly in the cradle of her thighs and she could feel him nuzzling against her folds.

'Yes, *yes,*' she said around his lips, wanting this part of him. Shifting her hips, encouraging. Needy.

He slipped inside her, just an inch, and she felt his big body shudder.

'So hot. So tight. I cannot…'

Skin damp, hair drenched, muscles flexing, he was struggling for control, she realised. But he felt sensational and she wanted more.

She lifted her hips.

He sank a little deeper. 'Claudia, *ángel,* give me a minute.'

He was loath to hurt her, and she adored him for it, but she'd wanted him for what felt like for ever.

Claudia pulled him up to kiss her, tangled her tongue around his, wrapped her legs around his waist, hooked her ankles and pulled him in. All the way.

The air locked in her lungs as she felt a tiny tear inside her. A red-hot arrow lancing up her core.

Lucas tore his mouth way. 'Claudia?' He held her face in his large hands, kissed her mouth. 'Breathe for me, *cariña*.' He skimmed his fingers lovingly down her cheek, picked up her hand, kissed the spot on her wrist where her pulse thrummed against the flesh.

Pain evanesced and she revelled in the fullness, the rightness.

'You feel amazing,' she whispered, staring into his eyes, nearly drowning in the liquid desire pooling in his sapphire depths. And right then, at that very moment, she knew the truth. She was falling. Falling so very hard.

She smiled, imagined it was close to something sad. So she made it brighter, cupped his jaw, massaged behind his ears, his nape, just the way he liked it. She smoothed her hands across his hips. His glutes were like stone. And thank heavens he melted before her eyes.

'I want it all,' she said. 'Take me.'

Even if it were just this once, she needed it to last her a lifetime.

'You feel like heaven,' he said, pulling out of her just a little and then sinking back inside. So gentle, giving her time to adjust. 'So perfect.'

In out, over and over, until all thought was banished and only pleasure remained. Until they found a glorious rhythm and he upped the pace, faster…faster…harder.

Kissing her possessively, he stroked every inch of her, his hand trailing down her thigh as he shifted slightly to deepen his thrust and grind against her where she needed him most.

The new angle spawned shockwaves of fresh sensations and then she was almost there, tightening, crying out, poised at the edge of paradise, reaching for the heights of bliss.

'Claudia…' His huge body stiffened above her and a keening moan seemed to rip from his throat. The exquisite sight of his face contorting with pleasure, tossed her over the edge until she was falling, falling, shattering, revelling in the sensations shooting through her like white-hot stars.

Face buried in the soft skin of her neck, Lucas bathed in her honeyed scent, luxuriating in the aftermath of pleasure such as he'd never known—sure he'd just tasted ecstasy.

Claudia clasped his head, holding him tight. 'Don't let go,' she whispered.

But he would crush her, he knew. So he gathered her in his arms, rolled onto his back until she was sprawled over his chest, her dark tumble of curls a provocative feast.

His heart turned over, struggled to pump blood round his veins, and he closed his eyes while a torrent of conflicting emotions bombarded him. His head was waging an almighty war. *More. Need more. Get up. Move away.* He'd slept with a few women in his time but, *Dios,* nothing like this. This wild, insatiable, clamouring need—this craving to keep her close and never let go. It scared him half to death.

'Lucas?' she said, lifting her head and resting her chin on the back of her hand as she looked up at him. Her eyes were fired with enough anxiety to make his guts clench. 'Was I…okay?'

He let go of the air locked in his chest and raked damp hair back from his brow. Never had he been asked that. But she was looking up at him, so damn trusting, her heart etched on her face, needing to know she'd been worth it. His stomach ached.

'Listen to me, *querida,*' he said, trailing the back of his finger over her temple, down her nose. 'When you are stripped bare and no longer able to hide you are breathtaking.'

As her bruised lips parted he traced them, following the sexy dip of her top lip. Her pink tongue snaked out and flicked the tip and a fresh spurt of heat shot down his spine, thick as lava, as he remembered the way she'd tasted him. Such a ferocious mind. Always learning, always desirous to be the best.

'You're the most passionate woman I have ever met.'

She blinked. Smiled the sexiest of satisfied smiles and dropped a lush, moist kiss on his chest.

'That's good,' she said, as she tiptoed her fingers down his abdomen, cruising over the ridges and down, down to where he was hard and ready for her touch.

Bolder now, she wrapped her fingers around his length and explored every inch of him, first with her hand and then with her eyes. Until the heat was a fiery ball and he was plunging past the point of no return. He grasped her wrist, flipped her over and pinned her to the bed, his hands holding hers above her head.

Her eyes blazed, glittering with shards of exquisite excitement.

'Ah… You like that?'

What she liked, he realised, was to be wanted. She loved his weight on top of her. His strength turned her on, heated her blood. She felt protected. *He* made her feel safe. *Dios.* His heart turned over again. He should not revel in that—he really shouldn't.

Licking her lips, she nodded, her breath quickening, her hips writhing in their own little way to drive him crazy with the need to be inside her.

Keeping her hands above her head with one hand, he trailed the other down the slope of her full lush breast. '*Dios.* You have the body of a goddess. Heavenly to look at. Sinful to touch. Makes me feel damn weak.'

He kissed the soft underside while his fingers trailed down her soft stomach, wanting to see if she was ready. 'You are not sore?'

'No,' she breathed. 'Need you.'

Her head tossed back and forth. Her dark curls fanned over his white pillow. His pillow. His bed. *His.*

Skating over the damp curls at the apex of her thighs, he dipped into her heat, felt warm moisture coat his fingers. A moan—his, hers, entwined—filled the air.

His heart struck up a ferocious beat. Blood roared through his head. Lucas knew he was flirting with disaster, stumbling across unknown territory, yet nothing could stop him. She would be gone soon enough.

'So wet, *cariña*. You want me inside you?'

'Yes, yes…'

Sweat beaded his brow as he settled between her legs, hard and achingly heavy. And when she moved against him for a frantic beat he wondered if he would last.

He grasped her hair, cupped her head in one hand and brought her mouth to his so he could plunder, drink in her cries when she came for him. With his free hand he caught her nipple with his thumb and forefinger, rolling the tight tip until she undulated against him, working up to a frenzy. Then he stroked down her toned thigh and sank into her with one deep thrust.

A hoarse cry broke from his very soul and poured into her mouth. Tight, hot, she gripped him in her slick heat, drawing him deeper under her spell until he didn't know where he ended and she began.

The need to watch her orgasm for him, so he could remember, became an almighty obsession. So he stroked down her waist, over her hip, round to the soft curve of her luscious rear and lifted her thigh-high over his waist to deepen his thrust and grind against her.

'Oh, Lucas…'

Her fingernails bit into the skin on his shoulders and a fever unlike any other took hold of his blood as a torrent of fire built inside him, far stronger than the first time, and Lucas knew— just knew—he would never recover from this explosion of feeling. Never in a million years.

Lips locked, she cried into his mouth, the sound of her sensual elation throwing him over the edge, tossing him into the black depths of ecstasy.

Hurling him into the unknown.

* * *

Light flickered in his brain and Lucas prised his eyes open to the darkness of night. He'd slept?

Warmth smothered the right side of his body and half of his chest…Claudia. She mumbled something, almost a cry, the high pitch snapping him to full lucidity, and Lucas tightened his hold on her waist.

'Claudia?'

She struggled against him and he instantly loosened his grip, cupped the back of her head, softly kissed her temple. 'Wake for me, angel.'

She stilled before the tension drained from her spine and she fell back against his chest. 'I'm sorry,' she said. 'I'm okay. Truly.'

'You were dreaming?'

'It's being back here. So strange.'

Her skin was damp, clammy. 'Not a good dream,' he said. Statement. Fact. Lucas knew too well the cold sweats, the shaking so hard it was impossible even to drink water.

'Not really,' she mumbled, snuggling into his side, hiding her face. 'It's nothing.'

His stomach tensed and he nudged her softly with his arm, needing to see her face. She turned her head and lay down, facing him. 'Do not hide from me, Claudia. I cannot bear it.'

Nibbling on her bottom lip, she gave him a searching look. 'I just have this nightmare sometimes. It's a memory, that's all.'

'Ah, that's all?' he said, trying to tamp down on the flare of anxiety because he knew the power of memories. How they could haunt you. Drain your very soul.

She had demons of her own; he'd known that, hadn't he? 'You tried to tell me on the plane, I remember.'

'Did I?'

That she couldn't recollect spoke volumes. But then he remembered her panic, the fear that had sliced through the very heart of him.

'Tell me your dream,' he said, sweeping a lock of damp hair from her cheek with his fingertip.

He could see the hesitation in her eyes, couldn't understand it. 'Claudia?'

Searching his eyes for a long moment, she seemed to look for sincerity or wonder if she could trust him—not with her body or her safety but with her secrets. Her past.

'Trust me, *cariña.*'

Wriggling from his hold, she rolled onto her back and pulled the sheet up to her neck. Lucas ignored the cold chill sweeping over his body; she needed space. He understood. So he moved onto his side to face her, bent his elbow and rested his head on the ball of his hand.

Staring up at the ceiling, she began to talk, her voice detached. 'I must've been twelve. It's my last memory of being here.' Her brow creased as she delved into the past. 'It was one of those hot clammy days that made me feel so sick I could hardly breathe…hardly walk. My mother took me to the hospital. I think they'd had some specialist flown in.' She shuddered, gripped the sheet at the delicate dip in her throat. 'I could hear every word through the open door, but my legs… I couldn't move to close it. I covered my ears but she was ranting at him. Railing. Going on and on. I'd never heard her in such an awful state.'

She huffed a laugh, the sound so damn hollow his guts twisted.

'You've met her, Lucas. So chillingly calm. So strong. But this day she was almost wild. *"Look at her!"* she screamed to the doctor, jabbing her finger in my direction. *"Just look at her. My beautiful daughter is no more. You have to do something."* On and on she went, for what felt like hours.'

Lucas watched her knuckles scream in protest as she twisted the sheet in her fingers, her eyes closed, her teeth sinking into her lower lip as she stifled her sorrow. And he'd swear his chest had cracked open.

'Someone carried me out to the car. She was so deathly silent and I was so numb. She couldn't bear to look at me. When we reached the Arunthe tunnel there was traffic everywhere.'

Her chest rose and fell with short, sharp breaths and the need to touch her, hold her, was so strong his arms ached.

'I think we'd been followed,' she continued, brushing hair from her damp brow with trembling fingers. 'There was always stuff in the papers, wondering what was wrong with me. Why I was kept under lock and key while my sisters enjoyed their independence. I think being so secretive must've made it worse.'

The room was dim, but Lucas saw one silvery droplet trickle down the side of her face. The pain in his chest tore up his throat. *'Querida—'*

'Suddenly,' she said, 'men were crawling over the car like locusts, banging on the windows so hard I thought the glass would shatter. They yanked at the door handles, over and over, trying to get in. And my mother… She pushed me down—said I had to hide, to stay out of view in case they saw me. *"No pictures of her,"* she was screaming. *"No photos. No photos."* Yelling. Crying. *"They can't see her like this."* I just wanted to die. That's exactly what I wished for.'

Her voice trailed to a pained whisper and Lucas strained to hear her.

'She screamed at the driver to move forward and he tried to switch lanes. He tried. He *tried.*'

Lucas ground his jaw so hard a shard of pain shot up to his temples. 'The car crashed?'

'Yes,' she said, her chest rising as she struggled to wrestle her emotions into submission. 'Next thing I knew I was in London. Hidden. Locked up.'

Her voice ebbed once more and Lucas leaned closer.

'The Princess in the Iron Mask.'

'What?' he said, frowning deeply, sure he mustn't have heard her correctly.

'That's what the other children called me. Although it was probably my own fault. I had at least two copies—you know, the novel by Alexandre Dumas? The mask they needed to hide the face of the King's twin?'

He jerked upright, shaking his head. Adamant. Goddamn furious. 'No, Claudia. *No.*'

'Yes.'

'That was just children being mean and spiteful because you are royalty. Most children dream of such a thing, *querida.*'

She dashed her hands across her cheeks. 'And my mother saying those things? Was *she* just being mean? Telling everyone I wasn't beautiful any more? That she couldn't bear to look at me? Touch me?' Her voice hitched on the last word and she flung back the covers and vaulted off the bed. 'I need to go now.'

'No!' he said, lunging, grabbing her hand, keeping her at the side of the bed until he stood before her. Cupping her face, he looked deep into her eyes. 'Listen to me, Claudia. I'd say your mother was past herself with worry because no doctor could diagnose or even help. She had to watch you suffer. Can you imagine that?' Lucas tilted her face, needing her to see the conviction in his. 'Think of how you feel when you sit with Bailey. It hurts you, *si?*'

She nodded, just once, eyes flooding, spilling. His heart tore.

'I'd say your mother didn't think or realise the words she spoke would affect you so. Whilst she is not the most affectionate of people, I believe in this case she was unthinking. Not uncaring.'

'You think she honestly cared about me? She cast me out. I was dispensable to them.'

'Impossible,' he said fiercely. 'You are far from dispensable, *cariña.* And you were *not* cast out. The accident, I think, was the last bullet for her. If I had been in the same position and you had almost died I also would've taken you away. Far, far away. Somewhere safe. Where you could get help. St Andrew's is the best—world renowned.'

'And would you have left me there, Lucas? Alone? They hardly came. I waited. And waited.'

His stomach wrenched. Little wonder leaving Bailey had killed her.

Would he have left her? The answer hovered on his tongue. For what peace would it bring her? He could never say the words pounding at his temples, fighting to break free.

'Your parents had a country to run, Claudia—a country in trouble at the time. I remember those years. Your parents had other children. Duty. Responsibilities.' Even as he said the words they sounded hollow, knowing the price she'd paid. Her parents had sacrificed her happiness for the good of thousands. Something he'd done over and over in his career.

'Trust *you* to see it that way,' she said, bitterness lacing her voice, twisting her head until his hands fell away—hands that now felt bereft. 'Of course you'd have left me. Duty. Obligation. That's all you ever talk about. You're just the same as them.'

He closed his mind to the disgust in her eyes. 'I see both ways. For a young sick girl to be left in a foreign country. Isolated in such a way.' His chest felt crushed by the impact. 'It must've been very hard for you.'

He knew all too well the emptiness, the fear she would have felt—could feel it now, brewing in his system like poison. Fear that made you weak. Angry. Resentful. Determined at any cost to close the door to your heart and never reopen it.

'*Dios.*' The truth slammed into him, almost knocking him off his feet. 'So blind,' he said, scouring her face, drinking in her amazing beauty and tender vulnerability while the last remaining fragments fell into place. The final piece of intelligence he needed to create Claudia Verbault.

'What happened when they came to see you, *cariña?*'

Her gaze fell, drifted to the window as the first strokes of dawn broke through the slit in the drapes. 'I wouldn't speak to them. Not one word. When I grew older, got better, *had* to speak, they started making demands for me to return. I pushed for my independence. I wanted my freedom.'

'No, Claudia,' he said, shaking his head slowly. 'You pushed them away because you were hurting. Your freedom was a ticket to a pain-free zone.'

Her teeth sank into her bottom lip and she finally looked up at him, her amber eyes huge, swimming with unwanted tears. 'Yes,' she whispered, broken, still hurting.

'You believed they would leave you alone. To live your own life.'

She sniffed. 'Hoped would be more like it.'

'Ah, Claudia, all the hope in the world cannot change who you are.' He knew that better than anyone.

No matter the man he'd become, underneath he was still Lucas Allesandro Gallardo—the boy who'd failed to protect and had lost everything. The man who'd fought for king and country and pledged an oath to honour and obey. The same man who'd just surrendered to his selfish desires and taken an innocent. One he'd sworn to protect. A woman he was beginning to doubt knew what she wanted from life, let alone how to find the love she so desperately needed.

She was blossoming before his very eyes—a butterfly emerging from the chrysalis. She deserved happiness and there was a man out there, perfect and strong and made just for her. And now Lucas had ruined her reputation. Lucas who had nothing to offer.

His chest seized, the pain dominant, punishing. She was so damn vulnerable she hadn't realised the consequences of her actions. That had been *his* job. And he'd failed. He'd allowed his emotions to reign. Again. He'd failed to protect. Again.

Lucas closed his eyes. What the hell had he done?

CHAPTER TWELVE

PADDING DOWN THE hallway, Claudia cinched her robe tight. Silence, even after years of it, made her cold from the inside out. What had happened she'd no idea, but after a night of heart-shattering euphoria Lucas was gone. *Her* Lucas, that is.

Lucas Garcia, Head of Security for Arunthia, was back in full military mode today. Distant. Guarded. Re-armed with enough strength to fight a seven-nation army. Even Armande had backed off, when Lucas had gone on a full-on attack over some keypad in his office. But she'd hazard a guess that had more to do with a delivery from the palace—a rack of dresses for the ball tomorrow night and an official-looking parcel for him. 'Business,' he'd said. One of the few words he'd spoken all day.

Feet bare, the chill of each wooden plinth penetrated her feet as she tiptoed down the staircase. Did Lucas blame her for hardening her heart to her parents? It was the hardest thing she'd ever done, and here she was doing it once more.

Thankfully she had more sense than to fall for a man who could make love to her with such glorious passion, then wrap her in one of his dark grey sheets and carry her to her room. Oh, and the real *pièce de résistance* had been the words, 'Go to sleep.' Before the door clicked shut with deafening finality.

He'd walked away—just as he'd warned her he would. So she'd no right to be hurting—*none*.

But...

Sleep? Wrapped in satin that smelt of sex and Lucas?

And still she could smell him—the musky potency that oozed from his every pore. Raw, addictive and utterly tormenting.

A moan snuck past her lips. She just wished she'd never told him the things she had. She might as well have ripped her heart from her chest, sliced it open with a scalpel and laid it on the table for his inspection. Obviously he hadn't much liked what he'd seen.

Pausing on the bottom step, she peered through the darkness, eyes slowly adjusting at the wide rack standing by the window, weighted with a colourful array of cloth. With sleep a pipedream tonight, she'd nothing better to do than make her choice.

Risking a glance at Lucas's office, she saw a thin sliver of light under the door; imagined him sitting there. Honestly, he was such a cold brute at times. Yet it was that very darkness that engaged her—locked her on target and drew her in.

The ivory moon hung low, casting the room in silver swathes—just enough light for her to take a peek at the dresses. When they'd arrived today her bruised heart had demanded they be returned. She could buy her own dress—one that wouldn't come with any stipulations. But then, thankfully, the red haze had cleared and the fact she'd been thought of at all was something. Despite everything they were her parents. And her mother *was* trying.

Trailing her fingers over the array of satin, silk and lace, she closed her eyes. Pale gold ruched satin whispered to her, called her name. Gripping the arch of the clothes hanger, she pulled it from the rack, held it up to her body and swayed gently, watching the frothy skirt swish around her legs. So beautiful. Created for a princess of the realm.

Ramming the dress back on the rail, she picked another. A vibrant aquamarine colour with a low dip at the back, a straight skirt. Full sleeves.

'Ah, Claudia, have I taught you nothing?'

The heavy weight rustled to the floor as she spun around and slapped her hand over her cantering heart.

Lucas lay sprawled on one huge aubergine sofa, where he had a prime-time view of every move she made. One arm bent, he propped up his head, wearing an expression that bordered on dark torment. Hair damp, the dark locks clung to his brow. The lack of light shadowed his blue eyes, transforming them to obsidian depths that drilled straight through her.

His other arm dangled off the edge of the seat, his hand a claw, holding a whisky glass from his fingertips. The crystal tumbler swayed back and forth lazily. Legs wide, one bent knee was resting on the back cushion, the other was long and straight in front of him.

To anyone else it was the insolent pose of a devil-may-care, but Claudia could feel the anguish rolling off him in waves. This devil *did* care, and something powerful held him in thrall.

She feasted on his bronze chest, the rippled curve of his abs and the tight waistband of his black hipsters…and lower to the snug, thick ridge of his erection. A shiver that had nothing to do with the room's temperature whistled through her.

Eyes fluttering shut, she bit hard on her lip, trying to remember why she was so angry with him, shovelling deep to dredge up hurt. She'd been dumped into her cold bed as if nothing had happened between them, then ignored, all day, and lest she forget he'd taken her parents' side over hers. But in all fairness she'd known he would. He was all about duty—just as they were. It shouldn't hurt. It *should* make her heart stronger. Harder.

Counting to three, she ordered her eyes to stay above his waistline and popped them open.

'You've taught me plenty, Lucas. How to reach the heights of passion only to fall from grace. And I have to tell you it's quite a drop. How easy it is to trust, open yourself wide, only to be rejected when you come up wanting. Have my confessions turned you cold? Because, honestly, it's freezing in here.'

'No.'

That was it? *No.* Did she believe him? He certainly didn't have any reason to lie.

Arm lifting, he took another lazy swig of Scotch, his shadowed face haunted, and a pang resounded through her heart.

'Talk to me, Lucas. Tell me what's wrong.'

'Go to bed.' His tone was icy cold, the dismissal cruel.

Curling her fingers into protective fists, she forced her heels into the rug, while the overwhelming urge to go to him, brush the hair from his eyes and kiss away the pain, warred with the fear of rejection. If she could hold him, help him, he might fall asleep in her arms like the first time. How many times had she needed comfort and it had never been offered? Then maybe— just maybe—he would tell her, he would share.

Pushing her pride deep down, knowing he needed her, desperate to console him, she implored, 'Will you come? Spend my last night with me?'

'No.'

One word, loaded with pain.

She took a fortifying gulp of air. 'I don't understand why you're being like this.'

The sound of glass clattering off oak, the slosh of liquid spilling, made her flinch. Not that Lucas seemed to notice.

'Do you realise what I've done, Claudia?' he said. 'Taken an innocent when you were in my protection. I should never have touched you.'

Wait a minute...

'No—*no!* For heaven's sake, I asked *you.* I wanted to make love just once in my life. You've taken nothing from me, Lucas. I gave it freely.'

'Pleasure does not come without a price, *querida*,' he countered fiercely. Then his lips twisted, one dark brow raised into a cynical arch. 'Make love, Claudia? Didn't I tell you I just have sex.'

The way he said *sex*, as if it was dirty, something to be ashamed of, scored at her heart, sent flames of dismay up her throat. He regretted making love to her—having sex—whatever the hell he wanted to call it, and—*oh, my God*—she had to stiffen to stay upright through the pain in her stomach, which twisted tighter with every second he stared, as if he couldn't bear the sight of her. One look that launched a thousand reasons to run. Leaving behind the main reason to stay. Ripping her clean in half.

He was in agony.

Lucas thrust his hands through his hair and tore his eyes from her while a dark torrent stormed through him, pulling, dragging him under. His chest heaved as he suffocated under the dense blanket of remorse.

Dios, he'd taken away her chance of marrying with honour. And that damn letter from her father, pouring out his gratitude to Lucas, had poured gasoline on the flames of his anger. In one night he'd dishonoured her and himself. *Dios,* if their affair ever became public knowledge…

Self-loathing sucked his throat dry.

His gaze landed on the original painting for the tenth time. The memories like a drum-beat, loud and disturbing, warning him to back away, turn her against him, make her leave.

'Who is she, Lucas? You know her. I can see it in your face when you look at her.'

'I do not know her,' he said, his throat thick as he stared at the past. Failure. His mistake. One he would never repeat. 'She reminds me of someone. That is all.'

'Someone you lost?'

He tried to swallow around the grenade lodged in his throat but it was damn impossible. 'Go to bed, Claudia.'

'Talk to me, Lucas,' she begged, taking a step towards him. 'Please.'

Fire and fury bubbled up inside him—a volcano erupting. 'Go to bed,' he repeated louder, far harder than she deserved, which made him feel even more of a bastard.

But, *Madre de Dios,* he was unsure how much more he

could take. Standing before him, she was so damn exquisite. Her eyes full of undeserved empathy.

'Why are you pushing me away?'

His tenuous hold snapped. 'Because I do not want you here. *Comprende?*'

As long as he lived Lucas would never forget the look on her face and his guts twisted, punishing. How could he say that to her? When she already questioned her self-worth? When it was he who was unworthy? And the pain—*Dios,* he hated seeing pain in her eyes. Pain *he* had put there.

Thuds hit his temples. He lifted his hands to cover his burning eyes, but not before a swish of satin whispered by. Like a drug addict grabbing for his next fix, he closed his eyes in ecstasy even as he hated himself for giving in to the hungering clawing need—he grabbed her wrist, pulled, needing to feel her against him and despising himself for his desperation.

Struggling, she pulled her arm away. 'Get off me.'

'Come to me.' *Dios,* the craving was so intense he shook with the power of it.

One quick tug and she was bent over him, her face hovering above his, the soft tumble of her hair brushing his chest and arms, the sweet honeyed scent of purity assailing his mind.

He captured a curl around his finger, mesmerised.

'Let me go,' she whispered, her chest rising and falling, her robe loose, gaping, taunting, teasing him with the lush swell of her breasts cupped in black lace.

Pounding sensations and emotions assaulted him. Relief she was close. Disgust at himself for being unable to let her go. Regret—yes, regret because she didn't deserve to be treated this way. And the ferocious need to replace the pain in her eyes with pleasure. *Will you come? Spend my last night with me?* The pleasure she'd obviously come for.

'Come to me, Claudia,' he said, gliding his free hand up her throat, across the warm skin of her shoulder. Sliding his fingers beneath the satin robe he pushed it down her arm. His sex throbbed for the tightness of her body, but first he needed to banish the anguish from her eyes. 'Let me hold you, *querida*.'

The fight left her then, her glorious body softening. His hand fell away as she stood tall and he watched, bewitched, as the black robe fell from her shoulders in a sensual glide to pool on the floor. It was a damn good job he was lying on his back or he'd be on his knees.

Scantily clad in low-cut lace and sheer black satin, slinking over her curves, she was his every fantasy come to life.

Blood roared through his head as the heat surging through his taut frame built to inferno proportions. 'You're incredible,' he said, grasping her satin-sheathed waist and lifting her over him.

Straightening his legs, he coasted the slippery sheath up her bare thighs so she could straddle him, revelling in the slick skin smothering his hips. He plunged his hands into the thick fall of her hair and pulled her mouth down to his. Kissed her hard, desperate to taste, remember.

He traced the seam of her lips with his tongue. 'Forgive me, *cariña*. It is myself I am angry with.'

'Let it go, Lucas,' she whispered, before her lips surrendered.

The sweet taste of forgiveness coated his tongue and for one blissful moment he allowed himself to savour, to indulge in the forbidden tang.

This was what she wanted, he told himself, what she'd come for. And he'd make it spectacular for her. Make her shatter over and over, make her beg him for more until that fierce brain could no longer think. Only feel. Him. Inside her. Surrounding her. A night she would never forget.

Tomorrow everything would come right. He'd meet with Henri and do what was necessary. And Claudia would stand in front of the nation and accept who she was. She would realise the extent of her duty and responsibilities; his promise to return Princess Claudine Verbault would be complete.

But for tonight she was still his.

Tonight she was still *Just Claudia*.

Her hot naked core nestled against his throbbing erection and she undulated against him with rhythmic serpentine movements that detonated a need that made his vision swim.

'Careful, *cariña*...' he growled.

She filled his mouth with her sweet moans of pleasure. Her hands were a firebrand smoothing over his chest, up the column of his throat, sinking into his hair, massaging the ultrasensitive skin beneath his ears. It was a confident touch that hummed through his body, and his hips jerked so hard he almost lost it.

In one deft move he broke their lip-lock, whipped the gown up and over her body, tossed it to the floor.

Her voice low and sultry, she began to tell him what she wanted—how hard, how deep, how much she wanted him. Only him. Words he knew were driven by her fierce need for fulfilment and yet he snatched at them, held them close, allowed himself to believe they were true just for a while.

'Lucas, *please.*'

Hand rough, unsteady, Lucas cupped the full swell of one breast, pushed his hipsters down his thighs with the other. She was there, poised, glorious above him. And when she sank down on his erection, sheathing him in hot tight ecstasy, a shot of nitrous injected his heart, stopped it dead.

Claudia's amber eyes locked on his as she flashed him one of her melt-your-knees smiles and flung her head back in wild abandon, arching sinuously. And suddenly that same heart was torn wide open.

He was the mightiest warrior. And he'd just been slayed.

CHAPTER THIRTEEN

A WARM SPLASH of crimson dawn flooded the room, washing his torso in a reddened hue, and Lucas flung back the covers of their makeshift bed, extricated himself from the heady scent of passion and launched to his feet.

Skin damp, flushed, feverish, his body shook as if under the power of some deadly virus. Breathing hard, he thrust his legs into a pair of creased trousers and tied the cotton bands at his waist. Only then did he glance down at Claudia, where she lay curled around his empty space, dozing, cashmere blankets draped over her sinful curves.

Something had gone wrong. Some time during the night. Hours of sex should have at least made him feel sated, at some kind of peace. He scrubbed his palm over the ridges of his abdomen, trying to ease the crush.

Lungs tight, his eyes bounced around the room. *Dios,* he could still see her spread across the glossy black top of his baby grand, open, needy. Still taste the exotic hint of mango on his tongue from when he'd devoured her body. Still feel her nails tearing at his skin.

'Lucas?'

Her voice—small, hesitant—snagged his attention and his gaze jerked back to the mound of pillows. To her.

Dios, the way she was looking at him…

'Come lie with me?' she asked, eyes brimming with hope and something soft and warm.

He shook his head slowly. 'I need to shower, dress.' *Walk away.*

'Okay, well…' She bit down on her bruised bottom lip. 'I've been thinking.'

'*Dios,* Claudia, I wish you wouldn't,' he said, scouring his nape with his palm.

She smiled. 'Ha-ha. Seriously, though, when I go back to London maybe you…'

Lucas closed his eyes as blood began to rush through his skull at a deafening speed.

He'd made a mistake. A colossal error of judgement—something that seemed to be happening with astounding regularity since this woman—*Dios,* no, this *reluctant royal*—had crashed into his life.

Last night she hadn't come to him just for sex, and once again he'd surrendered to his selfish desires. Now she was sussing him out with all the delicacy of a sledgehammer. And never mind London—she needed to take her place at court!

He hadn't heard a word she'd said, but he didn't need to. Her lips had stopped moving and she peered up through long sooty lashes. Coy, sanguine.

Dios, was she falling for him?

Lucas thrust his hands through his hair. Felt moisture coat his palms. 'Claudia, you must see this for what it is. Heat. Passion. That is all there could ever be. We made a pact, you and I.' He had nothing to offer but a dark soul. And he lived only to work—as he should. She deserved so much more—a chance to find the love she needed.

'I know that,' she said, brow creased, her gaze fastened on her nail as she scratched an invisible mark from the throw. 'I just thought if you were ever in London we could have dinner or something. I mean…why not?'

Good question. The answer, he knew, was the cure for the deadly tangle of emotions knotting his guts. Because if she left his life normality, a pleasing lack of feeling, would surely resume.

The only way out was to tell her the truth. Crush any spark, any kindling of emotion that was flickering to life inside of her.

Something made her move. Maybe it was the way his frame stiffened. Maybe his conviction scored his face or maybe she felt the sudden chill nip her skin. Because she bolted upright and tugged a fawn cashmere blanket up over her breasts, veiling herself. Protecting all her heaven while he took her on a trip to hell.

His blood turned black and weaved a poisonous path towards what was to come—the disappointment in her eyes, the mortification—when she realised what kind of man she'd given her body to.

'You asked me last night who she reminded me of,' he said, jerking his chin towards the famous painting. 'The real question is *what* she reminds me of. Tell me, what do you see?'

Her wide eyes flicked to the painting, back to him. 'Pain. She's in pain and she's shielding something. And when you look at her I can feel *your* pain.'

Not for much longer.

'They bear little resemblance, but I knew when I saw her she had to be mine. To remind me of the man I truly am. That I am responsible for her death.'

Drawing her knees up to her chest, she yanked the blanket up to her throat. Her white knuckles stood out starkly against her honey-gold skin.

'While you spend your every waking moment fighting to cure pain, I have *caused* it.'

He watched the flames of her amber fire snuff out. Felt the atmosphere crackle, scratch at his skin.

Fists clenched, he nodded slowly. '*Sí,* now you are wary. And so you should be.'

He hauled air into his lungs. Almost there. Any second now she would be gone from him. For ever. To take her rightful place.

* * *

Claudia trembled at the deluge of formidable power emanating from his frame as he paced the room, tormented by demons. Then he froze, closed his eyes as if reliving his darkest moments, and when they opened once more the pain she saw there was like a physical punch to her midriff, hurling her across the room.

'She reminds me that for the rest of my days I will pay for killing my own mother.'

Her stomach flinched so hard her gasp rent the air. She blinked wide, shell-shocked eyes. '*What?* No,' she said, shaking her head vigorously. 'No. You couldn't. I don't believe you.'

'I failed her,' he said, his eyes clouded, almost black. 'When I should have been protecting her. I am responsible for her brutal, agonising death.'

Some unseen hand gripped her heart and tore it from her chest. 'Your mother was…?' She couldn't say what was too horrific even to contemplate.

Lucas thrust his hands through his hair, twisted his fingers, punishing. 'Murdered,' he said, voice dark, haunted. 'I was working. We had no money, no food. So damn poor. He came for her when I should've been home, protecting her. Keeping her safe. *Dios,* I knew what he was capable of.'

He clenched his fists so hard she could see the dense muscle in his arms bunch and flex as if readying for a fight.

'Always I returned by nightfall, but that night I was careless. Missed my lift. Had to walk. Was too late. She was already broken. Her body twisted. Limp. Yet still she drew breath. And I stood, frozen. Weak.' His lips twisted with self-disgust. 'Did nothing to stop him walking free.'

She filled in the rest. It was oh-so-heart-shatteringly easy. He'd felt fear. For his mother. For himself.

'A coward,' he said, deathly quiet.

Oh, God. A sob threatened to tear from her throat as hot liquid splashed behind her eyes. Just in time she managed to swallow it whole. 'Don't you *dare* say such a thing. You told me you were young when your mother died.'

'*Sí.* I was fourteen. A man.'

'No, Lucas,' she said, her heart breaking in two. For him. 'A boy on the cusp of becoming a man.'

Such an emotionally tumultuous age, she knew. To lose his mother in such a way…

'No,' he growled, slashing an unsteady hand through the air. 'Do *not* look at me with pity. I don't deserve it. *Comprende?*'

Claudia nodded, schooled her features, determined to be strong—to be the woman he needed. Because she knew all about unwanted empathy. It would make him angrier still. 'Tell me what happened…to your mother. Please.' God, how she wanted to hold him. Comfort him. But she didn't have a hope of penetrating the dark forcefield shrouding him as he paced the floor. 'You knew the man who killed her?'

He stopped dead, no more than five feet in front of her, and sank his dark fierce gaze into her eyes. 'Of course I knew him, Claudia. He was my father.'

She tried—she really tried to keep still, to show nothing, but he must have seen the colour leach from her face. She could feel cold seeping through her body after all. *I knew what he was capable of…* 'Did he…?' She couldn't even say it. *Did he hurt you?* And no matter how hard she tried to stem the images they seemed to whip her mind, one after another.

His mouth twisted into a cruel sneer. 'Yes, Claudia, my father was the worst kind of man. He gambled every cent. Whored all over town. Drank himself into furious rages and beat her so badly she suffered severe internal haemorrhaging. Bled for hours before my very eyes.'

She drew her lips into her mouth, bit down hard, hauling every ounce of strength she could find to stop from crumpling to the floor. He had to live with his memories every hour of every day, and she felt damn pathetic for thinking *she'd* had a grim childhood. In comparison her life had been a bed of orange blossom.

She swallowed around the tight searing burn in her throat. 'I'm so sorry, Lucas. Truly.'

Claudia watched him slump into the deep sofa, bury his face in his hands. 'By the time I managed to get help, get her to the hospital, it was too late. I just sat there and watched her die. Powerless.' He spread his hands wide in front of him, looked down at his palms as if he was back there, in that very room. 'Blood dripped from my fingers. Pooled upon the floor. The longest six hours of my life.'

She scrambled onto her knees, then her feet. Wrapped the blanket around her body sarong-style and took a tentative step towards him, asking, begging. 'Let me hold you. Can I hold you? Please.'

'No!' he said, snapping upright, warding her off with one flat palm, eyes wild as pain howled through him. 'You stay away from me. I do not know what I'm capable of right now.'

Claudia slid back. Not because she was scared—no, she would never fear him—but because *he* was terrified. Terrified of the emotions pummelling through him. She wondered then if emotion reminded him of pain. Of weakness.

'I made a promise to her that day. That I would avenge her death.' His voice grew harder, darker, menacing. 'And I grew bigger, stronger—went after him. Ensured he was thrown into the worst hellhole on earth, where he died a befitting death. But that wasn't enough. Nowhere near enough. I went after every other murdering son of a bitch he was associated with. Hauled them one after another in front of every court in the land.'

'A vigilante.' *Of course.* She'd seen that roguish side to him from the start. The ruthless determination he radiated. The fierce power that held her in thrall. 'A hero.'

One corner of his mouth lifted in a satirical smirk. 'You think that, *querida,* if it keeps you warm at night.'

A blast of outrage stung her cheeks. 'I won't think it. I *know* it,' she said, her voice cracking as she thumped her heart with her fist. 'In here. Arunthia wouldn't be the country it is today without you. The people worship you. So don't you dare question your self-worth to me.'

He huffed a mirthless laugh. 'And right there,' he said, 'is the irony.'

'What do you mean?' she said, hating the cynicism, the disbelief in his eyes.

'Your father persuaded me to join the Arunthian Military. Taught me how to use power and strength for good, how to strive for honour by doing my duty to king and country. He saved my youthful dark soul. So when I came for you I had given him my word to protect you. And how do I repay him?' His lips twisted in self-disgust. 'I take your innocence. I ruin your reputation. I dishonour you and myself. Now I pay the price.'

The *price?*

'Oh, now, wait just a damn minute,' she said, her voice tremulous, her hand beseeching. 'I asked you to make love to me. I gave freely. I wanted you so much.' Her voice shattered along with her heart. Suddenly she didn't care what the admission would cost her, because he needed to hear it. 'Only you. It was never just sex for me, Lucas. I only wanted you. What's more, there was nothing, *nothing* dishonourable about what happened between us.'

Face contorting, he shook his head as if he fought an inner battle—his conscience warring with her words.

Then he flung his arms wide. '*Dios,* what is wrong with you, Claudia? Where is the hate?'

'In you, *cariño.* Never in me!' What was he thinking in that tormented mind? Realisation struck her down and she crumpled to the bed of pillows. Shook her head wildly. 'You could never, *ever* turn me away from you. Ever, *cariño.*'

His eyes flared with either anger or panic. She couldn't be sure. '*Dios,* do not call me that, Claudia.'

'Don't call you what…my darling?' Her voice turned hard, because she was so damn angry with him. 'Why? Because you don't deserve affection of the heart? You deserve it more than anyone, Lucas. Or is it because you intend to pay for the tragedy of your mother's death for eternity? Well, I say you've spent your whole life atoning for the past, and now it's your turn for some happiness.'

Eyes still haunted, he merely blinked up at her, as if horrified at the very thought. Either it had never occurred to him that she would forgive him or— *Oh, God.* Pain ripped through her. She'd been so sure something had changed during the night. She was scared, she realised, of his answer. But if this man had taught her anything it was courage.

'Or is it me?' she asked, wincing inwardly at the quiver in her voice. She cleared her throat, made it stronger. 'Am I not enough for you to try? Was it truly just sex for you?'

His jaw clenched, together with every muscle in his body, fiercely hard, resolute, and her stomach plunged to the floor.

'I warned you, did I not? I have sex. I walk away. I'm not a man to become attached to.'

Oh, it was far too late for that. Self-reliant Claudia had done the one thing she'd sworn she'd never do. She'd got close. And now just the thought of never seeing him again was like a huge gaping hole inside her—one that panged straight through her soul.

'You're right. You did warn me,' she said, trying for light, airy, scrambling for the cool, calm composure that had shielded her for so many years. She took a deep breath, trying to wrap her foggy mind around forming words. 'It's probably for the best. After all, a continent divides us in our desire to work, to atone, to give back. In that way we are similar, you and I.'

She tried for a smile but it felt brittle, edgy. Because she was about to lie outright. To relieve some of the strain marring his beautiful face and, though it pained her to admit it, she was still just a woman underneath. Pride she knew was a rare, fragile thing.

'Just as well I hadn't fallen for you.'

'Good—that is good,' he said, voice gruff, eyes drifting away from her. 'I have asked Armande to take you to the palace at noon. I have business in Barcelona, but I'll return for the ball.' Then he swung away to look out on the swirling mass of storm blowing in from the east. 'Tonight we keep it professional. You will stand in front of the nation and do your duty.'

She would have laughed if knives had not been tearing her apart. He thought of nothing, focused on nothing, but his duty to Arunthia. And wasn't that the story of her life?

Reaching for the anger, the hurt, she snatched at thin air. Because through it all she understood the rules he lived by. The horrific loss of his mother and his guilt dominated his every waking moment, and he found the honour he desperately needed by doing his job and fighting for the greater good. Just as Claudia had pledged her life to cure, to ease pain. She could never give that up, just as he couldn't.

All his rules made him the beautiful, strong, heroic man he was.

'Yes, Lucas. I'll do my duty. For *you*. On one condition.'

Lucas braced his arms against the plate glass as he stared into the turbulent froth of the ocean. Despite her words he knew she wished to see him again, and something close to need, yearning, clawed down his chest, lacerating his resolve.

Temptation was an ebb and flow of words in his mind. *Yes, I will come and see you, querido, hold you in my arms. I will try and give you everything you desire.*

Palms flat, he pushed off the window and turned to face her, guts twisting, his head in the midst of an almighty war…and his gaze crashed into the woman he'd failed. A woman sheltering a child from the storm, in pain, so much pain.

Claudia was wrong. He didn't deserve to be released from the shackles of blame.

Dios, how could he even think of allowing himself a relationship with Claudia? She made him feel every single emotion, and he knew the dangers of that. Loss of thought, of reason, control.

To this day he was plagued by his mother's death. What if

he had acted quicker, stopped the blood somehow, run faster for help? But he'd been afraid—yes, afraid—a destructive emotion that made you sloppy, careless, because love was so powerful it took away everything.

If he failed to protect her… *Dios,* just the thought made his blood run black. She was too precious.

Head high, the fawn cashmere blanket wrapped around her decadent curves, she walked towards him. Lucas stiffened, balling his fists to stop himself from reaching, from taking her one last time. To pacify the craving. Numb the pain. Because he refused to use her heavenly body in such a way.

Her step faltered and she sank her teeth into her lip. 'Did you hear me, Lucas?'

Like a potent aphrodisiac, her scent, *their* scent, curled up his nose, blurring thought.

'Ah, of course.' He'd almost forgotten. About her duty. His mission. That in itself should have told him something. 'Tell me your condition, Princesa.'

CHAPTER FOURTEEN

'*PROMISE ME YOU will let go of the past.*'

A cacophony of voices floated through the open window. Bristles stroked her scalp and diamond pins slid through lofty curls, yet through it all Claudia stared unseeingly into the gilt-edged dressing table mirror before her. Remembering the dark haunted look on Lucas's face as nine simple words tossed him further into purgatory.

So strong was his need to do his duty and get her to the palace, he'd given her his oath to try, however much it pained him. For, truly, what was the point of hurting, of living with such pain, when the past couldn't be changed.

'Claudine.' Her mother's serene face popped into view beside her. 'Where are you, I wonder?'

Thinking about my lover. Claudia winced inwardly as her cheeks rouged in the mirror and feathers of unease dusted her nape. 'Oh, nowhere in particular.'

Her mother arched one perfectly plucked brow, wholly unconvinced, and Claudia almost smiled. She could read her mother now, especially when they were alone, making her realise that Queen Marysse wore a mask of her very own.

'Pass me another pin, then, dear.'

Claudia reached for another pin, chose a pearl, and passed it over her shoulder. 'Don't you have staff to do this? Surely you don't have time.'

'Nonsense. I will make time. How many days and nights of my life have I spent wishing I could be there for you?'

Claudia closed her eyes, knowing it was time she listened to her own advice and let go of the past.

'I didn't know you felt that way, Mother.'

Perhaps Lucas was right. On that fateful day her mother had been unthinking, not uncaring. And maybe her parents had handled her illness the only way they knew how. By acting. Not by becoming overwrought with emotion—like her mother had during the accident. Her safety and health had been paramount to them. She'd never felt loved, but her parents must have cared. She only had to think of what Lucas had gone through and every memory seemed to fade. Diminish, somehow.

'Let us start over—could we, Claudine?' Her mother's warm fingers curled over her shoulder, squeezed through her cotton wrap. 'I am opening the new children's wing next week and I was hoping you would come.'

Claudia looked up…saw warmth and hope in her mother's gaze. She could do her duty while she was here, couldn't she? There was really no need for the frisson of panic that they might expect more. 'I'd like that.'

'Good. I have asked Lucas to arrange the security.'

Oh, honestly, even the mention of his name gave her palpitations. 'You saw Lucas this morning?'

'Briefly. Your father was in talks with Philippe Carone, but Lucas seemed anxious to meet with him. Henri saw him, of course, before he flew to—'

'Barcelona,' Claudia murmured through the clattering in her head.

Why had Lucas gone to see her father so suddenly? And why did her stomach scream at the thought? And why was her mother watching her so closely? They'd done nothing wrong. *Everyone* had sex. Right?

'Yes,' her mother said slowly, as she slid alongside Claudia to choose another pin from the gold tray. 'His headquarters are there.'

Some sixth sense told Claudia she should quit while she was ahead, but now she'd started talking her tongue didn't want to stop. 'Headquarters for what?'

Her mother's brow creased, amber eyes snapping up to Claudia's. 'LGAS, of course.'

Suddenly grateful she was sitting down, Claudia's mouth worked. '*The* LGAS? Lucas *owns LGAS?* How on earth did I miss that?' She slumped back into the chair. 'High-end security, renowned, the best in the world.' Always protecting, she mused with a secret smile...which then slid off her face. 'Wait a minute—doesn't LGAS have an aerodynamic wing? I travelled in one of his jets!' The word *wealth* didn't even begin to describe his inordinate success. God, she was so proud of him her heart ached.

'Of course you did, darling. Everyone important does.' Her mother heaved a theatrical sigh. 'Shoulders straight, Claudine. A hump is most unattractive.'

Claudia bolted upright. 'I can't believe I didn't see it.' For heaven's sake—did she go around with her eyes shut? What else had she missed?

'Lucas is a very private man,' her mother continued, her tone taut, her eyes narrowed on Claudia's face. 'Something I'm acutely grateful for. You are entitled to a private life, Claudine, I stress *private.*'

Claudia's stomach plunged. Was she so obvious? Or was the fact she'd been his guest enough to arouse suspicion? She'd never thought of that, had she? No, she'd just been desperate to stay with him. Only him. Because he made her feel safe. But how had it looked from the outside looking in? He worked for her father. He—

'Nothing is going on, Mother.' Well, apart from sex, and she wasn't telling her *that.*

'I am glad to hear it. The stakes are high. Think of your reputation. His work.'

She couldn't give two stuffs about her reputation. Despite every loaded inference to the contrary, she was going back to London! And Lucas was staying here.

Heart crashing against her ribs, she flinched at a brisk rap upon the door and the strutting in of her mother's PA, carrying a crushed velvet gift box.

Her mother passed the box to Claudia with a warning look. 'I will leave you now. Your father will be here on the hour.'

Waiting for the door to close, she felt a heady concoction of panic and excitement surge through her veins. At the click of the door she fumbled with the lid, tossed it to the floor and tore through layer upon layer of black tissue paper. Then time stood still as her eyes devoured the contents, her heart leaping up her throat.

'Oh, Lucas.'

Hand trembling, she picked up the thick cream-coloured card, ran her thumb over the strong, black masculine scroll. Laying the card upon the mirrored plate, just so, she returned to the box and lifted a pair of long pale gold gloves—exactly the same satin as the dress he'd known she was desperate to wear. The sheath, thank heavens, hung on the rack in front of her: a temptation she'd been unable to shake.

Twisting her hand this way and that, she saw small diamond studs wink at her from where they trailed up the full length of the cuff in a perfect row.

Tears glistened behind her eyes.

This from the man who professed he didn't feel. Oh, but she knew he *could* feel—every emotion, ten-fold. The power of which scared him to death.

Lucas cared for her. He must. Was he lending her his strength? God, how she ached for his touch. A touch she couldn't allow herself to hope for, because she was beginning to realise she'd put his position at risk. The honourable duty he lived for.

Dressing, she imagined him sprawled across the sofa, watching her, dark hunger glittering in his sapphire eyes as she smoothed sheer ivory silk stockings up her legs. Legs he'd kissed every inch of. Tying the ribbons on her corset, it was as if his fingers curled around the supple silk, pulling her, cinching her tight.

This from the man whose written words echoed in her head as she stood at the top of the opulent sweeping staircase holding onto her father's arm, her heart a thump, thump, thumping beat.

Hold your head high, Princesa.

Claudia lifted her chin. Opened her eyes on a monstrously titanic room where every sinister eye looked upon her.

Be proud of the woman you have become.

She took one step, then another, begging her feet not to fail her now. Down, down, down she went, gliding into the palatial, softly lit ballroom. The crowd hushed, her mind locked on Lucas…the satin caressed her wrists like a lover's healing kiss.

This from the man whose eyes sought hers as soon as her feet hit the polished floor with a look of such intense pride she had to grip her father's arm not to fall.

Her heart filled, gushed, overflowed.

This from the man she'd fallen deeply and irrevocably in love with.

This from the man she now had to protect.

Lucas stood in the midst of inane chatter, searching for the satisfaction of a mission accomplished. It was like digging for mines in the dark.

Statuesque, sanguine, Princess Claudine Verbault had finally taken her rightful place. The sight of which Lucas knew was his cue to leave. Yet his designer-clad feet were as if suctioned to the silver-toned marble as he hauled air into his tight lungs, clenched every hard muscle in his body until his bones ached.

That he'd lasted one hour and thirty-three minutes without manhandling her out of the room was a miracle in itself. And what the *hell* was Henri doing, throwing Philippe Carone at her every chance he got? The business magnate just happened to be one of the most eligible bachelors in Europe. And if the sleaze-bag danced with Claudia one more time—if he looked at Claudia one more time, stripping the tight sheath from her body with his marauding eyes—Lucas would launch the man across the room.

Thrusting his fingers to his throat, he yanked at the stiff collar.

Madre de Dios, surely Henri was not contemplating such a match? After everything she'd been through? Hadn't she paid enough of a price to Arunthia? To lose her parents, her home, while so tender and vulnerable.

Lucas closed his eyes, took a deep breath, infusing his brain with some sense. No, he was wrong, Henri wouldn't ask such a thing of her.

But *Dios—Carone*? The man wasn't much taller than she was. How could he possibly protect her? Lucas could do a better job with his eyes shut! What the hell had *ever* made him think otherwise? No longer was he fourteen years old. No longer did he doubt his own strength. Claudia had trusted him with her life—curled her naked body into his. Even after he'd told her the truth of his past she'd cared not. Still she'd trusted implicitly. Still she had wanted to be held. And he'd walked away. Focused on duty. Rammed her responsibilities down her pretty throat. And if Henri were serious about Carone she would be strangled by duty until the day she died. Lucas had never considered happiness important. Until her. Until now.

On the far side of the room he saw Carone set his sights and begin walking towards her.

Excusing himself from the cluster of foreign dignitaries, Lucas swerved through the crowd, eyes locked on Claudia, his arms begging to pick her up, take her away. If he didn't feel so damn sick he would laugh at the irony.

She turned, as if sensing him, eyes filling with an instant of warmth before veiling, cooling—a look he did not care for.

'Good evening, Your Royal Highness,' he said, with a formal nod. 'You look exquisite.'

'Thank you, Lucas, you don't look too bad yourself.' She forced a smile and his stomach hollowed…then shot to the floor when Carone sidled up beside her and Claudia offered the other man a sincere warm slide of her lips.

'This dance is *mine,* Carone,' he growled. 'Excuse us.'

Lucas slid a protective hand over the base of Claudia's spine, curled his fingers up around her waist and felt her muscles stiffen beneath his touch. He thrust away the sliver of panic; he'd wanted professional and now he was getting it.

'I have a better idea,' he said, tightening his fingers as they walked towards the dance floor—and took a swift unheeded side-step through the double doors leading on to the terrace beyond and the privacy of a star-studded sky. The chilly nip of the air did a miserable job of lowering his temperature.

'Are you sure this is such a good idea?' she asked, quickly sliding from his hold.

The loss of contact did abominable things to his mind-set. Lucas closed the doors, drowning out the noise with a satisfying click, and swivelled back to face her, taking a good swift kick to the guts as he drank her in.

All glamorous sophistication, she stood by the wrought-iron railings, pearly teeth gnawing at her rouged lip, top-to-toe in gold satin which hugged and caressed every voluptuous curve. His palms itched to indulge. Stroke. Cosset. *Dios,* would the craving ever cease?

He balled his hands. 'Claudia…' he managed, before wondering what the hell to say.

The lines of strain eased from her brow as her mouth tilted knowingly. 'Thank you for the gift.'

'You're very welcome,' he said, still loath to admit, even to himself, why he'd sent it. So she would feel his possessive touch around her beautiful wrists. A touch she'd discarded within minutes. 'You didn't seem to need them for too long.' Which was a good thing, he assured himself, ignoring the twinge in his chest.

'Ah, well,' she said, her cheeks pinkening to rose-gold, 'I'd quite forgotten how slippery satin was.'

Lucas swallowed hard. *Dios,* he was dying here.

Dying? No, it was worse than that. He felt as if he was about to lose the most important thing in his world. Again.

'So slippery,' she continued, probably in an effort to keep things light, oblivious to the dark storm raging inside of him, 'that after thirty minutes the caterers were three champagne flutes down and in all conscience I thought I better take them off.'

The tension in his midsection evaporated on a laugh. One side of her lush mouth curved and his arms ached to pick her up, carry her away.

Chin dipping, she peeked up at him through dense sooty lashes. 'I found out something else tonight. Or should I say *realised* something else. *You* gave me the money. The funding. My parents would never have offered. How it must have pained you to coerce me.'

He shrugged. Made it lazy. He would have given her one hundred million. 'I do not regret it.' How could he when he never would have tasted heaven otherwise? 'So do not forgive me,' he bit out.

'Oh, I will—and I do,' she said softly, her eyes now full— the first signs of a thaw?—brimming with a warmth that made his skin prickle, his heart thud. 'I'm in awe of you, Lucas. To come so far against all the odds.' She reached up, trailed one finger down his jaw. 'I'm so proud of the man you have become.'

Dios, he'd had it with this senseless woman.

Snap went his resolve, his strength. One step forward and he reached out...and every muscle in his arms, every vein in his body, froze as her lashes fluttered closed and she shook her head.

'I should go back inside,' she murmured. 'Thank you for everything.'

His head jerked. Thank you? For what…? *The sex?* Was *that* why she'd wanted him to come to London…for more *sex?* Something told him he'd slipped into the irrationality danger zone here, but *Madre de Dios*—thank you? As if she could just walk away and forget.

Like hell she would.

Ignoring the pop of her eyes, Lucas dug his hand into the hair at her nape, yanked her head back and flung his mouth against hers. He muffled her shock with his lips and kissed her irrational mouth while a noxious tangle of emotions knotted his guts. Plundering her mouth with his tongue, he curved his hands around the delicate span of her waist and crushed her against him.

A fist of anxiety clenched his heart when she stiffened… but then she wrapped her arms about his shoulders, thrust her fingers in his hair and tugged, giving as good as she got. The flush of relief turned to liquid fire as she blazed in his arms.

The crackle and hum of static energy surged between their bodies, bouncing from one point of contact to the other. *Dios,* they created enough electricity to power the eastern grid. He couldn't let her go. He needed…

A flash lit the sky. Then another. A slam. A door? Fireworks?

A gasp rent the air. Not his. Not hers.

Lips froze, still close, and Lucas could taste her panting breath as it whispered across his tongue.

Thuds hit his temples as reality cracked through his skull, his entire body vibrating with the force of it.

Hands falling from her pale, horrified face, Lucas took a step back, closed his eyes. No, no, *no! Dios,* her reputation would be in tatters.

Plink. Plink. One light after another lit the sky. Cameras. *Dios,* she hated cameras. She would run, he knew. Hide.

Hands fisting into a violent clench, his eyes flew open. And locked onto her amber fire.

Still here. Still standing tall. Regal. Brave. Courageous. After everything she'd been through he could not, *would not* walk away from her now.

Dark waves of fury poured from his rigid shoulders while an earthquake shook the paving beneath her feet.

Oh, God, why had she kissed him back? She was supposed to be staying away from him!

Her mother's voice came to her. *Think of your reputation... his work.* And the cold night began to seep through her skin, burrow into her stomach.

'Tell me this isn't happening,' she whispered.

'Consequences,' he said, his voice dark, fierce, harder than ever before. 'Now we face them.'

'Oh, Lucas, I'm so sorry.'

His words screamed in her head. *Your selfishness is astounding.* In all the years she'd loathed her own reflection she'd never envisaged disliking the person she was inside. Had she once given thought to the impact on Lucas should they ever be found out? No. She'd just wanted him. So desperately. Unseeing of the consequences.

Swarms of black locusts poured onto the patio—one brawny security man for every ravenous tabloid fiend.

'Tell me now,' he said, his eyes swirling with a turbulent storm. 'What do you want, Claudia?'

She wanted to fix it. Put everything right. Make good on the destruction she'd caused. The alternative didn't bear thinking about. But she *did* think about it. Because her brain wouldn't switch off. Would Lucas the Honourable propose? Be trapped *by her* for eternity? Or, worse still, would her father discharge him? Strip him of his honour?

Never.

Claudia could fix this. Make sure he kept his job. His life. Everything that made him the man he was. The man she loved. And she knew exactly how to do it.

'I will fight for you,' he avowed. 'Tell me what you want.'

Her throat stung. Still he would fight for her. Her brave knight. But even knights answered to their king.

'To be free. To go home. That's all I've ever wanted.' *Until you. Only you. God,* her heart was breaking.

His jaw hard, the shutters slammed down over his face. 'Very well.'

He took a step back and beckoned to Armande with a flick of his fingers, told him to corral all the reporters out front for Lucas to deal with.

Claudia inhaled his scent one last time as she snuck around him, raised her chin and strode towards her father.

She ignored the disappointment weighing heavy in his eyes. She'd make him happy soon enough.

'Can I speak with you, Father?'

'My office. Twenty minutes.'

Claudia spent the longest, most agonising twenty minutes of her life pacing the living room in the private quarters of the Palace. The silvery moon cast eerie shadows over the oppressive grandeur, making her shiver. But this way, *sans* artificial light, she could keep one eye on the grandfather clock and sneak a peek at Lucas out front, his huge body looming over a member of the paparazzi.

Thankfully they'd only had a small audience on the terrace but…God, the look on his face as they'd parted ways. She would never forget it. Fierce, yet strangely bleak. He must hate her for placing him in this position.

A loud gong echoed off the oak-panelled walls like a death-knell and she stiffened her backbone, swept through the room, down the cavernous hallway to her father's office. Palm flat, she pushed through the door, turned, closed it with a soft click and spun around to face him—sitting behind his wide desk in a high-backed brown leather chair, focusing his flinty gaze on her face.

'Claudine.'

'Father.' She strode towards his desk to stand opposite him

and lifted her chin. 'I have a proposition for you.' Even as she hoped to reach a compromise—something she should have considered well before now—she realised that on the back of ruining the Anniversary Ball her timing sucked.

'Let's hear it,' he said, barely suppressed temper firing his cheeks.

She kept her cool. Reached for her mask. Because she'd never needed it more.

'I apologise for any embarrassment I've caused you tonight. Truly. But the fault is mine and I'm quite willing to make it up to you.' Her voice almost cracked on the last, and she bit her inner cheek to stop from crying out, pleading with him.

'Unless you are willing to come home for good, I do *not* want to hear it.'

She tried to swallow but it was impossible. So much for compromise.

How right Lucas had been. *You cannot change who you are, Princesa.* And hadn't she suspected all along that the moment she stepped foot on Arunthian soil her freedom would be lost?

Brittle was surely the only word to describe her smile. 'All right, Father. I'll come home.'

His clipped grey brows hiked just a touch. 'You will give up your work?' he said, still disbelieving.

The lump in her chest caught fire and tore up her throat. Years of research…the children she'd left behind…Bailey. *Forgive me. I'll make it up to you. I swear it.* 'Yes.'

She would never have believed it possible of her autocratic father, but his head actually jerked. Strange how that small reaction pleased her—until she beheld the gleam in his eyes.

'Will you marry Carone?'

Whack—the first crack in her armour ripped through her stomach and she stiffened to prevent the flinch. She should have known there was some reason he'd been throwing Carone at her. She couldn't contemplate what such an allegiance would involve or she'd throw up on her father's pristine desk. Didn't royals marry for love these days? Then again, what did it matter when she couldn't have the man she loved? And if she lived elsewhere she wouldn't have to see him every day. She could forget. *Impossible.*

The effort to stand tall while her heart was bleeding made her legs throb. 'Yes,' she said, proud of the steel in her voice. 'As long as you do something for me.'

That cool, flinty gaze narrowed imperceptibly. 'I am intrigued to know what would make you give up so much, Claudine.'

'Lucas gets to keep his job, his honour, and to do his duty for Arunthia. You need him, Father, I know you do. And he… he needs it too.' She wondered then if the virtual stranger before her could hear the love in her voice. So she licked her dry lips and focused on the aspect that would carry more weight with this ruler of a nation. 'The people love him. He's their hero.' *And mine too.*

Her father nodded slowly, his bushy brows low over his eyes. 'I see.'

The stern lines of his face softened, to make him appear younger somehow. She blinked hard, wondering if the transformation was a mirage.

'Does Lucas know how you feel about him?'

A breath she'd had no idea she was holding whooshed out of her and her head bowed—her mask slipping to shatter upon the floor. 'God, I hope not.'

'Too. Late.'

Slam went her hand to her heart as those two little words delivered in that deadly fierce voice echoed around the room.

Slowly she turned. *Oh, no.* 'Lucas.'

Sprawling insolently, he encompassed one huge black wing chair, the tie of his tux loose around his neck, one devilish dark brow raised. And she'd swear she could hear his molars crack.

'Big mistake, *querida.*'

CHAPTER FIFTEEN

Having just spent the last forty minutes in the depths of hell, Lucas wasn't feeling so good.

'Excuse us, Henri.'

'Of course, my friend.' He heard the smile in Henri's voice, ignored it. God only knew what the man was thinking after Lucas had played every strategic manoeuvre to get Claudia back to bloody London!

Dios, he was going to make her pay.

Wide-eyed, still shaking like a blade of grass on a breeze, Claudia stood, her gaze flicking from Lucas to her father, back to Lucas.

Still she was unsure who held the power—over him, over her. He had no idea what had happened to make her doubt his dominant strength, but soon she would remember Lucas was his own man with his own damn rules. A fact Henri had always accepted.

'We leave. Now,' he said. Toxic nausea churned inside him, poisoning his voice.

Palm flat to the base of her spine, he gave her a deft push out through the door, down the hallway to the front of the private wing, farther still into the night.

'You're angry with me?' she asked, her voice small, quivery, as she lifted the skirts of her dress and negotiated the stone steps.

'Of course not. Whatever made you think such a thing?'

He jabbed at the open door, being held open by Armande, his voice petrifying the wildlife. 'Get in the damn car.'

Armande bowed his head shortly before they both slid into the stifling interior.

'It must have been Armande,' she murmured, plastering herself against the opposite end of the cream leather bench and nipping her plump bottom lip.

Dios, more enclosed spaces! He rammed his fingers down the inside of his shirt and tore another button free as the car meandered down the tree-lined incline.

'I thought it was you with the reporters outside.'

'Clearly.' Although he'd never been more grateful for *not* being somewhere in his entire life. To think she might have left!

He scrubbed his hands over his face, his hair. Checked the privacy screen. Unable to wait a second longer to vent all over her.

'I asked you on the terrace,' he said, hearing the dark blend of incredulity and anger in his own voice, 'what you wanted. That was a *very* simple question, Claudia!'

She winced, reached up, rubbed her brow. 'I know you did.'

'And what did you say to me? That you wanted to be *free!*' He balled his fists on his thighs as his volume soared. 'Yet now you will marry that sleaze *Carone?*'

'Well, I—'

'*Dios,* Claudia, I had a goddamn coronary right there in the room!' He laid a hand on his chest to check his heart was still there. Still beating. Like a pneumatic drill.

'You did?' she asked, turning to look at him, her brow pinched. 'Well, I was just trying to think of a way to fix things.'

'Do me a favour, *querida?* Do not over-think. It scares the hell out of me.' He could barely breathe just thinking about it. The way she had stood there—so calm, a stranger to him—telling Henri she would marry that tiny fool *before* she'd bothered to stipulate why. Drawing out his pain as if he was lying on some medieval rack in the dungeon.

And then there she was, his little warrior, no longer fighting for herself but fighting for him. And, *Dios,* still he could barely breathe.

Pursing her lips, she crossed her arms tight over her chest. Her lush breasts eased out of the ruched bands of her bodice and he had to tear his eyes away before he hauled her into his lap. Three minutes and they would be home. Surely he could wait that long?

Yet he could feel her skin start to bristle. She was thinking again. *Damn.*

'You both sat there, no doubt having sealed my fate, and let me say all that stuff!'

What was she? Embarrassed? 'Let me assure you there was no pleasure to be gained.' From the first part at least. And he would have made his presence known if her words had not struck him dumb.

'And how is it going to look now?' she said, her fiery temper bubbling to the surface. 'There were still some reporters milling around back there.'

Lucas snapped. 'To hell with the paparazzi! I do not care for other men's opinions. And you'd better get used to the attention, *querida.* I imagine once news of our engagement hits your face will cover every rag in the western hemisphere!'

Her small hand curled around the base of her throat. *'Engagement?* Oh, God, I should've known. What did he say? What have you done?'

He had done nothing bar fight for her freedom! But he wasn't done with punishing her yet.

'Did I not tell you that *I* make the rules, Claudia? And I assure you, your fate was sealed well before tonight, *cariña.'* Although, to be fair, for an intelligent man it had taken him a while.

'What's that supposed to mean?'

Lucas rocked forward as the car pulled to a stop and within twenty seconds he had her ensconced in the house. His house. Their house. Their living room.

Claudia stood in the middle of the floor, feet shifting, watching him warily. 'All my things are at the palace.'

'I will send for them tomorrow,' he said, tearing his jacket from his torso. 'You will stay here. With me. Always.'

'Lucas will you stop this? I haven't agreed to anything and I refuse to trap you!'

Grabbing fistfuls of his shirt, he ripped it from his body. Buttons pinged off every surface as he tore it off, tossed it to the floor. Then he swung back to face her, pointed at the gold sheath. 'Take it off.'

Her lips parted on an indrawn breath and she flushed crimson from head to foot. 'The *dress?* Why?'

'Because *his* fingerprints are all over it,' he ground out. 'And because I have just been through the worst forty minutes of my adult life and I need to *hold* you!'

'Oh.' Pursing her lips, she reached for the zip at her side and slowly pulled the metal pin down, inch by excruciating inch. His pulse spiked as the contaminated gold satin slinked from her luscious curves to pool on the floor at her feet, leaving her standing in...

'Madre de Dios.'

'You recognise it?' she asked, voice husky, sexy as hell.

Tight ivory cinched her small waist, widened at her full spilling breasts. Lace-top silk stockings and crystal-studded gold heels completed the evocative feast.

Lucas scrubbed his palm over his heart. Just to check again. 'The lingerie boutique. In town.'

'Ah. So I *did* have your full attention?'

'Always, *querida,*' he said, shucking off his trousers and shoes until he stood in snug black hipsters, never taking his eyes from those glorious centrefold curves. Curves he now gripped at the waist and hauled to straddle him as he plunged to the sofa.

Wrapping his arms around her, he buried his face in the soft skin at her neck and inhaled, over and over, rubbing his lips against her delicate collarbone, trying to pull her tighter into him.

She made that erotic purring noise that drove him *loco*.

'Agony,' she whispered. 'At least we're good at this, I suppose.'

'Stop it. You are thinking again.'

'Can't help it.'

'I know,' he said, pulling back to kiss the curve of her neck, the sexy dip behind her ear. 'That brain of yours was one of the first things that hit me. *Dios,* one look at you and it was like crashing headlong into a solid brick wall. Then every touch was like flirting with a minefield. Every look was a bullet between my eyes. And when you spoke those words tonight...'

He loosened his hold, just enough to sit back, cup her face and sink into her amber fire. 'So brave. My beautiful brave Princesa. I have never felt more proud or more love for you.'

Her long black sooty lashes fluttered while her delicate jaw went slack. *'Really?'*

'Claudia, Claudia. The night I took you I made a choice. I chose *you*. Not duty, not Arunthia. You. I knew then, *cariña*. One taste and I would lose it all. I knew then I would resign. And I would do it all over again in a heartbeat just to hold you.'

Moisture pooled in her eyes and his stomach twisted as one dewy droplet trickled down her face and slid over his thumb.

'You resigned?' she said in a teary whisper.

'*Sí.* I resigned this morning. I would've done so days ago, but I couldn't leave you long enough. Tonight was my final duty.'

'But you said...you told me there could never be anything more. I thought you would never open your heart to me.'

'It took me a while to realise you were already there. I could not get my head around deserving you. So long I have lived with the guilt. But then you told me you were proud of the man I have become. And if *you* thought I was worthy who was I to argue?' He shrugged, tried to make it lazy, still not entirely convinced, but...

'Guilt? I wanted to die when I realised I'd cost you everything. Have you ever thought for one moment that I don't deserve you?'

'No,' he said fiercely. 'And do not let me hear you say such a thing again.'

'Yes, Lucas,' she said, a mocking smile teasing her lips.

He growled. 'It scared the hell out of me that I might fail to protect you. But then I thought how could I possibly trust anyone else? It is impossible. Only me.'

'Only you.' She trailed her fingertips down the side of his face and he nuzzled into her touch. 'Although maybe if you eased off a bit...? I can paddle in the sea without disaster striking.'

He growled again—deeper, harder. That was the only answer she was getting right now. The roll of her eyes told him she knew it.

'But still I held out,' he said. 'Until I heard the words you spoke to your father. Filled with such bravery. And there was I—a warrior shielding my heart, without the courage to love you. After everything you've been through you stood there, my little warrior, and gave up your work and your freedom for me. I was humbled by you, *querida*.'

She reached up, softly brushed his hair from his temple. 'I'd do anything for you. I love you so much.'

Lucas closed his eyes. That was it. She'd said it. She was his. Always.

Claudia nestled impossibly closer, peppering kisses all over his gorgeous face. He'd chosen her and it was as if the Philharmonic Orchestra was playing in her soul, making her blood sing, her body hum in ecstasy—alive, so vibrantly alive.

And because she knew he needed to hear it Claudia said the words, over and over, as she kissed his warm lips. 'I love you, Lucas, only you.' She added that last bit because the insane man was jealous beyond belief and, knowing he felt every emotion ten-fold, he must be in serious torment.

His hands slipped from her face and he began to pull the pins from her hair. 'I want it down around your shoulders. Over me. And, *Dios,* I'll have to leave you and go back to your father in the morning. It is a question of honour.'

'Wait a minute… You mean you didn't ask him already? Well, what on earth were you talking about in there?'

'Getting you back to London,' he ground out. 'Like you asked!'

'Oh.' An inappropriate laugh burst past her lips. God, they made a sorry pair. Mind you, she couldn't regret a minute— not whilst in the midst of this heavenly pay-off. 'So why are we getting married?' It was obvious, but she couldn't resist.

'Because I damn well say so!'

Oh, he was so fantastically fierce. She had a huge grin on her face, she knew. 'You love me?'

'*Sí.* Desperately.'

'We're going to get married?'

'*Sí.* I can wait one week for you to arrange something.'

'One *week?*'

'Only one. My heart cannot take any more.' Her hair tumbled down around her shoulders and he groaned, thick and low. 'I will take you to visit Bailey and build you a new place for your work here. The best in the world.'

Claudia flung her arms around his neck, sank her fingers into his hair and breathed him in while her brain tripped. What else did she want? She was on a roll. She could have every little thing she'd secretly dreamed of.

She sprang back. 'Can we have a baby too?'

His throat convulsed. He went pale. Claudia's heart pinched, but she told herself not to be disappointed—it was only one little dream. She could push it back down.

'I never thought I deserved such a thing,' he said, wearing that haunted look that made her heart weep for him.

'Oh, Lucas, you deserve everything—and I'll spend my whole life proving it to you.'

One corner of his sexy mouth quirked. 'I want a baby girl with amber eyes and honey-gold skin.'

Typical, then, that she wanted a boy with rich sapphire blues. 'I don't think nature is going to listen to your rules, my darling.'

'Of course it will.'

She laughed. 'God, I love you.'

His hot gaze dropped to her chest. 'I love this thing you are wearing, but I want it off.'

'Pull the ribbons here,' she said, running her fingertip provocatively from the dip at the base of her throat to her cleavage, to rest on a line of tiny bows trailing down the front.

One after another he pulled the ties free—colour slashing his cheekbones as he unwrapped her. And if she'd thought he was hard beneath her already she'd been oh-so-very-wrong.

'Did you hear what I said about my dreams that day?' she asked, breathy as she undulated against him. Heat flooded her core, soaking her skimpy panties.

A husky groan poured from his mouth. 'I would not have a heard a freight train rolling through town, *cariña*. I was too busy imagining you in this sinful contraption.' The tight material gave way under the weight of her breasts, parting. 'My imagination was scarily accurate. *Dios,* Claudia, I need to be inside you.'

Lifting her arms, she peeled the corset from her body and let it fall to the floor.

His hot, heavy eyes raked over her flushed skin, his feverish hands following in their wake. He cupped one of her breasts, taking all the weight from her shoulder, and she leaned forward, needing the crush of his talented fingers.

'Tell me, *querida*. While I can still think.'

She licked her lips as he scraped his thumb over the tight peak, making her shudder.

'You said every princess dreams of Prince Charming. And I…I tried to tell you. I used to lie in bed and dream of one man.' Dreams…stories she'd passed onto Bailey. 'A warrior who would charge through the hospital walls…or in our case my lab. Sweep me off my feet. Save me from myself.'

She caught his questioning gaze, held it. 'I used to dream of being kissed by my hero. The Dark Knight.'

He grinned one of those gooey bad-boy smiles that made everything hot and wet, gripped the strip of lace around the top of her thighs and tore her panties clean off. 'I am adoring your dreams, *Just Claudia*.'

'Oh, I have tons more,' she said, sheathing him. Loving him.

He curled his hand around her nape, pulled her down to his mouth and murmured against her lips, 'And I shall make every one come true.'

Then he kissed her. Her hero. Her Dark Knight.

* * * * *

MILLS & BOON®
By Request

RELIVE THE ROMANCE WITH THE BEST OF THE BEST

A sneak peek at next month's titles...

In stores from 11th August 2016:

- **Heir to His Legacy** – Chantelle Shaw, Cathy Williams & Lucy Monroe

- **A Pretend Proposal** – Jackie Braun, Ally Blake & Robyn Grady

In stores from 25th August 2016:

- **His Not-So-Blushing Bride** – Kat Cantrell, Anna DePalo & Fiona Brand

- **Her Happy-Ever-After Family** – Michelle Douglas, Barbara Hannay & Soraya Lane

0816/05

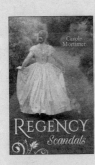

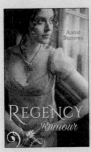

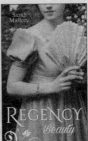

MILLS & BOON®

The Sara Craven Collection!

Dive into the world of one of our bestselling authors, Sara Craven!

Order yours at **www.millsandboon.co.uk/saracraven**